Lyn was born in Liverpool in September 1943. Her father was killed on D-Day in 1944 when Lyn was just nine months old. When Lyn was three her mother Monica married Frank Moore, who became 'Dad' to the little girl. Lyn was brought up in Liverpool and became a secretary before marrying policeman Bob Andrews. In 1970 Lyn gave birth to triplets – two sons and a daughter – who kept her busy for the next few years. Once they'd gone to school Lyn began writing, and her first novel was quickly accepted for publication. She has since written a further thirty-seven novels.

Lyn lived for eleven years in Ireland and is now resident on the Isle of Man, but spends as much time as possible back on Merseyside, seeing her children and four grandchildren.

Praise for Lyn Andrews' compelling sagas:

'An outstanding storyteller' *Woman's Weekly*

'A vivid portrayal of life' *Best*

'A compelling read' *Woman's Own*

'The Catherine Cookson of Liverpool' *Northern Echo*

'Gutsy . . . A vivid picture of a hard-up hard-working community . . . will keep the pages turning' *Daily Express*

By Lyn Andrews

Maggie May
The Leaving Of Liverpool
Liverpool Lou
The Sisters O'Donnell
The White Empress
Ellan Vannin
Mist Over The Mersey
Mersey Blues
Liverpool Songbird
Liverpool Lamplight
Where The Mersey Flows
From This Day Forth
When Tomorrow Dawns
Angels Of Mercy
The Ties That Bind
Take These Broken Wings
My Sister's Child
The House On Lonely Street
Love And A Promise
A Wing And A Prayer
When Daylight Comes
Across A Summer Sea
A Mother's Love
Friends Forever
Every Mother's Son
Far From Home
Days Of Hope
A Daughter's Journey
A Secret In The Family
To Love And To Cherish
Beyond A Misty Shore
The Queen's Promise
Sunlight On The Mersey
Liverpool Angels
From Liverpool With Love
Heart and Home
Liverpool Sisters

Lyn Andrews

When Daylight Comes

HEADLINE

First published in 2003 by
HEADLINE PUBLISHING GROUP

First published in this paperback edition in 2016 by
HEADLINE PUBLISHING GROUP

2

Cataloguing in Publication Data is available from the British Library

ISBN 978 1 4722 4637 0

Typeset in Janson by Avon DataSet Ltd, Bidford on Avon, Warwickshire

Printed and bound in Great Britain by Clays Ltd, Elcograf S.p.A.

Headline's policy is to use papers that are natural, renewable and recyclable
products and made from wood grown in well-managed forests and other
controlled sources. The logging and manufacturing processes are expected to
conform to the environmental regulations of the country of origin.

HEADLINE PUBLISHING GROUP
An Hachette UK Company
Carmelite House
50 Victoria Embankment
London EC4Y 0DZ

www.headline.co.uk
www.hachette.co.uk

This book is dedicated to the memory of Colette Grennan, who lost her battle with cancer early on Sunday morning, 10 November 2002. She was a lovely, vivacious woman, who enjoyed life to the full and gave so much of her time to helping others, not only within the parish and town of Tullamore, but also throughout the country, and especially the children of Belarus. She was a devoted mother to her young sons, the mainstay of her family, a much-loved member of St Carthage's Ladies Group, where I met her, and a shining example to everyone who knew her for the serenity and courage with which she faced her pain and her eventual death. God bless you, Colette, it was a privilege and great pleasure to have known you and to have been able to call you 'my friend'.

Also for Tony McCann, my art teacher, who has, with great patience, helped me achieve one of my greatest ambitions – to produce some fairly passable watercolours. Thanks, Tony, I must be one of your greatest trials!!

Lyn Andrews
Tullamore 2002

Chapter One

'DO YOU THINK THE weather will hold?' Maddy Brennan peered up at the April sky, a frown creasing her forehead.

'Oh, Mam, stop worrying, you're almost as bad as Aunt Jo! To say nothing of Aideen – she's had everyone in a state of nerves all morning!'

Maddy smiled at her daughter Jessica. Jess, as she was called in the family, was so like her. Of course she herself was a middle-aged woman now, but Jess's dark hair and eyes reminded her of the young Maddy Kiernan who had come to Liverpool from Ireland all those years ago. And she seemed to have inherited all her father's good points too.

'I wish Da was here,' Jess said wistfully, her eyes straying from the gardens to the wide expanse of the Mersey estuary beyond.

'So do I, but business is business,' Maddy replied firmly, patting the brim of her hat. Of course she missed Martin too but she had grown accustomed to his long trips away. As

1

Captain and owner of the Brennan Line, the sea was his life: she'd known that from the day they had first met.

'You do look lovely, Jess. I wasn't sure about that colour, especially the way Aideen described it, but you were both right.'

Jess smiled. There had been a couple of arguments over the yellow bridesmaid's dress and matching bonnet. She really hadn't minded what colour her cousin picked, it was Aideen's day after all.

Maddy sighed and her thoughts turned to her own outfit. 'I'm not at all sure about the feathers on this hat. There seem to be too many of them.'

Jess was mildly exasperated. 'Oh, Mam, it's the fashion! Everyone is wearing feathers on *everything*.'

'Then there must be desperate numbers of dead birds around the place!' Maddy replied, but with a smile. Both Jess and Aideen had always been followers of fashion and both, in their own different ways, were beautiful girls. She was so pleased, for Johanna's sake, that Aideen was marrying so well.

'What *is* Arthur like? You seem to know him quite well.'

'Not really, Mam. It's only since all the arrangements started to be made that I've had much to do with him. He seems quite nice. You know he's rich, of course, and from a well-connected Liverpool family, but what's good is that he really does seem to idolise Aideen. I gather, though, that his mother doesn't think Aideen is such a good catch.'

'From what I've seen of his mother she wouldn't think *anyone* is good enough for her two sons. Look at Edward, he's older than Arthur and not yet married or even engaged.

Aideen will have trouble with that one, you mark my words.'

Jess looked quickly around. 'Oh, Mam! Don't let anyone hear you saying things like that!'

Maddy shrugged. 'I think we'd both better go in and see how the preparations are going before this wind does irreparable damage to my hat.'

A scene of chaos greeted them in the wide, airy hall with its black-and-white-tiled floor, pastel-painted walls and impressive staircase.

'Oh, Maddy, I've been looking everywhere for you!' Johanna Kiernan exclaimed, clutching her sister-in-law's arm.

'You look very smart, Jo, but what's the matter?'

With a wave of her hand Johanna dismissed her russet taffeta dress with its lavish trimmings and the matching hat that had cost a small fortune. 'They've sent the wrong flowers and she's almost hysterical!'

Maddy glanced at the floral arrangements dotted around the hall. 'But they did all these last night.'

'It's not the arrangements, it's the personal flowers. I ordered roses and lilies at a cost that Tom nearly had a heart attack over, and you should see what they've sent! Oh, what am I going to do with her, Maddy? She's getting into a terrible state. I'm at my wits' end!'

A look of determination crossed Maddy's face. 'Leave her to me, Jo. Jess, go and see if you can find a glass of sherry for your aunt, she needs it.'

'And keep Tom away from the whiskey, he's had enough already!' Johanna called after her niece.

'I'm only the bridesmaid, how can I do that?' Jess answered

with spirit, thinking that she didn't really blame her uncle. The whole affair was degenerating into something resembling a three-ringed circus.

'Oh, God! You gave me a fright!' she cried as she hurried into her uncle's study in search of the decanter and glasses. A tall figure had risen from the depths of a deeply buttoned leather armchair.

Patrick Brennan grinned. 'Have you decided to hide too?'

Jess smiled back at her elder brother, marvelling yet again at how unlike each other they were. Two years older than herself, Patrick was tall, thin, fair-haired and blue-eyed.

'No, I came looking for the sherry for Aunt Jo, Mam says she needs one. Aideen is having hysterics.'

'When isn't she?' Patrick sighed, resuming his seat.

Jess poured a generous measure of sherry into a crystal glass. 'Well, don't just sit there, go and find Uncle Tom and try and keep him sober.'

Patrick frowned. 'I would have thought that was Ronan's job, not mine. He's his son, I'm only a nephew.'

'If Ronan's got any sense he'll have locked himself in his room! Oh, please, Patrick, try and be of some help!'

Reluctantly he got to his feet. 'All right, but I'm only doing it for Aunt Jo and Mother. Da should be here.'

Jess was exasperated. 'Yes, well, he isn't, so just go! Make some sort of an effort to be useful!'

With a very bad grace Patrick left. He was not looking forward to the rest of the day. It was typical of his uncle to spend so much money on Aideen, for whom he had little time. In his opinion she was totally selfish and as much a social climber as her father. Nor had he any liking for Arthur

Dempsey and his brother Edward who was to be best man. But – he shrugged – it was Aideen's life, not his.

'Ah, sure, don't you start giving out to me, Maddy!' Tom Kiernan exclaimed on seeing his sister approaching and noting the expression on her face.

'Your daughter has your poor wife demented and she doesn't need you adding to her worries.'

'Don't be such a killjoy, Maddy! Haven't I something to celebrate? I've got her married off to a decent young feller from a very good family. Not bad for a lad from the bogs of Ireland.'

Maddy smiled. 'I'll agree with that, but for God's sake, Tom, don't ruin it for the girl. Her future mother-in-law has a tongue that would cut the horns off a cow!'

'And you'd be an expert on that, having put up with old Mrs Buckley for all those years.'

'Don't you say a wrong word about that woman. She was the making of both of us and you know it.'

They both fell silent, thinking of the eccentric, imperious old lady who had taken them both in all those years ago. Maddy remembered the day vividly. She had been at her wits' end: destitute and without even a roof over their heads. She had once acted with kindness to the old woman's elderly butler and it had brought her the position of lady's maid, a comfortable home and ultimately the love of her life: Martin Brennan. When Mrs Buckley died she had left Maddy her house, her money and the two ships that were all that was left of a once thriving shipping line. A line that with hard work, self-sacrifice and dedication Martin and Maddy Brennan and

Tom Kiernan had built up into a now prosperous business. The huge, crumbling house in Faulkner Square had been sold and both families now lived in smaller but well-appointed houses in the suburb of Crosby where the gardens overlooked the shores of the river.

Tom raised his glass and drained the contents. 'To old Mrs Buckley, God bless her!'

'Amen to that – and that's your last, Tom Kiernan, until after the church service. Where's Ronan?' Maddy asked, to change the subject.

'He went for a walk by the river. I should have gone with him, is what I'm thinking. There he is now.'

Maddy looked out of the window to where her nephew was making his way across the garden towards the house.

'He's a fine lad,' Tom said proudly.

'He is so,' Maddy agreed.

'Now, if I could get him married off to some heiress . . .'

'Leave him alone. He'll marry when he's ready. That's the answer I get from Jess. That and she hasn't met anyone yet that she would consider walking out with, let alone marry.'

'They make a fine pair. The same stubbornness, the same trite answers. Ronan, lad, will you take a drink? You look to be in the need of it.'

'No thanks, Da. It's a bit early for me.'

'That was a nice try, Tom, but you've had your last for now.' Maddy laughed and her nephew smiled. He felt sorry for his father; all this fuss and palaver had driven Tom mad – to say nothing of the expense. He himself had nothing against Arthur Dempsey. Sometimes he almost pitied the lad, not only did he have his battleaxe of a mother to contend

6

with, now he was getting a wife who had been spoiled and petted all her life and who would expect the best of everything.

'Is there any word from Uncle Martin?'

Maddy shook her head. 'He should be back within the month though.'

Tom looked uneasy. There was so much riding on the return of Martin Brennan. Much more than anyone, including Maddy, realised. Money was tight and this wedding had cost him more than he could afford; but he had become carried away with Aideen and Johanna's plans and with the fact that she was marrying far above her station. The Dempseys were old money. The Kiernans, on the other hand, were new money, and from a background little better than that of a peasant farmer, which was what his father had been, back in King's County (as Offaly was called then). Tom's father had been struck down in the cholera epidemic, leaving Tom at nineteen the guardian and breadwinner for his sisters Maddy and Carmel.

They had been hard days, but they'd been lucky, having been taken in as servants by James Mitchell, the Agent for the Grand Canal Company. Tom had always had ambition, and he'd aspired to marry the daughter of the house but Maddy had put paid to that and he'd left to start a new life in Liverpool. His sisters had followed him soon after. He pushed away the thoughts; it was all a long time ago. He didn't want to admit to himself that uncertainty and financial worries were once again staring him in the face, just as they had when he'd left Offaly.

'Cheer up, Da, it's not that bad,' Ronan interrupted.

Tom smiled, a tight movement of the lips that never

reached his eyes. 'It's not, but I'll be glad when it's all over, Ronan.'

'Won't we all,' Maddy agreed heartily.

'Well, I wouldn't mind a honeymoon in Italy,' Ronan joked.

'You have to find a wife first,' his aunt commented drily.

Ronan laughed. 'Oh, please, don't you start!'

'Your da was just saying, you make a pair, you and Jess. I despair of ever getting her married. Sometimes she's too independent for her own good. Too much the "modern miss".'

'Well, just think how much she's saving you, isn't she, Da?'

Tom looked serious. 'I don't even want to think about the cost of all this, never mind calculate it.'

'Well, that's something you can look forward to, Tom!' Maddy quipped. 'But it shouldn't ruin you.'

Tom wanted another drink. Oh, if only she knew how matters really stood.

Jess came towards them, holding up her skirts so as not to trip. 'Uncle Tom, you're wanted above,' she informed them.

'Is it time already?'

'It must be, nearly everyone has gone. I'm going to look for Patrick and then we'll go. Jess, go with your uncle,' Maddy instructed, gathering up the train of her own dress and looking around for her gloves.

'You look lovely, Jess. I mean it.'

Jess smiled up at Ronan. She was fond of her cousin. He was quite a handsome man with his father's dark eyes and hair and Aunt Jo's softer features. He'd never seemed to bother with girls and she wondered if there was anyone special in his life.

'The colour of the dress is a bit . . . bright but . . .' he ventured.

Jess laughed. 'Oh Lord! Don't you start! We've had war already over this outfit.' She dropped her voice. 'Have they been trying to marry you off too?'

'They hinted.'

'Mam more than hints to me.'

'We must be two of a kind. Maybe we'll end up the old bachelor and old spinster.'

'Stop that! It makes me sound dreadful! "Spinster of this parish". It almost makes me want to rush out and find a husband!' Jess pealed with laughter at the idea. 'If I can find a man like Da, I might just do that!'

'You'll have a hard job to find someone like him.'

'I know. It might take a long time, but I'll keep looking.'

'It might take for ever.'

She looked up at him, knowing how fond he was of her da. 'It will be worth it, Ronan.'

Suddenly he was serious. 'It will, Jess.'

She smiled, touched. Then she said, 'I'd better go before there are more hysterics.'

He watched her as she went upstairs. She was so like her mother to look at, but her character was that of her father. She had inherited the best while Patrick, her brother, seemed to be like neither of them. He'd often heard his mother say that Patrick was very like their tragic Aunt Carmel, who had been, in his opinion, a rather pathetic figure. She'd been a sensitive, almost childlike girl who had never been able to cope with what destiny had planned for her. He sighed, pushing the thoughts away. Today was for rejoicing, not dwelling on the dark tragedies of the past.

'Thank God everything went so well.' Johanna was relieved.

'Well, she's his responsibility now. He can pay all the bills she manages to run up,' Tom answered.

'Tom! Hush, for heaven's sake, someone might hear.'

'Oh, you know what I mean, Jo.'

'Is there anything wrong?'

'No, I was just thinking of the cost of all this.'

'Oh, sometimes you exasperate me, Tom Kiernan! It was you who wanted to give her a "grand send-off".'

He smiled down at his wife a little ruefully. 'And we gave her one, didn't we?'

'You did her proud, Tom.'

Again there was the rueful smile. 'Well, we'd better mix and mingle, be the perfect host and hostess.'

'I don't think any fault could be found with the meal or the wine and they certainly couldn't look down their noses at the champagne. It was the best that money can buy.' Johanna sighed. 'I do hope she'll be happy.'

'Why wouldn't she be? He's a decent lad.'

Johanna shook off the mood. 'I'm going to rescue Maddy from Arthur's mother. Poor Maddy, her eyes have a sort of glazed look about them.'

'Miss Brennan, I believe your glass is empty. Would you like me to get you another drink?'

Jess looked up and found Edward Dempsey smiling at her. She smiled back.

'Thank you, Mr Dempsey. I'd like another glass of champagne.'

She watched him as he threaded his way through the throng of smartly dressed men and women in dresses of every colour imaginable, bedecked with jewellery and vying with each other in the style, size and heavy trimmings of their hats. He must be well over thirty. He wasn't bad-looking, with neatly brushed-back light-brown hair, grey-green eyes and strong features. She'd not had a proper conversation with him yet though; perhaps he was an almighty bore. She raised her hand to tuck a few tendrils of hair back under her bonnet, wishing she could take it off now the cere-monies were over, but convention decreed she must wear it until the last guest had departed. She caught sight of her mother being propelled across the drawing room by her aunt. Mam at least had escaped from the awful-looking Mrs Dempsey.

'Your uncle certainly knows his wines. Everything we've had today has been of excellent vintage.' Edward Dempsey handed her a tall crystal flute.

'He spent a great deal of time choosing them, I know that much. He usually only drinks whiskey himself.'

'Well, here's to the bride and groom – again!'

She looked up quickly and saw a flash of amusement in his eyes. 'You're not like your brother, Mr Dempsey.'

'I don't look much like him, I'll give you that.'

'I don't look a bit like my brother Patrick – and he's not like me in nature either.'

'I suppose it's not absolutely essential that siblings look alike, Miss Brennan.'

'Oh, please, call me Jess. You make me sound like a maiden aunt!'

He smiled at her and she thought how different it made him look. 'I don't think anyone would make that assumption, Jess, and please call me Edward. I suppose we're related now. My brother and I are also dissimilar in temperament, although, contrary to what some people think, I am capable of enjoying life.' He smiled ruefully and his gaze rested on his brother.

She smiled back. Despite his rather formal way of speaking she liked him. 'What do you do, Edward?'

'I work for my father. In fact I seem to do most of the work these days.'

'Doesn't Arthur work with you?'

'Yes, but his mind hasn't been on his work lately and neither has Father's.'

'Well, that's understandable. Everyone's mind has been on this wedding and now it's over perhaps we'll all get some peace.'

She was a very pleasant girl, he thought. Quite beautiful too, in a very different way to his new sister-in-law, although she obviously didn't realise it – whereas Aideen did.

'Your father is away at sea, so I hear.'

'Yes, he's due home towards the end of the month and I'll be terribly glad to see him. He seems to have been away for so long.'

Her expression had softened, he thought. She obviously was very fond of her father. 'Where is he coming from?'

'America. Charleston, to be exact.'

'He owns the line, doesn't he?'

'In partnership with my mother and, since last year, Uncle Tom.'

'How many ships are there?'

'Three, and a fourth is being built across the water at Cammell Laird's shipyard.'

He nodded, impressed and a little surprised that a woman was a partner in the business. It was unusual.

Jess sipped her drink, thinking of the row there had been over the fourth ship. Her father had said it was too soon to be buying another one; they hadn't finished paying for the third. Nor did he approve of having one built. It was terribly expensive and there were plenty of good, sound ships for sale. But Uncle Tom had won the day, backed up by her mother.

'You're looking very serious and concerned all of a sudden, Jess.'

She smiled. 'It's nothing. I'll just be grateful when he gets home and I know Mam will be too. Even after all these years she's not used to the separations.'

The strains of the small hired ensemble drifted in from the dining room. 'Ah, I believe the dancing is about to commence. May I, Jess?'

'Thank you, Edward. I must warn you though I'm not terribly good at it, despite all the money Mam spent on lessons.'

He laughed. 'I'm sure you don't mean that.'

'Oh, but I do, Edward!'

Chapter Two

———◆———

'MAM, WHAT ARE YOU doing?' Jess asked, finding her mother standing gazing through the circular window on the landing.

'Oh, Jess, I'm so worried. There's not a sign of your da's ship.'

Jess slipped her arm around Maddy's waist and peered out of the window that overlooked the gardens and gave a clear view right out over the Mersey estuary. It was possible to watch the movements of all the shipping coming in and going out of Liverpool from here.

'Maybe they'll come in at night.' She hated to see her mother look so anxious. In the darkness it wasn't possible to pick out individual ships. Only their navigation lights were visible, although it was possible to tell how large the ship was. *Brennan's Pride*, *Brennan's Promise* and *Brennan's Enterprise* would all come home together. They sailed in a sort of convoy, and they all carried the same cargo to the same destination: cotton for the thriving mills in Lancashire's small industrial towns. Cotton had made the Brennans wealthy; it had made the Dempseys very wealthy indeed, they having being cotton brokers for many years.

'I always hate the thought of them crossing the Atlantic. It can be treacherous at any time of year. I feel so . . . helpless!' Maddy banged her fist on the window frame. 'Oh, I wish I'd never had this window put in! Both your da and Aunt Jo tried to persuade me against it but I wouldn't listen to them. I thought it was such a good idea. I'd be able to see Martin's ship when it came into the estuary, which would give me some extra time to prepare a decent homecoming. I wish now I'd stuck to the old way.'

'Going down to the docks to stand and wait. We'd be there for hours on end, in all weathers, and you'd never move an inch. I remember those days very well. By the time we got to see Da, Patrick and I were tired out and often cold and wet.'

Maddy looked stricken. 'Oh, Jess, is that truly how you look back on those days? I never meant you to . . . suffer. I just wanted you to see as much of your da as was possible. That makes me feel so guilty!'

'Mam, don't talk like that! I should never have mentioned it. You did it for the best. You've always tried to do your best for us.'

'I felt I had to be mother and father to you both.'

'Mam, you *were*. Stop worrying and come away from that damned window.'

'Jess, I *know* something is wrong. I just *know* it!'

'Don't worry, Mam. They're not that late.'

Maddy nodded slowly. It was true they were only a few days late. That could be due to a variety of circumstances.

Delays in the cargo being transported to the docks. Delays in loading the cargo. Delays caused by the weather. Too much wind or not enough of it, although these days they no longer relied on sail alone. The ships could be steam driven when the need arose, not like the old days when they risked being becalmed. She had always been so close to Martin, so close that she often knew what was in his mind before he had even uttered a word. And she felt instinctively that there was a problem.

She twisted her hands together helplessly. 'I wish now I'd never agreed with Tom over the new ship. I feel as though I've let your da down.'

'Of course you haven't. It made sense. Trade is booming. Liverpool is the second port of the Empire, only London handles more tonnage, you know that, Mam. He was just being . . . cautious. He didn't want you to stretch yourselves too far. But sometimes you can be too cautious. Strike when the iron is hot, as Uncle Tom says.'

'Sometimes your uncle has too much to say altogether,' Maddy replied shortly.

'Mam, come away. It's a fine day; we'll have tea in the garden.'

Reluctantly Maddy let herself be guided out into the garden she had planned. As she waited for Minnie, the maid of all work, to bring out the tea, she relaxed a little. A few minutes in the garden always had this effect on her. It *was* a beautiful garden and it had been a labour of love. She'd come from Irish farming stock so she supposed that was where she'd got her love of the land, and it kept her busy while Martin was away. They always joked about it.

'And what new botanical delights have you in store for me this time, Mrs Brennan?' he would say very formally, but the amusement in his eyes gave the lie to his tone of voice. The garden looked wonderful in spring, everything so fresh and green. She had a new rhododendron bush covered in magenta flowers that she wanted to show him when he came home, she told herself firmly.

That night she awoke with beads of perspiration on her forehead and the bedclothes in a terrible tangle. She'd been having a dream, a bad dream, but she couldn't remember exactly what it had all been about. She pulled on her dressing gown and went quietly down the stairs as far as the landing, her gaze automatically turning to the window. She peered into the inky darkness. She could just make out lights on the horizon. Oh, please God, let it be Martin! Please, let it be him! she prayed. The ship was too far away to judge its size; she'd go down and have a cup of tea while she waited for it to draw closer.

Oh, how the time dragged by, she thought as she sat at the kitchen table, holding the cup with both hands. A few minutes later she was startled to hear the back door open. Her heart leaped and she jumped to her feet. He was home! Martin was home! He was coming in the back way so as not to disturb her! He was always so thoughtful.

'Martin? Martin, is it you?' she called softly.

Her heart dropped like a stone and disappointment washed over her as Patrick came through the door. 'I'm sorry, Mam. I forgot my front-door key and I didn't want to disturb you.'

Maddy bit her lip. 'I thought it was your father. I'm getting very worried about him.'

'Oh, he'll be all right, Mam. He's been late before. When we were children he was always late.'

'I know, Jess said that this afternoon. Perhaps I'm just being an eejit.' She managed a wry smile at her use of what Martin always called her 'Irishisms'.

'It's late, Mam. Go back to bed, you must be cold.'

'I know it's late! And just where have you been until this hour?'

'At my new club. There are some very interesting people there. It's much livelier than Da's, that's full of old bores. Tonight I got chatting to a fellow who's made a fortune out of stocks and bonds, and he's only a few years older than myself. He wants me to give it a try.'

Maddy looked sceptical. 'Really, and with what? You know money is tight.'

'It's only tight because you and Uncle Tom insisted Da buy a new ship. I don't know why Uncle Tom was so keen on that seeing he's had to dig deep into his pockets for that circus of a wedding.'

Maddy rose and rinsed out her cup. 'Patrick, let's not start on that again. What was this young man's name?' she asked to change the subject.

'Terence Shay. I liked him from the moment we were introduced. A very pleasant person indeed.'

'Good. You don't have many friends, Patrick. But let's wait until your da gets home and discuss stocks and bonds with him.'

Patrick nodded moodily. It was always 'wait and ask your father' with Maddy. It made him feel like a schoolboy who knew nothing about business. To be truthful, he wasn't in the least bit interested in shipping or cotton or corn or any other commodity that came into the docks, so he spent as little time in his father's offices as was possible. Stocks and bonds seemed to be far more intriguing. It entailed taking a risk. Gambling on the future. His new friend had made it all sound so exciting and his gambling had paid off, or so he had said. It would be great to have an income of his own, Patrick thought. Great not to have to ask for everything that he couldn't afford on his wages, which were hardly adequate to support his lifestyle. Three times over the last few months he'd had to ask his mother for money and he'd hated it. He also knew the fact would be passed on to his father who would lecture him about being wasteful and extravagant. To become a man of means appealed to him greatly, and his mood brightened at the thought. Then, just as quickly, some of his good humour left him. His father was a cautious, careful man. Patrick doubted there would be much use asking him about investments in stocks and bonds, but he'd try.

'Well, I'll go up, Mam. Don't you stay down here all night, it's cold.'

Maddy nodded. She wished her only son were more like his father or even more like Ronan. She knew he hated working in the shipping office. It was tedious and repetitive but he'd shown no inclination to take up any other kind of employment and that had angered Martin. It had been her idea that Patrick work in the offices of the Brennan Line. Just as it had been Johanna's idea that Ronan should *not* work with his father in his professional capacity, that of an accountant.

She poured herself another cup of tea and resumed her

seat. She knew she wouldn't be able to sleep and the range was still in, banked up for the night by the efficient Minnie. She moved her chair across to it and placed her feet on the hearth. Oh, she knew Patrick was unlike herself, Martin or Jess but he was very like Carmel. Carmel had been very beautiful but very quiet, sensitive and shy. She had never really grown up; she had remained childlike even when married. She had certainly been no match for Elizabeth Murgatroyd, her poisonous mother-in-law, although she'd been adored by her young husband, Charlie. Maybe Carmel's naïvety had been partly her fault? She would never get over the guilt she felt at neglecting to explain fully to Carmel what was expected of her in the physical side of marriage, which had been so repulsive to Carmel that her poor young sister had taken her own life. Never, if she lived to be a hundred, would she forget the sight of that pale lifeless figure in the bed, covered demurely by the bedclothes which when pulled back had revealed the slashed wrists and the scarlet, blood-soaked sheet. Patrick had been born the year her sister had died so tragically and he un- doubtedly resembled Carmel in looks and also in certain traits of character. Maddy shook herself mentally; she was being superstitious, but she supposed that went with being born and brought up in Ireland.

She stretched. She was stiff and she was cold, but that ship would be near enough by now to judge its tonnage. As she peered into the darkness she could see the red port light clearly and a glimmer from the wheelhouse and the saloon. She could almost taste the disappointment. No, it wasn't one of theirs. It was too small. Probably one of the night ferries from either Dublin or Belfast. The nagging doubts and fears came back as she wearily climbed the stairs. Her head was aching but there would be precious little sleep for her tonight.

It was Jess who woke her and she rubbed her eyes sleepily as her daughter drew back the curtains and the early May sunlight streamed into the room.

'Jess, what time is it?'

'A quarter to ten.'

Maddy threw back the bedclothes. 'Good God! Why didn't you wake me sooner?'

'Minnie said that when she brought up your tea you looked so peaceful she didn't have the heart to disturb you.'

'I couldn't get off to sleep last night. I tossed and turned for hours but then I must have gone into a deep sleep.'

'Uncle Tom is downstairs, Mam, and he . . . he doesn't look very happy. In fact he looks terrible. I think he's ill.' Jess couldn't meet her mother's eyes as she passed her her dressing gown. Her uncle did look terrible. He looked old, very old, but he wouldn't tell her what was the matter.

'Go back down, Jess. Give him some tea and I'll be down as quickly as I can.'

Maddy dragged on her clothes, brushed her hair and swept it off her face with two tortoiseshell combs. Oh, God! What was it that had Tom down here at this hour of the morning, instead of at the offices?

'Tom, what's the matter? Is it . . . is it Martin?' she faltered as she entered the drawing room.

Slowly Tom nodded and tried to gather his wits, which had been completely scattered since he'd received the news. 'I've had word that . . . that there has been a huge disaster off the coast of Newfoundland.'

'Newfoundland! That's Canada! It's miles off course! What happened, Tom? For God's sake, tell me!'

'There was a terrible storm. Dozens of ships were blown off course. Some were swamped, breached . . .' He shook his head again, trying to clear his mind of the mists of shock and disbelief that enveloped it.

'Oh, Holy Mother of God,' Maddy cried.

Jess went and put her arms around her mother, her eyes pleading with her uncle to get on with it, terrible as the news appeared to be.

Tom swallowed hard. 'We . . . we've . . . lost them all, Maddy. All three have gone down, God help us! And God have mercy on all their souls.' He dropped his head in his hands.

Maddy couldn't speak. She felt as though a hand had gripped her throat and was squeezing it tightly. It couldn't be true! Martin! Martin wasn't coming home! He was never coming home!

Jess buried her head on her stricken mother's shoulder and the tears filled her eyes. Her da! Her wonderful, laughing, loving da wasn't coming home! She'd never see him again. She'd never be able to throw her arms around him as she'd always done when he walked through the door after each voyage. Deep sobs racked her.

'Tom, go . . . go and tell . . . Patrick.' Maddy's arm was around Jess's waist as she forced herself to be calm. There would be so many days and weeks and months ahead for her to weep; now, this minute, she had to be strong for her children. She stood up and disentangled herself from Jess.

'Jess, he wouldn't have wanted you to be so terribly upset.'

Jess held tightly to the back of the chair, feeling almost faint. 'I know, Mam, but I . . . can't help it. I can't believe I'll never see him again! Why? Oh, why Da?'

'There are so many wives and mothers and daughters who will be asking the same question this morning. All three ships! Nearly a hundred men! Oh, but Jess, I know how you feel.' Mother and daughter clung together, bowed down with grief.

Tom came back, followed by a pale-faced, stricken Patrick. He was unable to take it in.

Maddy caught her brother's hand. 'Tom, are there any more details?' she begged.

'Not yet, but it's a major disaster not only for us, but for the city, the port—'

'Oh, I don't care about the city, the port! It's us . . . and the families of the men . . .' Maddy choked.

'Mam, sit down, you look terrible,' Patrick urged.

'We all look terrible. We all feel terrible. Look, I have to go. I have to try to find out more. Patrick, get dressed and come with me, lad.' Tom's voice was heavy.

Patrick frowned. 'Surely you don't need me today?'

Tom was in no mood for prevarication. 'Of course I'll damn well need you! Get dressed.'

Reluctantly Patrick left the room. He was terribly shocked and upset. He needed time to himself. He didn't want to go into those stuffy offices and be surrounded by people who wouldn't know the right thing to say or the right way to act in the face of such a disaster.

Tom turned to Maddy. 'Jo said to bring you both over to our house.'

Maddy nodded. She needed the comfort her sister-in-law could give. They had been close from the day they had first met. 'Jess, fetch our coats, luv.' She managed to keep her voice steady.

Maddy and Tom sat in stunned silence as Patrick dressed and Jess went for coats and hats.

Suddenly there was a crash followed by the shattering sound of breaking glass.

'My God! Now what?' Tom yelled, jerking to his feet.

Maddy ran to the door and through into the hall. Jess was standing on the landing with shards of glass all around her, a gnarled old walking stick in her hand and a trickle of blood running down her arm.

'Jess! Jess!' Maddy cried in fright.

'In God's name what possessed you to break the bloody window?' Tom shouted.

Jess was shaking. 'I hate it! I *hate* it! Now we'll never have to look through it again! The Widow's Window has gone!' she cried, tears streaming down her cheeks.

Tom turned away. He hadn't known what those circular windows were called.

Maddy took the stick from Jess's hands and drew her distraught daughter into her arms. The 'Widow's Window' was an apt name. How could she have forgotten it? Shaped like a porthole and set in the right position to look out to sea, its purpose was to enlighten the watcher of her status: wife, or – if the ship never returned – widow. Martin would never again sail across the Mersey bar and she, now a widow, would never look through that window again. Jess had done the right thing.

Chapter Three

———◆———

JOHANNA LOOKED PALE AND shocked, her pallor increased by the black high-necked dress she had changed into when Tom had informed her of the disaster. Tearfully she hugged Maddy and then Jess.

'Oh, Maddy, I'm so sorry, so very sorry. I can't believe it!'

Maddy grasped her hand tightly. 'Neither can I, Jo. Everything seems so unreal. Like a bad dream. Something I'm going to wake up from.'

'Tom is in a dreadful state. He looks so old and ill and, bad as this is, I'm sure there's something else he's not telling me.'

'What?'

'I don't know, Maddy, but I think it's something to do with money.'

Maddy groaned. 'Oh, it's that damned ship! I should never have agreed to it.'

'Mam, there's no use thinking like that.'

'I know, Jess, but I can't help it.' Maddy turned to Johanna. 'We shouldn't think of just ourselves, Jo. There are other wives who will be just as distraught and disbelieving.'

Johanna eased Maddy into an armchair. 'I know. Tom has gone to the offices to try to get names and addresses and see if there is any more news.'

Maddy shook her head slowly. 'All three! Jo, I can't take it in! Three! Martin was a good captain, he had years and years of experience and he hand-picked the other captains and officers. The crews were all well disciplined, good workers and many had years of sailing experience behind them.'

'The storm, the conditions . . . they must have been terrible, Maddy. They'd have all done their best, but we can't possibly imagine what it must have been like. People are saying it's the worst for fifty years.'

'Would it have been . . . quick?'

'I don't know. I honestly don't know, Maddy,' Johanna replied sadly.

Maddy jumped to her feet. 'That's what I can't bear, Jo, that we don't *know*! But Martin would have tried desperately to save his ship.'

'Oh, Mam, don't!' Jess cried, trying to dispel from her mind the terrifying images of her father battling the wind and the waves to save his ship and the lives of his men.

Johanna dabbed her eyes with her handkerchief. She felt so helpless. She wished she could be of more use to Maddy. 'I'll send for some tea. I think we all need a cup and I've also sent for Ronan to come home. Tom . . . we all need him here.'

Maddy dashed away more tears with the back of her hand. It was as though a huge black void faced her now; she prayed for the strength to cope with the rest of the day that lay ahead. She could think no further than that.

They were all sitting in dazed silence when Patrick and Ronan arrived, followed by Tom clutching a piece of paper.

'Tom, what news?' Maddy exclaimed as Johanna looked with concern at her husband. She'd never seen him look so ill. She knew he had been worrying about something – she'd thought it was the expense of Aideen's wedding – but as soon as he'd finished reading the note in his hand the colour drained from his face, leaving his lips bloodless and his eyes full of stunned disbelief. This was more than just the loss of Martin and the crews.

'Not much, Maddy,' he managed to croak.

'Tom, sit down, I'll get you a drop of brandy, you look as though you need it.'

Ronan looked around at the white, drawn faces of his aunt and cousins. 'I'll get it, Mother. And I think we should all have one for medicinal purposes.' He too was stunned. It defied belief. How could this happen to someone like his Uncle Martin?

'For God's sake, Tom, tell us what you do know,' Maddy pleaded.

Tom took the glass his son offered and drained the contents in one gulp. He twisted the glass around in his hands. A stark future lay ahead. He was facing ruin: how was he to tell them that?

'Six ships have been lost in all; four more are badly damaged but have made St John's, Newfoundland.'

'Oh, God have mercy on them all!' Johanna whispered, the glass in her hand shaking.

'The waves were fifty feet high, the wind hurricane force. Martin . . . Martin was a good seaman but . . .'

'With conditions like that, all he could do was trust in God and hope for the best,' Ronan said quietly, almost reflectively.

Maddy choked on a sob and Jess put her arm around her. It was tearing her apart to see her mother suffering like this. Her own sorrow was pushed into the background at the sight of Maddy's overwhelming grief.

'We've got all the names and addresses of the crews,' Patrick said awkwardly, wishing something would change the terrible atmosphere.

'Then I suggest we do something to alleviate their worry and fears,' Ronan said. 'I gather no one has informed them officially?

'Right then, Patrick and I will go and . . . talk to the families.' He felt he had to do *something*. He just couldn't sit here all day and witness such heartache. His father was in a state of shock and obviously not yet fit to do anything positive. But this wasn't their tragedy alone and as employers they had responsibilities.

Patrick looked up. Having to listen to the mumbled words of sympathy, having to look at the stricken faces of the clerks in the offices had been bad enough, but he'd made no protest. He'd just wanted to go home. To go to his room and try to take in his own loss and look to a future that had changed so dramatically.

'I . . . I don't think I can . . . face that,' he ventured.

Ronan glared at him. The useless, weak-willed, selfish sod! It was typical of Patrick. 'It's not a matter of being able to face it, it *has* to be done.'

'You can't do it all by yourself, lad. There're . . . there're so many of them,' Tom said woodenly.

Johanna got to her feet. 'I'll go too.'

Tom looked at her with concern. 'Jo, it's no place for you.'

'I'll come with you. I . . . I know how they'll be feeling. It might help. A few words of comfort from me,' Maddy offered. If she could just do *something*, she might feel better. If she had to sit here all day she'd go mad.

'Mam, if you're going, then so am I,' Jess stated firmly. It wasn't going to be easy but Ronan was right, someone had to do it. All those poor women would have heard would have been rumours, nothing official. She could only guess at their bewilderment and fear.

'At least you two are brave enough and concerned enough,' Ronan said quietly, looking pointedly at his cousin Patrick.

'Oh, I'll go with you, Ronan,' Patrick said with a bad grace. It was just typical of Ronan to make him appear heartless and selfish.

'Jo, I don't think any of you should go,' Tom interrupted.

'For God's sake, Tom Kiernan, what are we supposed to do? Sit here lost in our own grief!' Maddy exclaimed with some of her former spirit.

Tom shrugged. 'Oh, go then, Maddy! I'm too ill to argue with you.' This was typical of Maddy: always going out of her way to be of use to others. Well, she'd not be welcome in those homes when the news got out about their financial position.

Johanna put her arm around her sister-in-law. 'Maddy, are you *sure* you feel up to this? It's going to be very hard.'

Maddy nodded. 'It's better than just sitting here brooding. There'll be so much time for that in the future and I feel it's my responsibility.'

Johanna nodded sadly.

With a very bad grace and beneath the hostile gaze of his cousin, Patrick got to his feet. Oh, would this terrible day never end?

It was a question echoed by Maddy, Jess and Johanna at the end of a long, harrowing afternoon. In a way her mother had been right, Jess thought. Because Maddy too was now a widow, the women to whom she had to break the devastating news drew some comfort from her presence. The homes they'd visited were nearly all poor and the families large, but one in particular stuck in her memory. The room had been very sparsely furnished but it was clean, as were the numerous children. The two youngest had clung to their mother's skirt while she nursed a baby in her arms. She'd taken the news well. At least there had been no screams of disbelief or hysterical sobbing. With heartrending simplicity and with tears in her eyes, she'd asked, 'How am I to feed them all now, Mrs Brennan?' Jess'd watched her mother fight to control herself and then Maddy had taken out her purse.

'Take this, Mrs Cleary, it's all I have now but I . . . I'll find a way to make sure you can feed them. That's a promise.'

As they'd left, she had said, 'Oh, Jess, what else could I do? She was so brave.'

It was something that was weighing heavily on Maddy's mind when they all returned to Jo's house that evening. She'd made a promise and she'd do her best to see she kept it. She felt exhausted and drained and yet thankful that she'd gone personally. She was glad she had been able to reach out with understanding and pity to those women: women who already bore the cares and anxieties of their harsh lives etched on their faces.

'You did well, Jess,' Ronan said as he helped her off with her coat.

'It was terrible but I think it helped Mam. I couldn't let her go alone, and it was best that I was with her and not Patrick.'

'Patrick is a coward. He has no spirit, unlike you, Jess.'

'It did take . . . courage and Patrick is sensitive.'

'Don't try to defend him, Jess.'

She shook her head. Ronan's vehemence had surprised her, but she knew what her da would have thought and said about Patrick's unwillingness to help.

Johanna had sent for tea and sandwiches, for they were all utterly worn out. When Maddy took the teacup from Johanna, she returned to the subject of the Clearys. She was determined: 'We have to do something for them.'

'But what can we do?' Tom asked irritably.

'We can try to give them a bit of money in compensation. They have no other means of support. Some have seven or eight children. What are they to do?'

Tom wasn't interested. He had too much on his mind. More fool them for having all those kids they couldn't hope to feed and clothe properly. 'Maddy, don't you understand? We're not in a position to give them anything. Unfortunate as it is, if they can't manage, it will be the workhouse for them.'

Maddy's temper flared and for a second she forgot her own loss. '"The workhouse"! "Unfortunate"! How can you be so callous? They've lost their men! They've lost more than just a husband and father, they've lost their breadwinner!'

Tom's own temper rose. 'Maddy, there *is* no bloody money!

31

Can't you understand that? We've *nothing* to be giving to them. We could be facing the workhouse ourselves!'

'What in the name of heaven do you mean?' Johanna cried.

All eyes were focused on him and Tom knew he'd have to tell them now, this very minute. It could be postponed no longer. The day and the hour he had dreaded had arrived.

'We've lost three ships and three cargoes. We haven't finished paying for the third and then . . . then there's the fourth.'

'What about the fourth? Oh, I should never have let you persuade me, Tom! I must have been mad!' Maddy cried.

'Does that matter now?' Ronan said quietly. He'd been watching his father closely and he knew something was desperately wrong.

'To pay for the fourth, we . . . I . . . had to raise money—'

'We know that!' Maddy interrupted.

'I had to have some collateral for the bank, and the shipyard wanted a large sum before they began work . . .'

'Tom, what have you done?' Johanna implored.

Tom covered his face with his hands. He almost wished he too was lying at the bottom of the cold northern ocean, like Martin Brennan. He couldn't look at either his wife or his sister.

Maddy was on her feet. 'Tom Kiernan, what have you done?' she repeated Johanna's question. When she had been a young girl living in Ireland he had deserted her and she had the distinct feeling that somehow he was doing it again.

'I mortgaged this house, and yours, Maddy. Now, with Martin and . . . everything gone we'll have to cancel the order with Laird's and they won't refund the money, the keel has been laid. They'll have to cut their losses by finishing the work and then try to sell the ship.'

'And so the bank will foreclose,' Ronan finished.

'Mother of God! Tom, what . . . what does that mean?' Johanna cried.

'It means that we'll all be thrown out! You, me, Aunt Maddy, Jess and Patrick! For Christ's sake, what did you think you were doing?' Ronan demanded, rounding on his stricken father.

'Did Martin know about this?' Maddy snapped.

Tom shook his head. 'God help me, I glossed over the true cost of the ship.'

Maddy sat down. Suddenly she felt faint. This just wasn't true! It wasn't happening to her. After losing Martin it looked as if she was losing her home too. It was just too enormous a realisation for her numbed mind to take in.

'I wanted to expand and Martin was so . . . cautious,' Tom tried to explain.

Ronan exploded. 'And he had every right to be!' He had loved, respected and admired his uncle.

Slumped in a chair, Patrick couldn't take it in either. The events of the day had been harrowing enough but now was destitution really staring him in the face?

Johanna pulled herself together. 'And you went ahead with Aideen's wedding knowing we could lose the roof over our heads?'

'I didn't bloody know this disaster would happen! I've enough on my plate, Johanna, without—'

Jess was on her feet. 'Enough on your plate! You've got

enough on *your* plate! What's going to happen to us, Uncle Tom? Haven't we suffered enough today?'

Tom didn't answer and Johanna looked pleadingly at Ronan but he turned away and poured himself a drink.

He was fuming. How could his father have been so stupid and irresponsible? Had he not thought it through? Why, oh why had he been so adamant that they needed a new ship? And knowing the risks he had gone ahead with that bloody wedding! It defied belief.

Maddy got up. 'We're going home. We've got to try and make some sense out of all this, try and think what we can do. But I'll never, ever, speak to you again, Tom Kiernan, for as long as I live! You've taken everything! Everything was handed you on a plate but you weren't satisfied, you wanted more and more! You'll never change!'

Johanna held out her arms and tears filled her eyes. 'Oh, Maddy, please don't leave this way.'

Maddy shook her head. 'I'm sorry, Jo, you know this has nothing to do with you or how I feel about you, but he . . . he's despicable! I never want to set eyes on him again!' She walked from the room followed by Jess and Patrick.

Johanna gazed after them sadly. What would Maddy do now? What would they *all* do now? Tom's selfish ambitions had ruined them all. She turned away and caught the furious gaze of her son. Oh, she was too weary and too worried to listen to the huge row that was clearly brewing between her husband and her son.

'I'm going to bed. It's been a terrible, terrible day,' she said quietly.

* * *

Maddy went straight to Martin's small study and sank down in the well-worn leather chair. Her head was aching and a terrible sense of desolation hung over her. She was exhausted both physically and mentally but she doubted she would ever sleep again.

Everything in this room reminded her of him: the prints of sailing ships that hung on the walls; the set of miniature nautical brass instruments that she'd had made for his last birthday: the pens, pencils, silver ink pot, blotter and notepaper on the desk. One of his uniform caps lay on the top of the teak sea-chest.

She rose, picked it up and buried her face in it. It smelled of Martin, the only man she had ever loved. Then the tears that had been forced back all day began to fall. How could she go on living without him? She was alone. Part of her was dead.

Jess found her curled up in Martin's chair, sobbing into the old cap. Her heavy heart went out to her mother and she put her arms around her.

'Oh, Mam, please go to bed. Try to sleep.'

'How can I? How can I face the future without him? How can I sort out all the problems that face us without him?' Maddy sobbed. Never again could she take a worry or concern to him to discuss until a solution was reached or he had calmed her fears.

Jess fought down her own tears. 'Mam, I feel lost too. I'll miss him so much. But you've always been a fighter. You've always been strong. Da told me all about how you left Ireland and were living in a cellar half starved when you first came to Liverpool. Mam, you *have* to find some ray of hope! How will *we* cope without your strength?'

'I don't have any strength left, Jess. He was my strength.' But looking at her stricken daughter, Maddy knew she had to pull herself together. 'I'm sorry. I don't want you to worry. We'll share this grief together, all of us.'

'And Uncle Tom and Aunt Jo?'

Maddy's expression changed. 'I meant what I said. I never want to see *him* again!'

'But Aunt Jo?'

'Oh, I don't know, Jess. We have always been close friends, but he's her husband when all's said and done and she has to try and keep her family together.'

'Please, Mam, don't fall out with her. It's not her fault and she loves us all. Things will be hard for her too.'

Maddy nodded slowly. Jess was right. It wasn't Jo's fault and she'd be so upset if the rift between herself and Tom became a rift between them all.

'I'll get Minnie to make some tea and then I think we should all try and get some rest.'

Maddy caught her daughter's hand. 'You are a great comfort to me, Jess.'

'We'll manage, Mam. Somehow we'll manage.'

Maddy touched the girl's cheek. 'You have your da's optimism and determination.'

'And your strength, Mam.'

Chapter Four

———————

WHEN SHE AWOKE NEXT morning Maddy's head felt muzzy and she struggled to raise herself on one elbow. What had happened? Why was there such a feeling of despair hanging over her? Then she remembered. She dropped her head onto the pillow. Martin! She'd lost Martin for ever! All the tearing emotions experienced during the long dark hours of the night returned. She didn't want to face the future without him. She just wanted to lie here and cry for him. Cry and cry until there were no more tears left.

A quiet knock on the door forced her to raise her head and Minnie, her face white with concern, came in with the tea tray.

'I . . . I wasn't sure, ma'am . . .' the girl said timidly. No one had needed to tell her what had happened. The terrible news was all over the city.

'Thank you, Minnie. Just put it down, please.'

The girl twisted the hem of her apron. 'Ma'am, I just want to say how . . . sorry I am.'

Maddy nodded and bit her lip. Minnie was a good girl but

she was going to have to let her go. There was no money to pay her.

When the girl had gone, she forced herself to sit up and drink the tea. There were still so many problems facing her. She wished she could push them away, banish them from her mind completely, but she couldn't. Time was not on her side. Her worries for the future of her family surmounted her grief.

She got up, washed and, as she searched her wardrobe for something suitable to wear, she realised that black mourning clothes were another problem that had to be dealt with.

Jess was sitting in the small morning room, sunlight streaming in through the window. The room looked so bright with its yellow and green chintz curtains and matching chairs and sofa. A large jug of flowers sat on the window ledge, china ornaments were arranged on the mantelpiece and top of the bookcase. How could there be so much sunshine and cheerfulness in a home that had just lost its dearest member?

'Did you get any sleep, Mam?'

'Not much. When I woke, just for a few seconds I didn't remember, I thought . . .'

'I know, Mam. So did I.' Jess poured her mother a cup of tea and Maddy sat down, weary already.

'Where's Patrick?'

'Out. I don't know where. Minnie said he went very early and with no breakfast.'

'He's probably gone to his new club. Maybe he thinks being with his friends is better than being here with us. Oh, Jess, I don't feel up to it, but I've got to face the fact that we could lose our home.'

'Patrick should be here, Mam! It's his problem too. He's part of this family and just running off and shutting himself away in some club isn't going to make the problems go away! It's not fair to leave it all to you.'

'I know, Jess, and I wish he were different.'

'What will we do? Is there *anything* we can do?'

'Try to get as much money together as we can and . . . and then I'll have to find myself a job.'

'Mam, you're not used to working!'

'I was once and I can do it again,' Maddy replied with some determination.

'Then so will I. All night I've been thinking of what I can do in the way of work. I'm not formally trained for anything, but my English is good, and so is my arithmetic. Maybe I could get a job as a bookkeeper or a clerk.'

'Those are men's jobs, Jess. No one would employ you.'

Jess became impatient. 'There must be *something* I can do.'

'We'll think about that later. The first thing I'm going to do is see the bank manager. Mr Frederickson knows me well, maybe he can offer some advice. Then I'm going to sell all our jewellery, the silver and china, and as much of the furniture as I can. Poor Minnie will have to go, I'm afraid.'

'We'll both help, Mam. Patrick will have to find other work and he can give up that stupid club for a start.' She knew there would be an argument over it but she didn't care. She was determined he was going to pull his weight and not shirk his responsibilities by skulking behind the closed doors of a gentleman's club.

Maddy looked closely at her daughter. 'Jess, I feel as though there should be some sort of service – a memorial for all who were lost.'

Jess was about to reply, but stopped and looked puzzled as the sound of the front-door knocker came to their ears.

'Minnie will go,' Maddy said as Jess started to get to her feet.

They heard the sound of voices and then Minnie appeared. Behind her was a pale-faced, haggard-looking Johanna.

'Oh, Jo!' Maddy cried, tears starting in her eyes.

Johanna instantly hugged her.

'Aunt Jo, I'm so glad you came,' Jess said thankfully.

'Maddy, how are you? I've not had a wink of sleep all night, thinking about you . . . about everything.'

'I've not slept much myself, Jo.'

Jess poured her aunt some tea as she removed her coat and hat.

'Has Tom said anything more?' Maddy demanded.

'No. There was a terrible fight last night between him and Ronan. You know Ronan's got a fierce temper when provoked. I went to bed; I couldn't stand trying to calm them both down. Oh, I still can't take it in, Maddy, the fact that he would put our home in danger on a whim, for his ambition. Ronan says the ships were insured with Lloyd's but Tom said for only a fraction of what they were worth and that money will have to go towards the debts. We'll have to sell up, find somewhere smaller, very much smaller so Ronan told me this morning. Tom . . . Tom's going to ask Arthur's father for a job and, if we sell as much as we possibly can and with Ronan's help, well, in a small house, we could just manage. But it's you, Maddy, I'm worried about.'

'We'll have to sell things too, Jo, and I've decided to go and see Mr Frederickson at the bank, to see if he has any ideas and—'

'And Patrick and I will both get jobs. I don't care what I do as long as it brings in some money!' Jess interrupted.

'You're a good girl, Jess, I know you'll be a great comfort. I also know that Patrick can be . . . difficult.'

'He's more than difficult, sometimes he's utterly useless.'

'He tries to shut himself away from problems and I suppose up until now he's been able to do that.'

'But now that Da and the money have gone, he'll just have to face up to things,' Jess said firmly.

'Oh, please, don't you two start falling out!' Johanna pleaded. 'And, Maddy, if there's anything I can do . . . ?'

Maddy managed a smile. 'Thanks Jo, but you're going to need every penny you can get yourself.'

'Mam was just saying that she feels there should be some kind of memorial service for everyone.'

'You see, Jo, there's no grave. There's nowhere to go to grieve. It doesn't seem final. With a grave and a headstone you *know* it's over, that they've . . . gone!'

Johanna nodded. She could understand that. 'I agree, Maddy. I'll speak to Father Miller at St Anthony's, our old parish, and then I'll come back and see you later.'

When her aunt had gone Jess went up to her room and sorted out her belongings. She had a few pieces of good jewellery. The diamond and aquamarine necklace and earrings that had been her twenty-first birthday present. A gold locket; two gold bracelets. A silver filigree necklace set with pearls; a pretty enamelled fob watch and four pairs of earrings. A gold cross and chain and the jewellery box itself: ebony, inlaid with mother-of-pearl and ivory. She also had some pretty Dresden china figurines and her silver dressing-table set. She'd pack them together and Mam could take them with all the other things. Patrick had some gold cufflinks and shirt studs, two gold watches with gold and garnet fobs, two signet rings, a silver-backed gentleman's dressing set, plus some other bits and pieces. And if they both got jobs maybe, just maybe they could manage to keep a roof over their heads. Perhaps not this roof, but, like Aunt Jo, something very much smaller. It was upsetting to have to part with so many things that held sentimental value, but she felt a sense of strong determination wash over her. She *had* to do this. It was what her father would have expected of her. She had to make an effort. She at least had to try and not just give in!

Maddy was sitting at the desk in Martin's study, surrounded by lists she had made. Lists for the invitations to the service, lists of jewellery, silver, china, antiques.

'I've packed up my things, Mam.'

Maddy passed a hand across her eyes. They felt as though they were burning. 'Oh, Jess, even with the sale of all these I don't know how we're going to manage.'

'Patrick has things too and, as I said, we'll both get jobs. I can teach children. I can be a governess.'

'It wouldn't pay much, Jess, and you'd have to live in.'

'Maybe not, if I got somewhere local.'

Maddy sighed. 'Oh, we'll see, Jess.'

'That's Patrick,' Jess said as she heard the front door. Judging from the way it slammed, he wasn't in a very good mood. She went into the hall.

'So, you're back. Where have you been?'

'To my club. I felt I couldn't stay here. The sense of loss and uncertainty was too overpowering.'

'Mam's in the study, we're getting everything together that we can sell.' She looked closely at her brother. 'You seem rather pleased with yourself.'

'I am. I've got the solution to all our problems.'

'Patrick says he has the answer,' Jess informed her mother as brother and sister entered the study.

Maddy looked up hopefully. 'Have you, Patrick? Have you really?'

'I think I have. I've been to the club. I went early. I couldn't stay here – can you understand that?'

Maddy leaned back and pressed her fingers to her throbbing temples. 'I think so. And . . . ?'

'I was talking to Terence, you remember I told you about him? He often stays overnight at the club.'

'Your man who is so good with the stocks and bonds?'

'Yes. I was telling him about the . . . disaster and . . .'

'And what?' Jess demanded. This was the first she'd heard of either this person called Terence or stocks and bonds.

'He said if we put as much as we possibly can into stocks that he has a lot of faith in, in a couple of months our money problems at least would be over.'

'And how does he know?' Jess demanded. It seemed too easy.

Patrick became impatient. 'Because he's made a fortune that way. Aren't you glad I met him, Mam? We won't be forced to leave here, we'll have money to buy back the things have to sell . . . it's so simple.'

Maddy sighed heavily. At least he was trying to help. 'It's too simple, Patrick. That's what worries me. No one makes a fortune gambling and if they do they always lose it again by continuing to gamble.'

Patrick ran his hands through his hair, a habit he had when he was impatient or annoyed and he was both now. There was nothing wrong with the scheme, he trusted Terence's judgement completely so why were they both being so suspicious? 'Mam, what choice have we got? We've got to give it a try.'

'We haven't got much to invest. The money we make from selling our more valuable possessions won't be enough to buy stocks or bonds and we can't wait a couple of months! Besides, I have to give the families some kind of compensation, no matter how small. I *promised*.'

Patrick was astounded and outraged. 'You're going to give everything we have to those . . . those . . . people!' he spluttered.

'It's little enough for their loss.'

He looked at them both aghast. 'What about *our* loss, Mam? What about *our* future? Forget them!'

Maddy became cold. 'You sound just like your uncle! I *won't* forget them! It's my moral duty to try to help them and I won't go back on a promise!'

'What can you do for them, Mam? The few pennies you can manage to give won't keep them from the workhouse, so why bother?'

'You don't understand, do you? Da would have understood, it's what he'd want us to do,' Jess said angrily, thinking how cold and cruel her brother could be.

'Would he? Would he really, Jess? Would he be happy to see us flung out on the road while Mam gives away every penny we have?' Patrick cried.

'Things wouldn't be at this pass if he was here and, yes, I think he would have wanted us to do what was right for those poor souls!' Jess shouted back.

Maddy stood up. 'Stop it! Stop it both of you! It's not helping!'

'Oh, I give up! I give up with both of you!' Patrick cried, wrenching open the door.

'Where are you going now?' Jess called after him.

'Back to the club where I can get some peace!'

Maddy covered her face with her hands. He was no use at all when faced with anything difficult.

'Well, he was a lot of help!' Jess said bitterly. 'He thinks that hare-brained scheme thought up by a stranger will miraculously solve our problems! Can't he see how . . . how pathetic he is?'

Maddy looked sadly at her indignant daughter.

'Oh, Jess, I wish he were different, but he's not. He'll get over his anger and frustration but in the meantime we have to try to sort things out.'

'Are you really going to try to give every family something? You only promised Mrs Cleary.'

Maddy nodded. 'I am. I can't give to one and not the others.'

'I don't suppose Uncle Tom will help?' Jess ventured.

'You heard him. He won't. Come with me, Jess, please? I have to talk to Minnie to explain . . . and she's going to be upset and I really can't face it alone.'

Jess took her hand. 'You know you can always count on me, Mam.'

It hadn't been an easy interview. Minnie had been very tearful but at least she understood and Maddy had promised a glowing reference. It was a subdued, red-eyed girl who ushered Johanna in later that afternoon.

'I can see you've told her,' Johanna remarked.

'We both did. Naturally she's upset. How did you get on, Jo?'

'Father Miller said he will say a special Mass on Monday morning at eleven o'clock. Most of the families live in either his parish or the surrounding ones. He asked if there were any special hymns or prayers you'd like? I can choose them if you don't feel up to it, Maddy.'

Maddy thought for a few minutes. 'I'd like the reading from St Matthew's Gospel. Chapter eight, verses twenty-four to twenty-six.' Her voice dropped, and quietly she recited, ' "And suddenly a great tempest arose on the sea, so that their boat was covered with the waves. But He was asleep.

' "Then His disciples came to Him and awoke Him saying 'Lord, save us! We are perishing!'

' "But He said to them, 'Why are you fearful, oh ye of little faith?' Then He arose and rebuked the winds and the sea and there was great calm." ' She paused, gathering her thoughts. 'And then from the Beatitudes, number two, "Blessed are those who mourn for they shall be comforted." I think they'll be soothing.'

Johanna nodded, her mood equally subdued. 'And the hymns?'

'The sailors' hymn, "Eternal Father, strong to save", and "Hail, Queen of Heaven, the ocean star". They're both appropriate.'

'I'll make sure he knows. Has Patrick come home yet?'

'Been and gone. He had this eejit of a scheme to invest what little we do have in stocks and I told him it wouldn't work. I also told him I intend to give a few pounds to each bereaved family. He didn't agree and there was an argument and he stormed off again.'

Johanna sighed. 'They have so little, Maddy. I'm afraid I won't be able to persuade Tom to do the same, but I wish I could.'

'No, you won't, Jo. He's no compassion or sense of duty.'

'He'll be at the Mass. We *all* will,' Johanna said firmly. She knew she'd have no trouble with Ronan. Tom would be a different kettle of fish, although surely he wouldn't refuse to attend? Well, if she needed Ronan's help to persuade him she knew she'd get it. She felt sorry for Maddy. Patrick was little better than useless now that his safe world had crashed around his ears. She too was reminded of how like Carmel Patrick was. Carmel hadn't been able to cope with anything.

Chapter Five

MR FREDERICKSON WAS FULL of sympathy as he ushered Maddy into his office. He had known her for years, ever since she had been Mrs Buckley's maid and companion, and he'd watched her grow from a pleasant, generous young girl into the strong, loyal and still generous woman. She'd had her fair share of tragedy in the past, but nothing on the scale of what now faced her.

'Mrs Brennan . . . Maddy, on behalf of myself and the staff of the bank, please accept our condolences. It's a terrible tragedy. It's hit the city hard.'

'I know and thank you for your concern.' She was trying to sound brisk and businesslike; she didn't want this meeting to degenerate into a morass of self-pity. 'Apart from everything else, I find I'm in a desperate position financially.'

He frowned as he shook his head sadly. 'Due to the loss of three ships and their cargoes. Were they not insured?'

'They were but not substantially. My brother dealt with that side of the business and he's always tried to cut corners.

That money will have to go to pay the debts and it won't clear them.'

'I understand.'

Maddy looked at him sadly. 'No, I'm afraid you don't. Due to the high-handed, eejit actions of my brother we are in danger of losing our home.'

The man leaned forward. 'How is that possible, Maddy?'

'My brother doesn't bank with you, so you won't know his financial position. He misled Martin over the cost of a new, fourth ship by a large amount. To raise the extra money he mortgaged his own house and mine. With the loss of the ships and the fact that we haven't finished paying for the third one, his bank will foreclose.'

He was shocked, even though he knew a little of her brother's character. There had been that unsavoury business all those years ago of Tom Kiernan increasing Mrs Buckley's housekeeping cheques without her knowledge and for his own personal gain. It had been one of the reasons Tom Kiernan had taken his business elsewhere.

'Maddy, my dear, this is indeed terrible news.'

'I've come to you for advice. I know I'll have to sell most of my possessions, and both Jess and Patrick will find work, but will that be enough? In addition I have promised to pay every family who lost their breadwinner when the ships sank a small compensatory sum.'

He looked grave. 'You have no other savings or investments?'

'Albert, you know we haven't. We ploughed everything back into the business, apart from money to run the house and keep us.'

'Then I'm sorry to say that I'm afraid you will lose your

home,' he said regretfully. He admired her sense of duty and generosity in wanting to do something for the unfortunate families, but was it wise when she was in such a dire predicament herself? 'This may sound harsh, Maddy, but you really can't afford to give money away. Please, think very carefully about it.'

'I *have* to, Albert. I've promised and I know that Martin wouldn't want me to renege on that promise, even though it means hardship for my family. We have so much more than any of those poor women have.'

'I think your best option is to try and raise enough money to purchase or rent a small house in a . . . less . . . er . . . select neighbourhood.'

'I'll try. I'll have to get the best price I can for . . . everything.'

'Make sure you do it quickly. By rights Tom's bank may be entitled to it. And please think carefully about reimbursing the families. Perhaps I could give you a small loan? A personal loan, nothing to do with this bank.'

He didn't have much and he was saving it for his retirement, which wasn't that far off, but he couldn't see her thrown out on the streets.

Maddy shook her head. 'Thank you, I really do appreciate that, Albert. It's so generous and kind of you, but no. How could I pay it back? There will be little enough money coming in for the bare necessities.'

'Well, if you change your mind, please call in to see me. I'll do anything I can to help.'

Maddy stood up. There was nothing more to say. The interview hadn't helped to ease her mind. Albert Frederickson had only confirmed what she already knew: that the house would be sold to reimburse Tom's bank. Well, she might as well go home, she thought dejectedly.

Jess knew by the look on her mother's face that the visit had been fruitless.

'Did he give you any help, Mam?'

'No, Jess. He was very kind and he did offer me a loan from his own savings but I refused it. I'm in enough debt already. He suggested buying or renting a small house in a poorer area.'

'Then we'll have to sell—'

'Everything – and before Tom's bank and their bailiffs get their hands on it!' Maddy interrupted. 'Is Patrick back?'

'No.'

Maddy sighed. 'Oh, maybe it's for the best that he stays there. Perhaps it will give him time to sort himself out.'

Jess nodded but without conviction. 'Ronan called. He only stayed a few minutes.'

'That was good of him. What did he say?'

'That he's very sorry he can't do more to help us, but he has to think of Aunt Jo first. He has a little money of his own and if things get really bad, well, he'll do what he can.'

Maddy nodded. 'Let's make an inventory and then this afternoon we'll take it down to the Auction Rooms in Hanover Street. They'll collect large items by cart and they have auctions nearly every day. I'll take the jewellery to Boodle & Dunthorne's.'

'Wouldn't it be better to take it to a pawnbroker?'

'No, I'll sell it, Jess, not pawn it.'

'How much will the auction bring in?'

Maddy shrugged. 'Maybe forty guineas, maybe less.'

'Is that all, Mam?' Jess cried.

'Jess, it's not all antique and you only get half of nothing for second-hand furniture.'

Jess glanced around her sadly. Was that all they would get for a home that had been furnished lovingly over as many years as she could remember? Home – this house – meant so much to her. All her memories were here.

'It's no use moping, let's have something to eat and then we'll start. At least it will give us something to do to keep us occupied,' she added with a catch in her voice.

Midway through the afternoon Patrick arrived home.

'What's going on?' he demanded, looking around to where pictures, ornaments, silver, china, crystal glasses and cutlery were piled on tables and sofas.

'Nearly everything is to go for auction, so we're making an inventory. Mam's going to take our jewellery and sell it.'

'Would you get your things together for me, Patrick? I'm sorry, but we have to find the money to pay for a roof over our heads.'

He was annoyed. 'If you'd only listen to me, none of this would be necessary.'

'Please, don't let's start an argument, Patrick?' Maddy begged.

Oh, he looked so petulant, like a spoiled child, Jess thought to herself.

'I . . . I'd like to keep my things. Well, at least the money they make,' he said mutinously.

'What for?' Jess demanded.

'I told you. There's a good investment in certain stocks and

I intend to put as much as I can into them. Terence says it can't fail.'

Jess lost her temper. 'Oh, Patrick Brennan, you selfish *eejit!*' she cried. 'Don't you understand that we've got to get as much money together as we can to be able to afford a roof over our heads? And not a very good roof either. Probably somewhere in Everton or Anfield. Just who is this Terence? He certainly seems to have taken you in. If it was that simple to make a fortune, then how come half the city isn't wealthy?'

'I don't expect you to understand, Jess! He's a friend, a good friend, and he's promised to help me all he can.'

'Then he's as much a fool as you are!' Jess said scathingly.

Patrick lost all patience. 'Oh, you're both impossible!'

'I suppose you're going running back to this Terence and your club – again!' Jess mocked.

He ignored her jeering and turned to his mother. 'So, can I keep my watches and cufflinks and studs?'

Maddy nodded. She was too weary to argue.

'I hope you'll be sorry after you've sold them and lost the money! The day you make a fortune from gambling in stocks is the day pigs will fly!' Jess called after him.

'Jess, there's no use you getting into a temper, he'll not change his mind. He can be so stubborn at times – just like you!'

'All right, Mam. I'll put the kettle on; we'll have a bit of a break,' Jess replied, resignedly.

Maddy had made an appointment to see the manager of the jeweller's after lunch on Monday.

'I'd hoped to make it much earlier than that. I wanted to

have got it over with before the Memorial Mass, so I could give the widows something afterwards.'

'Well, it can't be helped, Mam.'

They were all dreading the Memorial Mass. It was going to be an ordeal and Maddy would be so glad when it was all over. Jess resolved to help her mother all she could. Patrick's sole contribution was the fact that he had actually agreed to go, she thought angrily. He hadn't been home at all, all weekend, and she knew her mother was worried and disappointed with him.

The church was packed with women and children, and there was a fair scattering of men too. Maddy ignored Tom completely although she did manage a nod and a smile for Johanna and Ronan as she took her place on the opposite side of the church. She was surprised to see Mr and Mrs Dempsey, Senior, and Edward Dempsey in the pews near the front. She thought of Arthur and Aideen who were still on honeymoon and what an awful shock Aideen would have when she returned.

Throughout the service she kept her head bent and fought to control her emotions. There was so much sorrow and grief in the church. She could hear the stifled sobs, the muttered prayers and exhortations, and her heart, full of her own misery, went out to the women who from now on would find life a hard-fought, relentlessly grinding battle against poverty and destitution. A battle some would lose, ending up either taking to the bottle and the temporary oblivion it provided or in the place they feared and dreaded most – the workhouse.

The readings and the hymns gave her little comfort. The heartbreak and loss were too raw, her anger against her brother too consuming and she still had another hurdle to overcome, one she prayed she could get through without breaking down completely.

Jess too felt desperately miserable. She longed for the strong, comforting arms of her father and his ability to put everything into perspective. She could only hope that, after this service, time would heal their pain.

Patrick's anger and resentment smouldered on. It was inconceivable to him that his mother was going to give away what little they had to this crowd of weeping, poorly dressed and, in some cases, not very clean women and their numerous offspring. It wouldn't have been so bad if she'd taken his advice. Well, when he made his promised fortune he wasn't going to see a penny of it passed over to anyone. It would be *his* alone, to do with whatever he wished.

At the end of the Mass, Father Miller announced that Mrs Brennan wished to say a few words and he encouraged Maddy to go up to the altar-rails.

Jess clasped her hands tightly together in her lap. Her poor mother would need every ounce of her strength in the next few minutes. She glanced across to where her uncle sat, staring straight ahead, his face a mask of disapproval. There would be no last-minute offer of help or support from him, she thought bitterly.

Maddy cleared her throat and prayed that somehow Martin would help her. This was something she *had* to do.

'I . . . I'm so sorry that we have all had to come here at all this morning. I share your loss and your heartbreak, and I hope you will all feel that now there has been this service, this blessing, perhaps we can feel comforted. Our husbands, fathers and brothers have no grave except the sea, but we will always remember them, pray for them and as Father Miller has said, "when the sea shall give up its dead we will be reunited".' She swallowed hard and fixed her eyes on the statue of the Blessed Virgin at the back of the church. 'I know that their deaths will cause great hardship for so many of you and while I too have suffered financially, I feel it is my duty, and something my dear husband would have agreed with, to try to give you all a few pounds to help you over the dark and lonely days that lie ahead of us. God bless and keep you all.'

She could barely see her way back to the pew, so blinded was she by her tears.

Jess took her hand and squeezed it, blinking back her own tears. 'Oh, Mam, you were so strong and sincere.'

Maddy nodded, unable to reply. Today was almost as bad as Thursday had been, but she had no choice except to get through it.

In the churchyard, Maddy was soon lost in a crowd of grateful women. It was so rare for anyone to help them but Mrs Brennan was trying, even though she shared their grief.

'Jess, may I say how sorry I am?'

Jess turned around. Edward Dempsey was looking at her with pity in his eyes.

'Thank you, Edward. It was very kind of you to come.'

'It's a terrible tragedy. How are you coping?' He seemed genuinely concerned about her.

'We're doing just that – coping – but it's not easy.'

'Your mother is a very strong, thoughtful, generous woman. I admire her tremendously.'

'She . . . she feels very strongly about helping.'

'I was a little puzzled. She said you are suffering financially?'

'Well, we have lost three ships.'

'But they must have been insured.'

'Yes, they were,' she replied flatly.

'I'm so sorry, I shouldn't be asking such prying questions.'

Jess managed a smile. 'That's all right, Edward. I know you are concerned and thank you.'

'May I offer you a lift home? I do have my own transport,' he added, seeing her gaze settle on his parents who were talking to the priest. He'd also noticed the rapid departure of her uncle and his family.

'That would be grand. Mam has to go into Liverpool: some business matter, and she refuses to let me go with her.'

'Your mother seems to know her own mind.'

'She does. She's a very strong person, much stronger than me or Patrick.'

'Your brother seems to have left.'

'He has,' she replied sharply.

Here was another area where he obviously had to tread carefully. He regarded Patrick Brennan as something of an oddity although he really didn't know him that well. It was just his mannerisms, and his rather bland, weak-looking features. He had none of the vivacity and vitality his mother and sister had shown before this tragedy struck.

As the carriage made its way towards the suburbs, he kept up a steady flow of small talk on everyday topics that didn't need replies; Jess found his company restful. He was very sure of himself in a quiet way and she wondered idly why he had not married. In certain quarters he would be considered quite a catch. He was older than Arthur and therefore would inherit his father's position and most of his wealth.

'I realise you are in mourning and it's very soon to be asking, but I wonder would you consider having dinner with me, when you feel up to it?'

Jess dragged her mind back to the present. 'I'd like that, Edward, but not yet. Perhaps in a couple of weeks?'

'I understand. It was rather crass of me to ask but . . . the truth is, I hold you in very high esteem.'

Jess looked at him. 'You do have a very formal turn of phrase, Edward.'

'I suppose I do. It's the way I was brought up,' he said apologetically.

She smiled. She imagined that many girls would find his formality off-putting, but she quite liked it. Beneath the outwardly stiff person was a polite and sincere man.

He continued to chat until they reached the house, where he helped her down. 'When can I call on you, Jess, or perhaps it would be better if I wrote?'

She remembered their dire financial position. 'I think it would be better if I were to write to you. Things are a little . . . confused.'

'Of course. I'll wait, then, for word from you. Goodbye, and please give my condolences and regards to your mother.'

She smiled up at him and was startled when he took her hand and kissed it. It was something so completely out of character, she imagined, but just what did it signify? Well, there were other more important things to worry about, she thought as she opened the front door.

As she sat in the hackney cab on her way to town Maddy felt emotionally drained, and physically exhausted too. She'd had hardly any sleep lately but at least the service was behind her now. She leaned her head against the padded leather back of the cab. This would be one means of transport she'd have to give up. From now on it would be trams or Shanks's pony. She wondered just how much money she could raise from the contents of the black leather Gladstone bag that rested on the floor by her feet. It had to be substantial and she would haggle like any market woman.

To save money she asked the cab driver to set her down at the bottom of London Road. She'd walk from there. It was quite a long walk to Lord Street but it was a fine day, it would do her good. Perhaps it would clear her head: she needed to concentrate, something she hadn't been very good at lately.

Gripping the handle of the bag tightly, she crossed over to the huge, impressive colonnaded façade of St George's Hall. It really was a magnificent building, she thought, gazing at the four bronze lions on their marble plinths that guarded the approach to the plateau and the numerous steps that led up to the building itself. She'd walk down to Ranelagh Street, up Church Street and into Lord Street. It would be quicker that way, despite all the traffic. She would keep away from all the expensive shops in Bold Street where she had often taken her business in the past.

She walked on, deep in thought, oblivious of her surroundings, until she realised that people around her were shouting and screaming and waving at her. She was puzzled. What was wrong? What did they mean? Why all the urgency? And there was another noise too, like a drum being beaten. She turned around and her eyes widened in horror. She was rooted to the spot with fear. It was too late! Far too late! The last thing she saw was the flying mane, the eyes rolling in terror and the white-flecked muzzle. She went down under the huge flying, feathered hooves and the crazed horse galloped on, the broken traces trailing behind it, its driver and a young policeman racing in grim pursuit.

Chapter Six

————◆————

THE POLICEMAN WAS STILL there when Johanna and Ronan arrived. Johanna was half out of her mind with worry. All she'd received was a scrawled note in Jess's handwriting saying: *Please come quickly. Mam's had an accident.*

She looked around the clean and tidy kitchen but there was no sign of either Jess or Patrick.

'What happened? Where are my niece and nephew? Have they gone to the hospital?'

The man looked perturbed. 'The young lady is upstairs, ma'am. She appears to be alone.'

Ronan frowned. Patrick was missing again; typical, he thought.

'But what's happened to Maddy? Mrs Brennan? Is she badly hurt?' Johanna pleaded for information.

The constable shuffled his feet. She didn't know. God, this was terrible, having to break the news a second time. 'Did no one tell you, ma'am?'

'Tell me what?'

'She . . . she's dead, I'm afraid.'

Johanna stared at him in horror. 'No! No! She can't be!' She clutched the edge of the table for support. She felt faint.

'Sit down, please, ma'am. I'll get you a glass of water. Sir, she's not well.'

Gently Ronan eased his mother into a chair while the constable filled a glass with water.

'What happened to her? It's only a couple of hours since she was . . .' Ronan was shocked to the core. It was just too much. This would kill Jess. Her father and mother dead within a matter of days. Not even a week had elapsed.

'A runaway horse. It couldn't be stopped and she either didn't or couldn't hear all the warnings. It was over in a couple of seconds. A doctor was called but she was already dead. Killed instantly, a blow to the head or so the doctor said. If I had a pound for every damned horse that bolted in this city I'd be a rich man, and I know of a couple of colleagues who've been killed trying to catch and hold them. Those shire horses have the strength of a dozen men. I know, I stopped one myself. The Humane Society gave me a medal for it.' The constable brought himself up short. He was babbling. 'I'm so sorry for your loss.'

'Oh, Ronan! She must have been too distraught to hear anything until it was too late! Oh, poor, poor Maddy!' Johanna began to sob, covering her face with her hands.

'Mam, Mam, please!' Ronan looked at the policeman for support. He didn't know what to do for the best. He'd never seen his mother so upset before, but of course she and his Aunt Maddy had been very close.

'Best leave her to cry it out, sir.'

Ronan nodded. 'How did Jess, my cousin, take it?'

'I don't think it sank in, sir. She didn't say a word. There wasn't a tear either. She just asked that her note be sent to your mother and then she went upstairs. It's not natural to be so calm. It may be the calm before the storm, so to speak.'

'I know it's not the normal course of action, but I think I should go up and see that my cousin is all right. She won't be alarmed, when we were children we often played in our rooms together, all four of us, and Mother . . .'

The other man nodded. 'Best leave your mother here until she's composed herself. I'll keep my eye on her. Can the brother be contacted anywhere?'

'Black's Club in Islington. He's probably drowning his sorrows. There was a Memorial Mass at St Anthony's for those lost in the storm off America last week.'

'A bad business that,' the other man said grimly.

'My uncle, Jess's father, was one of them. He was the captain of the *Brennan's Pride*.'

'Oh, the poor girl!'

'I'd better go up.'

He paused outside Jess's door, nervous about what state he would find her in. He should have had a drop of brandy first. This was terrible but he had to make sure she was all right. He knocked gently and heard the muffled response.

Jess was sitting on the edge of the bed, staring straight ahead of her. Her pallor startled him.

'Jess, it's Ronan. How are you?'

She turned towards him and he thought he'd never seen

such emptiness in anyone's eyes. They looked utterly blank – dead even.

He reached out and took her hand and she clasped his tightly. 'Oh, Jess! I'm so sorry! Truly.'

'This isn't happening, Ronan. It *can't* be!'

'Jess, I'm afraid it *is* true. Mam is downstairs, but she's in no state to see you just yet.'

Jess didn't reply at first. She was looking past him at the photographs on her dressing table. She felt cold. It was as if the blood in her veins had turned to ice water and a lump of lead were sitting in her stomach. Apart from that everything seemed so . . . normal. Everything in this room was exactly the same as it had been five days ago, before . . . Her father smiled at her from the photograph, his eyes and his smile so like her own. Her glance fell on her mother's photograph. She dragged her mind back to the situation.

'What will I do, Ronan?'

Instantly he was at her side. 'Don't worry, Jess. I'm here. I'll take care of you.'

She looked up at him. He'd always been there to help her, even when they'd been children. He'd always fought her battles and backed her up. He was more than just her cousin, he was like an older brother and they were similar in so many ways.

'But what will happen?' she queried.

How he wished he could turn back the clock. 'Leave everything to me, Jess. I won't let you down, I promise.'

'Patrick?'

'They're sending for him.' He wished he could do more for her. The constable was right, she was too calm: she seemed broken. However, his words seemed to have given her some impetus. She stood up.

'I'll come down. I can't leave Aunt Jo alone.'

Ronan took her arm gently.

'It's all right, Ronan. I'm fine. I can manage.'

But he put his arm around her. 'Jess, you're not fine. You've had a terrible shock.'

When they reached the kitchen he was relieved to see that his mother was more composed.

As soon as she saw them Johanna rose and held out her arms to Jess.

Jess hugged her. 'I'm fine, Aunt Jo, really.'

Johanna glanced at Ronan who shook his head.

'Oh, Jess, what can I say? It's too much . . . just too much to bear.'

Jess held her hand. 'Don't be too upset. At least she's with Da now.'

Her tone struck fear into Johanna's heart. Jess had adored her mother. This wasn't right.

'Ronan, she'd be better coming home with me . . . us. So I can keep a watch on her.'

Jess snatched away her hand as though suddenly scalded. 'No! No, I'm not going to stay under Uncle Tom's roof! This is all his fault!' she cried forcefully.

'Oh, Jess, I know, but please?' Johanna begged. Jess's behaviour – the vehemence of her tone – had scared her.

Jess shook her head. 'I'll be all right here.'

'Then I'll stay with you. You shouldn't be on your own.'

'Patrick will be—'

'Not much use, if his track record is anything to go by!'

Ronan interrupted bitterly.

'Please, Ronan, don't say things like that. Will you go and tell your father everything?'

Ronan looked grim. 'I will, but don't expect me to have any consideration for him, even though Maddy is . . . was his sister. As Jess says, it *is* his fault!'

Jess turned to her cousin and clutched his arm tightly. 'Ronan, don't let him come here! I never want to see him again. If he does come I'll . . . I'll ask the constable to throw him out!'

Johanna bit her lip. Oh, what had things come to? She, too, blamed Tom but he couldn't have known that his pride and overweening ambition would lead to such terrible consequences. And he was far from well with the worry of it all. In fact she was afraid of what this news would do to him.

'Well, now you have everything . . . in hand, I'd better get back to the station house. My sergeant will be wondering what's the matter.' Privately, the policeman thought the last thing he wanted to be was caught up in a family feud.

Ronan pulled himself together. 'Thank you, constable, for your assistance. You've been very considerate and obliging.'

The young man's expression became grim. 'I hate this part of the job.'

Ronan nodded. He could understand that very well.

When both men had gone it was Jess who made a pot of tea and cut some Madeira cake.

Her manner was frightening Johanna. 'Jess, I couldn't eat a thing. Do you really and truly feel so in control of yourself?'

'I do. It's very strange but I feel as though I have to cope with everything, because it's what she would have done. What she *was* doing, until . . . I know what she would have wanted, and that's for me to carry on as best I can.'

Johanna couldn't reply. She was afraid that all this might have a terrible effect on Jess's mental health. This behaviour certainly wasn't normal.

'I have some laudanum somewhere, will you have a few drops? It might help,' Jess asked her.

'Not yet, Jess, maybe later. Why don't *you* have some?'

'Before I go to bed perhaps.'

Johanna watched her move around the kitchen. Oh, she just hoped Jess wasn't losing her mind. Surely, something, something must make her break down and cry? It wasn't good for all the grief to be kept inside. She herself had cried so much of late that she thought she had no more tears left.

They were sitting in the drawing room, where Johanna had drawn the curtains, as a sign to the neighbours that the family had suffered yet another bereavement, when Patrick arrived home.

He looked pale and stricken. 'Aunt Jo, is this right? They . . . they told me exactly what happened but . . . ?'

'They were right. Oh, Patrick, I'm so very sorry and Jess . . . well, Jess is—'

'I'm fine, Patrick, really I am.'

His face crumpled. 'What are we going to do now? You know I can't stand all this tragedy.'

'We're going to carry on as normal. It's what Mam would have wanted,' Jess replied steadily.

He looked disbelievingly at his aunt who shook her head. 'I'm staying here, Patrick, so don't worry. We'll get through the next few days somehow.'

He nodded wordlessly and turned towards the door.

'Where are you going?' Jess demanded.

'Up to my room.'

'I thought you were going back to your club.'

'No. Not yet, at least. I need time. Time to myself.'

Johanna sighed with relief. The last thing anyone needed right now was friction that would lead to another argument. They were alone in the world now. They needed each other.

Patrick sat down on his bed. What was happening? His world was crashing around him. First Father, then the ruination of the business, now Mother. He caught sight of his reflection in the dressing-table mirror. He looked awful, but who wouldn't? This was all his uncle's fault, he thought angrily. Never in his life had he felt so insecure. Never in his life had he needed to worry about anything – except perhaps money – but now . . . What would happen to them? A thought suddenly occurred to him. He was now the heir to his father's estate, such as it was. He had to make his own decisions, something else he'd never had to do before. Well, of one thing he was certain. He wasn't going to give a single penny away, regardless of what his mother had promised. He couldn't, wouldn't be bound by promises she'd made. They would go to the grave with her. He just might be able to hang on to the house, if the bank could be persuaded to give him more time. If not he would definitely be able to buy something smaller, but still in a decent area. Another thought occurred to him. There was something that hadn't yet been mentioned. Hastily he went back downstairs. His aunt looked at him questioningly but he turned to his sister.

'Jess, did the police say anything about the jewellery Mam was taking to sell?'

Jess hadn't even thought about it. 'No, why?'

'Because we'll need that money. I'd better go down to the police station and see them. The stuff the old lady left to Mam was very valuable.'

'Patrick! Do you have to go right now? Can't it wait?' Johanna asked.

'No. Don't you see, we *must* have that money.'

'What for?' Jess demanded.

'So we won't have to sell up.'

'Is that all you can think about? Don't you care for anyone other than yourself?'

'Jess, it's for *us*. This is something that has to be done right away. It's very important that we find out.'

'Ronan will go,' Johanna offered.

'No. It's something I have to do myself.'

'Oh, let him go,' Jess said wearily, and Patrick, more animated than she had seen him in days, rushed from the house.

Johanna couldn't settle. What was happening to the family? She couldn't understand the attitudes of either her niece or nephew. 'Will I make more tea?' she asked at length. Jess had said nothing more. She just gazed into space.

'Not for me, thanks. Will we have to go to identify her formally?'

'I don't know, Jess. Perhaps Patrick and Ronan could do it? Oh, now what?' Johanna cried as there came a loud hammering on the front door.

A grimy young lad stood on the step with a note in his hand.

'This is for you, missus. The feller gave me a penny to bring it.'

Johanna took the folded piece of paper and opened it gingerly. Folded pieces of paper were proving to be harbingers of bad news. As she scanned the lines, her hand went to her throat.

'Oh, Jess, I'm so sorry but I have to go home. It's Tom.'

'What?' Jess hadn't really been taking much notice.

'He's ill. This is from Ronan, saying he has called the doctor. He found Tom collapsed.'

'Then go. You *have* to, Aunt Jo. He's your husband.'

Johanna nodded. How much more could they take? How much more could *she* take? She prayed nothing would happen to him. 'Jess, I . . .'

'Go! Go, quickly! Don't worry about Patrick or me, but let me know if . . .'

'I will. Promise me you'll take something to make you sleep?'

'I will.'

Time seemed suspended. After Johanna had left, she'd gone back into the kitchen. There was no clock but it was growing dark outside. Jess rocked herself back and forth in the old chair by the range. She knew the way she was feeling and behaving wasn't right, but she felt detached in some way. It seemed as though no matter what fate threw at her, she was able to cope with it. It was as if all her emotions were frozen, enabling her to rise above everything. Everything except the fact that it was all her uncle's fault. Her anger against him was the only thing that caused her heart to quicken.

The room darkened but she didn't get up to light the lamps.

The darkness and the silence were comforting.

She didn't know whether it was hours or minutes before she heard Patrick return.

She didn't speak as he came into the room.

'Jess? Are you still in here?' She heard him fumbling with a match and then the yellow glow of the oil lamp partly illuminated the room. 'It's gone, Jess.'

'What has?'

'The jewellery. There was no bag handed in. Someone in that crowd certainly took advantage of the situation. I don't understand just what the police were doing, not to have noticed it and taken charge of it and I told them too!'

He was incensed. They'd treated him as though he were a half-witted child. Was he absolutely sure there had been a bag? Shock, grief and bereavement could make your mind play tricks. Maybe it had been yesterday when his mother had had a bag with her? How the hell could it have been, he'd shouted, yesterday was bloody Sunday. There were no jewellers open. The sergeant had raised his eyebrows and exchanged glances with his colleagues. Expressions that said, 'Humour him, he's harmless.'

'Oh.'

'Is that all you can say, Jess? It was worth hundreds of pounds! Money we need!' he cried angrily.

Jess got to her feet. 'Money we need?'

'To keep a roof over our heads. I was going to ask the bank to give me more time. We have to live! Neither of us are used to doing without.'

'We'll have to get used to it, won't we?' she said coldly.

He was losing patience with her. 'No, we won't! But there'll only be the money from the auction and that won't be much. I . . . won't be able to invest as much as I thought I'd be able to.'

She stared at him, anger rising in her. '*Invest!* You're going to invest it in that mad scheme?'

'There's no other way of us making enough to keep this house. To keep *any* house!'

'You'll lose the lot! You know what Mam said about investing.'

He balled his fists in his pockets and his expression became hard. 'Well, she's not here. She didn't make a will. I *know* that. Dad did and he was always reminding her to do the same but she never did. Everything belongs to me now. What's left of it. It's mine.'

Her eyes widened and she too clenched her fists. 'Yours!'

'Yes, *mine*, Jess. Of course, I won't see you out on the street, but—'

'Oh, you fool, Patrick! You bloody fool! Don't you realise that you'll have us both out on the street with your stupid investments?'

Patrick lost his temper. 'I'm not standing here listening to any more of your insults! You just don't understand, Jess! You'll never understand!'

'No, I won't! I'll never understand why you are so much of an eejit!'

He snatched up his hat.

'Don't tell me! You're running back to your friend who'll tell you a pack of lies and you'll go on believing him!' she cried derisively.

'Oh, go to hell, Jess!' he yelled, slamming out.

Jess stared at the door and then it was as if the force that had been holding all her emotions in check was suddenly removed. Darkness crept over her, she stumbled and then slid senseless to the floor.

Chapter Seven

———◆———

WEARILY JOHANNA LET HERSELF in, then steeled herself for what lay ahead.

Ronan was waiting in the hall looking anxious.

'I'm sorry about the note. I couldn't leave him and there was no other way of contacting you even though I knew it'd be yet another shock.'

'Ronan, where is he?' Johanna interrupted.

'In bed. Dr Phillips is with him. He does seem a little better, at least he's making sense, knows where he is, things like that.'

Wordlessly Johanna went up the stairs and Ronan followed her.

The doctor turned towards her looking cheerful. 'He's a lot better now, Mrs Kiernan, I'm glad to say.'

Johanna crossed to the bed and took his hand. 'Oh, Tom! I was worried! It's been one thing after another and I was afraid that you too—'

'Ah, hush now, Jo. I'm fine. It was just a little turn and is it any wonder?' he interrupted a little testily.

'Now, Mr Kiernan, that's not strictly true. You'll *have* to take things easy and I won't hear another word on the subject.'

'Tom, you'll have to do as Dr Phillips tells you, no matter how hard it is. You'll just have to put . . . things . . . to the back of your mind.'

'Aye, well, that's easy enough to say, Jo, but not so easy to do.'

'Father, you need peace and quiet and rest.'

'I've left some medicine for him. Keep him on a light diet and no alcohol. I'll call again to see him tomorrow but if you need me before, just send for me. I wonder, Mrs Kiernan, might I have a word?'

Johanna reluctantly followed the doctor out of the room.

'How bad is he?'

'He's had a heart attack. He was lucky it was a mild one, but he should take it as a warning. He has to rest and if possible not to worry about anything. Ronan has already told me of the terrible tragedies you've all suffered, so it won't be easy for any of you. How is young Miss Brennan taking it all?'

'She's very calm. So calm, it's not natural. She idolised both her parents, and I'm afraid it will affect her mind.'

'Grief affects us all in different ways. We all have our own methods of dealing with it, but I would keep my eye on her, if you're able, Mrs Kiernan. Now what about you? How are *you* managing?'

Johanna managed a tired smile. 'I'm holding up as best I can.'

'That's good. I've noticed over the years that you women are much stronger than us men, especially when it comes to the really big problems in life.'

'Maddy – Mrs Brennan – was a very strong woman.'

'Then maybe her daughter takes after her. The young are very resilient. They usually cope with change well, something that it's harder for us to do. So, you see your husband *must* have rest and if possible some relief from the worry.'

'Doctor, I don't know how I can possibly ease his mind.'

'Just try. Now, remember, if you need me day or night, send word.'

'Thank you, doctor. I'd better get back to him now.'

'Goodbye, Mrs Kiernan.'

Johanna closed the door and leaned against it. Would life ever be uncomplicated again?

'Was it his heart?'

Johanna looked up to see Ronan descending the stairs. 'Yes. He has to rest and not worry! Two things your father has never been good at doing. Things can't get any worse, surely.'

'And what about you?'

'Oh, I'll manage – somehow.'

'I'll take care of everything and I mean *everything*. A house, the bills, the sale of what we have left, some sort of a job for him, if he's able. I don't want *you* to worry, Mam.'

'Oh, Ronan, what would I do without you? I'm hoping that Aideen will help out too.'

'Don't bank on it, Mam. She may ask Arthur's father for a job for Father, but I don't think we should expect more.'

'Perhaps you're right. Now, I have to get back to him. Thank you, Ronan, you've eased my mind a great deal.'

He watched her go quickly up the stairs and sighed. What else could he have done?

Johanna sat by the bed and took her husband's hand. 'Tom,

you really must do what Dr Phillips says. You've had a mild heart attack. He said it was a warning and . . . and I've lost so many people who were dear to me that if anything happened to you . . .' There was a catch in her voice.

Tom patted her hand. 'Oh, Jo, I'm so sorry for what I'm putting you through. I'm not a bad person, you know that.'

She nodded. 'You're *not* bad. It's just that you were never satisfied with what you had, that was your downfall.'

'I couldn't help being ambitious, Jo. I always wanted to get on in life, even when I was a lad back in Ireland. I wanted the best for all of you. I wanted what Martin and Maddy had. Money and a position in Society so no one could look down on me and say, "There goes that poor gossoon Tom Kiernan."'

'I know, Tom, but we were happy and comfortably off, we didn't need any more than that.'

'I'll suffer this guilt and pain for the rest of my life. And what will the future bring?'

'You're not to worry about the future, Tom. Ronan has promised to sort everything out and he will. We can be proud of him, Tom, we couldn't have a better son. He's very practical and sensible.'

'Just like you, Jo.'

She shook her head. 'No, I don't think I'm very sensible at all. I should have put my foot down over Aideen's wedding. We both should have.'

There was a silence until Tom faltered, 'I . . . I'm so sorry about Maddy. I really am. Oh, she irritated and exasperated me most of the time but she was my sister and she was good to us despite everything I did.'

'I know. But she would never really have been happy without Martin.'

'Well, she's with him now, and we should be thankful for that at least,' Tom answered.

'We'll have to take care of Jess and Patrick, they have no one else now.'

Tom regained some of his former spirit. 'Patrick will need taking in hand. The boy's a fool. Maddy indulged him because she had some strange notion that because he was born the year Carmel died Patrick was like her and needed even more support than Carmel did, God rest her. Maddy thought she had let Carmel down, but Carmel was a fool with not a brain in her head. Martin worried about Patrick too. He told me often enough that he didn't know how the lad would turn out. Jess is a different matter altogether. She's like Maddy and Martin. She'll make her way in the world.'

'But she'll need help, Tom, and we'll always be here for her. Now, try and rest. Everything is in safe hands and I don't want to lose you or have you an invalid for ever.' She bent and kissed his forehead. He had caused terrible suffering and family strife, and being inactive would be so very hard for him, but he was her husband and she still loved him.

Patrick downed the brandy in one gulp. Oh, how he needed that.

'So, all in all you've had a bloody awful day.' Terence Shay looked and sounded sympathetic as he turned the stem of the brandy glass between his fingers.

He had been fully aware of the animosity directed towards him by Patrick's family. It didn't bother him, in fact he could smile sardonically about it. He had almost everything in life he had craved. Money, a decent place of his own, expensive and fashionable clothes, the membership of this club: not bad for a lad from the slums of Manchester. And he owed it all to luck, to the gift he had for backing a winner, whether it be horses or, more recently, stocks and bonds. However, someone from his background (although he never freely disclosed that information) and with his accent was not readily accepted by his betters, so Patrick Brennan's friendship was something he was very keen on cultivating. Patrick's family had risen from obscurity in one generation. They had built up a very successful shipping line which would have continued to grow steadily under Martin Brennan and Tom Kiernan. They had amassed wealth and, because of both Martin and Maddy's personal characteristics, had been accepted by the upper echelons of Liverpool business society. They were even connected to the Dempseys. Yes, Patrick Brennan might provide the last thing he longed for: social cachet.

'It's been a dreadful day and Jess, well, Jess is impossible!' Patrick fulminated.

'Leave her alone, she'll get over it, women always do. They carry on like that just to annoy us, I'm sure.'

'She'll *have* to get over it!'

'You're sure your mother left no will?' Shay probed.

'Positive, but what does it matter now? The house will go to the bank, there are no savings, the jewellery has gone. There's only what I'll get from the auction and that won't go far.'

Shay noticed a passing waiter and indicated that two more brandies were needed. Then he turned back to Patrick. 'Pat,

I've told you not to worry. I'll take care of all your expenses until you get back on your feet.'

'I can't let you keep me, Terence,' Patrick protested.

'I won't be. It will be a sort of loan, until the investment pays off and it will, believe me. It's just a shame that you haven't more to invest but all that means is it will take a bit longer for you to recoup your losses. Trust me, I haven't lost a penny yet.'

Patrick mellowed a little. 'You really are a generous fellow. I . . . I never had many friends. Well, none at all really, just acquaintances, and now, when I'm really down and out, you offer me more than my family has. I'm truly grateful.'

Shay smiled. 'Well, what are friends for? And I know you'll reimburse me when you get back on your feet. Believe me, in a couple of months you'll be able to look back on all this and say, "Did all that really happen?" You'll be in a fine house with money of your own in the bank and no one will be able to look down their nose at you. This is just a temporary setback. Now, what about the funeral?'

Patrick looked confused.

'Your mother will have to be buried,' Shay said quietly.

'I suppose I'll have to see to it,' Patrick answered unenthusiastically. He hadn't even thought that far ahead but he now realised that he didn't relish taking it on.

'Why don't you leave it to me? It won't be that difficult, there are any number of good undertakers who will see to everything from the obituaries to the order of service. Just give me an idea of what you'd like and leave it in my hands. You've had enough to contend with lately.'

Patrick was effusive in his thanks. 'Would you *really*?

I don't want to see any of my family until I have to and it's so . . . painful.'

'Then it's as good as done. Now, here come our drinks and I'll tell Maitland that you will be staying here for the immediate future.'

Patrick felt as though a great weight had been lifted from him. He wasn't used to taking control and in his present state of mind everything had seemed dark and daunting.

'I really can't thank you enough! And as for the other matter, I'll be glad to reimburse you twice over.'

'I'm sure you will, Pat. I'm certain of it.'

Jess woke with a violent throbbing pain above her left temple. Her mouth felt dry and her eyes were burning. As she dragged herself up slowly she realised that she was fully dressed. It must have been the laudanum. That was what was the matter with her, it must be. She'd never taken it before; obviously she'd taken too much. She must somehow have dragged herself upstairs and collapsed on the bed. She vaguely remembered that she'd fainted and had come to on the kitchen floor.

She lay down again and closed her eyes. She felt awful. In fact she'd never felt so awful in her life before and yet there was something . . . something beneath the effects of the drug that was worse.

She was drifting off again when the sound of the front-door bell aroused her. She groaned and struggled off the bed. She felt weak and dizzy and clutched the doorpost for support. The sound of the bell seemed to be echoing in her head as she struggled downstairs.

'Jess! You look terrible!' Johanna took her arm and guided her into the drawing room. 'Where's Patrick?'

'Patrick?' Jess repeated sounding puzzled.

'Jess, sit down. I'll make some tea, you look as though you need it.'

'It's the laudanum . . . I feel . . .'

Johanna was very concerned. 'How much did you take?'

'I don't remember. It was after Patrick left . . .'

'He *left*! You haven't been here all night on your own?'

Jess nodded but the pain in her head made her gasp.

'Lean back against those cushions, I'll be back in a few minutes,' Johanna advised, feeling very guilty.

Jess felt a little better after the tea.

'Oh, Jess, I should have come back. What happened?'

Jess was trying to recollect but it was hard to concentrate. Slowly the events of yesterday came back. Mam was dead. A terrible, terrible accident, but she hadn't collapsed or been hysterical. She'd been filled with a strange calmness. Patrick had come home and then Aunt Jo had had to leave.

'Uncle Tom?' she asked at last.

'Is fine. He had a mild heart attack and has to rest. But what happened to you?' Johanna had never seen her niece look so ill. She was sure it wasn't just the laudanum; the realisation of Maddy's tragic death must have hit Jess at last.

'We had a row. Patrick . . . Patrick is taking everything. He won't honour Mam's promise, he's going to invest everything . . .'

'But what about you? He can't just abandon you,' Johanna cried.

'He did say he wouldn't see me without a home, but he'll

lose it all! I know he will! We'll have *nothing*!'

This was a far worse situation than Johanna had expected. 'Where is he?' she demanded.

'At that club with his friend,' Jess replied tiredly.

Johanna got to her feet. 'Right. I'm going to sort all this out. He's being totally irresponsible! He *can't* do this and he must be *made* to understand that. It's his duty – as your poor father would have wished – to take care of you.'

'I can look after myself. All I need is a bit of money to tide me over. I can work.'

'No, Jess, you can't look after yourself, not at this moment. Everything has been too much for you. When you feel a bit better, I want you to collect a few things and then you're coming home with me and Ronan can go and find Patrick and—'

At her aunt's words, Jess felt anger stir in her. The same anger she'd felt yesterday. Anger at her brother, but much stronger was the sheer fury she now felt for her uncle.

'No! I'm *not* going with you! This is all Uncle Tom's fault and I'll never forgive him!'

'Oh, Jess, please! He's sorry. He's so very sorry, he never intended any of this,' Johanna pleaded, upset and surprised at Jess's vehemence.

'I don't care! It is his fault, *all* of it! How could he do this? Oh, God! My head feels about to burst!' she cried, holding her head with both hands, as if to physically stop it from exploding.

Johanna was practical. 'Then it's back to bed for you. I'm staying here until you feel more yourself. All you can do is sleep it off.'

'I'm still not going home with you, not even when I feel better.'

'We'll talk about that later,' Johanna said firmly. 'Now let's get you upstairs. I'll make some cold compresses, they should help.'

As she helped Jess to her room, Johanna thought about her words to Ronan last night that things couldn't get any worse. Obviously she'd been wrong.

She sat in Maddy's morning room, her head in her hands. Oh, Maddy! Maddy, help me! she begged silently. Give me strength, please? Just give me a little of the strength you always had!

After a few minutes she pulled herself together. This wasn't helping anyone. Firstly she had to get a note to Ronan. Patrick's behaviour had to be sorted out.

When Ronan read his mother's note he felt the burden of responsibility settle even more heavily on his shoulders. Was there no end to it all? A fine mess his father's actions had left everyone in.

'How is Jess?' he asked his mother as he arrived.

'Not much better. The poor child took too much laudanum last night, I've sent her back to bed. Oh, I'm so worried about her, Ronan, she won't come home with me. She is still very very angry with your father.'

'That I can understand,' he said tersely.

'Ronan, please? I know it *is* his fault, but he didn't mean for all this to happen and you know he's ill.'

'I'm sorry, Mam. Now what is all this about Patrick?'

'The young fool is determined to lose every penny they

have by putting what money he'll make from the auction into stocks. They had a fight over it and he walked out and left her last night. I don't know what to do.'

Ronan looked grim. 'I do. Where is he? At his club – again?'

Johanna nodded.

Ronan picked up his hat. 'You stay with Jess until she wakes. I've asked Mrs Turnbull from next door to keep an eye on Father; she knows you're here. Leave Patrick to me. I'll sort this out.'

Johanna felt so relieved and thanked God that her son was not like his cousin.

Ronan had never been in Black's before and while the steward went to find Patrick he gazed around. It wasn't furnished or decorated in the dark, heavy way his father's club was. It was far more modern, which was probably why it appealed to younger men. These clubs had their place in Society, but he'd never felt the need to join one. Men came here for companionship, to discuss business, to get some peace and quiet away from their families and, like Patrick, to escape the pressures of life. Some even lived permanently in them. Ronan wasn't sure if such clubs were essential or even desirable.

When Patrick finally appeared, Ronan was surprised to see that his cousin wasn't alone. He was accompanied by a man of about the same age with dark hair and even darker eyes that darted about missing nothing. He was impeccably dressed in expensive clothes and a heavy gold watch chain was visible in his waistcoat pocket.

'Is there somewhere we can talk privately?' Ronan asked, looking pointedly at the other man.

'This is my close friend and business associate, Terence

Shay. Anything that has to be said can be said in his presence,' Patrick announced sharply.

'Really,' Ronan replied coldly. He had taken an instant dislike to the man. A sardonic smile hovered around Shay's mouth but his eyes were cold and calculating.

Patrick led them all into a small room that was obviously used for playing cards and smelled of stale tobacco smoke and hair oil. Both he and Shay sat but Ronan remained on his feet. He hadn't come for a social visit.

'So, what is all this nonsense about you taking control of what little there is of Uncle Martin's estate? You should be looking after Jess, not chasing pipe dreams and evading your responsibilities.'

Patrick looked annoyed. 'I *will* be looking after Jess and it's *not* a pipe dream. You tell him, Terence.'

Shay leaned back and pressed the tips of his fingers together. Obviously Ronan Kiernan disliked him, but the feeling was mutual. He cleared his throat. 'I have reliable information that stocks in a certain animal feed company will increase in value over the next couple of months,' he said slowly, as though talking to a not very bright child.

His manner infuriated Ronan. 'Indeed! And where does this "information" come from? Has an angel appeared to you in your sleep and urged you to buy Silcock's shares? I presume it is Silcock's you're referring to?'

'Ronan, I don't like your tone!' Patrick said angrily.

'It's all right, Pat, I'm used to dealing with sceptics. No, there was no angel. I don't need one, my own judgement is enough. I've made my own fortune that way,' Shay replied confidently.

'And what happens when you lose what money you have, when this deal falls through? How will you live then, Patrick?'

Shay did not let Patrick answer. 'The same way he is living now. Like a gentleman. I will support him – financially. It will only be for a short while. The deal won't "fall through", they never do.'

Ronan's dislike was turning to hatred. Just what kind of hold did this arrogant, supercilious, jumped-up, petty clerk have over Patrick? Shay didn't speak like a gentleman. He had an accent that for the minute Ronan couldn't place, but he was certain he came from poor stock. Of course his own father had come to Liverpool a penniless Irish emigrant, but with hard work and good fortune had become a wealthy and respected man and he himself was a member of a successful profession. If Shay had any kind of profession he doubted it was a respectable one. Couldn't Patrick, young fool though he was, see through him? He doubted very much that the man had a great deal of money. He was what his Aunt Maddy and his father would call a chancer.

'So, you are quite content to abandon your sister and let this . . . person pay your bills?'

Patrick jumped up, his face red. 'You don't understand, Ronan! Terence is my closest friend! He's goodness itself. I'm not abandoning Jess. I'll look after her even though she's stubborn and hot-headed and thinks I'm a fool. I'll look after Jess, when I can. Terence has even offered to pay for the funeral. Now that's what I call true friendship and generosity!'

Ronan's temper flared. '*He's* going to pay for your mother's funeral? Him? An outsider that no one knows anything about!

Keep your money, Shay! I'll pay for it. Patrick, you know she was dead set against this idiocy! I won't have her laid to rest with *his* money!'

Patrick was equally angry. 'She was *my* mother! It's *my* decision. It's none of *your* business, in fact this is all *your* father's fault so you can go to hell!'

'No sense in getting upset about it, Pat,' Shay intervened.

Ronan turned on him. 'I don't know what your game is, Shay, but I'll be watching you and if you put a foot wrong, by God you'll regret it!'

Patrick felt humiliated and furious. 'I won't have you speaking like that to my friend! Get out of here, Ronan, none of this is your business!'

Ronan turned on his heel and walked away, his fists balled in his pockets. He was filled with impotent anger. The plight of his own family, and the fact that his father possibly might no longer be fit to work, put a heavy strain on his finances, but he could have afforded to have given his aunt a quiet but respectable funeral. He had a horrible feeling that Patrick would turn it into a show of his own strength and position, aided and abetted by Shay. How would Jess take that news?

Jess looked around at the almost empty room. Just the bare essentials remained. It was the same in every room in the house. There wasn't a rug or carpet, ornament or picture, nor even a curtain at the window or a glass mantle over a gas jet. All the things she'd grown so used to, taken for granted, had been sold and they had brought only a pittance. A quarter of what they had cost over the years that Maddy and Martin had built their home. To watch everything being loaded onto the auctioneer's cart had been yet another heartbreaking experience.

She leaned her head against the windowpane. In ten short days her life had changed beyond all recognition, yet somehow she had coped with it all. Her father and mother had both gone and with them the money and security. Her home was being sold over her head and her brother didn't care. He had turned into a petty tyrant, aided and abetted by his so-called friend.

Anger was the only emotion that stirred in her now. Anger against her uncle and her brother. She had screamed at Ronan when he'd told her that he hadn't been able to change Patrick's mind and that Shay was paying for the funeral.

'NO! I won't stand for it! I'll pay! I'll find some way!' she'd cried, beating her fists against his chest.

'Jess, you have *nothing*! I said I'd pay. I wanted to, but I was told it wasn't any of my business.'

'Oh, Ronan, I can't let this happen! She would hate it!'

'There's nothing either of us can do. I know there's no money now but your father left everything to your mother and, as she died intestate, Patrick can do as he likes and no one can stop him!'

She'd clung to him and he'd held her tightly as she'd sobbed in anger, despair and grief.

He'd tried to soothe her. 'Jess, you don't have to go. Everyone will understand.'

Jess had raised her head. 'Ronan, I can't not go to my mother's funeral! I couldn't let her down like that.'

'She'd understand, I know she would.'

'But Patrick wouldn't. He'd think I was too weak, too

cowardly. That it would be my way of showing how . . . how I can't cope and am afraid of him and this weasel Terence Shay. No, I'll go, Ronan. I *have* to.'

'If you're sure, Jess.'

She'd nodded. 'I am.'

'What about . . . Father?'

She'd drawn away from him. Her expression had changed. 'What about him?'

'He is *really* sorry.'

'It's too late to be sorry now! I can't bring myself to speak to him, Ronan. I don't think I will ever change my feelings towards him,' she'd replied coldly.

'And Mam?' he ventured. It would hurt his mother terribly if Jess ostracised her too.

'I love Aunt Jo, it's not her fault.'

'But she'd be so much happier in her mind if you came to live with us. It would help her enormously.'

'Don't say that, Ronan! Don't try to blackmail me.'

'I'm sorry, Jess. That was unforgivable of me.' He'd meant it. Now part of her wished she could have agreed and had gone to live with them, but the other part – the stronger part – repudiated that wish. She had made up her mind what she would do.

She had made a parcel of the few things she had left that she cherished: a couple of photographs; an old cap and a broken pocket watch that had been her father's; her mother's small sewing box; the little enamelled brooch, a replica of the flag of the Brennan Line. There certainly wasn't much to show for all her years of growing up in this house that tomorrow she would have to leave. She would always think of this house, bare and forlorn though it now looked, as her home, but in her mind's eye she would remember it the way it had been. Not the way it looked now.

'Are you ready, Jess?' Johanna's quiet voice broke into her reverie.

'Yes.'

Johanna looked pale and tired and harassed as she took her niece's hand. 'I wish you'd reconsider,' she pleaded.

'I can't. It's nothing to do with you, Aunt Jo, you know that. I just *can't* bring myself even to speak to Uncle Tom.'

'I worry about you so much, Jess. You've had so much to bear and you're so resigned.'

'As I told you after we heard the news, it's very strange but I do feel calm. I know it's what she would have wanted me to be. I'm alone now and I'll manage.'

'Oh, Jess, you're not alone!' Johanna protested. 'You'll never be alone, not while you have me and Ronan and, if you ever need him, Tom. And I pray that God will change Patrick's mind about everything.'

'He might, but I don't think so. Patrick has always been different to me, different to all of us.'

'Except Carmel and I pray to God he won't end up the same way she did. So terrified and disgusted with life that she had to end it herself.'

'Mam would never talk about it.'

Johanna nodded. 'I know. It was terrible. She was so young, so beautiful and she had so much to live for – if only she'd have confided in us. We would have helped her.'

'I'm sorry, I've upset you.'

'Just don't cut yourself off from us, please?' Johanna patted her arm and dismissed the memories of her tragic sister-in-law. Carmel and now Maddy had suffered premature and tragic deaths, as had Martin. She hoped there would be no more.

The church was full and Father Miller had come to assist the parish priest. Jess kept her head down and refused to meet the gaze of either her uncle or her brother. She also kept her gaze from the coffin covered with expensive flowers, wherein lay her mother.

Before the Mass began the parish priest announced that this requiem was for the souls of both Martin and Maddy Brennan, as requested by their son, Patrick.

Ronan shot a quick look at his cousin and was annoyed to see that Terence Shay was sitting in the pew behind Patrick, as if he were a close family friend.

Jess didn't give either of them the satisfaction of looking up. She had seen her brother's friend when they had arrived at the church and she didn't like what she saw. And he was paying for everything, something she would never forgive Patrick for, even if he repaid the debt a hundred times over. Johanna was crying softly and her heart went out to her aunt. She and Mam had been closer than many sisters.

She struggled with her emotions all through the service, knowing the worst part was yet to come. She prayed hard that she would have the strength not to break down completely at the graveside.

She clung tightly to Ronan's arm in the cemetery, thankful that the shoulder-length black mourning veil hid her face as she tried in vain to hold back the tears. She felt that, in a way, both her parents were being laid to rest, for the priest included both their names in his eulogy and she knew that the headstone was being inscribed 'In Loving Memory of Martin and Magdalene Brennan', even though she had never heard her mother ever being called anything other than 'Maddy'.

'Jess, I'm so very sorry. It's tragic, just tragic!'

She lifted the veil and looked up into the concerned face of Edward Dempsey. She was taken aback. She hadn't seen him in the church.

'Thank you, Edward. Everything . . .' She lifted a black-gloved hand. 'Everything is so unreal.'

'It must certainly seem so. I really can't find the correct words. It's . . . stunning. If there is anything, no matter how small, that I can do to help, you will tell me?'

'Thank you, you're very kind.'

'And very concerned about you, Jess.'

'I'll be fine.'

He admired her courage enormously. He was sure that his mother, who was inclined to be domineering, would have taken to her bed if faced with so many overpowering disasters. He assumed she would now make her home with her aunt and uncle, just as he assumed her brother would make his own way in the world as any son of a man like Martin Brennan should.

'Please don't forget to write to me, Jess, when you are feeling up to it, of course.'

'I won't,' she replied politely, while wondering what possible use it would be to write to him or see him again, even though she did like him.

'Ah, here's Ronan. Well, goodbye, Jess, and please do take care of yourself.'

She nodded as Edward shook Ronan's hand and moved away. 'Jess, it's time to go,' her cousin said.

'Can I stay a bit longer?'

'If you want to, but everyone is leaving.'

Jess looked around and saw that they were virtually alone. 'You'd better go and help Aunt Jo.'

'Jess, I can't leave you.'

'Yes, you must! I'm fine, really I am. I just want some time to . . . be alone with her. To say my goodbyes to them both. By myself.'

He understood but was still anxious. 'But how will you get back?'

'By tram.'

'Jess, I can't let you do that!' he protested.

'Ronan, please? Please, I don't want any fuss.'

He took out some coins and a small roll of notes and pressed them into her hand. 'Take this, Jess. It's not much but it will see you over the next couple of days. Either Mam or I will come round later on to see how you are. It's your last night.'

'Thank you, Ronan.' She slipped the money into her purse as he turned reluctantly away.

She looked down at the freshly dug mound of earth and the wreaths of flowers. She knew what she had to do now.

She bent and plucked a white rose from one of the wreaths Patrick had bought. She'd keep it always.

'Give me the strength to be like you, Mam. Help me to make my way in the world, Da, so that when I see you again – whenever that will be – you'll be able to say you're proud of me. I have to go now, to start a new life away from wealth and the house I've always called home. A life in which

I'll work hard, at anything, the way you did, Mam, when you first came to Liverpool. I won't fall by the wayside. I won't do anything you'd be ashamed of. I know I'm not really alone, you'll always be with me, both of you. And one day I'll keep the promise you made, Mam, to all those poor bereaved women, so your name will be honoured. I promise you all of this, just help me along the way, please.'

Chapter Eight

J ESS LOOKED AROUND THE room with tears in her eyes. It was dreadful, really dreadful. There was a small window that overlooked the yard, its panes of glass dirty and fly-speckled. On the ceiling and part of the fireplace wall, large patches of damp discoloured the plaster. The woodwork was all rotten and the floor was flagged with uneven stones. It was dark and squalid, airless and dirty. The furniture consisted of an old table, a chair, a stool and a mattress on the floor covered with two thin grey blankets. There were a few pots and pans.

She had been here in Bevington Street for a week now and at first she had cheered herself up with the thought that she'd get used to it once she'd cleaned it up a bit and hopefully bought some more bits of furniture and a rug for the floor. Now she realised that she would never get used to it.

Mrs Scragg, her landlady, had said she was very lucky to get it. If her two eldest boys and one of her daughters hadn't left home she would never have had a room to rent and a furnished one at that.

'So, yer could say it's yer lucky day, girl. It'll be three shillin's a week.'

'There's no water, what do I do?' she'd asked, feeling close to despair.

'Yer 'ave a bucket or a big jug an' go out ter the standpipe in the street an' wait yer turn with everyone else, luv. There's no fancy way of goin' on round 'ere. Yer 'ave ter share the privy in the yard an' all. Us women try ter keep it decent, like, but the fellers around 'ere are worse than pigs!'

Jess had felt physically sick at the pictures the woman's words conjured up in her mind. She prayed she would get work soon. Animals were better housed than these people. She had never known such poverty existed, but realised that she would be living cheek by jowl with it now.

She had gone to a second-hand shop and had spent more of her precious money than she had intended on crockery, pans, towels and bedding. She'd haggled with the shopkeeper over two rugs, a small wooden chest and two oil lamps and he'd thrown in a bucket and a large enamel jug. He'd delivered them that afternoon and each piece was noted and commented on by her landlady. She had no intention of staying very long, but the things she'd bought were more in the way of necessities than luxuries.

She shook herself mentally and pulled the three-legged stool over to the tiny fireplace in which she would soon have to light a fire if she wanted a cup of tea and something to eat, although she didn't feel hungry. What little food she had was in an old tin box, to prevent the vermin devouring it.

She took out her purse and emptied the contents onto her lap. Five shillings was all she had left of the money Ronan had given her. If she didn't find work soon she wouldn't even be able to afford to stay here. And she had had no luck so far. She pulled out the list of names and addresses she had copied from the Kelly's Street Directory in the public library. There were three more names of wealthy families who lived in Abercromby Square, after that she would have to start on Rodney Street.

'This is not getting you anywhere, Jess Brennan!' she told herself firmly. She'd make a cup of tea and then write to the remaining families who just might need a governess.

She lit the fire, made a mug of tea and pulled the rickety table across to the window. It didn't give much light but there was enough for her to see what she was doing. She commenced writing her letters, wishing she had an address more imposing than Bevington Street. When she had finished she decided she would post them. It was a fine evening and she would enjoy the walk, once she left these mean dirty streets behind and got onto the main road.

Mrs Scragg and one of her neighbours were sitting on the front doorstep.

'Are yer goin' out, Jess?'

'Just to post a few letters. It's a nice evening.'

'It's that all right, luv. I said the same thing meself, didn't I, Dora?'

The other woman nodded, her eyes taking in Jess's clothes and the fact that she wore a hat. No one around Bevington Street even owned a hat.

Mrs Scragg was obviously in a gregarious mood, Jess thought irritably.

''Ave yer 'ad any luck gettin' work?'

'Not yet but I'm sure I'll get something soon. That's why I'm going to post these.'

'Funny way of goin' about gettin' a job, if yer ask me,' Dora McCreedy muttered.

Jess ignored her and smiled cheerfully. 'Enjoy the evening and the fresh air.'

Nellie Scragg grimaced. 'It's not so bloody fresh around 'ere, luv, but I expect yer've noticed that.'

Jess just smiled and turned and walked up the street.

'She's a strange one.'

'Not used ter livin' like this, Dora. All them posh clothes an' fancy way of goin' on. Like I told yer, only in the place five minutes and she's spent a fortune on furniture an' stuff. Yer should 'ave seen 'er face when I told 'er she 'ad ter share the privy!'

'What kind of a job is it that yer 'ave ter write a letter? I've never 'eard of the like. Yer go an' ask them.'

'Dunno, but she's out all day long. I don't expect she'll be 'ere long. Pity, them few extra shillin's are great. As long as our Mogsy doesn't get 'is 'ands on them first an' use them fer booze!'

'Iffen she does go, she might leave yer the stuff she's bought, Nellie,' Dora mused. They fell silent as Jess turned the corner and was lost to sight.

It wasn't far to the postbox but Jess really didn't feel like going back. She walked on down Scotland Road, up Everton Valley and along Walton Breck Road until she reached Stanley Park. At least here she could forget for an hour or two that dreadful room and everything about Bevington Street. It was a lovely evening. She'd always loved the early summer months and the park looked beautiful. The paths were tidy, the flower beds a riot of colour, the grass verdant and springy, and the trees covered with pink and white blossom and sap-green leaves. Many other well-dressed people were out walking too, and the park keeper made sure that no riff-raff got past the gates which were securely locked at night.

Oh, it was heaven just to breathe in the scent of newly mown grass and blossoms. She'd go and spend half an hour in the huge glasshouse with its palms and exotic flowers. She followed the pathway that led towards the glasshouse and the lake but as she turned a corner she stopped dead. Johanna was coming towards her and there was no way of escaping her.

'Jess! Oh, Jess!' Johanna cried, hurrying to throw her arms around her niece. 'Where have you been? I've searched everywhere, and so has Ronan, but no one knew where you'd gone. When you didn't come home from the cemetery we were all worried sick. Why did you leave like that without telling anyone where you were going?'

Jess disentangled herself and taking her aunt's arm led her to a bench in a small arbour set off the pathway.

'I'm sorry if I worried you, I really am. I had to go. You know I had to leave the house and I couldn't live with you, so . . .'

Johanna was both relieved and concerned. 'Jess, are you all right?'

'I'm fine.'

'Where are you living? How are you managing?'

'I'm living in a nice room, not far from here in Winslow Street,' Jess lied. 'I have a little money and I'm expecting to be employed as a governess very soon. I had an interview this afternoon, in Abercromby Square. A very nice family. I'll live in, of course.' Fleetingly she thought of that interview. It had been no more than a cursory inspection and her lack of experience had very obviously been taken into account. She had definitely not been suitable. Still, she managed to appear cheerful and confident. There was no way on earth she would live in a house with her uncle, but she really didn't want her aunt to worry.

'You look fine.' But Johanna couldn't hide the doubt in her voice.

'Really, I am. Oh, Aunt Jo, this is something I have to do. I have to make my own way in the world, it's what they would have expected. How is Patrick?'

Johanna shook her head. 'Still living at that club and being financed by that friend of his, so Ronan told me. But I'm more worried about you, Jess. It's not easy for a young girl alone.'

Jess changed the subject. 'What are you doing here in the park? It's miles away from Crosby.'

'*We're* miles away from Crosby, Jess. Ronan has found a house for us in Claudia Street, number twenty. It's near here and it was such a lovely evening that I told him I'd take a short walk. We only moved in today. The house was sold very quickly.' Johanna sighed sadly. 'It was such a lovely place.'

'At least this is a fairly respectable neighbourhood,' Jess pointed out.

Johanna smiled. 'Yes, it is. It's far better than anything Tom and I had when we were first married, in fact things were pretty grim until we moved in with Maddy and Mrs Buckley.'

At the mention of her mother's name Jess's composure slipped.

Johanna took her hand. 'I'm sorry, Jess. It was thoughtless of me.'

'I do miss her.'

'So do I and I feel as though I'm letting her down.'

'Why?'

'Because I'm not looking after you.'

'She won't blame you. It's my fault that I can't . . . won't live with you.'

'Jess, will you promise me something?'

'If I can.'

'As we both live near the park, will you meet me here once a week? Say on a Sunday afternoon? When you get a position as a governess you'll have time off and usually it's on a Sunday afternoon. I'm sure there will be no objections to your meeting your aunt. That way I can at least see how you are managing.'

Jess nodded. There was nothing else she could do. She didn't want to cause her aunt any more upset. 'I'd better be getting back. I have so many things to do.'

Johanna got up. 'I find it's better to keep busy. How are you for money, Jess?'

'I have enough, really I have,' Jess said, adding another lie to the one about having so much to do.

Johanna kissed her on the cheek. 'Then I'll see you on

Sunday afternoon. Take care of yourself.'

'I will. Don't worry about me. And don't worry if I . . . don't arrive on Sunday. I can hardly ask for time off as soon as I start, unless of course they offer. If they don't, I'll try and get word to you.'

They parted company with an embrace and Jess walked quickly away towards the main road. A tram passed her and she wished she had the money to spare for the fare. She didn't want Johanna to see her walk past Winslow Street.

The sun was sinking fast as she at last turned into Bevington Street. She was exhausted and downcast. She hated to have to lie to her aunt but if Johanna ever saw where she was living, she would have ten fits and would feel dreadfully worried and guilty.

She looked up as she heard someone whistle. A group of men and boys were hanging around the corner of Titchfield Street and Bevington Street. All were staring at her, some with mocking grins on their faces. They wore the uniform of the poor: moleskin trousers, a greasy half-threadbare jacket and, despite the warmth of the evening, the grubby white muffler around the neck to hide the collarless shirt. Some had caps of rough tweed on their heads; all wore heavy boots.

She quickened her steps. She had no intention of crossing the road to avoid them even though she was very uneasy.

''Ere, girl, lend us yer 'at, we're 'avin' soup!' one called and they all laughed.

Jess's cheeks burned with anger and humiliation but she ignored them. She took a deep breath as she drew abreast of them. She had to show that she wasn't afraid of them otherwise she would be an object of their derisive humour for ever.

Quite suddenly it seemed as though they had closed in and surrounded her. Three of them faced her and she could smell their breath. Odours of beer, tobacco and neglected teeth made her wrinkle her nose with disgust. 'Let me pass, please,' she said coldly.

'Oh, get 'er, don't she talk dead posh!' a lad about her own age yelled mockingly.

'I don't think she fancies yer, 'Arry, lad! Look at the gob on 'er!'

Jess glared at them. 'Will you please let me pass. I'm on my way home!'

'Yer don't belong round 'ere, do yer? What fancy street did yer cum from?'

'Don't yer like talkin' ter fellers like us? Are we too common fer yer, is that it?'

She looked around helplessly. What would they do if she started to scream?

'For the last time, will you let me pass or I'll have to—'

A red-veined face with bleary eyes and dark stubble-covered chin was shoved close to her own. 'Yer'll do what? There ain't no scuffers around 'ere, girl!'

She stepped backwards but the circle seemed to have grown smaller.

'That's a nice birrof jewellery, girl. Might fetch a shillin' or two.' Another fingered the small pin on her lapel: the enamelled replica of the flag of the Brennan Line.

She knocked his hand away. Anger was beginning to replace fear. 'You keep your hands off me and don't you dare touch that brooch!'

'Oh, get 'er! Right little 'ard case! What's so special about that brooch then?'

'It belonged to my mother. My father had it made for her, so keep your hands off it!'

'I'se seen that flag thing before somewhere,' the younger lad said.

'Yer liar!'

'Liar yerself! I tell yer I'se seen it before!'

'We know where yer live, girl.'

'Indeed!' Jess said coldly.

'Oh, Christ! 'Ere cums Mogsy Scragg and 'is mates!' someone cried and suddenly they dispersed.

Jess looked around and saw her landlady's husband and two of his friends coming towards her. She felt relief flow through her. He was a big man with a barrel chest, a shock of iron-grey hair and had a reputation of being a hard case who stood no nonsense from anyone.

'Oh, Mr Scragg, I'm so pleased to see you.'

'What 'ave them 'ooligans been sayin' ter yer, girl?'

'Oh, nothing much. I think they were just trying to . . . frighten me.'

'I'll bloody "frighten" them! Shower of no-marks! Bloody cowards! Cum on, girl, I'll see yer 'ome.'

He had been drinking, she could smell it, but she didn't care. She was just thankful he'd come along.

Mrs Scragg and her neighbour had vacated the step but the door, as was usual in this neighbourhood, was wide open. She hurried inside and turned before opening the door to her room. 'I really am grateful, Mr Scragg. Goodnight.'

He grunted and walked past her.

Inside she sank down on the stool. Oh, God! What would have happened if he hadn't come along? The incident had frightened her. She couldn't count on her neighbour to be around all the time to protect her. She touched the little brooch, her fingers shaking. It was the only piece of jewellery she had but she knew any one of them would steal it, given half the chance.

Chapter Nine

———◆———

B Y THE END OF the following week Jess was desperate. She had received no replies at all to her letters and writing paper, envelopes and stamps cost money she could now ill afford.

Mrs Scragg was demanding the rent; after she had paid that there was hardly enough left to buy food, never mind things like soap or other necessary toiletries. For the first time in her life she was hungry and afraid. She could pawn the few things she had but who around here had use for photograph frames, a broken watch, a cap and a sewing box? Nor did she want to part with them. She looked around at the few items she'd bought. If things got worse she would have to sell or pawn everything. It didn't bear thinking about.

She held her father's cap to her cheek, fighting back the tears. It was so hard to be alone. So hard to know where to turn next.

'Jess, are yer in there?'

Jess closed her eyes. Oh, not again! She couldn't put

off paying her landlady any longer.

'Come in, Mrs Scragg,' she said, opening the door.

'I thought yer was in. Can yer see yer way ter pay me the rent money?'

'Yes, of course. I'm sorry, I was going to call with it later on,' she lied, rooting in her purse for the coins and noting just how little there was left.

'Ta, luv. 'Ave yer 'ad any luck with work, like?'

'Not really, but I'm still hoping.' She tried to sound optimistic.

The woman glanced around the room and her gaze rested on the naval cap.

'It belonged to my father. He . . . he's dead.'

'That's a shame, luv. What about yer mam?'

'She was killed in an accident with a runaway horse.'

'Them bloody 'orses are a menace! I seen one only last week. A feller shouted ter 'is mate across the street an' the bloody animal is up in the air an' off like a shot with the cart draggin' behind. It run over three people before it were stopped! They should bloody shoot them if they carry on like that, that's what I say! Yer're not safe ter walk the streets with them boltin' at the drop of a 'at.'

Jess nodded but she wasn't really listening. She had come to a decision.

'Mrs Scragg, do you know the name of the nearest pawnbroker?'

The woman's eyes narrowed. 'Is yer that 'ard up, girl?'

'Just a bit. I need something to tide me over until I get work, can you understand that?'

Her landlady nodded. 'Oh, I can that, girl! Me weddin'

ring spends 'alf its life in O'Malley's.'

So, the girl was hard up. How much longer could she afford to pay her rent? She could rent out this room to half a dozen people and for a couple of shillings more if Jess left all the furnishings. She couldn't afford to be out of pocket.

'O'Malley's is on Scotland Road. 'E's not the nearest but 'e always gives yer a fair price which is more than yer can say fer Kelly's or Bloomberg's. What 'ave yer got, like, apart from what yer bought at Hardcastle's?'

'My mother's sewing box and a watch of my father's, but it's broken.'

'Not much call fer stuff like that round 'ere, Jess. Nothin' else? Yer 'at an' coat might bring a couple of bob. The weather's fine now an' if it turned cold yer could gerra shawl. They're great things ter 'ave.'

Jess nodded her thanks.

'What about that little brooch yer've gorron yer coat?'

Jess shot her a guarded look. 'It was my mother's and I'd like to keep it.'

Mrs Scragg sniffed. 'It's up ter you. I was talkin' ter a woman yesterday an' she said 'er 'usband was drowned when the *Brennan's Pride* were sunk. I was wonderin' iffen yer were related, like? Yer name bein' Brennan an' all?'

Jess nodded slowly. 'My father was the captain of the *Brennan's Pride*.'

'Is that right? Well, yer never know the minute, is what I say. Do yer want me ter cum with yer ter the pob shop? Introduce yer, like?'

'Thank you, that would be . . . helpful.'

'Well, if yer've nothin' else ter do, we'll go now.'

Jess realised she would get no peace, so reluctantly she wrapped the sewing box and the watch in her coat and picked up her hat.

'Off we goes then, luv,' Mrs Scragg said cheerfully. At least the girl would be able to pay next week's rent, she'd make sure Charlie O'Malley gave her at least three shillings.

It was a humiliating experience to have your belongings carefully scrutinised and haggled over, Jess thought. The shop was small, dark, dusty and smelled of stale body odour, as did its owner who shook his head and tutted to himself as he examined everything.

'Come on now, Charlie, give us a good price. That there's a good quality coat with no holes or tears in it. And that 'at must 'ave cost a few bob.'

'When it was new,' came the terse answer.

'Well, what about the little sewin' box? It's good wood an it's gorrall kinds of things inside it. Useful things, like.'

'Useful for who? How many women round here can even sew?'

'God, would yer listen ter 'im! Right bloody miser yer are, Charlie O'Malley!'

'I'll give you five shillings for the lot and that's more than you'd get anywhere else,' he stated firmly.

'Five shillings!' Jess cried.

'She'll take it, Charlie.'

He counted out the coins and Jess slipped them in her purse. The hat alone had cost twelve shillings.

''Ave yer any decent shawls, Charlie? She might need one. It can get cold of a night.'

'No! No, really I won't need one,' Jess protested.

'I can let you have this one for one and six. It's a good heavy one, lined too.' He held out the garment for inspection and Mrs Scragg fingered it.

'We'll give yer a shillin', there's a couple of 'oles in it.'

'All right. You drive a hard bargain, Nellie.'

'Well, in our position yer 'ave to!' she retorted, handing the shawl to Jess who put it over her arm. It wasn't cold enough to wear it, was what she told herself, but really she was reluctant to admit that she now would be forced to wear this garment, as much a badge of the poor as were the men's mufflers.

On the way back she was thoughtful and at last she asked her landlady the question she'd had at the back of her mind all evening.

'What other kind of work is there for women in this part of the city?'

'What can yer do?'

'I can keep house and my writing is good, so is my arithmetic.'

'Well, yer won't find many jobs that call fer all that, not round 'ere. Yer might get factory work in a rope works or feed factory or makin' matches, things like that.'

'What would I have to do?'

'Whatever the foreman tells yer ter do. It'd be 'ard on the likes of youse. It's dirty work an' they pay yer buttons fer standin' on yer feet fer twelve hours an' only fifteen minutes fer yer dinner. Them factory girls are dead rough, like. God knows 'ow they'd take ter yer, what with the way yer talk an' yer "please" an' "thank yer" all the time. Or yer can go cleanin'. Scrubbin' offices, like, but that don't pay much either an' it's usually married women what do it. Some take in washin', but I 'aven't got the room fer all that an' Mogsy says 'e ain't 'avin' the place like a public wash'ouse.'

It all sounded grim, but she'd promised to work at whatever she could get. The same way as Maddy had done when she'd first come to Liverpool.

'I think I'll try the cleaning. At least I know I can do that. I wasn't utterly spoiled.'

'Suit yerself, girl. Go down ter India Buildings early termorrer mornin'.'

They had reached the house. 'I will and thank you, Mrs Scragg, for . . . everything.'

She hung the shawl on a nail embedded in the wall and sighed heavily. Well, five shillings was five shillings more than she'd had a few hours ago. She prayed the weather would hold at least until Sunday afternoon. Aunt Jo would be horrified to see her wearing a shawl. She'd still be missing her hat but she could explain that away. She'd go into town very early tomorrow. She would have to walk and that would take her longer. Wearily she got undressed and lay down on the straw-filled mattress. She'd better try and get some sleep.

She was up at five, thankful for the fact that it was light, and began the journey through the eerily silent, sun-dappled streets of the city. The only other people she saw were women who were obviously also going cleaning and men making their way towards the docks in the hope of a morning's work.

When she reached India Buildings she met a hostile reception from the women she asked who she should see about getting work. They eyed her with suspicion. She was young, obviously unmarried, and far better dressed than they were. At last, however, she was directed to a tiny room in the basement.

'And what can I do for you?' asked the small, balding man with yellowed teeth who stood in front of an empty fireplace smoking a cigarette.

'I've come in the hope of getting work, cleaning.'

He looked her up and down. 'You don't seem the usual sort that goes cleaning.'

'No, but I can work hard. Truly I can.'

'You married?'

'No.'

'The others won't be happy, they look on this kind of work as theirs. Up and out, get it done, then back home to see to the old man and the kids and their own housework.'

'I understand, but I really *do* need the work.'

He looked thoughtful, then nodded. 'I'll give you a trial. It's half five to half eight, Monday to Saturday; you get Sunday off. It's six shillings a week. We supply the buckets, brushes, soap and floorcloths.'

Jess just nodded. It wasn't much but it was better than nothing.

'What's your name and can you start now?'

'It's Jess, Jess Brennan, and yes, I can start right away. Thank you, Mr . . . ?'

'Rodgers. Ted Rodgers. Go and get your stuff from Maisie. She'll tell you what to do.' He stubbed out the cigarette and wrote her name down in a ledger on the desk. Jess hoped 'Maisie' would be friendlier than the women she'd encountered so far.

By the time she'd finished she felt as though every muscle in her back and arms had been stretched on a rack. Her hands were red and smarting from the strong carbolic soap and her clothes were sticking to her with sweat. She'd never worked so hard in all her life. The other women left her alone although they laughed and chatted amongst themselves. Well, she didn't care. It was work. Honest work. But she'd never realised before how hard life was for the poor working class. She wished she had enough money for the tram fare home but she didn't. Not if she wanted to eat. Maybe next week, after she'd been paid, she could afford that luxury.

She was bone weary as she walked along the now busy and bustling streets. She was starving; she'd not bothered to have anything to eat before she'd left home. She'd get herself something to eat, have a wash, rinse out her blouse and then try and have a sleep, although that might prove difficult. The house and the street were noisy all day long.

When she turned into Bevington Street she noticed that already there were women standing on their doorsteps, gossiping. They stared at her and she nodded to them as she passed but it wasn't until she reached Nellie Scragg's house and saw the expression on her landlady's face that she realised something was wrong.

'Mrs Scragg, what's the matter? Has anything happened?' she asked apprehensively. Had Aunt Jo somehow managed to find her? Was it Patrick? Was it Ronan or even Uncle Tom?

'Oh, aye, girl, somethin' 'as 'appened all right!' Nellie cried. 'We'se found out about yer. Who yer are, an' what yer mam said. What she promised – the lyin' bitch!'

Jess's heart sank. 'What do you mean by that?' she demanded.

Two other women had joined her landlady.

'Yer mam was that Maddy Brennan, wasn't she?' Nellie stated, staring pointedly at the brooch Jess wore.

'Yes, but—?'

'An' she stood up in church, at the altar-rails an' all, an' said she'd give all them women some money fer losing their fellers—'

'An' it was all lies, bloody lies!' Dora McCreedy interrupted.

'It wasn't! She was killed. I told you that!' Jess cried defensively.

'Oh, very 'andy that!' Nellie mocked.

'We had no money! My uncle mortgaged the house and we couldn't pay our debts! She was selling all our things but she was determined to give everyone something, no matter how small. She *was* going to. Mam never broke a promise.'

'Pull the other leg, it's got bells on! She wasn't goin' ter give a bloody penny away. It was all just talk, tryin' ter ease her mind, like, after yer da went and lost all them men an' boys,' Dora screeched.

Jess rounded on her. 'My father was a good captain! I know he would have fought hard to save his men and his ships! And my mother meant what she said. It was my brother's fault that they got nothing. After she was killed he took over everything and he wouldn't pay out, even though I begged him to! Why do you think I'm living here, in one filthy room, and going out scrubbing floors? If I had money, would I be here at all?'

She looked around but could see her words were falling on deaf ears. They didn't believe her.

'Did yer 'ear that? One filthy room! Well, yer're not livin' 'ere any longer! Yer're out on yer ear! We mightn't 'ave much round 'ere, but we 'as our own rules. We don't give the time of day ter people like youse! Yer auld feller made a fortune out of the fellers who worked fer 'im. Paid them buttons ter risk their lives an' when it's all gone, yer cum down 'ere whinin' and whingin' and callin' us filthy! Clear off! Go back where yer belong! Back with yer lyin', cheatin' family!'

They didn't even allow her to collect her few belongings; she was manhandled up the street despite her protests until they reached the main road where they might possibly encounter a policeman who would want to know what was going on.

A big blowsy woman caught her by the shoulders and shoved her hard against the wall of a pub. 'Clear off! The likes of youse aren't welcome 'ere an' iffen we see yer again, yer'll not like what 'appens ter yer!' she said menacingly.

Released from their grasp, Jess turned and ran blindly across the road, narrowly avoiding being run down by three carts whose drivers shouted abuse after her. When she was finally out of breath she sank down on the doorstep of a rickety-looking old stable and covered her face with her hands. Oh, God, what was she going to do now?

Chapter Ten

———◆◆———

I T WAS NEARLY DARK when she made her way back down the alley and squeezed through the gap in the crumbling wall of the stable. Inside it was warm and the mingled odours of straw, manure and horse flesh hung heavily in the air. In the gloom the two old, scrawny workhorses snuffled and shifted from leg to leg and she patted them as she crept past and climbed the ladder up to the tiny loft where at least the straw was fresh. She sank down on it, dropping her head in her hands. This had been her home for over a week now. She had had nowhere else to go. She had no money.

At first she had continued to go to India Buildings to clean but she was too weak from hunger to sustain the sheer effort and energy required. There had also been the deepening hostility of the other women, which had eventually erupted into anger when someone finally realised who she was. That had been the final straw and she had begged Mr Rodgers for the couple of shillings she was owed before leaving.

'Please, please, I need that money desperately,' she'd implored, near to tears.

He'd delved into his pocket and thrust a handful of small coins at her.

'Here, take this and go. I can't have all this yelling and shouting and my workers up in arms about you. You're more trouble than you're worth. I should have known that as soon as I set eyes on you!' he'd said angrily, dismissing her.

That money had been spent and for days she'd had hardly anything to eat. In desperation and humiliation she'd been reduced to begging and even that hadn't been successful. She'd had to compete with hordes of ragged, starving urchins who were far craftier than herself and more appealing in their desperation. Twice she'd been moved on by the police for she hadn't known it was against the law to beg. For the last two days she'd been reduced to eating the bits of half-rotten fruit and vegetables that had been left for the old horses whose home she shared.

She lay down, the warm straw soft to her aching body. Tears prickled her eyes. Oh, how long could she go on like this? She had deliberately cut herself off from everyone. Aunt Jo would get so worried if she didn't turn up in the park this Sunday. But how could she appear looking like this? Her aunt would know things were very bad and would insist that she return home with her. 'Would that be such a bad thing?' a small, nagging voice inside her asked. She could live comfortably with them, maybe have a better chance at getting a job – one that didn't entail scrubbing floors. No! She had sworn never to live beneath the same roof as her uncle and she *wasn't* going to change her mind. But what was she going to do now?

She was too weak to tramp the streets. Too dirty and unkempt even to be considered for work should she turn up at the gate of any factory. She now looked exactly what she was. A destitute beggar. There was of course the final degradation for those who had nothing. To throw themselves on the mercy of the parish and be kept, albeit barely a step above destitution, in the dreaded workhouse. Her mother had refused to consider it, even in her darkest, despairing days in Liverpool, and nor would she.

She turned over and buried her face in the straw. 'Oh, Mam, Mam, please help me. Don't desert me now.' Her miseries overtook her until her body was racked with shuddering sobs. She had nowhere to turn. What use now all her resolutions, her spirit and strength? They had all deserted her.

Gradually exhaustion claimed her and she fell into a shallow sleep, tossing and turning restlessly. She was tormented by dreams and memories until at last she awoke, her head aching, her heart thudding, her clothes stuck to her with perspiration. She sat up, running her hands through hair that was becoming matted. She was certain something, some noise, had woken her and she peered around. Above her head was a tiny, dirty skylight and for an instant she thought she saw a shape outlined against it, then something fell onto the straw beside her. Tentatively she reached out. It was a bird. That was the sound she had heard in her troubled sleep: the beating of wings against the glass. It didn't move and she gently picked it up. No tiny heartbeat fluttered in its breast. It was dead, defeated by its fruitless efforts to escape. Just like herself. She stroked the soft feathers. Poor thing. Is this how she too would end her life? Defeated by her own frantic efforts to escape from her prison of poverty and despair? Would someone find her emaciated lifeless body stretched on the straw? Such soft feathers, she sighed. So beautiful even in this dim and dismal light.

'I'm not at all sure about the feathers on this hat. There seem to be too many of them.'

The voice startled her. It was Mam's. She shook herself. Was it? Had she really heard it or was it just inside her head? But she remembered the words well. Mam had spoken them on the morning of Aideen's wedding, and what had she said in reply?

'Oh, Mam, it's the fashion! Everyone is wearing feathers on *everything*!'

And then what had Mam said? She racked her brains, her mind turning back to that April morning not so long ago. That was it!

'Then there must be desperate numbers of dead birds around the place!'

Jess looked down at the bird. 'Dead birds,' she said aloud. Was Mam trying to tell her something? She parted the feathers with shaking fingers. There was a *huge* demand for feathers for decoration, but how . . . where would you find so many? Did you buy them and, if so, where from? And then who did you sell them to? Milliners and dressmakers, she assumed. Gently she laid the bird down and covered it with straw. In the morning she'd bury it properly. Briefly, she felt calmer – Mam *was* looking out for her. She was certain of it – but despair soon washed over her again. Where would she get the money to buy anything? She had no money even for food. But she was determined not to give in. Mam had shown her a way out. Tomorrow she would go and ask in the milliners' shops and something, *something* would turn up. She'd find *some* way of getting the money. She lay down and stared up at the minuscule patch of indigo sky visible through the skylight. If she could just get a start she would make a go of it, even if she had to starve and work her fingers to the bone. She wasn't finished yet.

When she awoke the sunlight was struggling in through the grimy, fly-speckled glass. There was no sound from below so the horses must have been taken out for their day's work. She had to get up and out before the lad who came to muck out the stable arrived and climbed up here for the fresh bedding. She picked as much of the straw as she could out of her hair and brushed down her dress. Hunger gnawed at her but resolutely she ignored it. She retrieved the bird, stiff now, from its temporary resting place and took it down with her. She found a shovel in a corner and managed to scrape a shallow hole in the earth floor and then buried it.

When she emerged from the dimness of the narrow alleyway the sun was warm on her face and gave her strength and hope. It was quite a long walk into the centre of town but she didn't care. She stopped at a horse trough at the top of London Road to drink and splash water over her face and hands, hoping to remove some of the dust and grime. She caught sight of herself in a shop window and was horrified. Could that really be her? That painfully thin girl in the stained and creased dress, with the tangled hair and wild eyes? She tried to smooth her hair and twist it into a coil but she had nothing to hold it up with and soon it began to fall and straggle around her shoulders. Respectably dressed people gave her a wide berth and she couldn't blame them. She looked terrible. How on earth was she going to get over the doorstep of any shop without being flung out on her ear?

Her spirits began to desert her as she finally made her way up Bold Street. Oh, how often had she come with Mam to shops like Cripps and the exclusive workrooms of dressmakers' like Drinkwater's? There had never been a problem getting across these thresholds then. But now, one look from the uniformed doorman at the wrought-iron façade of Cripps was enough to make her turn away. How, just how could she get the information she needed? She walked slowly on, and then stopped outside the window of Val Smith's Milliners. The hats on display were all adorned with feathers that had been dyed every possible shade and hue.

She turned as the shop door opened and a tiny old woman, dressed entirely in black, stepped out. Well, it was now or never. She took a few steps towards her then flinched as she saw the woman tighten the grip on her handbag.

'Please, madam, there's no need to be afraid. I mean you no harm,' she said quietly and respectfully.

At the cultured voice, something she had certainly not been expecting, the woman relaxed a little. 'Then what do you want, girl?'

'A small favour – and not money,' she added quickly. 'Would you, could you please go back inside and ask them where – how they obtain the feathers for decorating their hats?'

'Whatever for, child?' The old lady was intrigued.

'Madam, I can't go and ask them myself, not . . . not in the state I'm reduced to.'

'I can understand that, child. But why do you wish to know? Curiosity?'

Jess shook her head. 'More than that, ma'am, it might help me to improve my circumstances.'

'Are you perhaps a milliner?'

'I only wish I were.'

The woman nodded. 'Very well, child, wait there.'

Jess sighed with relief. Thank God someone was prepared to help her. In a few minutes the door opened and the woman came out smiling.

'They purchase them, usually at an auction or directly from importers, although they said smaller milliners do buy them from wholesalers, who in turn purchase them from the importers. Auctions are held once a month at rooms down by the Canning Dock. Fielding's Imports and Auctions, so they tell me. I hope that will be of some use.'

Jess could have hugged her. 'Thank you, thank you so much, ma'am!'

'I'm glad to have been of some help to you. These days I seem to be of so little use to anyone,' she added a little bitterly. 'Here, child, take this and buy yourself a decent meal, you look as though you need one and it might help your . . . circumstances. You are obviously not used to such hardship, neither did you ask for money. You are no ordinary beggar. Good luck with whatever it is you hope to do to improve yourself.'

Jess took the coin she offered and thanked her profusely. It was the first time in weeks she'd had a kind word from anyone.

When the woman had walked away she opened her hand and gasped. A golden guinea glinted in the palm of her hand. A whole guinea! Not enough to buy a shipment of feathers but certainly enough for a meal, a bath, a new dress and somewhere to stay while she tried to raise enough money to bid for a part-shipment that maybe she could sell on to small milliners. Oh, she had known something would turn up, that Mam was watching over her; now, because of the kindness of an old lady, a perfect stranger, she felt she at least had a small fingerhold to claw her way out of the terrible predicament she'd fallen into. Once, an old lady had helped her mam when she'd been at her wits' end, destitute and with her young sister Carmel to care for. Mrs Buckley had reversed Mam's fortunes. Now she wished she'd asked the name of her benefactress.

Even though she was starving she forced herself to think clearly. She would be denied entrance to any decent café looking the way she did, and more so somewhere respectable to stay. And she had no desire at all to return to the likes of Nellie Scragg and Bevington Street.

She turned her steps towards Church Street and the small branch of Marks & Spencer. There she could buy some new underwear and stockings, a skirt and a blouse and a cheap hat. A decent pair of shoes, nothing fancy, could be bought from any of the cheap shoe shops in the side streets.

She received some suspicious glances as she entered the small shop where the goods were displayed on counters, their prices clearly marked. But once she showed the assistant her money she was treated with more respect. Her purchases were wrapped in a brown paper parcel and she made her way out along Whitechapel towards Victoria Street where she knew there was a public bathhouse.

She paid her tuppence to the large woman at the door who handed her a towel and a small piece of soap.

'Down the corridor an' in the second cubicle. I'll be along in a minute ter turn on the tap,' came the reply to her queries as to what she should do next.

The room was tiny, most of the space being taken up by a huge cast-iron bathtub on claw feet. The walls were tiled in white and on the floor was a wooden slatted platform. She had just started to strip off her clothes when the woman arrived with a large spanner in her hand and proceeded to turn a large brass screw. The hot water gushed from the tap, filling the room with clouds of steam.

'Yer can turn the cold tap on an' off yerself, an' don't scald yerself, I'm not responsible fer yer. The brush is attached ter that chain,' the custodian of the hot water informed her when she had deemed there was sufficient hot water in the bath.

Jess turned on the cold tap while she removed the rest of her clothes and left them in a heap on the floor. Oh, it was pure heaven to ease her body into the hot water. It was so long since she'd had a bath. After a few minutes of blissful soaking, she took the soap and lathered herself all over, then using the long-handled wooden brush, stamped with the words 'Liverpool Corporation', she scrubbed herself vigorously. Using the last of the soap she washed her hair and then she stepped out. It was as though she had washed the past dreadful weeks away. She felt almost new. She towel-dried her hair and then dressed in the new clothes. She had almost forgotten what it felt like to be clean and fresh. She used the bathbrush to brush her hair, then she twisted it into a coil on top of her head and placed the hat over it. All her old clothes she wrapped in the brown paper: she'd ask the woman attendant to dispose of them. Next she'd find a café and have her first decent meal in over a week.

After a huge plate of bacon, sausage, black pudding, eggs and fried bread, washed down with a pot of tea in a café on the corner of Davies Street, she walked up and along Ormond Street where she found a house with the words 'Mrs Templeton's Select Boarding House' painted above the door.

Inside the hall was painted in brown and cream. The wooden floor was highly polished, as was the small desk on which a large aspidistra in a ceramic pot took pride of place. There was no one in sight so Jess rang the brass bell that was obviously there for just such a purpose.

A tall, thin woman appeared. She wore a black dress in an old-fashioned style and a pair of pince-nez were balanced on her nose.

'Good morning. May I help?'

'You are Mrs Templeton?'

'I am and you are?'

'Miss Brennan. Miss Jessica Brennan. I would like a room, please, if that is possible.'

'For how long, Miss Brennan?'

'Oh, er . . . how much do you charge, Mrs Templeton?'

'Half a crown a week. That includes towels, soap and use of the bathroom. And the sheets are changed every four days, that's something you won't find in many places, nor indeed will you find many bathrooms. I pride myself on my superior accommodation and modern appointments.'

'I can see that, ma'am. It will be for a week, to . . . er . . . start with.'

'To be paid in advance, Miss Brennan.'

'Of course.' Jess handed over the coins.

The proprietress looked suspicious. 'You have no luggage? I must stress that this is a select and respectable establishment.'

'Oh, of course! It . . . it's following. My plans were a little uncertain.' Jess hoped the hasty explanation would suffice.

The woman nodded curtly. The girl spoke well, her manners were good even if her clothes were cheap. She took a set of keys from the desk drawer. 'Would you follow me, please?'

Jess walked behind her up the carpeted stairs and along a narrow landing until Mrs Templeton stopped and unlocked a door with the number three on a small brass plaque attached to it.

Jess was surprised at how clean and well furnished it was. There was a single bed neatly made up with a blue and white cotton counterpane. A well-polished single wardrobe and a chest of drawers, a small marble-topped washstand with a blue and white delftware jug and bowl and two clean white towels. Set in the tiny bay window were a fragile-looking writing table and a chair.

'This is very nice, Mrs Templeton. Very nice indeed,' she enthused. It was indeed a very far cry from the room in Bevington Street and an entire world away from the loft in the stable that she'd left that morning.

The woman permitted herself a tight smile. 'This is the key to the bathroom. You will be permitted one bath a week, hot water will be brought each morning and of course it goes without saying that I expect everything to be left in good order. I do not permit visitors, unless by prior arrangement and agreement and then not in the rooms. There is a small parlour for such purposes.'

'That is very considerate of you but I'm sure I won't need to avail myself of the . . . privilege,' Jess answered very formally.

'I do not permit food to be eaten in the rooms. It encourages vermin.'

'Precisely. Is that all?'

'Except for one thing. The front door is locked at ten o'clock sharp. If you will be coming in later than that, special arrangements will have to be made.' Her tone implied that no respectable woman should be out later at night than that.

Jess nodded.

'Then I'll leave you. If there is anything else, just ask.'

'Thank you. I will.'

When she'd gone Jess sank down on the bed. Oh, what a day it had been but she felt so much better. She had somewhere decent, with some privacy, to stay for at least a week and she was certain that in that time she would have thought of some way to raise some money. She even had enough money left to last for meals, if she was careful. If she had a decent breakfast and dinner she could manage without lunch. She would have to go out later and buy a brush and comb and some hairpins but now she could rest.

She took off her shoes and hat and then stretched out on the bed. Oh, she could sleep for hours. 'Thank you, Mam,' she whispered before drifting into a deep and untroubled sleep.

Chapter Eleven

———◆———

AFTER HER BREAKFAST NEXT morning Jess studied the advertisements in the *Daily Post*, hoping to find something which would give her some idea as to how she might raise a small sum of money. Ten pounds or even, at a push, five would be enough. She couldn't go to a bank or even a pawnbroker. There had to be some way. She scanned advertisements that said things like 'Small Investors Needed' and 'Excellent Returns on Small Investments' but she had nothing to invest. She needed someone to 'invest' in her but she had no money for newspaper advertisements. Finally she made up her mind to at least go and find the premises of Fielding's Imports and Auctions at Canning Dock. She had to do something positive.

She enjoyed the walk; it was a beautiful morning and the sight of the river sparkling in the sunlight lifted her spirits. As usual it was busy, criss-crossed by ships of all shapes and sizes, and the forest of spars and rigging stretched as far as the eye could see. Despite the recent tragedy, business in the port of Liverpool was still booming.

She threaded her way between the crowds along the dock road, peering at the names of the businesses housed in the Gorree Piazzas that flanked it. It had to be along here somewhere. Strange as it may seem, in all the numerous times she'd walked along here, she'd hardly noticed the names of anything. But then, she mused, she'd never needed to before.

Finally she stopped outside a large soot-begrimed building and made out the faded lettering. It must be here and she wondered if there was any information to be had about when the next auction would be. There was a printed notice on the door and she bent to read it. The next sale of 'Imported Ladies' Millinery and Mantle Embellishments', which she concluded must mean feathers, was to be on Tuesday June 3 at ten a.m. 'Catalogues available on June 1 from these premises', the notice also stated. The next auction was at the beginning of next week. So, she had until then to find some money. Still, at least she knew where the auction would take place and where to get a catalogue.

She turned away, undecided what to do next, until she caught sight of one of the Mersey ferries ploughing its way across to the far bank. Well, it only cost tuppence, it was a lovely day for a sail, and she had time to kill and needed time to think.

She was trying to cross the road when she heard someone calling her name and looked around, a little fearfully.

'Jess! I thought it was you. How are you?' Edward Dempsey was smiling as he caught up with her.

'Oh, Edward! How are you?' She'd completely forgotten that he came down here quite often. It was part of his responsibilities to check on the manifests of the incoming cargoes, and because Dempseys' were a big operation it demanded a good portion of Edward's time.

'I'm fine. How are you, Jess? Where are you going?'

'Oh, I'm well. It's such a lovely morning that I had just decided to go for a sail on the ferry.'

She was glad to see him but a little apprehensive. She wondered if he had heard that she had 'disappeared'.

'To where?'

'Oh, I don't mind. Birkenhead, Wallasey, even New Brighton.'

He laughed. 'New Brighton it is. It's further.'

She was surprised. 'You'll come with me?'

'Of course. I can escape now and then. It's very nice there. The new promenade is lovely, so I hear. As I told you once before, Jess, I *do* know how to enjoy life. Who could pass up an outing and maybe lunch on such a glorious day?'

She smiled up at him. 'I would have thought your tastes would have been more . . . sophisticated.'

'Ah, then you don't know me.'

'Obviously I don't, Edward.' She laughed but an idea was forming in her mind. Why not ask him for a small loan? He knew her circumstances were strained but obviously not quite how much.

'Have you heard anything about Aunt Jo?' she ventured as they walked along.

'Not much, except, of course, that your uncle has been ill and that they have moved to somewhere near Stanley Park – and that you won't go and live with them?'

'No! I . . . I will never do that.'

Edward was thoughtful. It really wasn't any of his business

nor was it his place to tell her what to do with her life. He was disappointed that she hadn't written to him but obviously she had been busy.

They walked the rest of the way in silence and when they reached the ferry berth he paid their fares.

They climbed the stairway to the upper deck and sat at the bow.

'You'll have to be careful of your hat, Jess, there's always a breeze on the river. Ships generate their own wind,' he advised.

'I know that, Edward. I'm a captain's daughter, remember,' she reminded him, not unkindly.

'You look different, Jess,' he ventured as the ferry got under way. She did. She was definitely thinner and her clothes were not as stylish.

'I am. I live a very different life now. Much . . . simpler.'

'Would it be prying to know where you do live, Jess?'

'In a boarding house. A very select one. Mrs Templeton prides herself on that,' she added, seeing the surprise in his eyes and cringing inwardly as she pondered what he would have thought had he seen the state she was in a day ago. He wouldn't have recognised her at all, she was sure of it.

'And what are you doing?'

She took a deep breath. Now was her chance. 'I'm trying to start my own business, Edward.'

He was a little surprised. 'Doing what?'

'Supplying trimmings, feathers to be exact, to milliners and dressmakers for ladies' hats and dresses. In case you hadn't noticed everything seems to be weighed down with them. It was something Mam said about the hat she wore for Aideen's wedding that gave me the idea.'

'That's very enterprising.' He was full of admiration for her.

'It would be, but there's just one problem.'

He looked a little perturbed. 'And that is?'

She sighed heavily. 'Well, you know that financially things are . . . difficult, and I just don't have the necessary . . . capital, is that what you call it? The money necessary to buy the stock in the first place.'

The answer came to him at once, but he had to tread carefully; he didn't want to offend her and she was fiercely independent. 'Jess, would you like me to give you the capital?'

She looked up at him hopefully. 'No, Edward, I'd like you to *lend* it to me. I won't need much really and I would pay you back, every penny and with interest . . .' Oh, please let him agree. She couldn't let him just give her the money. That would never do.

'How much would you need? Thirty, forty, fifty pounds or more?'

She was staggered. 'Good grief, no! Ten, maybe fifteen.'

'Are you quite sure? That doesn't seem like much.'

'Quite sure. I don't intend to start in a big way. I'm quite prepared to work and build up a business slowly, the way Mam and Da did.'

He didn't miss the catch in her voice when she spoke of her parents. It must be very hard for her and she seemed to be doing so well, although he hated to think of her living in a boarding house, no matter how select. 'Then let's say twenty and there's no rush to repay it.'

'I'll repay it as soon as I possibly can, I promise.'

He reached inside his waistcoat, produced his wallet and

withdrew four large white five-pound notes and handed them to her.

She took them gratefully and smiled at him.

'Thank you, Edward. You won't regret it. Now, shall we enjoy the rest of the morning?'

She had enjoyed the trip. They had walked along the new promenade and then he insisted on taking her into one of the even newer hotels for lunch. It seemed such a long time since she had been in any building quite so magnificent and she felt decidedly underdressed, but her spirits rose when she noted that every other woman and girl in the room wore hats that were festooned with feathers; some even had them attached to jackets and the bodices of dresses.

He apologised for the fact that he really must get back to the office and, after thanking him and promising to be in touch, she left him at the bottom of Water Street.

As she walked back to Mrs Templeton's she clutched the money tightly in her hand. Now she could go to the auction and buy her stock. She could go on living in the boarding house: it was reasonably priced, clean and comfortable, but she realised that it wouldn't go down too well with Mrs Templeton if it were reported that she was keeping bundles of feathers in her room. She would have to find somewhere to store them. It wouldn't need to be anywhere large. Just a small room, or even part of a room to start with, and she would have to buy a small case or Gladstone bag in which to carry her samples when she visited her prospective customers. Oh, there was so much to think about, to plan, but she felt elated.

'Mrs Templeton, may I sit in the parlour, please? I need

some time to think . . . plan my future,' she asked, seeing her sitting behind the desk in the hall.

The woman noted the folded newspaper tucked under Jess's arm and nodded. She seldom enquired into the lives of her paying guests, as she liked to refer to them – boarders was such a common expression – but she couldn't fathom this young girl at all. Miss Brennan had obviously been well brought up and, she suspected, came from a moneyed background, and she was intrigued by the girl's reference to 'planning her future', but she wouldn't ask. It wasn't her way. She handed Jess a small key.

'Just leave it on the desk when you've finished, Miss Brennan.'

In the small, cool, dark room Jess sat at the oval table and opened the paper, turning the pages until she came to 'Premises for Rent'. She quickly scanned the lists. Everything seemed too big and too expensive. Tucked away at the bottom was a tiny notice. A 'Small workroom, part furnished, would suit an independent small businessman. Rent two shillings a week. Apply *Liverpool Daily Post & Echo*, Victoria Street.'

Two shillings wasn't cheap and she had a good idea of what 'part furnished' meant. Not a great deal. But there seemed to be nothing else on offer at a price she could afford. She folded the paper and got up. She'd go and see it before going shopping. She had no nightdress, no change of clothes, no toiletries and she needed a case. That would take up the rest of the afternoon, then she would have her evening meal and then tomorrow she would go to Stanley Park and hopefully see Aunt Jo. At least she would have some good news to tell her.

The clerk at the newspaper offices informed her that the

premises she was interested in were in Hunter's Yard, off Shaw's Alley, just off the dock road. 'Not a very nice area for a young woman though,' he finished.

'Oh, that won't worry me. I've coped with worse,' she replied, thinking of Bevington Street.

'Well, it's a Mr Harry Cartwright you've to ask for and – ' he leaned across the desk – 'if you ask me he wants too much in the way of rent. I've heard that you can hardly swing a cat in the place.'

'Thanks, I'll see if I can beat him down. "Part furnished" probably means there's a chair and a cupboard and nothing else,' she said, smiling.

It took her quite a while to find it. It was in one of the maze of alleyways and entries that ran off Shaw's Alley. The building was like all the others surrounding it: dilapidated, soot-blackened and with rubbish scattered on the broken and worn steps.

She knocked loudly on the door and waited until it was opened by a small, rotund man in a collarless shirt and a very grubby checked waistcoat and trousers. He mopped his forehead with a large red handkerchief. 'Yes?'

'I've come about the business premises to let.'

He looked at her suspiciously. 'What business are yer in, girl? I've never 'eard of a decent woman being in business around 'ere.'

She looked at him coldly, knowing exactly what he was implying. 'I supply feather trimmings to milliners and dressmaking establishments. A perfectly respectable business. I need somewhere to keep my stock,' she answered as briskly as she could. 'Now, may I see the premises?'

He looked at her closely. She certainly didn't look like a trollop nor, certainly, did she speak like one, but women were often more trouble than they were worth. Reluctantly he nodded and took a bunch of keys from his pocket. 'Follow me. It might not be suitable.'

'I think I'm the best judge of that – Mr Cartwright, is it?'

Again he nodded and indicated she follow him.

The dark and musty-smelling passageway led to the back of the house and into a small cluttered yard where there was little more than a falling-down outhouse.

Inside it took a few moments for her eyes to become accustomed to the gloom. It consisted of two small rooms. One was completely empty and in the other there was, as she'd suspected, only a battered table, a straight-backed wooden chair and a cupboard. A series of shelves were attached to one wall. A small grimy window on the opposite wall let in a little light.

'Well?' he asked impatiently.

She walked slowly around. 'It's exceedingly dirty and dark. Is there no gas?'

He indicated with a stubby finger a mantleless gas jet on the wall.

It would suit her very well, after it was cleaned up. 'I'll give you one and sixpence a week, which is all it's worth.'

'It's worth two shillin's. It's . . . private,' he blustered.

'It's not, unless there is another entrance?'

'There ain't, but it's lockable, no one will touch yer things. I could let it ter dozens of people.'

'Then why haven't you?'

'It's part furnished!'

'Is that what you call it? One and sixpence, a month in advance. That's my final offer.'

He knew he was beaten. He'd been trying to let it for months. 'Done, but yer drive a 'ard bargain. An' I suppose yer'll 'ave all sorts traipsin' in an' out.'

'No, there will be just myself.' She delved into the battered purse she'd bought and handed him the money. 'If you've no objection I'll come early on Monday morning and give the place a good clean.' She wrinkled her nose. 'What *is* that smell?'

He looked around mystified. 'The factories, I suppose. Can't say I notice it much meself. There's a tannery further down.'

'I suppose I'll get used to it.'

He fumbled with the bunch of keys and then handed her one. ' 'Ere's the key. Yer can let yerself out. What's yer name?'

She was about to reply 'Brennan' but stopped herself. She wasn't going to leave herself open to abuse again. Mam's maiden name had been Kiernan but that was her uncle's name too. 'The name of my business is . . . "Mitchell's Trimmings",' she replied.

'Right then, Miss Mitchell. Lock up after yerself.'

Once he'd gone, she smiled to herself. Mitchell had been the name of the canal agent who had taken in Mam and her uncle and her dead aunt, Carmel, back in Ireland when they'd been orphaned and she wondered what had made her remember it. Still, it sounded good. 'Mitchell's Trimmings'. Quite professional.

She sat down on the edge of the chair. It wouldn't be too bad once it was cleaned up. It was just the right size and those shelves would be very useful. It wasn't much but it was hers. Her very first business premises. It was a start and she hoped it wouldn't be long before she would need to move to somewhere larger. Well, she couldn't stay here all afternoon, she still had shopping to do. She'd head back to Church Street and pay another visit to Marks & Spencer.

For the rest of the afternoon she'd been busy. She had been passing a ship's chandlers when she realised that she would need cleaning materials. So she'd gone in and ordered scrubbing soap and brushes; Jeyes Fluid and buckets; poison for the vermin that infested all such premises; a glass gas mantle; some bleached calico for the window and to cover the table; and a dozen small open-topped wooden boxes, the type a ship's carpenter would use for nails. They would be useful for keeping different size bunches of feathers in. She arranged for everything to be delivered to Hunter's Yard first thing on Monday morning.

It was early evening when she returned to the boarding house, having had a simple meal at the café she now frequented, and clutching the parcels that contained the additions to her meagre wardrobe and a small leather case.

Mrs Templeton nodded her approval of what she considered 'luggage'.

Jess had considered asking to take her once weekly bath but, dusty and sticky though she felt, she realised that she would need it more after she'd finished cleaning her business premises, as she would always refer to them. Instead she asked, as a great favour and one for which she would gladly pay, for a jug of hot water to be brought to her room. Tomorrow she would be glad to see Aunt Jo, to be able to tell her all her news and put her mind at rest. She was on her way up again, and with no help at all from her uncle, she thought with great satisfaction.

On Sunday morning she enquired as to the whereabouts of the nearest Catholic church. That and the fact that she wore the cheap but smartish navy blue skirt and short jacket she had bought the day before, with a plain white blouse, had further increased her standing with Maud Templeton.

'After that I'm meeting my aunt in Stanley Park but I'll be in by seven at the latest,' she finished, smiling at the woman.

After Mass and a late breakfast, for the first time in weeks she took a tram out to Stanley Park. It was a luxury to ride instead of walk and she didn't begrudge the tuppenny fare. It was a joy to stroll amongst the green stretches of lawn and colourful flower beds that filled the air with their heavy perfumes. It seemed a world away from the dusty crowded streets of the docks and the city. Many other people had also come to the same conclusion and already the park was filling up with couples and family groups enjoying the summer sun.

She'd walked almost the entire circumference of the park, taking in the boating lake and the glasshouses and the pavilion, and was relieved when at last she saw the small and slightly plump figure of her aunt coming towards her.

Johanna's face broke into a smile of joy and relief. 'Oh, Jess, I'm so glad to see you! I was getting so worried about you. You didn't come last week and I was praying I'd see you today.'

Jess hugged her. 'Let's go and sit over there by those bushes. It'll be nice and cool. It's getting very warm, isn't it?' She led her aunt to a bench in a small arbour off the pathway.

'Did you get a job? Would they not let you have time off? You should have sent word to me, Jess.'

Jess took her hand. 'I'm sorry, but I've been really busy. I didn't get a job as a governess, I've got something much, much better.'

Johanna looked troubled. 'What?'

'I'm starting my own business. I've rented premises and I'm going to an auction on Tuesday.'

'A business? An auction?'

Jess nodded, her eyes dancing. 'You are looking at the owner and founder of Mitchell's Trimmings.'

Johanna looked mystified.

Jess laughed. 'Feathers! I'm going to supply feathers for trimmings. Oh, Aunt Jo, I know it's going to be successful!'

'But surely there are plenty of people who do that already?'

'Yes, but I intend to charge much less. I'm going to start in a small way—'

'But, Jess, you don't know anything about . . . business. Any business,' Johanna interrupted.

'I can learn and quickly and I don't mind how hard I have to work or scrimp. I've become used to that,' Jess said firmly.

Johanna nodded, but she wasn't at all sure about this. She would have much preferred Jess to be working and living as a governess. It would have eased her mind considerably.

'And I've moved.'

'Where to?'

'Mrs Templeton's Select Boarding House in Ormond Street. It's reasonable, clean and comfortable, and very respectable.'

Johanna nodded. Why had she ever doubted her niece?

She was certainly Maddy's daughter. 'And where are your premises?'

'Off Shaw's Alley. They're very small, little more than a shed, but once I've cleaned them up they'll be fine. They really are filthy.'

'Would you like me to come and help you?' Johanna offered.

Jess hesitated. She would prefer her aunt to see them when she'd finished. 'No, I can manage, truly. It won't take me long and I'm sure you have enough to do.'

Johanna nodded. She did. Tom was proving a terrible patient and Aideen was being no help at all. She seemed totally indifferent to her parents' plight. Only Ronan gave her no cause for concern.

'How is everyone?' Jess felt she should ask.

'Oh, not too bad. Ronan is very good and he's heard a little of Patrick.'

'Really?' Jess replied flatly. She was still furious with her brother.

'He is still living at the club, at the expense of that . . . that friend whom Ronan dislikes so much.'

'And his efforts to make a fortune?' Jess asked sarcastically.

'Apparently he has made a little money. He was at great pains to inform Ronan of that.'

'It won't last. Patrick is a fool! He knows nothing of stocks and he can be talked into anything!'

'That's what I too am afraid of.'

'Well, don't worry about him. He's made his bed, chosen his life.' She wondered whether she should tell her aunt that Edward Dempsey had lent her money but decided against it.

That was between herself and Edward and she knew he would never disclose the fact to her aunt, should he ever meet her, which was unlikely. At least until such time as her uncle was employed by the Dempseys. 'Let's not talk about Patrick! Shall we walk for a while?'

Johanna smiled tiredly. At least Jess was in good spirits and she looked well. The navy and white costume suited her, although it wasn't of the quality Jess had been used to. But her own wardrobe would have to last a very long time now. She stood up. 'Or shall we walk to the pavilion and have some tea? I could certainly do with a cup.'

Jess slipped her arm through her aunt's, feeling happier and more energetic than she had done for weeks. 'That would be nice, and when I have my place decent you must come and visit me for tea.'

Chapter Twelve

———◆———

I N THE EARLY MORNING light the tiny rooms in the rubbish-strewn Hunter's Yard looked even more dismal than they had done on Saturday, Jess thought as she let herself in. Thankfully, she had seen no sign of her landlord. She wrapped the large coarse calico apron around her and started to collect some of the rubbish together. After what seemed only minutes she heard her name being called and then realised that her cleaning supplies had arrived.

For what seemed like hours and hours Jess swept and scrubbed, wiped and polished, her work made harder by the fact that all the water had to be dragged from a standpipe out in the street. She had enlisted the help of two women to heat it up for her in the copper boilers they were using to do the weekly wash.

'Yer've got yer work cut out there, girl!' one had said dourly, nodding her head in the direction of her two rooms and pocketing the coppers Jess gave her for her help.

'I know! I'm worn out already and it's not nearly finished,' she'd replied grimly.

By late afternoon the place looked decidedly better, she thought. At least it was clean. It could do with a coat of whitewash on the walls and ceiling but that would have to wait. To her surprise the table, chair and old cupboard had polished up well and she'd lined the shelves with a roll of white paper she'd bought. Even the mantle now covering the unlit gas jet made the place look somehow more decent.

She was tacking the calico over the now clean panes of glass in the window when she realised she was being watched. She turned suddenly, catching a movement close to the open door.

'Who is it? Come out, I know you're there!' she demanded sternly. Probably the odious Mr Cartwright spying on her, thinking to increase the rent. She was very surprised to see a child emerge from behind the door.

'Hello, who are you?' she asked more kindly.

'I'se didn't mean no 'arm, miss. I was only lookin', like.'

Jess smiled. 'Come here to me so I can see you properly.'

The little girl moved forward a few paces and Jess squatted down on her heels.

'What's your name? Mine is Jess.'

'Tilly, miss.'

'That's a pretty name. How old are you?'

'I'm ten.'

'Really?' She was so small and thin that she looked to be only six or seven. She had a mop of thick brown curly hair that needed a good brush and dark eyes that looked huge in her pale pinched face. The dress she wore was too short and torn in places and her feet were bare.

'Are yer goin' ter live 'ere in ol' 'Arry's out'ouse?'

Jess smiled. 'No, but I'm going to work here. It's taken me hours to clean it up.'

The child traced an imaginary pattern on the floor with one foot. 'I'se know, I'se been watchin' yer.'

'Have you? Well, I could have done with some help. I've nearly finished now.'

The child nodded. 'It looks great now, honest it does. It's better than our 'ouse, yer've even got that fancy glass thing on the gas. We ain't got nothin' like that, we ain't got no gas even an' no candles most times either.'

'Where do you live, Tilly?'

'Down the end of the alley.'

'Won't your mother be worrying about you?'

The child looked scornful. 'Me mam don't worry about none of us. She's down the alehouse with me da.'

'Oh, I see. How many of you are there?' Jess was quite taken with the child and she felt sorry for her.

'Eight, iffen yer count our Davy, but 'e run away ter sea, like, ages an' ages ago. 'E's fourteen.'

Jess nodded and straightened up. 'Well, if you hold the end of this piece of material while I finish tacking it up it would help.'

Seeing that she wasn't going to be bawled out and since the lady was being very nice to her, something she wasn't used to from adults, Tilly readily agreed. She had discovered by listening to people's conversations and asking questions that the lady was going to have her own business, selling feathers for hats. That was something she knew about and liked. Secretly, she hoped the lady might offer her some work.

'Then, when that's done, I was going to go and get myself something to eat. I'm starving. Are you hungry, Tilly?'

'Oh, yes, miss!' The dark eyes lit up in expectation. This was far better than she had hoped for.

'Then you can show me where we can get a pot of tea and something to eat, if there is anywhere nearby, that is.'

'There Rosie's. It's a cannie.'

'A what?'

'A sort of 'ouse yer can get tea an' things ter eat. Dead cheap an' all.'

Jess wiped her hands on her apron. 'Right, let me find my purse and then we'll go to Rosie's.'

She locked the door behind them and then, taking the grubby little hand in her own, she laughed. 'Lead the way, Tilly!'

Rosie was a big, buxom, cheerful-looking woman who had enterprisingly turned the front room of her tiny slum house into a sort of cheap café.

'What can I get yer, luv?'

'A pot of tea and what have you to eat, for both of us?'

Rosie grinned at Tilly. 'On the cadge again, I see.'

'She's been helping me. I've taken Mr Cartwright's storerooms.'

''Is bloody auld shed more like! I 'ope yer aren't payin' 'im more than a shillin', the auld robber!'

'One and sixpence and it's nearly worn me out cleaning them.'

'I'll bet it 'as. Tell 'im seein' as 'ow yer've done 'im the favour of doin' them up, yer'll only pay 'im a shillin'.'

'I've paid him a month in advance.'

'Yer must be mad, girl! Now, will it be pie and mash or

scouse an' bread? Iffen yer'd cum sooner I'd 'ave still 'ad some sausages left.'

'Pie and mash sounds wonderful. For both of us, please. She looks as though she needs a good meal,' she finished in a lower tone of voice.

''Alf starved, the poor kid is, like all Maisie Dobbs's gang. She's a bloody disgrace, iffen yer'll forgive me language. Drunk mornin', noon an' night! Now sit yerselves down and I'll fetch it fer yer.'

The two big dishes arrived and they both tucked in. Jess found it was surprisingly good, as was the tea, and Rosie had also brought two big thick slices of bread and dripping.

Both she and Jess watched with sympathy as the child devoured the food, Jess thinking that she too knew how it felt to be starving.

'What do yer intend ter do with them rooms, like?' Rosie asked.

'I'm starting my own business. Tomorrow I'm going to Fielding's auction.'

'Are yer? Goin' ter buy them feathers?'

Jess nodded, her mouth full.

'What will yer do with them? Stick them on 'ats?'

'Not myself, I'll sell them to the people who make the hats, they can "stick them on".' She laughed.

'Well, good luck ter yer, girl. I expect I'll be seein' more of yer.'

'Oh, you will. Your meals are very good, Rosie. May I call you that?'

The woman laughed. 'Everyone else does, luv. What's yer name?'

'Jess. Jess . . . Mitchell.'

'Well, Jess, yer'll be seein' a lot of that one there too, iffen I'm not mistaken.'

Jess smiled at Tilly. 'I will. I hope she's going to come and help me around the place, when she's not at school.'

Tilly shot her a suspicious look.

Rosie laughed. 'Oh, she don't go ter school no more, luv. She's ten, the School Board don't expect it, not of kids around 'ere, an' they get no joy out of the parents either. Kids of 'er age 'as ter work, when they can get it.'

Jess was surprised but then realised just how little she really knew of the lives of the children in the dockland slums. Maybe she could help the child. Ask her to do some very light work around the place and pay her for her efforts. It might mean the child could at least buy food. 'Then she'll work for me.'

'Can I, really, miss? An' yer'll pay me an' all, like?'

Jess nodded. 'Yes, how about sixpence a week?'

'Sixpence!'

'Give 'er threepence, it's more than she'll get offen anyone else,' Rosie advised.

Tilly glared at her. She would have been rich with sixpence a week! Still, threepence was better than nothing at all, which was what she usually had.

They had parted company at the end of the alleyway and Jess had told Tilly to be waiting for her late tomorrow morning at Harry Cartwright's.

'You can help me sort out the things I buy at the auction and then we'll go to Rosie for our dinner. Now off you go home.'

To her surprise the child grabbed her hand, kissed it and

then ran off. Jess watched her, smiling. She was a funny little thing, but very endearing. She had probably never known any affection in her short life.

Next morning Jess was a little apprehensive as she studied the catalogue she'd bought on her way home yesterday. There were quite a lot of terms she didn't understand: 'down', 'half-quilled', 'full-quilled', 'crested'; but 'tail' and 'wing' were at least self-explanatory. She was thankful to see that there were part lots and small bundles, as well as full consignments and half-consignments. She just hoped the prices weren't high.

She sat at the back of the dingy room, clutching the number written on a piece of cardboard that she'd been given. She appeared to be the only woman there, which surprised her, and she received a few curious and faintly hostile looks. Well, she didn't care. She had twelve pounds to spend and she intended to spend it as wisely as she could.

She watched in silence as the bidding for the large consignments got under way and was surprised at the prices they commanded. There must be a fortune to be made, she deduced as she watched and listened closely.

She had marked on her catalogue the items she intended to bid for and the maximum she intended to pay, hoping her lack of knowledge wouldn't lead to expensive mistakes. At first she was hesitant but when she realised that she had obtained her first purchase for the sum of six shillings, less than she had budgeted for, she became more confident.

As the morning progressed more notice was being taken of her and her stock increased. By half past eleven she had bought all the lots she had marked for nine pounds and ten shillings.

Feeling very pleased with herself, she went to collect the boxes. They presented a problem as there seemed to be so many of them.

'Will you need transport, miss?' the young lad in charge asked.

'Er . . . no. I think I can manage, if you could perhaps tie them all together for me.'

He looked pained but did as she asked. As she struggled out a middle-aged man with a florid face and execrable taste in waistcoats looked derisively at her.

'Neither use nor ornament those part-quilled!' he mocked. 'Bloody women!'

'Really? And I suppose you're an expert on making ladies' hats and I don't think!' she replied cuttingly.

Her arms were aching when she finally arrived at Harry Cartwright's and found Tilly waiting for her. The child looked overawed.

'Did yer buy all them?'

'I did. Now, let's go and start sorting them out. I just wish I really knew what I'd bought.'

The array confused them both. Some she'd seen before, others she hadn't. Quickly she realised that 'down' consisted of tiny, fluffy, flyaway and rather useless-looking feathers. There were some tail, wing and crest feathers that were lovely and she wondered what kind of birds they came from and, rather sadly, just how many had been killed to provide them. Not this many could possibly have died of natural causes.

'Well, we'll just sort a few of each kind and tie them together so I can take them with me in my case.'

'Take them where?'

'To shops that make hats.'

The child shrugged. 'When will yer go?'

'This afternoon.'

'Can I cum with yer?'

Jess shook her head. She couldn't trail this little urchin around with her. 'No, I need you to stay here and carry on sorting and to look after the place.'

The child's expression changed.

'But we'll go to Rosie's first. As soon as we've finished. I could murder a cup of tea.'

Tilly's face brightened. A meal was far better than visiting hat shops.

Jess had made a note of some of the small millinery shops over the last couple of days and decided to try the first two on her list; one in Hood Street, the other in Dawson Street, both near Williamson Square. She had also worked out just what she would say.

'Good afternoon, may I speak to the proprietor?' she asked of the young woman who sat tacking a band of pink petersham ribbon to a light straw hat.

'Who shall I tell Mrs Cummings is asking to see her?'

Jess smiled. 'Miss Jessica Brennan, of Mitchell's Trimmings.'

The girl looked a little startled but disappeared into the back.

Jess looked around at the hats on display, feeling that her own was very inferior. She at least should have bought a decent hat, suitably trimmed with feathers. Preferably her own feathers.

'Mrs Cummings, how nice to meet you and how good of you to see me without an appointment.' She offered her hand to the unsmiling woman who appeared.

'What is it you are selling, Miss . . . Brennan?'

'Feathers, ma'am. For decoration and at a very competitive price.'

'Indeed?'

'May I show you some samples?' She sounded more confident than she felt and hoped the woman would ask no awkward questions.

Mrs Cummings nodded.

Jess placed her case on the counter top and began to remove her samples.

'They're not made up?'

'I'm sorry?'

'My usual supplier makes them up into small bunches. It makes things easier.'

'Oh, that would be no problem at all.'

'And what about colours? I need them dyed to match the fabrics.'

Oh, that was something she hadn't thought about. She could have kicked herself for her naïvety.

'I'm sure that can be arranged. If you were to give me some small samples of fabric?'

'And what prices are you offering?'

'A penny for a small cluster. Three farthings for two crest feathers, and twopence halfpenny for a fine tail feather such as this.'

'Hmm. Fine tail and crest feathers, undyed, are usually only called for for autumn and winter hats.'

'Perhaps some lighter-coloured ones? I do have some back at my premises?'

The woman fingered a few samples.

'I am just starting my business, ma'am, so I'm prepared to offer dyed feathers at the same prices.'

'Very well. I'll take a selection and if you can match my fabrics and bring me some cream or white tail feathers then I'll consider a bigger order. But the dyed feathers *must* match, Miss Brennan.'

'Of course. Thank you so much, Mrs Cummings. Now, when would you like delivery?'

'As soon as possible, please.'

'Shall we say Thursday?'

The woman looked surprised. 'That's extremely fast service.'

'It's one of the things I pride myself on. Prompt efficient service, at competitive prices. Now, if you could let me have the fabric samples I'll see you on Thursday, Mrs Cummings, and thank you.'

When she was once more on the street she let out her breath slowly. Oh, there was so much about this business that she didn't know! But she had to learn – and fast. She and Tilly could easily put together little clusters of feathers and hand-tie them but with a rapidly sinking heart she acknowledged that she knew absolutely nothing about dyeing feathers and didn't know where to start to find out either. And she'd promised them by the ridiculously short time of two days! She must be mad!

She was a little more cautious visiting the second shop and had more difficulty in persuading the owner to place an order until she decided to buy a decent hat. She chose a navy blue sugar-spun straw trimmed with a navy and white striped ribbon around the crown, finished off with a large bow of the same ribbon at the back. It cost her nine shillings but she felt it was a worthwhile investment. Mrs Cummings's decidedly disparaging glances at her old one had not gone unnoticed.

'I'se sorted them an' put some of them in them little boxes,' Tilly announced proudly when she returned.

'Good girl. Oh, Tilly, I've got a big problem.'

'Didn't yer sell none?'

'Oh, yes. You'll have to help me tie some into little bunches.'

'I can do that. I'm not daft.'

Jess managed a smile. 'I know you're not. But I've got to dye them and I don't know how to start.'

'I do,' the child stated.

Jess looked at her closely. '*You* do?'

Tilly nodded. 'I'se had a job in the dyeworks until me mam came lookin' fer me money. She were dead drunk an' started shoutin' and yellin' an' they give me the push.'

'Do you really know how to dye feathers?'

'Yus, an' I know 'ow ter mix the dyes an' all – I watched the women. But yer 'ave ter bleach them first. I watched them do that an' all.'

Out of the mouths of babes, Jess thought with such a surge of relief that she caught the child in her arms and hugged her. 'Oh, Tilly, what would I do without you?'

The child looked a little fearful. She'd never known anyone carry on like this before and all because she'd said she could dye feathers. It was something she'd enjoyed doing until she'd been forced to leave through no fault of her own. It had been easier than a lot of the other menial jobs she'd managed to get, but not keep, thanks to her mam's habit of coming looking for the money for more ale.

'Come on, let's go and buy the bleach and the dyes and then I'm going to treat you to a meal in a proper café. And to a new dress and a pair of shoes. You're my little angel, that's what you are.'

A huge smile lit up the child's face and Jess realised that she was in fact beautiful.

Chapter Thirteen

———◆———

TWO FRANTIC DAYS PASSED with many disasters, at the end of which she returned to Mrs Templeton's exhausted and with her hands stained with all colours.

'Good heavens, Miss Brennan! Your hands!' her landlady remarked when she paid her her rent.

'Oh, I know! Please, please don't ask, but I can assure you it's a necessary sacrifice. My business will be successful if I can just get the colours right, so it's a small price to pay.'

She had told the woman a little about her business venture which surprisingly had met with approval. Unlike so many of her generation Maud Templeton was very much in favour of women making their own way in the world, providing what they did was honest and respectable. Hadn't she done so herself?

'I would invest in some white cotton gloves, Miss Brennan,' she advised and Jess had thanked her and bought two pairs.

'Well, what do you think?' she asked Tilly as, with heartfelt relief, she placed Mrs Cummings's order in her case on Thursday morning. They had worked like demons but she was very pleased with the results.

'I'se think we done great, Jess.'

'I think we did very well, Tilly,' Jess corrected, smiling.

The child smiled back. She was getting used to Jess and some of her 'daft' ways, as she thought of them. Still, it was the first time anyone had looked out for her. These days she had two meals a day; a new dress and shoes (well, the dress wasn't exactly new but it was better than anything she'd ever had); and stockings and even knickers. Things she'd never had in her life before. Jess had even marched her to Victoria Street Baths and she'd had her very first bath. She'd been frightened to start with, terrified of the water that came gushing from the tap in clouds of steam and of the enormous, deep bathtub, but once she'd got over her fear she'd loved it, splashing about and laughing until Jess had scrubbed her mercilessly and washed and brushed her hair.

'Now you really do look like a little angel,' Jess had said with admiration at the transformation of the child.

Despite everything that had happened to her, as she walked towards Hood Street Jess felt happy and confident. She caught sight of herself in a shop window and thought how smart she now looked in her navy and white outfit with her stylish hat and the white cotton gloves, which she did not intend to take off and thereby disclose her inexperience.

Mrs Cummings was quite amazed and did not hide it. 'Well, I certainly didn't expect to see you until next week, Miss Brennan.'

Jess smiled. 'You doubted me, ma'am?'

The woman smiled back. 'I did indeed. You are very new to all this, aren't you?'

'I have to admit that I am.'

'No one submits single samples, Miss Brennan, except for tail and crest feathers. And the look on your face when I asked about dyed trimmings was a picture!'

'Oh, Mrs Cummings, so it was obvious that I was inexperienced?'

'Indeed it was, but I have to admit you are a fast learner and a very determined young woman. I like that. These are splendid. The match is very good and they are tied so well. They're very fiddly to do.'

'I had quite expert little fingers to help me.'

'Well, shall we go through to the back and have a cup of tea while we sort everything out?'

Jess was surprised and relieved. 'That would be lovely.'

'You know my usual supplier was very sceptical when I told him your prices and delivery schedule, but then he's a very sceptical man and can be quite . . . condescending.'

'He isn't a red-faced man with a dreadful taste in waistcoats, is he?' Jess asked, thinking of the very rude man she'd encountered at the auction.

'Indeed he is.'

'Then I've met him. It's nice to know I've proved him wrong!'

Something in the other woman's expression told Jess that she heartily agreed.

'He won't be very pleased to learn that I'll be decreasing my order, either.'

Jess was very pleased with herself as she returned to

Hunter's Yard, but before she reached the door she heard the sound of raised voices: a woman's and the shrill, hysterical pleading of Tilly.

'Just what is going on here?' she demanded as she entered.

The woman – a filthy slattern who was obviously drunk – was shaking Tilly and trying to tear the dress from her back.

'Jess! Oh, Jess, I'm glad yer cum back! Me mam's lookin' fer money an' I told 'er I ain't got none an' she said she's goin' ter take me frock an' shoes ter Uncle's instead!' Tears were streaming down the child's face and her shoulders were scratched.

Jess's temper burst forth. 'Take your hands off her! I bought those clothes, not you!'

'She's my kid! She's got money, I know she 'as!'

'She hasn't! I just feed her, since you certainly don't! In fact you are a disgrace and you have a flaming nerve even to call yourself a mother!'

The woman let out a curse and lurched towards Jess. Tilly broke free and ran and hid behind Jess, clinging tightly to her skirt.

'Yer toffee-nosed bitch! I'll swing fer yer!'

'Get out of here now or I'll call the police. I mean it! You're on my property and if you threaten me or her I'll make sure you end up in Walton Jail! Get out!'

'Yer don't scare me! There's no scuffers around 'ere!'

'Tilly, run along to Wapping and tell the desk sergeant that Miss Jessica Brennan, of Mitchell's Trimmings, requires assistance immediately. A drunken trespasser! Say exactly that, he'll believe you!' she instructed coldly.

The child turned and ran.

'Now do you believe me? You can get out and never come near me or her again, or you can go to jail. I mean every word I say.'

Despite her drunken state the woman realised Jess really did mean it, and was certainly not afraid of her. Muttering more curses, she staggered out.

Jess sank down on the chair and after a few seconds Tilly crept back into the room.

'I . . . I watched 'er. I was frightened ter go ter the polis station. I don't like scuffers. They belt yer.' She sniffed.

'Come here to me,' Jess said, opening her arms and lifting the bruised and frightened child onto her lap.

'I don't never want ter go back, Jess. I'se been hidin' me stuff from 'er every night but she must 'ave watched me and folleyed me.'

'Well, you don't have to go back.'

'Where can I go?'

'How would you like to come and live with me, in the place I stay, that is? If I can persuade my landlady to let you? You'll have to be very good and very quiet and learn manners and how to speak . . . nicely.'

The child's face lit up. 'Can I? I don't mind bein' good and learnin' things, honest I don't, Jess! She never gave me nothin' but belts!'

'Well, I can't promise, but I'll certainly do my best. Now, let's try and get you tidied up and then we'll go and get something to eat. Afterwards we'll see what Mrs Templeton has to say.'

* * *

As Jess had feared Mrs Templeton had quite a lot to say.

'I am absolutely adamant, Miss Brennan. No children!' She cast a piercing glance at Tilly who was hovering by the door, her thumb in her mouth, her eyes wide at the pristine hallway.

'Mrs Templeton, I beg you. She has nowhere else. Her mother is the most dreadful drunken slattern who beats her and lets the child go hungry and in rags. She's a good girl, she works hard, she's honest and when I've cleaned her up and taught her manners she'll be no trouble at all. She will be out with me all day and will be in bed early. You will hardly notice her.'

'Children should be seen and not heard, Miss Brennan, but quite often children of a certain sort are very visible and very noisy.'

'Mrs Templeton, please? I'll guarantee her behaviour and I'll pay for her. I can't let her run the streets at night, my Christian conscience wouldn't allow me to. I could never live with myself if anything happened to her.' She had emphasised the words 'Christian conscience' and saw that the woman had taken her meaning.

'Don't you think that if we can save one little soul from all the depravity of her world, a world she was born into through no fault of her own, it will assure us of our place in heaven?' It was a speech worthy of her mam in full flow, Jess thought with some amusement, but no hint of that amusement showed in her face or her voice.

Maud Templeton grimaced, but how could she, who indeed thought of herself as a God-fearing woman, resist such a plea? 'You drive a very hard bargain, Miss Brennan.'

'She's had a very hard life, Mrs Templeton.'

'Very well, I'll give her a trial, but any nonsense and out she goes. She will have to share your room and your bed and it will be another one and six a week. She is . . . clean? I'll have no lice or bugs in this house.'

'She is! I'll give her a bath and tomorrow she will have more respectable clothes, I promise.'

'And perhaps you could do something with that frizzy mop. Little girls' hair should be braided and tidy and kept out of their eyes!'

Jess nodded and sighed inwardly with relief. It had been a hard-won battle.

'What is her name?'

'Matilda Dobbs. Tilly.'

'I don't want to hear a sound out of you, girl!' Mrs Templeton said sharply as Jess called Tilly to her.

'Tilly, say thank you to Mrs Templeton. She has very kindly said you can stay here with me and she doesn't usually do that,' Jess prompted the sullen child.

'Ta, missus.'

Jess nudged her. 'Thank you, Mrs Templeton.'

The child repeated the words grudgingly then allowed Jess to propel her up the stairs.

'I don't like 'er,' she stated as Jess fumbled with the key to the door of her room.

'You don't have to. Just keep out of her way and when you do see her, talk to her politely.'

'What's "politely"?'

'Nicely, properly. Say "Good morning, ma'am" or "Good evening, ma'am".'

'I don't think I'm goin' ter like . . .' She fell silent as Jess gently pushed her inside.

'What's the matter now?'

'Am I goin' ter stay 'ere?' The child had never seen a room like this.

'You are.'

'Am I goin' ter sleep in that bed? I'se never slept in a bed, it's always been the floor.' She touched the blue and white counterpane almost reverently.

Jess shook her head. Such terrible hardship in such a short life. 'You are and you are going to get washed every morning and every night in that big bowl on the washstand and get dried with those big white towels.'

'Two times a day! I 'ave ter get washed two times!'

'Indeed you do,' Jess said firmly, beginning to realise that she was going to have her work cut out to 'civilise' and 'put manners on' this child, as her mam had been wont to say. 'Now, it's bathtime and in the morning we're going shopping. And we're going to have to do something with your hair.'

Tilly looked fearful. 'What's wrong with me 'air?'

'It's like a furze bush, as my mam used to say. I'm going to turn you into a neat, tidy, clean and well-mannered little girl, even if it kills me!' Jess said grimly.

The child Jess took with her to the park on Sunday bore little resemblance to the little slummy Tilly had been at the beginning of the week. Her cloud of brown hair had been, with some difficulty, plaited and tied with two bows of ribbon. She wore a Miss Muffet print dress with a white starched and frilled pinafore over it. Jess frequently had to tell her to stop lifting up the hem of the dress to admire her flounced petticoat.

'Why?' Tilly had demanded.

It was a word that Jess was becoming heartily sick of. 'Because nice little girls don't do things like that.'

'Is it "manners" again?'

'It is,' Jess had replied wearily.

Tilly was also very taken with her new black buttoned boots and Jess constantly had to warn her that she'd fall flat on her face if she didn't look where she was going.

There had been a small argument over the straw hat too.

'Yer can't see me nice ribbons now!' Tilly had protested.

'Oh, Tilly, of course you can and all—'

'Nice little girls wear 'ats,' the child had interrupted and Jess had been forced to laugh at the expression on the pert little face framed by the ribbons and topped with the straw boater.

'Now, if you promise to behave yourself I'll buy you some sweets, as long as you don't get all sticky and ruin your clothes.'

'Sweets! Can I really 'ave some, Jess?'

'What would you like? You can have a halfpenny twist.'

'Oh, aniseed balls. Yer can suck them fer hours. Our Billy give me one once, ages ago. 'E nicked them, like.'

Jess raised her eyes to the heavens. 'Just don't go saying things like that to Mrs Kiernan!'

Johanna was very startled to see Jess appear with a child in tow.

'Who on earth is she?' she whispered as Tilly, with her mouth full of sweets, tried to repeat, 'Good afternoon, Mrs Kiernan,' after Jess.

'Why don't you go and play with those children over there? If you give them a sweet they might let you play with their hoop,' Jess encouraged and, prompted by curiosity but determined to keep her precious sweets to herself, Tilly walked towards a boy and a girl of her own age.

Jess told her aunt the sad little tale and Johanna shook her head.

'Jess, don't you think you're taking on too much?'

'She's a bit of a handful but I couldn't just abandon her.' She didn't add that she knew what it was like to be hungry, dirty and an outcast. 'She's been a huge help to me. I would never have got a single order but for her. Believe it or not, she knows how to bleach and dye feathers. She had a job in a dyeworks.'

'So young?'

'She's ten. Starvation and neglect have taken their toll.'

'Well, tell me all about your week. You got an order?'

'Indeed I did,' Jess laughed and for the next hour aunt and niece chatted and exchanged news while Tilly played with her new friends, but kept a watchful eye on her benefactress and her sweets.

'Would she like some milk or lemonade while we have tea?' Johanna asked at length. At least the child did seem to be behaving herself.

'Probably lemonade. I doubt she's ever had it before and it should keep her quiet.'

Jess got up. 'Tilly, say goodbye to your friends now, we're going for some tea and Mrs Kiernan says because you've been so good you can have a glass of lemonade,' she called.

The promise of lemonade had the desired effect and all

three of them took the path to the pavilion.

'Jess, I would very much like to see where you are living, to set my mind at rest. I feel I owe it to your mother's memory. Oh, I miss her so much, Jess.'

'So do I, Aunt Jo, but I often feel as though she's sort of . . . with me.'

'I'm sure she is, Jess, although what she would have made of this little one, I don't know.'

'Oh, you know what she was like. She would have done the same thing.'

'Yes, she probably would. She was always so generous and kind-hearted, just as you are. Well, can I visit you?'

Jess nodded. She had no wish to add to Johanna's worries.

'And Ronan would like to see you, too, Jess. I know he worries about you.'

Jess smiled. 'Oh, in that case I'll have to ask Mrs Templeton's permission. She's very strict about "gentlemen".'

'He's your cousin!'

'But will she believe that?' Jess laughed, thinking of her landlady's face.

'She will if he accompanies me! What kind of a woman is she, for heaven's sake?'

'One who runs a very nice boarding house and who has already done me a huge favour.' She nodded towards Tilly who was totally engrossed in her glass of yet another treat.

'Well, then, ask her. Shall we say Wednesday evening at seven o'clock? If it's not possible, you could send word. You have the address.'

Jess nodded and wondered how this request would be met.

* * *

To her surprise Mrs Templeton didn't object.

'Providing he is accompanying your aunt, I can see no problem.'

'Thank you. Tilly will, of course, be in bed.'

The woman nodded. So far, to her surprise, the child had been no trouble. With her new clothes and her hair braided, she looked very respectable and she was a pretty little thing. Jessica Brennan was constantly rising in Maud Templeton's esteem.

'I could provide tea,' she offered. Very few of her guests availed themselves of the parlour and she was curious to see just what the relations of this very unusual young woman were like.

'Oh, that would be very kind of you. Would you object if I bought a cake?'

'Not at all.'

Tilly had wanted to stay up, she had liked Johanna and was hoping for another treat, but Jess was firm.

'This is a grown-up time,' she had insisted, tucking the child in.

They were very punctual, Mrs Templeton thought as she ushered them into the parlour, and the young man was very polite. They were obviously not short of money, judging by the quality of Mrs Kiernan's clothes and hat.

'Oh, Jess, this is lovely!' Johanna cried, taking Jess's hands.

'I told you it was.'

'Jess, you look very well,' Ronan said, smiling as she bade them both sit down. He had been concerned about her. There had been nights lately when thoughts of her and her predicament had kept him awake.

'Would you like me to serve tea in about half an hour, Miss Brennan?'

She beamed. 'Oh, yes, please! Isn't Mrs Templeton thoughtful?'

'You are indeed,' Johanna agreed.

'What kind of a place did you think I was living in?' Jess asked when they were alone.

'Well, I really did wonder, Jess.'

'It hasn't been easy, I'll admit that.'

'But you're a survivor, Jess. Just as Maddy was.'

'And I hear you have started your own business,' Ronan said. He noticed she looked thinner and there were the beginnings of frown lines on her forehead.

'I have. Oh, it's nothing much. I've sold a few feathers but the more I learn the better I hope business will become. What I have discovered is that you have to sell an awful lot to make a decent profit.'

'Will you be trying the bigger establishments?'

'Eventually, and the dressmakers, although I suppose the competition will be stiff. They probably have their long-established suppliers.'

'If you could find some sort of new approach, or offer them something . . . different, it would help,' Ronan suggested. He wanted her to succeed, if only to show her feckless brother that she could do better than him.

'I'll have to try and think of something. How are you, Ronan?' She thought he looked a little tired. He was really only a young man and should be enjoying life, going out with friends – even girls. He had a lot to offer. Instead he was busy shouldering all the family responsibilities.

'I'm doing all right. Things will be better when Father starts with Dempseys'.'

'Oh, and when will that be?' Jess asked in a clipped voice.

'At the beginning of next month. Arthur's father came to see him at the weekend, after Mother cleared it with Dr Phillips.'

Johanna looked a little uncomfortable, knowing Jess's views on Tom.

'Did you find it hard to raise the capital for the business, Jess?' Ronan asked to change the subject.

'Not really. I didn't need much. Twenty pounds. I . . . I borrowed it from Edward Dempsey.'

'Edward Dempsey! Why him? Jess, why didn't you come to me?' Ronan was perturbed. She should have come to him. She should have shared her plans with him. They could have discussed things, the way they always used to, and he would have helped her make plans.

'I just happened to meet Edward and when I explained, he offered. In fact he offered simply to give it to me but I couldn't accept that. So, it's a loan, and I'll pay him back, with interest.'

'It appears this family is doubly indebted to the Dempseys.' Ronan sounded bitter.

'Edward is very . . . nice. He took me for lunch in New Brighton.'

'Really? You never told me, Jess.' Johanna was surprised.

'Oh, it's nothing like that, Aunt Jo! I had decided to go for a sail, it was a lovely day and I had time to kill, and he said he'd come with me, that's all.'

For some reason that fact didn't seem to please Ronan either but she assumed he was upset over her loan. Still, she couldn't have asked him. He had enough on his plate keeping the wolf from his mother's door and a roof over their heads.

She was quite relieved when Mrs Templeton appeared with the tea tray.

She invited her landlady to join them and was amused to hear her quizzing Johanna – in a roundabout way – about her background. When Johanna finally informed her that Jess was the only daughter of the recently and tragically deceased owners of the Brennan Line, the woman nodded slowly. She'd thought as much. The girl had definitely come from a good background.

'A terrible tragedy. It must have been dreadful for you. I'm so sorry.'

Jess smiled sadly. 'It was and now you can see why I couldn't leave Tilly uncared for and friendless.'

'Her mother was exactly the same. She took us all in when I was first married and Ronan and Aideen were babies.'

'Well, I'm sure Miss Brennan will make her way in the world. She's an exceptional young woman.'

Jess looked embarrassed. This was high praise indeed. She only hoped she could live up to it.

Chapter Fourteen

⬦

J ESS LOOKED UP FROM her desk as the door opened but she was surprised to see Ronan come in.

'Oh, I thought it was Edward.'

'Disappointed?' he asked with a lop-sided smile.

'No, of course not! In fact I'm glad you've come. I don't see enough of you.'

'That's because you are always so busy, Jess.'

She smiled. 'I know, but you have to agree it's paid off.'

She was very proud of her achievements. In just a year her business had gone from strength to strength. It had been hard work. She'd spent long hours gaining new customers, working with Tilly to get the orders out and going to two or three auctions a month. After six months she had moved from Hunter's Yard to much bigger premises and now employed four women who did the bleaching, dyeing and hand-tying and – for special orders – selecting and stitching complete 'embellishments', as she called the highly decorative complete arrangements ready for instant attachment to hats, jackets and dresses. They were her speciality and she selected and assembled them herself. Her customers were not only milliners but some of the large dressmaking establishments and 'Mitchell's Trimmings' had become 'Mitchell & Brennan's Ladies' Ensemble Embellishments'. She had also had the good fortune to be able to purchase two smaller businesses similar to her own that had come up for sale. She had got them at a good price and had turned their fortunes around. They now formed a lucrative part of her assets.

Ronan nodded, smiling. He was equally proud of her. She'd achieved so much and virtually on her own. These days she was very confident and her past experiences seemed only to have increased her self-assurance and independence. She had blossomed too. She had put back the weight she had lost and her clothes were once more fashionable and expensive. It was a great relief to his mother.

'And how is Tilly's education coming along?'

Jess grimaced. 'She's still not at all happy at being sent back to school, but I told her she would never make her way in the world unless she had a decent education.'

He smiled. 'I didn't think she would need to "make her way". You spoil her shamelessly, Jess.'

'Well, you never know what the future holds, Ronan, and I would hate her to be . . . left, as I was.'

'Jess, you wouldn't accept help,' he reminded her. It had pained him greatly that she had not had sufficient faith or trust in him to have asked for his help.

'That's true, but just the same I intend her to be able to earn her own living, and a decent one, should she ever need to.

You have to admit, Ronan, she's much better than she used to be.'

'Oh, yes. You'd never dream she'd been born and brought up in Hunter's Yard now. Quite the "posh" little madam. To use one of her own expressions.'

'And Aunt Jo is teaching her how to cook and manage a household properly,' Jess added.

Ronan thought of Tilly's once-weekly visits. The kitchen usually ended up in total chaos and his mother invariably took to her bed. Tilly's efforts at self-improvement were best confined to school, in his opinion. She was the most precocious eleven-year-old he'd ever met.

'So, is Edward's visit a social one or is it business?'

'Social. He's taking me out to lunch. Believe me, it's a rare treat.'

She had become quite friendly with Edward Dempsey. Oh, he was still very formal and serious and sometimes she felt she could scream at him, he was so pedantic, but there were times when he amused her, even made her laugh and forget her worries and problems for a few hours. His advice was always sound; she had been able to pay him back, with interest, after two months and often asked his opinion as the business expanded. Ronan helped too. He did her accounts.

'We're celebrating,' she informed her cousin.

'What?'

'Well, you should realise how well things are going . . .'

'I do. Are you expanding?'

'Ronan, I'm always expanding. I'm almost certain I've got the Marshall's account and you know what that means?'

He nodded. Marshall's were the biggest suppliers of

part-made ladies' dresses and costumes in the city. They had quickly seen the advantages in the new 'ready-made' ranges that were becoming very popular.

'And I'm looking into new lines. Feathers on everything can't last for ever and I'll need to have other irons in the fire.'

'Very wise.'

'Edward's advice.'

'So, what are you celebrating? Marshall's?'

'Yes and . . .'

'And what?'

'I've decided to buy a house – and not just any house.'

Her eyes were sparkling and he smiled. 'Dare I ask?'

'Mam's house. It's up for sale again.'

He became serious. 'Jess, do you not think it'll be . . . too painful? All those memories?'

She shook her head. 'I've thought about that and no, there are so many *good* memories. It was my home. All my childhood was spent there.'

'Will it not be too big?'

'No. I can use Da's study as an office and of course Tilly will have a bedroom and somewhere to keep her ever-increasing collection of dolls, although why she seems to need so many is quite beyond me. I never had that many, but she says when she was little she never even had a single one. Her "family", she calls them, and she's very proud of them and keeps them immaculate.'

'What are they asking for it?'

She pushed a letter across the desk towards him.

He scanned the lines. It wasn't extortionate.

'I can afford it.'

'It will need furnishing.'

'I know, but I can take my time.'

'Will you try to track down some of Aunt Maddy's things?'

Jess shook her head. She'd thought of that but realised it would probably be a fruitless search and would take too much time. 'If anything comes up, of course I'll buy it. I'll go to the Auction Rooms in Hanover Street for most of the things I'll need.'

He nodded. She was always practical. 'Maud Templeton will miss you.'

'I know, but I couldn't stay there indefinitely, even though Tilly has her own room now. I know sometimes she is a bit too much of a chatterbox for Maud.'

That was true, Ronan thought. Maud Templeton was not really fond of children although she and Jess got on well enough; in fact, the older woman admired Jess tremendously and Jess was very good to her. These days the woman was far better and more stylishly dressed, courtesy of Jess. He always extolled his cousin's virtues and achievements to his mother whenever Johanna visited Jess, which was frequently, although Jess never visited their house.

He frowned, his thoughts returning to the purpose of his visit.

'What's the matter, Ronan?'

'The reason I came to see you, Jess, is that I've heard that Patrick is looking for you.'

'Patrick?' She seldom thought about her brother. She had still not forgiven him.

He nodded.

She turned away. 'Well, I don't suppose I'm *that* hard to

find. He has sense in his head. My business is called Mitchell & Brennan.'

'Would you see him, Jess?'

She picked at an imaginary thread on her cuff and shrugged. 'I . . . I'd prefer not to.'

'If he should come to me, asking . . . ?'

She turned towards him. 'I can't tell you what to do, Ronan.'

'Then I won't tell him. I can never forget or forgive what he did to you, Jess.'

She nodded. In some things Ronan was implacable and just as stubborn as herself. She supposed they had both inherited the trait from their parents.

'As I said, it's up to you but I really do have no wish to see him. I told him to go to hell and I meant it. Have you told Aunt Jo?'

'No.' He smiled wryly. 'You know what she's like. Ever the peacemaker.'

'I know. She . . . she still hasn't given up on me and . . . your father.' She refused even to call him 'Uncle Tom'.

'And I don't suppose she ever will.'

Jess was thoughtful. 'Ronan, there is something I've been wanting to ask you about.'

'What?'

'I've been thinking about it for quite a while. You remember Mam promised some compensation to the widows and I wanted to honour that promise until . . .' She pushed to the back of her mind the dreadful memories of her eviction from Bevington Street at the hands of Nellie Scragg and her neighbours. 'Now that I have money, I feel I can.'

'Jess, it's very honourable of you and in principle I agree, but why not wait a while? Perhaps until you have sorted the house out, and you have more security behind you, for both yourself and Tilly. Look at it again in say three or four months.'

Jess twisted her hands together. 'They must already have suffered so much, Ronan.'

'I know, Jess, but that couldn't be helped and, apart from wanting to honour Aunt Maddy's promise, you really don't have any obligation to them. You lost everything too.'

She sighed. She had and she had lived like them in poverty and despair, even if only for a short time. 'If you think I should wait, I will.'

'I do,' he replied firmly. 'Well, I suppose I had better be going before Edward arrives.' He stood up, feeling a little jealous of the attention Jess seemed to give his sister's brother-in-law. Edward was a dry stick, in his opinion, and he hoped the fellow wasn't just going to string Jess along. He didn't think Edward had any serious romantic intentions where Jess was concerned.

Jess got to her feet too. 'I'd better make myself presentable. We're going to the Grand, the new one in New Brighton. It only opened last week and it's supposed to be very "posh", as Tilly would say.'

'Well, he can certainly afford it, Jess.' He knew he sounded a little bitter, but it was true. Edward Dempsey didn't have to virtually support his mother and father. Ronan's father's income was now very modest.

Jess wondered if Ronan were jealous of Edward. Oh, that was being fanciful! she told herself. Was it that Edward was taking time off for lunch? Ronan rarely did, but he had even more responsibilities than Edward. Still, she wished her cousin would take more time to enjoy himself.

As usual she had enjoyed her lunch but she had insisted on returning to work.

'I have a great deal to do, Edward, really,' she'd protested. 'But I have enjoyed myself.'

'So have I, Jess. I mean that. You are always so animated and interesting, but you are always so busy.'

'And so are you. The only other man I know who works so hard is Ronan.'

'We both have to, Jess. Father isn't getting any younger and I can't leave everything to Arthur, much as I'd like to. Perhaps we can have dinner one evening?'

'When I've sorted out the house and Tilly, that would be lovely.'

'You are taking on a great deal with that child, Jess.'

'Oh, she's not that bad. She's better than she used to be,' she said lightly. She often had the feeling that Edward had as little time for Tilly as Maud Templeton did.

Jess decided to finish early just the same. She'd call into the offices of Worrell and Hackett who were selling her former home and tell them that she wished to purchase it. It would make her feel so much happier. Then after supper she would take Tilly to see what would be her new home.

She left Mary, her most senior worker, to lock up and walked quickly towards the corner and the tram stop into town, but as she reached the end of the road a man stepped out of a doorway and into her path.

'Patrick!' She was shocked to see him.

'I . . . I finally found you, Jess.'

'Ronan said you were looking for me,' she supplied coldly.

'You seem to have done well.'

'I have, but with no thanks to you!'

'Jess, please . . . ?' He could see she hadn't forgiven him.

'So, what do you want? I'm in a hurry. I have an important appointment.'

He shifted his weight from foot to foot. 'Do you think we could perhaps go for a drink?'

'I don't frequent public houses. You should know that.'

'Tea then?' He didn't want to have to carry on a conversation in the street.

'Why? Why now, Patrick?' She was impatient.

'Oh, Jess! You're still my sister!'

She relented. 'Just fifteen minutes. There's a Kardomah Coffee House around the corner. It will have to be coffee.'

He walked in silence beside her until they reached the coffee house but waited until the waitress had served them before he spoke again.

'Jess, I don't blame you for still being angry with me—'

'Angry! I was furious!'

'I thought it was for the best,' he pleaded.

'Obviously it wasn't.'

'I did make some money—'

'I heard,' she interrupted, 'but you lost it. I knew you would.'

'It was just bad luck!'

'You make your own luck, Patrick. And what about your friend? The one who was so sure you'd make a fortune?'

'Terence has been very good to me, Jess, but he lost money too and he just couldn't afford to go on . . . bailing me out.'

'I see.'

'No, Jess, you don't. I . . . I'm broke. I have nowhere to go.'

'I thought you were staying at your club?'

'I can't afford . . . Terence can't afford for me to stay there any longer. I have nothing, Jess, and I must owe a small fortune!' he pleaded, close to tears. The last months had been terrible as one after another his investments had failed to bring in a return. Now he didn't know where to turn.

For the first time Jess looked closely at him. He was thinner, there were lines at the corners of his eyes, his hair needed cutting and his clothes were shabby.

He leaned across and caught her hand. 'Jess, please, you've got to help me! I've nowhere to go and no one else to turn to.'

'Neither had I, Patrick. I was reduced to living above a rundown old stable and begging for food.'

'Oh, God! Then you know how desperate I am. I know you've worked hard and I'll help, I'll do anything, anything at all! I'll sweep floors, cart rubbish. Please, Jess, don't desert me? Mam . . .'

At the mention of her mother Jess knew she had lost this battle of wills. Mam had looked out for her; Mam would never forgive her if she failed Patrick. He'd never cope if he tried to live on the streets. Slowly she nodded.

'Mam wouldn't have wanted me to just abandon you. She knew you would never be able to manage.'

'I know. I'm not like you. I suppose I *am* like Aunt Carmel. Oh, Jess, you won't regret it.' He was so thankful.

'I hope I won't, Pat. Now, you'd better finish your coffee and come with me.'

'Where to? You said you had an appointment.'

'I have. I'm going to buy back the house in Crosby.'

He was astounded. 'You've got *that* much money?'

'I've worked damned hard for it and I'll have to go on working damned hard to furnish and run it.'

'I'll help you all I can, Jess. I promise.'

She managed a smile, wondering just what Tilly would make of her brother. 'You'll have to be prepared to share it.'

He was curious. He knew she still would have nothing to do with their uncle. 'Who with?'

'Tilly.'

'Who?'

'Tilly Dobbs. She's eleven and I suppose you could call her my adopted sister. She's been living with me for a year now.'

He said nothing, amazed. What on earth had possessed her to take in an eleven-year-old child? No doubt he would soon find out.

Chapter Fifteen

———◆———

TILLY HADN'T HAD A good day at school. There was so much she didn't know and she was so far behind everyone else. She hadn't wanted to go back to school at all and she certainly didn't see the reason for it. Wasn't she fine as she was? She had learned a lot already and she was a great help to Jess, a 'credit' to her now, as Mrs Kiernan – or Aunt Jo as she now called her – often said.

She dawdled along, dragging her bag of school books along a low garden wall. She had a wonderful life now, compared to her years with her mam in Hunter's Yard. She looked down at her neat buttoned boots. She had four pairs of boots now, where once she had none, and a whole wardrobe full of clothes. In winter she had thick stockings, a heavy coat, hats and scarves and gloves. There was always plenty to eat and she had a lot of toys. She had a whole new family too. She liked Aunt Jo enormously: she was so patient and kind; but Mr Kiernan was another kettle of fish altogether, often abrupt and quick-tempered. She didn't know why Jess would never speak of him, some fight in the past so she'd heard. She liked Ronan too, although he was a bit serious. But all the good things hadn't helped her at school today. The class bully and her gang of friends had been tormenting her about her reading, mimicking her stumbling pronunciation until she'd lost her temper and had flown at the girl. Then Miss Thomas had blamed her for starting a fight and she'd been made to stand in the corner for the whole afternoon. Well, she'd just tell Jess that she wasn't going to school any more. Not after today. After she told Jess about how awful the other girls had been she was sure she could talk Jess around.

She worked out what she was going to say when Jess got home. She didn't do her homework, she just sat in the parlour and pretended to do it in case Mrs Templeton should check on her, which she often did until Jess arrived. To her surprise Jess didn't come straight in as she usually did, but she heard her talking to Mrs Templeton in the hall. She couldn't think of any misdemeanour she had committed but Mrs Templeton would find something to complain about if you were a living, breathing saint.

When Jess finally came into the room Tilly was surprised and annoyed to see that she was not on her own.

'Tilly, this is Patrick, my brother. He's coming to stay here with us and I've got another surprise too,' Jess announced with a bright smile at the child who was looking with suspicion at Patrick.

Tilly nodded at Patrick who smiled back politely. She looked to be a sharp little minx.

'What surprise?' Tilly asked, suddenly feeling ill at ease. He didn't look in the least bit like Jess, she thought. In fact you wouldn't think they were even related – and she didn't like the suspicious way he was looking at her.

'I'll tell you over supper. Now, put those books away and get your things. Have you finished?'

'Yes,' Tilly lied determinedly. Now how was she going to tell Jess she wasn't going to school any more?

In the café, Jess watched Patrick bolt his food. He must be starving. How long was it since he had had a proper meal? Well, she would have a word with him after Tilly was in bed. She would have to have a talk with Maud Templeton too, she had just skimmed over Patrick's predicament and only the promise that it wouldn't be for very long had induced the woman to let him stay at all. It wasn't that she had taken a dislike to him personally, Maud Templeton seemed to dislike all men, only tolerating those who were her paying guests because they were just that.

'So, what is the surprise?' Tilly asked, her mouth still full.

'What have I told you about talking with your mouth full?' Jess rebuked her.

'Sorry,' Tilly muttered, annoyed with herself for letting Jess down. Patrick's expression seemed to suggest he took it for granted that that is what she normally did, knowing no better.

'You'll be pleased to know that we're leaving Mrs Templeton's very soon.'

Tilly's eyes widened. She hadn't expected this. 'Why?'

'Because I've now got enough money to buy a house. The house I used to live in, in fact, where I was brought up.'

'Before you lost your mam and da and all your money and he left you?'

'I didn't leave her! She left me,' Patrick interjected, stung by the implication and the fact that the child knew so much.

'Never mind who left whom. But, yes, that's the house.' Jess poured herself another cup of tea. 'I went to the agents on my way home to tell them definitely.'

'When can we move?' Tilly demanded.

'When I've got some furniture and all the legalities are sorted out. In about three weeks.'

'Can I have my own room? A whole room to myself?' the child begged.

Jess smiled. 'Yes, and then you'll have plenty of room for all those dolls you collect and which I seem to find in the oddest places. Now, how did school go?'

Tilly looked glum. How could she tell Jess now, with *him* looking at her as though she was something that had crawled out from under a stone. He didn't like her, she could tell. Oh, well, soon she would be going to a new school: maybe she'd make some friends there, and maybe the teachers would be kinder and have more patience and not rap her knuckles all day long or make her stand in corners.

'I . . . I haven't finished my homework.'

'You said you had.'

'I know but . . . but it's so hard. I do try, Jess!'

'Maybe I can help you with it,' Patrick offered, sensing that to stay on the right side of his sister it would be best if he showed some sign of friendship towards this little 'adopted sister' as Jess called her. She was obviously very fond of the child, which he found incomprehensible.

'Would you really, Patrick? I have to go and have a long

talk with Maud so it would be a great help. She does have a lot of catching up to do.'

'Of course I will. I have to do something to repay your . . . kindness.' He smiled briefly but there was a note of bitterness in his voice.

'You don't have to "repay" anything. You're my brother.'

She was grateful to him but judging by the look on Tilly's face the plan certainly didn't meet with her approval.

When Tilly and Patrick were settled in the parlour, Jess went to look for Maud Templeton.

'Can I explain about my brother and the future?' she asked her landlady who was seated at the desk in the hall, seemingly checking the laundry receipts.

'Come through to my sitting room. We won't be interrupted there.'

Jess was surprised. Although Maud Templeton had thawed lately she'd never been invited into this sanctum before. It was a small, rather gloomy and austere room although what furniture there was had been well polished and cared for.

'Now, I think you *had* better explain, Jessica,' the woman said ponderously as she indicated that Jess take a seat on a small, deeply buttoned leather chair at the opposite side of the fireplace.

Jess nodded. She had asked Maud to call her 'Jess' but Jessica was as far as she would go towards informality.

'Patrick finds himself in a . . . predicament. He lacks sufficient funds to maintain a place of his own and I *have* to help him. I hope you can understand that. As I said, it won't be for very long as I'm buying a house in Crosby.'

'Oh, I see.' The woman frowned. 'Won't that be a bit far away from your business?'

'Yes, it will be much further, far more travelling. I'll come into town by tram. It's a special house. It's where I was brought up.'

Maud Templeton digested this thoughtfully. 'You know, Jessica, you have done very well indeed and it's not easy, this being a man's world.'

'Don't I know that well enough.'

'Your poor mother would have been proud of you. *I* am very proud to have known you and had you staying beneath my roof at what must have been a very difficult time in your life. What little I do know, your Aunt Johanna has informed me of.' She leaned forward a little. 'Are you quite sure about . . . your brother? He hasn't treated you very well, has he?'

'Patrick isn't like me, it's *difficult* for him to have to stand on his own two feet.'

Maud sniffed derisively. 'It's a common failing in a lot of men.'

Jess ignored her. 'He'll be fine now he's back with me and living somewhere decent.'

'Where *has* he been living?'

'At his club, as far as I know.'

The older woman sniffed again and raised her eyes to the ceiling. Typical! Living the high life, doing nothing, while Jess had worked and scrimped and saved and taken that little urchin under her wing and transformed her into something closely resembling a child from a respectable background.

'It's a lovely house, really it is, and as soon as I'm organised you must come and visit, you've been so good to me. I know it's not always been easy,' she added, thinking of Tilly's first few weeks under this roof.

'That's very kind of you, Jessica, I'd be delighted to visit.' Maud meant it, even if only out of curiosity. 'So, when do you think you will be leaving me?'

'In about three weeks. I have a lot to do, I've no furniture or . . . well, anything.'

'I'll take you to Ingrams. I deal with them a lot and I'll make sure you get good value for money. They're not the cheapest but you do get good quality merchandise for your money. I'll miss you, Jessica, and I'll miss your Aunt Johanna's visits. She's a very pleasant woman. Very pleasant indeed.'

Jess smiled. 'I'll miss you too.'

'I presume your brother will now find himself some employment, to help you out?'

'I'm sure he will. He used to work for my father – in the offices – so it shouldn't be too hard.'

'I hope he pulls his weight. You have enough on your plate with the child.'

Jess smiled. 'You won't be sorry to see the back of Tilly, I know.'

'I won't pretend I like children, I don't. But you have done so well with her, I simply hope you don't spoil her. Just remember you can take the child out of the slum, but it's another matter to take the slum out of the child.'

Jess nodded, but she didn't really agree. Give anyone half a chance to better themselves and they would, she was certain of that.

She rose. 'Well, I think I'd better go and see how they're

doing. She doesn't find schoolwork easy and Patrick, who's helping her, isn't the most patient person.'

'Just let me know when you want to visit Ingrams and if there is anything else I can help with.'

'I will, and thank you.'

Maud Templeton looked reflectively at Jess. She was a very brave young woman and she was certainly taking on a lot with that child and a brother who, although older, didn't look as if he was going to be of much use to her. Hardly two words to string together. She knew the type. In her business you became a good judge of character and in her opinion Patrick Brennan was going to cause Jess trouble.

In three whirlwind weeks the paperwork was completed and Jess had duly been to Ingrams with Maud Templeton and had bought everything she would need to set up her own home. Some rooms would still be sparsely furnished and of course the furnishings were nothing like those that had formerly graced the house, but she hoped that in time it would become more like the home she had once known and loved.

Every night Patrick helped Tilly with her homework, which surprised Jess. She knew Tilly was wary of him and she sensed that the child was jealous, which in her opinion was ridiculous. But at least Tilly was making some improvement and seemed happier to go to school. Even so, she felt that Patrick was still trying to repay her and that he really didn't approve of the time, affection and care she afforded the child.

The day before they were to move into the house in Crosby, Maud Templeton and her maid of all work, Eliza, helped Jess give the house a good clean.

'It is a lovely house, Jessica,' Maud remarked admiringly. 'And you know that gentleman, Mr Dempsey, is a very pleasant and handsome man.'

'Edward?'

'Yes, he called when you were out. I told him you were moving: he seemed a little surprised.'

'He probably was. Oh, he did know I was intending to move, but not when.'

'You could do a lot worse than him, Jessica. He's very nice indeed.'

Jess smiled deprecatingly, secretly amazed at what Mrs Templeton was suggesting. Was there something about Edward that she was missing?

Maud decided she had said enough on the subject of Edward Dempsey. 'What an unusual window.'

Jess looked up towards the landing and suddenly felt overwhelmed by her memories. She'd smashed that window the day she'd learned that her father wasn't coming home ever again. The day Uncle Tom had come to give them the dreadful news and not only of her father's death.

'I'm going to have it bricked in! It's called a "Widow's Window" and my mother used to stand and watch there, waiting for my father's ship. I *hate* it! I will never forget the day when we heard the news.'

'I can understand that,' Maud answered gently, concerned at the effect her words had had on Jess. 'Right, now I'll go and clean the bathroom and then we'll have a cup of tea. Eliza, did you bring the cups and the kettle and the other things?'

'I did, ma'am,' the girl answered dutifully.

Tilly arrived after school with Patrick who was bursting to

inform Jess that he had obtained a position as a clerk.

'Oh, Jess, it seems so strange to be back here,' he said as he came into the hall and looked around.

'It does, especially seeing it empty. I don't know what kind of people they employed to clean but it was far from that.'

'I can vouch for that,' Eliza muttered resentfully.

'Well, it won't be empty for much longer. The furniture arrives in the morning,' Maud interrupted, shooing Eliza, who was laden down with buckets and mops, ahead of her towards the kitchen.

'Isn't it big!' Tilly exclaimed, gazing around in disbelief.

Jess laughed. 'This is just the hall.'

'And there's a garden, too,' Patrick informed the child, amused by her astonishment. 'You can play in a garden, instead of the street.'

Tilly looked at him to see if he was being sarcastic. 'I don't play in the street any more. It's . . . it's not nice.' She cast a surreptitious look at Maud Templeton. It was she who had said that when Tilly had once asked if she could play out.

'Come and see your bedroom,' Jess instructed, taking her hand.

The room was bare but Tilly didn't care. She turned to Jess with shining eyes. 'This is *mine*? All *mine*?'

Jess nodded and the child ran to the open window. 'I can see for miles and miles! Right out over the river and to the sea!'

'Yes, you can. That's why I thought you'd like it.' It had been her room and for that very reason she had felt unable to occupy it again. She didn't want views over a river down which her father would return no more. 'Tomorrow, when the furniture arrives, you can bring all your things up and sort them out.'

'What will I have, apart from all my clothes and dolls?'

'Well, let me think now. There'll be the bed, of course, and a wardrobe and a tall chest. A bedside table with a lamp, a towel rail, a chair and a small desk and then there's lots of space under the window seat. Look, it lifts up.' She drew up the lid of the upholstered seat that was set into the bay window. 'You can put all your toys in here.'

Tilly peered suspiciously into the space. 'Not my dolls, though? I don't want to shut them up in the dark.'

Jess smiled. 'They won't mind, Tilly. They're only dolls.'

'They're my *family*!' the child protested indignantly. '*I* wouldn't like being shut up in the dark!'

'Oh, all right! You can put them where you like, as long as you keep them tidy. Now you have a room of your own I expect you to keep it nice.'

'Oh, I will, Jess, I promise! Oh, if only Mam could see the style of me now!'

'Yes, well, the least said about her the better,' Jess replied grimly.

'Jess, do you think we'll be happy here again?' Patrick asked tentatively as they stood looking over the gardens that Maddy had planted and tended with such care.

'I hope so, Patrick. The hardship I suffered – and believe me, it *was* hard – sort of helped me to overcome some of the memories. It made me look on things – and living in this house again was one of them – in a very different light.'

'This house doesn't have all that many happy memories for me, Jess.'

'How can you say that? We had a wonderful childhood,' she cried.

'We did, but . . . but the last years . . .'

'They were difficult for you, but not me.'

'That's because you always knew what you wanted from life, Jess. I didn't. That was something I could never really explain to either Mother or Father, particularly Father. I hated the shipping business.'

'I know.'

'And that was a big disappointment to him. I know he wanted me to follow in his footsteps, go away to sea, learn the business from the bottom up, but I couldn't, Jess.'

'Well, it's all water under the bridge now. So, you have a job?'

'I do. It's only as a clerk but I'm used to that. The pay's not much, but at least I will be able to help out, pay my way, Jess. I won't be living off you.'

'You were quite happy to live off your friend.'

'No, I wasn't. Terence insisted but I wasn't happy. I owe him so much.' He had hated to leave Terence owing him such a debt of gratitude, not to mention money.

Jess didn't want to go down that road again. It was enough that Patrick did at least seem to want to work and help out with the expenses of running a home. She prayed they would all be happy in this house. That there would be no more friction, no more rows, no more unhappiness.

Chapter Sixteen

———◆———

To JESS'S RELIEF THE peace she'd longed for seemed to be within her grasp at last. Although she still had the feeling that Tilly and Patrick really didn't like each other, they both seemed to be trying to overcome the feelings of mutual hostility.

Patrick worked long hours but didn't complain a great deal and Tilly seemed to have settled better in her new school. Patrick still helped her with her work, when he could. Jess had no way of knowing if Patrick kept in touch with Terence Shay but she suspected he did. He had asked that a small amount of his salary be kept back for 'personal expenses'. She'd agreed. He did need some money of his own to spend and even if he was paying part of it to his friend to reduce the debts he had accumulated, she didn't mind. It was only right that he paid what he owed.

The house looked infinitely better too, she thought as she folded Tilly's clean clothes and put them away. The child did keep her room very tidy. She smiled at the row of assorted dolls, some of them rather battered, that sat in a line on the bed. How Tilly managed to sleep with that collection beside her she didn't know. Tilly was almost fanatical in her devotion to them and Jess wondered whether it was something to do with her very bleak and deprived early childhood. There had been very little love and affection in her life until now.

As she took her own freshly ironed clothes into her bedroom she was surprised to hear the garden gate creak. Peering out of the window she saw Edward Dempsey coming up the path. She dumped the clothes on the bed, glanced at her reflection in the dressing-table mirror and tidied away a few tendrils of hair that had come loose. Did she have time to change her blouse? No, she sighed to herself as the sound of the doorknocker echoed in the hall.

'Edward, how nice to see you,' she greeted him. 'Please do come in.'

He looked a little hesitant. 'I hope it's not inconvenient, Jess.'

'Of course not. You're my first visitor, apart from Aunt Jo, of course.'

'As I hadn't heard from you, I took the liberty of calling on Mrs Templeton who told me you had indeed moved here.'

She ushered him into the sitting room.

He looked around approvingly. 'The place looks well, Jess.'

She smiled a little ruefully. 'But not quite the same as it used to.'

'Well, I'll have to take your word for that. I was never here before. But these things take time. I brought you this, as a sort of "welcome home" gift.'

'Oh, Edward, how thoughtful of you.' She was genuinely touched.

He watched her as she unwrapped the paper. She was so composed, so self-assured, quite unlike any other girl or woman he knew. He would really like to get to know her better but felt he was perhaps a bit too old and staid for her. But he was glad he'd come, especially as Mrs Templeton had informed him that Patrick was living with her now. He felt the lad had treated her very badly, but perhaps he'd seen the error of his ways. He sincerely hoped so.

'Oh, Edward, it's lovely!' She stroked the blue and gold Crown Derby vase almost reverently. Mam had had one just like it and she wondered . . . but no, Edward couldn't have known that. It must have cost him a pretty penny just the same.

'My mother has one very similar which she prizes, so I thought . . .' He smiled and shrugged.

'It's very good of you.'

He shrugged again. 'So, you really didn't mind me just calling in?'

'Heavens, no! It's lovely to see you and if it hadn't been for you, Edward, I wouldn't be back here in this house at all.'

'All I did was lend you a small amount of money, Jess, the rest you did yourself through sheer hard work, determination—'

'And a lot of luck!' she finished, placing the vase carefully on the mantelshelf. 'I'll organise some tea, or would you prefer something stronger?'

'No, tea will be fine.'

The sound of the front door opening and then closing made her look up. 'Ah, that's Patrick.'

'I heard he was back.' Edward couldn't keep the note of disapproval from his voice.

'I couldn't turn him away. I just couldn't.'

'Of course not,' he murmured but his eyes became hard as Patrick entered the room.

'Look who's come to see us. Perhaps you could keep Edward company while I make some tea?'

The two men eyed each other with suspicion. Patrick had never liked Edward Dempsey. But, to be fair, he'd never liked any of the Dempseys.

Edward spoke first. 'I just called to see how things were progressing. I heard you were back.'

'What is that supposed to mean?' Patrick asked curtly.

'Nothing. It was just a simple statement. I presume it's accurate or is this arrangement of a temporary nature?'

Patrick was stung. 'I'll get back on my feet and I'm not sponging off Jess. I pay my way.'

'I didn't assume for one minute that you were "sponging", as you call it, but Jess has been through some very difficult times and I for one don't want to see her in such a predicament again. You do understand me?'

Patrick was fuming. Just what was Dempsey getting at? And what were his feelings for Jess? Before he had time to reply Jess was back, informing them that Tilly would bring the tea.

'Is she capable?' Patrick asked irritably.

'Yes, she is. She's a very capable child,' Jess replied. You could feel the tension in the air, she thought, wondering what Edward had said to make Patrick so on edge.

'And how is the child coming along?' Edward asked with genuine interest.

'Very well indeed. She actually likes her new school. She says her teacher is kind and patient and the other girls are friendly and don't bully her because her home and clothes are better than theirs. She still has quite a lot of catching up to do, though. Patrick's very good, he often helps her with her homework.'

'Indeed,' Edward answered. He was surprised that Patrick Brennan would do something so unselfish and helpful but perhaps he was just doing it to get on the right side of his sister, seeing she was so fond of the child.

When Tilly brought in the tray both men watched Jess fuss over her: Patrick with annoyance and Edward with benign amusement, thinking she was an endearing girl who was very bright and had improved immensely. Patrick for the life of him was unable to understand why Jess had wanted to saddle herself with another burden on her time, money and emotions. But then Jess had always had a soft side. It was just a pity that she had taken such an irrational dislike to Terence when she hadn't even met him and therefore didn't know how amusing and charming and clever he could be. He accepted the cup from Jess with a muttered 'thanks' and hoped Edward Dempsey's visit wouldn't last too long.

Before Edward left he tried to warn Jess not to be too trusting of her brother.

'Jess, I don't want you to be upset by him again,' he said as they stood in the hall.

'I think he's learned his lesson, Edward. He is trying very hard, he works long hours in that office even though I know he isn't cut out for that kind of employment.'

Was he cut out for *any* kind of employment? Edward

wondered to himself but said nothing. His own father had once remarked that a man like Martin Brennan must find such a son a great disappointment.

'Jess, will you let me take you out to dinner? Now there is Patrick to keep his eye on the child, whereas before . . .'

Jess smiled at him. She'd been putting him off for far too long. He was really a very thoughtful, caring man. And she remembered what Maud Templeton had said about him. He was indeed a handsome man and also a very desirable one because of his nature. 'I'd love that, Edward, really I would.'

'Then what about Saturday? The theatre?'

'Would be lovely.'

'And supper?'

'Edward, you're spoiling me.'

'It's about time someone did, Jess. I'll call for you at seven-thirty.'

'I'll look forward to it and thank you again for the beautiful vase.'

Jess returned to the sitting room and found Patrick pouring himself a whiskey from the decanter that always stood on the sideboard. 'What was the matter with you two?' she asked.

'Oh, he's so pompous and suspicious!'

'He's a bit formal, I'll give you that, but he's a very pleasant and admirable man.'

'He insinuated that I was living off you and more or less warned me not to upset you again. The nerve of the man!'

'Oh, Patrick, I suppose it's his way of being protective of me. He's asked me out on Saturday night.'

'Are you going?'

'Yes, I've put him off for far too long.'

'That's no reason to accept.'

'Yes it is and besides . . . I quite like him.'

'He's dry and sanctimonious, and he's old.'

Jess laughed. 'Then I've nothing to be afraid of, have I? And really, Patrick, he's not *that* old.'

'Be it on your own head then,' Patrick muttered into his glass. He wondered just what Edward's feelings towards Jess were. Had he any intention of asking her to marry him? He couldn't really see Jess married to someone like him. Mentally he shrugged. He didn't think his sister had marriage on her mind at the moment, she was too involved in her business. The fact that she had been so successful had surprised him. She'd had no training or experience and yet somehow she'd done it. He was glad but in a way a little jealous. His parents would have been proud of her, of that he was certain. Especially his father. Jess had always been his favourite. He drained his glass. The thought made the whiskey taste sour in his mouth.

Jess had enjoyed herself. As the evening progressed, to her surprise Edward had become far more informal and she caught a glimpse of the man beneath the rather serious exterior. He had bought her sweets, the seats were of the best and supper had also been a lavish affair. He was sparing no expense and she began to wonder just how she felt about him. She wasn't in love with him. That much she did know. But she did like him a great deal and she had agreed to go out with him again one evening. Well, it wasn't exactly a promise of betrothal, was it? she told herself with some amusement.

Johanna was thinking the same thing after Jess had told her about her evening out, the following Sunday afternoon when they met in the park. During the summer months it was a tradition they kept up. It got them both out of their respective houses for a few hours. Tilly enjoyed her weekly treat of sweets and lemonade and there were always other children there for her to play with.

'Do you think he's serious, Jess?' Johanna asked, neatly tucking her skirt around her feet as they sat down on a bench.

'Oh, Aunt Jo, not you too?' Jess laughed.

'Why, who else has commented?'

'Patrick.'

'I see,' Johanna mused.

'I wish I did!'

'Perhaps Patrick's afraid Edward will oust him in your affections.'

'Oh, that's nonsense. It's an entirely different thing. Patrick's my brother and Edward is . . .'

'What?' Johanna quizzed. She for one thought it no bad thing for Jess to be courted by Edward Dempsey.

'A friend. He's been good to me.'

'He has and he's not a bad catch.'

Jess pealed with laughter. 'Do you think you can marry me off to a Dempsey too?'

'No one could "marry you off", Jess. You're much too stubborn. But it's something you'll have to consider, Jess. I've never heard of him courting any other girl.'

'He's not *courting* me!' Jess protested.

'Isn't he?' Johanna smiled.

Jess became serious. 'Oh, Lord, you don't really think so?'

'It's something to think about, Jess, I mean it. Even his mother couldn't complain about you. You wouldn't be going to him almost empty-handed like Aideen went to Arthur. No, you're a successful woman who has money and property of your own. And he is the elder brother, he'll inherit almost everything and that's not to be sniffed at, Jess.'

'Stop it! I . . . I haven't even thought of anything like that. I'm just too busy with the business and madam over there.' She nodded towards Tilly who was playing cherry wobs with two small boys.

'And how *is* Patrick?' Johanna asked to change the subject.

'He's fine. He's working hard and does try to help in the house.'

'No more talk of investments?'

'No. Thank God. I think he's got that out of his system. He . . . he's not very happy about me seeing Edward.'

Johanna raised an eyebrow.

'Patrick says he's pompous and suspicious.'

'Suspicious of what?'

'Of Patrick doing something stupid again, I suppose.'

'You see, he does care for you, Jess.'

'Oh, for heaven's sake, stop that! Will we go for tea? I foolishly promised Tilly that if she were good I'd take her for a trip on the boating lake but I'll need a good strong cup of tea first.'

'You're never going to trust yourself to row around in one of those flimsy little things?'

Jess smiled. 'I told you it was a foolish thing to do.'

Johanna laughed. 'Well, don't expect me to come too. I'd never trust anything smaller than one of the Mersey ferries. I'll watch.'

* * *

It was almost dusk by the time they reached home. The trip on the boating lake had taken far longer than Jess had imagined and they had been the last ones to leave the park before it was closed.

'Oh, I'll be late getting the supper now,' Jess grumbled.

'I'll help you. I know how to peel and boil vegetables. Aunt Jo showed me,' Tilly offered. She at least had enjoyed their trip even though she hadn't been much good with the oars and had almost lost one.

'You'll have to if we're to get anything to eat this side of midnight,' Jess sighed as she took off her hat and hung it on the hallstand.

'There's someone here,' Tilly hissed, having gone towards the kitchen but stopped when she heard voices from the sitting room.

'Oh, damn! I hope it's not Edward. I haven't time to sit and talk to him.'

'I don't think it is,' Tilly said confidently.

Patrick was talking to a young man with dark hair and eyes, dressed in a well-cut lightweight wool jacket and flannel trousers. Her brother seemed very animated and a little flushed, Jess thought.

'Ah, Jess, you're home at last,' Patrick cried, getting to his feet.

'We were detained on the . . . er . . . boating lake,' she replied, smiling apologetically at the stranger. 'A little matter of not being able to get the boat in question to go in the right direction.'

The man stood up and smiled back. 'A tricky business that.'

'Very. I apologise for my lateness.'

'Jess, this is my friend Terence Shay. You remember I told you how good he's been to me.'

Jess's smile froze. So, this was the man who had fed her brother all those lies and false hopes and expectations of fortunes easily come by.

'It's a pleasure to meet you, Miss Brennan,' Terence Shay said, still smiling. He could see she wasn't very pleased to see him.

'Have you come here with more hare-brained schemes? If you have, there's the door. I'm not the fool Patrick is. I've earned my money the hard way.'

This wasn't going to be easy and yet it was imperative that he got on the right side of her. Before the introduction she had been pleasant and he had to get her back into that mood.

'Miss Brennan, please, let's not start off on the wrong foot,' he said convivially.

Jess was not going to be put off. 'We're not "starting off" at all.'

'Jess, please? Terence is my friend. I owe him a debt of gratitude.'

'And of other things too, so I understand. If you've come for money, Mr Shay, you're out of luck. Patrick has none and I—'

'He hasn't come looking for money, Jess!' Patrick interrupted heatedly. Why did she have to be so suspicious, so blunt?

'What has he come for then?' she demanded of her brother.

'Perhaps I'd better explain.'

'Perhaps you'd better,' Jess said coldly, sitting down.

Terence Shay also sat and began to twist his hands together.

He had to word this correctly and it wasn't going to be easy. Well, he'd just have to eat humble pie. He wasn't in a position to do anything else.

'I admit that I might have been at fault in persuading Pat to invest what little money he had, but I did it in good faith, Miss Brennan, you have to believe that. I honestly thought – no, was *convinced* that I could help to restore the family finances and that then Pat would have been able to have kept you in the way you'd been used to.'

'Really?' Jess queried coldly. Quite apart from her initial prejudice, she realised she *didn't* like him. He was just too . . . glib. He obviously had this little speech well rehearsed. She glanced at Patrick and saw to her consternation that he was hanging on Shay's every word.

'Yes, *really*, Miss Brennan. I really am most truly sorry that that didn't happen. The last thing I wanted was for anyone to suffer.' He paused and shook his head. 'I tried to look after Pat as best I could, hoping things would change, that our investments would eventually pay off, but . . .'

'But they didn't.'

'No. It was very bad luck for both of us. And now—'

'And now what?' she interrupted again.

'Jess, please, won't you let Terence explain?' Patrick begged.

'Please do.'

'Now I find myself in more or less the same position as Pat and as I've no one, no parents, no brothers or sisters, I've come to throw myself on your mercy, Miss Brennan.' He looked down at his hands. He hoped he appeared contrite enough. He hadn't a place to lay his head and was counting on Patrick. He cursed himself for the fool he'd been. He'd gambled and spent extravagantly, always telling himself that there would be plenty of money. Didn't everything he touched turn to gold? But it hadn't and now he needed a place to live and escape his creditors. Jess Brennan could supply that.

Jess's eyes narrowed. 'On my mercy? What exactly is that supposed to mean?'

'After paying my debts – all of them – ' he glanced pointedly at Patrick – 'I have hardly a penny to bless myself with and no roof over my head.'

'Your club?' Jess asked coldly.

'Are refusing to keep a room for me unless I can pay in advance.'

'You see, Jess, he's nowhere to go and it's partly my fault. He used his own funds to keep a roof over my head.'

'And so he should! It was he who persuaded you to risk your money.'

'Jess, we can't turn him out. Not after he's been so good to me. Does that count for nothing in your eyes?'

Jess didn't answer. She didn't want him here under her roof and yet . . .

'Miss Brennan, if I have to beg I will. It will only be for a short time, I promise.'

Jess was weakening. 'And do you intend to seek work?'

'Of course!'

'Please, Jess? He was my saviour.'

'Don't be so dramatic, Patrick!' Jess snapped.

'He was, in a way. I would have gone out of my mind after Father, then Mother . . . and all the worry of the loss of the business and the house,' Patrick pleaded sincerely.

'And how do you think I coped with it all? By running away and hiding?'

'Jess, you know I'm not like you. I never will be, it's not my fault.'

There was a whining note in her brother's voice that grated on her nerves. 'Just don't say it's because you're like Aunt Carmel, Patrick, or I'll scream!'

'Jess, please? Do this one favour for me? Terence will be no trouble, really, and I do owe him so much.'

Jess looked down at her hands. What was she to do? She had forgiven Patrick, up to a point, but to have to put this so-called 'friend' up in her own home was a difficult pill to swallow.

'Miss Brennan, please?' Terence Shay said quietly, hating having to debase himself before this uppity, self-righteous slip of a girl.

Jess sighed. How could she refuse? She nodded slowly. 'What can I say? As long as it is only for a very short time. I have enough on my plate as it is. And I insist it is a formal agreement. You will become a lodger in this house. You will pay rent – when you are able – and you will abide by my rules. I am a respectable woman and wish to remain so in the eyes of my friends and neighbours. This way there will be no irregularities, proprieties won't be offended. Those are my terms.'

Slowly Shay nodded his agreement. The bitch! She was certainly making him eat humble pie, but there was nothing he could do.

'I say, aren't you taking things a bit too far, Jess?' Patrick felt humiliated himself.

'No! I have my reputation to think of, not to mention Tilly. That's my final word.'

Patrick glanced sympathetically at Shay but there was nothing he could do.

Chapter Seventeen

————◆◆————

JOHANNA WAS FAR FROM happy when Jess informed her of Terence Shay's presence in her home and had conveyed her fears to both her husband and her son.

'She's so pig-headed you'll do nothing with her, Jo,' Tom said grimly. 'Look at the way she rejects all my apologies and all *our* efforts to be reconciled. She wouldn't let us help her when she needed it.'

'What could she do? She doesn't like it one bit, but he was good to Patrick.'

'Good!' Tom cried derisively. 'He filled his head full of eejit ideas! Lost him what little money he had. You call that "good"?'

'I'm with Father on this. She should never have agreed to it,' Ronan had said grimly. He vividly remembered his one meeting with Shay. The man was arrogant and unscrupulous and Ronan certainly didn't trust him. He was certain Shay had an ulterior motive.

'But what are we to do?' Johanna had protested.

'I'll go and see Jess and . . . *him*,' Ronan had promised.

It was Tilly who let him in. 'She's in the kitchen.'

'Where's Patrick?'

Tilly jerked her head in the direction of the sitting room. 'He's in there with *him*!'

Ronan looked at the child. She wasn't a fool. In fact she was quite bright. 'You don't like him, do you?'

'No. I . . . I don't like either of them, but *he* hates me.'

Ronan was perturbed. 'Why do you say that? What's he done?'

'Nothing. He hasn't belted me or anything like that, but he just sort of watches me, all the time.'

Ronan nodded. Terence Shay was a nasty piece of work and it really worried him that Jess had no one close at hand to protect her.

'Tilly, if anything . . . anything happens that you don't like or you think I should know about, you will tell me?'

She nodded.

'You can tell me when you come to see Mother. I don't want you to be afraid or upset, either of you. Promise me?'

'I promise I'll tell you or Aunt Jo.'

'Preferably me – first at least.'

'I will,' Tilly promised.

'Good girl.'

Jess was up to her elbows in flour, baking, but she was always pleased to see Ronan.

'You can see now why I didn't come to the door myself. Sit down.'

'I hear you've been pressed into having Shay stay.'

She nodded. 'But not for long, I hope. And I've insisted he is a lodger here, not a guest. He'll pay rent and I won't have him treating the place as if *he* owns it.'

'How *is* he behaving?'

'Well, I have to say, very politely. I don't like him, Ronan, but I can tolerate him for Patrick's sake, as long as he's not always under my feet and isn't rude or arrogant.'

'I've found him to be both.'

'But he wasn't living under your roof.'

'Jess, if ever he does or says anything, anything at all that upsets you—'

'I'll throw him out, you can be assured of that.' She banged the rolling pin down hard on the pastry as if to emphasise her point.

'Do you think he has some sort of ulterior motive?' he pressed. He was certain of it.

'Like what?'

'Like trying, through Patrick, to gain control of your business?'

'My God! I never thought of that! No, Patrick isn't that much of a fool to believe I'd let him share any part of my business.'

'Don't be too sure, Jess.'

'Patrick has no head for business, Ronan. I had to learn the hard way but Patrick . . . well, he'd never learn in a million years. That scheme to make a fortune from stocks and bonds came to nothing. It must have been a hard lesson for him, at least I hope it was. But if there ever is anything . . .'

'Send Tilly for me, Jess. I worry about you being here in this house with both of them.'

She looked a little concerned, but shrugged. 'Don't worry about me. I can take care of myself.'

'But I do, Jess.' He did. In some ways Jess was her own worst enemy. Too trusting, too ready to forgive Patrick.

She smiled. 'I really *can* look after myself.'

'And the child?'

'She has nothing to fear from him. I'd kill him if he touched her.'

'She doesn't like him.'

'I know that only too well. She doesn't like Patrick either and neither does Edward.'

'Edward Dempsey?'

'Yes. I've been out to the theatre with him a couple of times.'

Ronan didn't reply. He'd heard from his mother about these little outings. She hoped it would mature into something more permanent but inexplicably he didn't. Was he jealous, he wondered? Was it natural to experience these feelings whenever he looked at Jess? He steadied himself. She was his first cousin. It was just protectiveness, concern and . . . affection. It was all it could be. It wasn't against the law to marry a cousin, even a first cousin, but the Church and his family didn't favour it. Still, Edward Dempsey wouldn't be much use to her in dealing with the likes of Terence Shay.

He stood up. 'I suppose I should look in and see Patrick on my way out.'

'You should. He's still your cousin.'

'And Father is still your uncle, Jess, and he *is* sorry. He was only saying so the other day and he means it.'

'Ronan, please don't start that again. I don't want to fall out with you.'

He nodded, and fell silent. He knew Jess's position had not changed but he had to keep on trying, if only for his mother's sake. Johanna still hated there to be such a rift in the family.

Terence and Patrick were playing cards and laughing as Ronan entered the room, but the laughter died as soon as they saw him.

'How are you, Ronan?' Patrick asked stiffly, getting to his feet.

Terence didn't move but eyed Ronan with a mirthless grin that bordered on the arrogant. Ronan's intense dislike was apparent and it amused him.

'Well, and yourself?'

'Well. You know Terence, of course.'

'Had to swallow your pride, Shay, and beg for lodgings?' Ronan said cuttingly.

Shay flinched and a flush of anger tinged his normally sallow cheeks. It took a great effort not to snap back. He'd have his revenge on Kiernan in the fullness of time, he told himself.

'Now, that's hardly a pleasant thing to say,' Patrick cried. 'And Terence is more of a guest.'

'That's not what I've heard, and neither of you were very civil to me the last time we met, if I remember correctly, Patrick. Jess has been good enough to take the pair of you in but just remember that I'll still be watching you. Even more closely now that you're living here with her.'

Patrick was annoyed. 'If you've nothing civil to say, Ronan, then I think you'd better leave. Whether you like it or not, this is my home now. Jess would never turn me out on the street.'

'Then just watch that you don't give her cause even to contemplate it. Either of you. Goodnight.'

Terence Shay watched Ronan's receding back with narrowed eyes. 'Don't let him upset you, Pat. If you ask me he's more interested in your sister than he cares to admit.'

'Oh, that's preposterous, Terence! He's our cousin and a first cousin at that.'

'Well, it's happened before, Pat. Don't look so surprised.'

'I'll admit that they've always got on well together, and Aideen as well before she was married. I'm the odd one out.'

'You're not. You're just different, that's all, and much nicer.' He shrugged elegantly. 'But maybe she'll marry the very worthy and wealthy Mr Dempsey. That would put paid to any ideas your cousin might have.'

Patrick laughed, good humour restored. 'Sometimes you are so droll.'

Tilly was very troubled and found it hard to wait until her next visit to Johanna's to talk to Ronan about what she had witnessed. She couldn't tell Jess about it either. She had tried but the words wouldn't come and she'd given up.

'Can I stay until Ronan comes in, please?' she asked Johanna who was teaching her to sew and knit, although she appeared to be hopeless at both pastimes.

'Only if you can manage to do one square without dropping any stitches. Whatever you attempt always finishes up looking like a dishcloth.'

Tilly pulled a face. 'I can't help getting so many holes in it. I never seem to know where I've dropped the stitch.'

'Go more slowly. You rush at things, Tilly, that's your trouble.'

Tilly bent her head over the knitting again and prayed Ronan wouldn't be late.

The square was finished to Johanna's satisfaction and she was sitting at the kitchen table with a glass of milk and a biscuit when Ronan came in.

'I want to talk to you,' she hissed, jerking her head in Johanna's direction.

'I've a book I want to lend Tilly, it might help her with her geography lessons,' Ronan announced and Tilly slid off the chair.

'Can't it wait until she's finished her milk?' Johanna asked.

Tilly gulped down the remains of the drink. 'I've finished,' she announced.

'Come on with me then. Is Father in the sitting room?'

'No. I told him a short walk would do him good. He's gone to buy a newspaper.'

'What's the matter?' Ronan looked tensely at the child as he sat down. 'Has he said or done anything to hurt you?'

'No, but . . .'

'But what?'

Tilly fidgeted with the edge of her jacket.

'What has he done? Was it Shay or Patrick?'

'Sort of both of them.'

'How "sort of"? Tilly, you can tell me.'

'Well, they didn't say anything or do anything to me . . .' She paused.

Ronan was becoming impatient. Why on earth was the child beating about the bush?

'Tilly, for heaven's sake, spit it out!'

'Well, I was going to get my school books and ask Patrick if he could help me – I . . . I don't understand all those different kinds of clouds. They didn't hear me open the door and . . . well . . . do men . . . kiss?'

'Do they what?' Ronan thought he must have misheard her.

'Kiss.'

Ronan was totally disconcerted. 'I . . . well, I suppose sometimes they might sort of . . . hug each other, in friendship . . .'

'No, they weren't just hugging. It was like men and women do. I used to see it all the time when I lived in Hunter's Yard.'

Ronan felt cold all over. In the name of God, what had the child seen? 'You're absolutely certain, Tilly?'

She nodded vigorously. 'I'm not making it up because I don't like them, honestly! I tried to tell Jess, but I couldn't.'

'No, don't tell Jess. I will. You were right to come to me, Tilly. Now, put it out of your mind. I'll deal with it.' He stood up and took a book from the low bookcase. 'Here, you take this book and get off home now or Jess will begin to worry.'

When the child had gone he poured himself a stiff whiskey and sat down. The child wouldn't lie about something like that. He gulped down his drink and poured another. Patrick had always been sensitive, almost effeminate in his ways. Never joining in the rough and tumble of their games when they'd all been young. Always shying away from what he called 'manly pursuits and hard decisions'. Weak, that's what Patrick was. Weak and effeminate, easily manipulated by someone as ruthless as Terence Shay. Left to his own devices he was certain Patrick would never have gone down that particular road, but with Shay? And what of Jess? Jess, living unaware of this . . . Would it be better to tell her, warn her, or to leave her in ignorance? Would she even thank him if he enlightened her? Would she even believe him?

For almost an hour he struggled with his conscience. What could he do? It was against the law but the only proof he had was Tilly's word and they could laugh that off or say the child was lying out of jealousy and spite. Could he confront them? What if Patrick went to Jess and told her a pack of lies about Ronan himself trying to discredit him? There was no love lost between himself and Patrick. What then would Jess think of him? No. He could say nothing. Reveal nothing. He would just have to bide his time and be more watchful.

'You're very late. What kept you?' Jess asked when Tilly returned. She had been getting worried. The meal was ready to go onto the table and Patrick had already demanded why they had to wait for a tardy child.

'I . . . I needed a book, this book, for my homework. Ronan promised to lend it to me but Aunt Jo didn't know where it was, so I had to wait,' she replied, placing the book down on the table.

'Well, go and wash your hands and then sit down. We're all starving.'

Tilly did as she was told but refused to meet either Patrick or Terence's gaze.

Terence picked up the book. 'Aren't you a bit young for all this?'

'No,' she answered sullenly.

'What is it?' Patrick asked and Terence passed the volume over to him.

'Surely this must be way above you? *Climatic Influences*,' he read aloud and then looked suspiciously at her.

'Tilly, are you sure this is the right book? Ronan didn't make a mistake? It's very grown up,' Terence asked.

Tilly felt afraid. Did he know? Had he guessed? Had she been right when she'd said they hadn't seen her? Maybe they had. She glanced at him quickly. He was looking at her with such nastiness in his eyes. He must know why she'd been to see Ronan.

'I . . . I . . . didn't really look at it. It must be the wrong one,' she muttered.

'I don't know what's wrong with Ronan, giving her a book like that. How old does he think she is?' Jess grumbled as she served the vegetables.

Tilly didn't dare look up and so didn't see the looks that were exchanged between Patrick and Terence Shay. Looks that said they would have to be careful. Little pigs had big ears and even bigger eyes and perhaps even unguarded tongues.

Chapter Eighteen

JESS WAS CONCERNED. She hadn't really noticed the discrepancies at first, thinking she must be wrong, that it must be her own mistakes, her forgetfulness. She had been very preoccupied lately. Her business was still growing and she was having to think about moving again to bigger premises. There would be more staff to employ, her own packaging to design and have printed and Tilly's education still took up quite a lot of her time.

Strangely, of late Tilly had flatly refused to let Patrick help her and she'd noticed that not only was the child very quiet when either Patrick or Terence were around but she seemed to be watchful. Jess could get no sense out of her as to why this change in behaviour had occurred.

'I can manage my homework on my own,' Tilly had declared firmly.

'But you can't. You're always asking me questions.'

'You always helped me before *he* came, why can't you do it now?' Tilly demanded.

'You don't really like him, do you?' Jess probed.

'No. I can't help it, honestly I can't, and I don't like that other feller either.'

'Well, I have to agree with you there. But if Patrick upsets you so much then I suppose you'd better go on asking me to help,' had been her final words on the subject and Tilly had seemed relieved.

Now she counted the notes and coins from the black cash tin where she kept the housekeeping money. It was always kept in the study but the drawer had been slightly open when she'd gone to her desk and that had alerted her. There were definitely two white five-pound notes missing and some change. Her eyes narrowed. It had to be Terence Shay. She was certain that neither Tilly nor Patrick would steal from her.

She sat down and leaned her head on her hands. If she confronted him he'd deny it and she had no proof. Oh, she should have known that things were going too well and that he, although he had a job of sorts, wouldn't be content to live on her sufferance. She was going out with Edward that evening; she'd ask him for his advice. She knew she could go to Ronan but then there would be an almighty scene which would upset everyone. No, she preferred not to go along that road until it was absolutely impossible not to do so.

She had just finished getting ready when Tilly put her head around the door. 'You look beautiful, Jess, honest you do.' Tilly was full of amazement.

'Do I really? You don't think I'm, well, too dressed up?' Jess stared at her reflection in the dressing-table mirror. Edward was taking her to a rather grand concert in St George's Hall and she'd chosen a pale apple-green taffeta dress, the neckline and sleeve edges trimmed with ecru lace, the bodice decorated with tiny clusters of white feathers. An advertisement for her own wares, she'd laughingly remarked to the dressmaker. Her dark hair had been piled up on top of her head and a band of pale green ribbon, set with two white egret feathers fastened with a diamond clip, circled her forehead. She wore tiny diamond stud earrings and a gold locket and chain around her neck.

'Didn't you say it was a "posh" concert?'

'I did.'

'Then you're just the right amount of "dressed up",' Tilly said with conviction.

Edward was of the same opinion when he came to collect her. 'You look absolutely stunning, Jess!'

'Thank you, Edward.' She laughed. 'Tilly assures me I'm not overdressed.'

'She's right.' He smiled. She did look very beautiful, he mused. He'd been thinking very seriously about her lately and he wondered if tonight he should declare his feelings and his hopes. He knew he was what some people would call a 'dry stick' but he had a lot to offer her and they did get on well together. But she was so full of life, spirit and self-confidence, would she find him too dull? He also had to admit to himself that she was a good catch for any man. Something even his mother had remarked upon, which was surprising as she seemed to hold very few girls in such high esteem.

'After the concert we'll have supper in the North-Western Hotel, it's just opposite St George's Hall and is very nice, so I've heard.'

'Won't it be very late?' Jess queried as he placed her evening cape around her shoulders.

'No. The concert should be over by ten.' He made up his mind. He would ask for a table in a quiet part of the room and then take the bull by the horns and tell her how he felt.

Jess had enjoyed the concert enormously. The organ was huge and its notes resounded magnificently in the high-ceilinged hall. It was quite amazing and made the hair on the back of your neck stand up, she told him as they crossed Lime Street to the hotel, which was next to the station.

'It was a spectacular performance,' Edward agreed, holding open the door for her.

'It's . . . magnificent,' she whispered. It was decorated in royal blue and gold and huge crystal chandeliers bathed the room in dazzling light. The carved and gilded tables and chairs looked so fragile and there were individual crystal candlesticks on each table. The crisp snowy tablecloths were set off by the floral arrangements in shades of blue and lemon and white and beautiful pedestal arrangements of similar flowers were dotted around the room.

As she handed her cape to a waiter Edward spoke to the maître d' who then led them down the room and towards a small area half screened by potted palms and flowers.

'Oh, this is lovely, Edward.'

'I have to agree. I've never been here before but it came highly recommended.' He smiled and passed her the menu. 'I think we'll have a bottle of champagne, your best,' he instructed the hovering wine waiter.

'Are we celebrating?' Jess asked, a little surprised. Edward wasn't mean with his money but he wasn't given to outright extravagance either.

'I hope so, Jess.'

She looked thoughtful. She really didn't want to spoil the evening so she'd better get the unpleasant matter of the missing money out of the way now.

'Edward, I'd like your advice on something that's rather . . . delicate?'

He was surprised and perturbed. 'Of course.'

'Just recently I've noticed that money is going missing from the household budget.'

'Missing? You mean stolen?'

She nodded. 'Today when I counted it there were over ten pounds missing. I'm certain it's not Tilly.'

'Then Patrick or that Mr Shay?'

'I don't think Patrick would steal from me. Oh, I know he hates having to ask for money, but he does ask and I never refuse him.'

Edward looked grave. 'Then it's Shay.'

'Yes, but I can't prove it.'

He had only met the fellow briefly, but he knew the background. Nor had he liked what he'd seen. The man was arrogant and supercilious; like Ronan, Edward would have been happier to see him leave Jess's house.

'Why don't you just tell him to leave, Jess?'

She sighed. 'Because of Patrick. There would be the most awful row and I don't want to fall out with him again.'

'I can understand that but, Jess, it has to stop. You can't have a thief in the house.'

'I know, but what *can* I do?'

He turned his knife over thoughtfully in his hand. 'We had a case of this in the office once. Father instructed that a dab of printer's ink be smeared on certain notes. It's extremely difficult to wash off. We soon found the culprit and he went to jail. Do the same, Jess, and then watch Shay carefully. If you catch him with ink on his fingers he can't deny it and surely even Patrick can't refuse to see what's before his own eyes.'

She nodded. 'Thank you, Edward. I'll do that, unpleasant though it will be. You're right, it has to stop and I'll be glad to see the back of him. I dislike him intensely.'

Edward nodded his agreement. 'There is something very odd, almost sinister about him. I've made some enquiries but no one seems to know anything about him. Where he comes from, his family, his connections, anything. I think he's gone to a lot of trouble to cover his tracks. I'll feel better when he's no longer under your roof.'

'Oh, let's forget all about him. Why spoil a lovely evening.'

Edward left it until they were taking their coffee to broach the subject that had been foremost in his mind all evening.

'Jess, before we go there's something I'd like to ask you.'

Jess was a little startled and wondered for one frantic minute if it was going to be a proposal of marriage. That was something she hadn't thought about much but she had no desire to upset him. Oh, God, give me the right words, she prayed quickly.

'We . . . we seem to get along very well together—'

'Oh, we do, Edward. You're a great friend,' Jess interrupted.

He managed a smile. 'Well, that's just it, Jess, I look on you as more than a friend. I had hoped we were . . . close. I . . . I'm very fond of you.'

'Oh, Edward, I'm very fond of you too but . . . but I haven't really thought seriously about any relationship.'

'Do you think you could think about it?'

She toyed with the hem of her table napkin. 'I could *think* about it, but I don't want to promise anything. I don't want to hurt you, Edward, you've been very good to me.'

'Jess, I did what anyone would do. I lent a small amount of money to a friend.'

'But you will never know how much that meant to me at the time. It was all that was standing between me and . . . and destitution. I mean that, Edward.'

'Oh, Jess, I never realised that things were *that* bad!'

She nodded. 'They were. In a way you were my saviour and for that I'll be eternally grateful.'

'So will you think about it, Jess, please?' he urged.

Slowly she nodded. 'Yes. Yes, I promise I'll think about it seriously but please, Edward, don't press me for an answer too soon.'

He felt so relieved and happy. 'I won't, I promise. It's enough that you've agreed to contemplate it.'

She reached across the table and patted his hand. 'Dear Edward, always so formal, but it's part of your charm.'

She really *didn't* want to hurt him. She was fond of him; he did have a lot to offer her. But was it enough?

She was preoccupied when she reached home. She knew she had a difficult decision to come to, one that could not be taken lightly, and she hoped she wasn't in for many sleepless nights. There was a light burning in the sitting room but she went straight into her study and closed the door. She draped her cape over the back of the chair and sat down at the desk. 'Oh, Da, what shall I do?' she whispered into the darkness. Da would have approved of Edward, she was almost sure of that. He was conscientious, hard-working, honest and steady. He was an attractive man. He was the heir to a substantial fortune and greatly respected name, but was all that enough to base a marriage on? Marriage was for ever. Da had had all those qualities when Mam had married him. The fortune had come later. Together they'd worked hard for it and their prestige in Society.

She pushed the matter to the back of her mind. She would think about it, hard, but later. She was tired. She rose and lit the lamp and then rooted in the bottom drawer of the desk for the small bottle of printer's ink that was kept there. She withdrew three five-pound notes from her purse and, using a letter opener, smeared a little ink on the corner of each. Then she got up and walked into the sitting room with them in her hand.

'Did you have a good evening?' Patrick asked, looking up from his book.

Terence ignored her.

'Very. The organist was a very talented man and the North-Western Hotel is quite splendid.'

'He doesn't mind spending his money on you, does he?' Patrick remarked.

Jess shrugged.

'And talking of money, why are you wandering around with that in your hand?' Patrick demanded.

'Oh, heavens, I almost forgot I had it. I took it from my purse, I'll put it in the cash box. Well, goodnight then.'

Patrick shook his head. Sometimes Jess acted very strangely.

'She looked as though she had something on her mind,' Terence said thoughtfully.

'Edward Dempsey probably. I wonder if he will ever get round to asking her to marry him?'

Shay looked speculatively at Patrick. 'Then will she let you stay in the house or will she sell it? I shouldn't think he would want to live here.'

'I don't know. I hadn't really thought about it, but I'm sure she wouldn't leave me homeless and she knows I can't afford to buy or even rent anything decent.'

'Don't worry about it too much. Our fortunes will improve before long.'

'How? We've hardly any money between us,' Patrick complained.

'I'm working on saving some stake money and this time I'll be very very careful how I invest it. No more long shots. We'll soon be out of here and in a place of our own.'

'Well, it can't come soon enough for me with Jess holding the purse strings and wanting to know all my business – and that sly little minx watching every move and sneaking off to bloody Ronan.'

'Relax, Pat. She *didn't* see anything and she *won't* see anything.'

'She makes me uneasy.'

'Oh, she's sharp all right, but don't worry, I'll attend to her in my own good time.'

At every opportunity Jess looked closely at the hands of both Patrick and Terence Shay but as the days passed she was disappointed that obviously neither of them had been prying into the little black cash box.

Tilly had noticed Jess's preoccupation but hadn't asked the reason. After dinner was over and cleared away she took her books into the dining room but found her usual place occupied by Patrick who had the newspapers spread over the table and was studying long columns of names. She didn't want to disturb him so she backed out and headed for Jess's little study. She had barged in, closing the door behind her, before she realised she wasn't alone. Terence Shay was sitting at Jess's desk with a small black box in his hands.

He jumped up on seeing her and she shrank back against the door.

'What do you want, sneaking around the place?' he demanded. Her sudden appearance had startled him. He knew Jess was fully occupied in the kitchen, that Patrick was reading the financial papers, so he'd assumed he was safe. He'd forgotten about Tilly.

'I came to do my homework! What are you doing in here? Is that Jess's money?' she demanded, beginning to feel angry as she realised just what he was doing.

'That's none of your damned business, you impudent little chit!'

'It is! You're . . . you're stealing from Jess!' She gave a yelp of pain as he caught her roughly by the arm.

'You can't prove it. So you've seen nothing, do you understand?'

'I'm going to tell Jess anyway! I hate you!' Tilly cried.

'You're not going to say anything because if you do then something very nasty is going to happen to you.'

'You . . . you don't scare me!' Tilly tried to sound defiant but he *was* frightening her and he was hurting her arm.

'Well, I should. You're a nasty little sneak and that should be beaten out of you.'

'If you hurt me Jess'll call the police.'

He raised his arm to strike her but stopped. 'What the bloody . . . ?' he cried, catching sight of the black ink stains on his hands. The bitch! The bitch had set a trap and he'd walked straight into it. He was certain it was printer's ink and the damned stuff wouldn't come off. Suddenly he caught hold of Tilly's free hand and stuffed the notes into it. His mind was working quickly. He'd say he caught her stealing the money and had tried to take it off her, hence the stains on his hands.

Tilly stared down at the money in her hand, a hand that was now smudged with black ink. 'What did you do that for? I don't want Jess's money!'

'Oh, yes you do! That's why you came in here and I caught you stealing it.'

Tilly's eyes widened. 'No! No, you're a liar! Jess won't believe you!'

'We'll see,' he spat, preparing to act out the most important part in his life to date.

Chapter Nineteen

———◆———

BOTH JESS AND PATRICK came into the hall to see what all the commotion was about and found Terence Shay shaking a frightened and crying Tilly.

'What's going on? Take your hands off her!' Jess demanded.

'I caught her in your study, rifling your cash box!'

'I wasn't, Jess! I wasn't, it was him!' Tilly cried desperately. Jess wouldn't believe him. She *couldn't* believe him. She hated him, but she was also afraid of him. He was a grown-up and often other grown-ups believed their peers, rather than children.

'She was stealing! Look at her hands!' he demanded.

'*I* wasn't! *He* was the one taking your money, Jess. He *was*!'

'When I took it off her I got covered in this damned ink!'

'Jess, surely you don't believe Terence was stealing from you? Why would he?' Patrick protested. It was unthinkable in his opinion. Terence would never steal but Tilly, oh, that was a different matter altogether.

'Why indeed? Why on earth would Tilly steal from me? She's never done anything remotely like it before. I can't say the same for him, I hardly know him.' Jess stared at Terence coldly. She didn't trust him an inch. Who knew what kind of background he came from? It could have been somewhere as bad as the slum she had rescued Tilly from, despite all his fancy ways. Oh, he was clever – sharp, even – but it cut no ice with her.

Patrick was outraged. 'Jess, you've got to believe it's not Terence! She . . . she comes from Hunter's Yard, from a festering slum. You can dress her up all you like, Jess, but underneath she's a little slummy and always will be. She's probably been stealing since the day she could walk!'

'Pat's right, Jess. You can't trust her, it's the way she is, it's in her nature!' Shay added defiantly.

Tilly threw her arms around Jess's waist. 'I didn't steal, Jess! Honest to God, I didn't! I've never taken anything that didn't belong to me, not even when I was hungry and cold.'

Jess held the sobbing child to her and her eyes narrowed on Terence. 'I don't believe a word you say. Just why were you going into my study in the first place?'

'Why was she?' Terence blustered.

'I was going to do my homework but Patrick was using the table!' Tilly cried.

Jess held Shay's gaze steadily. 'I'm asking you again, why were you going into my study?'

'I was looking for an envelope,' Terence Shay lied grimly. 'I'd been writing a letter to . . . to a colleague. Go and look in my room if you want to, it's there. I needed an envelope.

I knew there would be one in your study, and when I went in I found *her*.' He would just have to risk her calling his bluff. He wasn't going to give up easily. He had a comfortable home in this house and a decent if limited lifestyle and that little slummy wasn't going to ruin it all.

Jess glared at him. She didn't believe him but she knew Patrick would side with him and demand she did nothing further about it because, when it came down to it, whose word would the police believe? That of a respectable businessman or a dressed-up little slummy? Maybe she'd given him a fright. Maybe he'd learned his lesson and would watch his step in future.

'I don't believe you but I'll let the matter drop this time. I'm not a fool, I know money has been going missing. This isn't the first time but it will be the last because if there is any more trouble from you, then you can pack your bags! Come along with me, Tilly, let's try and get you tidied up.'

'I don't know what's got into Jess lately, I really don't.' Patrick shook his head as he followed his friend into the sitting room.

Terence was relieved to an extent. He had misjudged the depth of Jess's feelings for the child, but at least Jess hadn't thrown him out. He would have to be careful in future and now there was no way he could supplement his savings at Jess's expense. But Patrick still needed to be reassured.

'I wouldn't steal from her, you know that, don't you? Everything I said was true. When I walked in she was standing there bold as brass with the money in her hands. You're right, Pat. A leopard can't change its spots. She's a thieving little slummy and always will be.' He was smarting with the humiliation of it all. He'd been careless. He should have known Jess suspected, but instead he had taken her for a fool, something he would never do again. It had been easy. The odd five pounds here, a couple of guineas there, all to add to the small sum that was building up and which he intended to use as his stake money to rebuild the fortune he had stupidly gambled away on cards and horses.

'Of course I know you're no thief,' Patrick said with conviction.

'She . . . she's just impossibly stupid about that child,' Terence fumed.

'I know. I've tried to tell her but she won't listen. Come and have a drink, it's been a bad experience for you,' Patrick soothed.

Shay nodded grimly. It had indeed been a bad experience for him but it would prove to be an even worse one for that child. He hated her and a burning desire for revenge was coursing through him, blinding him to caution.

Tilly was still very upset. The incident had shaken her.

'I don't like him, Jess.'

'Neither do I and I *won't* have him blaming you for things you've not done.'

'Why does he have to stay, Jess?'

Jess sighed. 'Because if I went to the police over it, Tilly, there would be a terrible fuss and it would upset you even more. You know how you feel about the police.' Although, God knows I've tried to change your attitude, she added to herself. The unfortunate denizens of the slums had little time for the members of the Liverpool City Police Force.

'Don't worry, he'll never do anything like it again – not if he wants to stay here. Now, I think I've got some chocolate somewhere. Try and get some of that ink off your hands while I look for it.' Jess patted the child's shoulder comfortingly.

Tilly had calmed down considerably but she was even more wary now of Shay and when she next went to Johanna's she resolved to tell Ronan what had happened.

He'd listened in silence, his expression grim. 'So she's letting him stay?' he asked when she'd finished.

Tilly nodded. 'She said she'd be watching him carefully now and that he won't dare steal again, but I . . . I'm frightened of him. He was going to belt me, I know he was!'

'He won't touch you, Tilly. If he does he'll have me to answer to, but you're right to tell me.' He was even more uneasy in his mind now. Of course Patrick would back up any story Shay told. He wished Jess had told Shay to go. If things got any worse he would have to talk to his father about how to get Patrick out of Shay's clutches.

Tilly felt much better when she returned home. Ronan knew everything now and he wouldn't let Shay hurt either herself or Jess. She trusted him and Aunt Jo and she supposed Mr Kiernan was all right too – even if Jess didn't think so.

Jess wasn't home yet but that wasn't unusual these days. She was very busy moving and keeping up with her increased orders but she still found time to sit and talk to her about her day. Jess always found time for her, that's why she loved her so much. The house was quiet so she went into the kitchen to make herself a sandwich. It would be a long time before she got her supper tonight. Thankfully neither Patrick nor *he* as she always called him appeared to be home yet. As it was Friday she didn't have much homework to do and it was still very warm so she decided to take some of her dolls and go and sit in the garden, it was nice there and you could even smell the sea.

When she opened the bedroom door her eyes widened in horror. Sawdust and stuffing were strewn across the floor as were the arms and legs and heads of her precious family of dolls. Their clothes were torn to pieces and scattered around the room. She dropped to her knees, tears pouring down her cheeks. Who had done this terrible, terrible thing and why? She lovingly picked up a limp torso that still had a head and two arms attached and held it to her. Maisy had been her favourite and now all her lovely hair had been cut off and her dress was in ribbons. Overwhelmed by loss and desolation she sat with her back to the wardrobe, nursing the pathetic, broken toy and crying as though her heart was broken.

Jess was annoyed with herself for being so late. She should never have got into an argument with the removal men. They had been employed to move the boxes she and Mary had carefully packed with samples to the new premises and place them in the rooms designated and not pile them all in the office. She should just have refused to pay them, instead of arguing over it. Oh, well, she would sort it all out tomorrow.

The house was quiet and she wondered where Tilly was. She'd been in the kitchen, she could tell that. Very probably she was upstairs or out in the garden.

When she opened Tilly's bedroom door her horrified gaze swept the room before she dropped to her knees and gathered the sobbing child to her.

'What happened? What happened to them all?' she cried.

'Someone . . . someone killed them, Jess! They killed my family!' Tilly sobbed into Jess's shoulder.

'Hush now. We'll take them to the dolls' hospital and get them fixed and if they can't fix them I'll buy you some more,' Jess soothed.

'I don't want more, Jess! I want . . . them!'

'Come on, Tilly, don't upset yourself so much.' She was about to say, 'They're only dolls,' but she stopped herself. To Tilly they were more than that. They represented the secure and happy life she now led as opposed to the miseries of her early childhood. Anger began to burn in Jess. Oh, she knew very well who had done this. Let him deny it all he liked, this time he was going. He had unerringly picked the things that Tilly treasured most and destroyed them, knowing it would devastate her.

'Hush. Hush now. We'll pick them all up very carefully and put them in boxes and in the morning we'll go and see what can be done for them. When they're mended Johanna will make them all new clothes. Hush now, dry your eyes!'

Tilly had gradually calmed down but Jess's anger grew as she watched the child carefully place her damaged toys into the boxes she had found, writing out labels with all their names.

They had just finished the task when she heard the front door open and then close.

'You stay here while I deal with them!' she instructed grimly.

She went swiftly down the stairs to the lower landing. She saw both Patrick and Terence Shay hanging up their jackets.

'Don't you bother to take your coat off, you're not stopping! I want you out of here in five minutes!'

Patrick looked up at her in astonishment. 'Jess, what on earth is wrong?'

'Ask him,' she snapped, her eyes blazing.

'Me? What am I supposed to have done now?' Shay looked mystified and hurt.

'You deliberately destroyed every single doll Tilly had! You're despicable! You're beneath contempt!' she spat.

'Dolls! In the name of God, Jess, what are you talking about?' Patrick demanded. Was she beginning to lose her reason?

'Some time today he came back here and tore apart all her dolls and ripped their clothes and left it all for her to find.'

'I did no such thing, I've been at work all day!' He'd known it was a childish act but it had given him great satisfaction. He had told himself that if he denied it vehemently enough and with enough scorn, he'd get away with it. He knew he could count on Patrick's support, but he hadn't reckoned on the fury it would arouse in Jess. He had made a serious miscalculation.

'Jess, you're being hysterical. Why on earth would Terence do something as petty, as . . . stupid as that? I really do think you are losing all reason where that child is concerned!'

'I am *not* being hysterical or losing my reason! It's to pay her back for catching him stealing my money. She loved those dolls, they meant a great deal to her. You are a vicious, vindictive, no-good thief!'

Terence *had* to make this denial plausible. 'I can assure you that I didn't lay a finger on her precious toys. She will have done it herself, no doubt knowing you will buy her more. I have far more important things to do with my time than mutilate a collection of ridiculous dolls!' His tone was scathing in the extreme.

Jess was totally unmoved. 'You can deny it until the Last Day but I don't believe you. I want you out of here in five minutes, or I'll call the police.'

'Jess, for heaven's sake, this is stupid! It's ridiculous! All this over a few bloody dolls!' Patrick cried in disbelief.

'Don't you swear at me, Patrick Brennan, and this is not some prank. It's a deliberate, cruel and calculated attack on a child's feelings and if you feel so strongly that your precious "friend" is being wronged then you can go with him. You can both get out!'

Patrick was struggling with his emotions. This was all utterly preposterous, but neither of them had anywhere else to go. If he stayed he could perhaps calm Jess down and persuade her to take Terence back. He would really have to try to wean her away from this absurd fondness for a common slummy.

'I think you're being very hard, Jess,' he said at length.

'It's up to you, Patrick,' she replied coldly. She was adamant that Terence Shay wouldn't spend another hour under her roof.

Shay knew he was defeated. 'There's no point in you leaving, Pat. Don't worry about me. I'll manage, I have before.'

'I'll help you pack,' Patrick muttered and Jess turned away, leaving them in the hall to discuss their plans.

When Ronan heard from a very upset Johanna what had transpired he looked grim. At least Shay had gone but that wasn't to say that Patrick wouldn't see him again and then any liaison between them was open to far more public inspection and scandal. It was time to have a serious talk with his father.

Tom Kiernan looked older than his years. His ambition had very nearly destroyed not only himself but his entire family and it weighed heavily on his conscience these days. Especially after the heart attack he'd suffered. He realised how close he'd come to meeting his Maker and having to answer some difficult questions. His one great sadness in life was the fact that Jess still wouldn't forgive him or even see or speak to him.

'Dad, I need to talk to you about something . . . important and not very pleasant,' Ronan said haltingly, finding Tom alone in the sitting room reading the newspaper.

'Then spit it out, lad. Is it about your sister?' In Tom's opinion his daughter had turned into a snob of the highest order.

'No, Aideen is fine, as far as I know. It's about Patrick.'

Tom looked grave. He had no great opinion of his nephew. Patrick was a great trial to Jess. 'What's he done now?'

Briefly and with great embarrassment Ronan told him.

'He's *what*? He . . . he's one of *those*?' Tom roared, jumping to his feet, his face almost puce.

Ronan nodded. 'I'm afraid so.'

'God in heaven! I never wished it before in my life but I'm glad that neither Maddy nor Martin are here to see this day. Does Jess know?'

'No.'

'And that's the way we'll keep it – and not a word to your mother either. She would be terribly, terribly upset. God above! The scandal this would cause if it got out! I dread to think what the Dempseys would do!'

'I know, but what are we to do about it?' Ronan demanded.

'This Shay feller, he's gone? He's definitely left?'

'He has.'

Tom looked thoughtful as he paced the floor. There was only one thing to do. 'Well, we'll have to get him married off. That's the only thing that will scotch any . . . rumours. And I'm sure if he were married to an attractive young girl he could be persuaded to change his ways. I'm convinced that would solve the problem.'

'Married? Who to?' Ronan was taken aback.

Tom's mind was already working. 'Catherine Grainger. She's a pretty, respectable girl, no parents, lives with a maiden aunt who would be glad to get her off her hands, according to your mother.'

'But would she agree? Would *he* agree?'

'I think she would, we could leave that in your mother's capable hands, and as for *him* – leave him to me! By God, by the time I'm finished with him he'll be glad to marry her!'

Ronan pondered this. It was a solution but was it right to trap a naïve, trusting young girl into marrying a man she believed would love and cherish her? But on the other hand, maybe it would be the making of Patrick. He nodded. 'So, what will you do?'

'Firstly, speak to your mother. Persuade her that it is a good idea and then . . . then I'll send for him. This is at least something I can do to help protect the family and Maddy and Martin's memory.'

Chapter Twenty

————

JESS WAS SURPRISED AT Johanna's visit. It wasn't often she called during the week knowing how limited Jess's free time of an evening was.

'Is something wrong?' she asked, leading the way to the sitting room.

Johanna smiled. 'No. Does there need to be something wrong for me to visit you?'

'Of course not. Sit down.'

'I have come for a reason though, other than to see you, of course. How is Tilly now?'

Jess frowned. 'She's still upset although three of them can be mended and I've bought her two new ones. It still makes my blood boil when I think about *him*!'

Johanna nodded. 'It was a wicked thing to do. I'm so glad you got rid of him, Jess, I never liked him.'

'Patrick isn't very happy but I told him if he feels so strongly then he can follow him. Oh, I've no patience with Patrick these days!'

'It's Patrick I've come to see you about.'

Jess raised an eyebrow.

'Tom and I were talking. Jess, it really is time that Patrick was married. It would steady him.'

Jess was taken aback. 'Married? Who to? He doesn't *know* any girls, let alone court one.'

'We realised that that was a problem but I have a friend who knows a very suitable girl.'

Jess smiled ruefully. 'Aunt Jo, you can't arrange marriages in this day and age.'

Johanna looked serious. 'Sometimes, Jess, these things *have* to be arranged. Sometimes it's better that way. I'd say young Catherine Grainger would be the making of Patrick. I've met her on a number of occasions. She's a lovely girl. Attractive, pleasant, placid and altogether very amenable. I'm sure she'd suit him down to the ground.'

Jess looked interested. Johanna was serious. 'Who is she?'

'Her aunt is the friend of my friend Elinore. Do you remember her? She was at Aideen's wedding?'

Jess nodded. Elinore Parsons had seemed a pleasant enough person.

'Poor Catherine lost both her parents in an accident when she was only fourteen. She's an only child and her aunt is the sole relative she has in the world. She's been well brought up and is from a good family. There's no money to speak of, of course, but Elinore tells me that Catherine's aunt wishes to see her settled.'

'Wants to get rid of her?'

Johanna frowned. 'Jess, that's a bit blunt.'

'But true.'

Johanna nodded. 'True indeed.'

'But will she want to marry Patrick? Surely she must have some say in the matter?'

'Patrick isn't a bad catch, Jess. He's quite handsome, well educated, cultured and although he has no money of his own—'

'I do,' Jess interrupted with a smile.

'Would you object, Jess?'

'I don't know. It's not me who's going to marry her.'

'But if they came to live here?'

'Aunt Jo, I'd have to meet her before I could make a judgement. I think I should meet her anyway. Has any of this been mentioned to her?'

'Not yet. Your uncle wants to speak to Patrick and then . . .'

'So, Uncle Tom is going to browbeat Patrick.'

Johanna was quick to notice that Jess had called Tom by his name for the first time since Maddy's funeral. 'It's not going to be a question of that, Jess. He's going to persuade him, make him see it's for his own good. At the moment his life has no purpose. He's just drifting along and in the company of such undesirables as Terence Shay. He has to *do* something with his life. He can't just waste it, Jess.'

Jess nodded her agreement. If Patrick could be persuaded and if this Catherine Grainger was suitable and agreeable it would certainly be a worry off her mind. She had no wish for Patrick to go on 'drifting' as her aunt put it.

'Well, depending on how things go, I'll bring Catherine to meet you. I'm sure you'll like her, Jess.'

Jess smiled. 'I'm sure I will, but will Patrick? Now, shall we have some tea?'

Johanna agreed and leaned back in the chair. She had told Tom that she was sure Jess would put up no obstacles and she too would be very relieved to see Patrick as a steady, married man, with hopefully – in time – a family of his own. Johanna hoped they could bring this off. She felt she owed it to Maddy.

Patrick was a different matter. He was annoyed that he had been summoned like a child and probably to account for all that stupid carry-on with Tilly that had resulted in Jess being so utterly unreasonable towards Terence. He wasn't an errant schoolboy to be hauled up before the headmaster, he was a grown man.

He was surprised to see Ronan sitting with his father. They both looked far from amiable. He realised for the first time how closely his cousin resembled his uncle and also how much he disliked them both.

'Sit down, Patrick, I have something to say to you.'

Patrick sat uneasily on the edge of the sofa, feeling more and more irritated. How dare they sit there glaring at him with disapproval!

'If it's to do with Jess's totally hysterical behaviour over those stupid dolls, then all I can say is I just don't want to hear any more about it. That child is a menace!'

Tom got to his feet. He had prepared all this carefully. He had anticipated all Patrick's questions, denials and excuses: his nephew wasn't going to wriggle out of this. Oh, no, he owed Maddy this much. He'd let her down badly, was partly responsible for her death; now the least he could do was spare Jess any more heartbreak and shame, and his sister's reputation and good name. 'It's not Jess's behaviour I want to talk about. It's yours with that . . . Terence Shay.'

Patrick blanched. Just what did his uncle mean?

'Don't try to deny it. I . . . we know what you are and what he is.'

'He . . . he's a friend, that's all!' Patrick blustered.

'Oh, no, lad, he's more than that! You were seen!' Tom banged his fist down hard on the top of the sideboard and spat, 'By God, your poor father would turn in his grave if he had one.'

Patrick jumped to his feet, his cheeks burning. 'I'm not staying here to listen to . . . to . . . this!'

'SIT DOWN!' Tom thundered.

Patrick sat, refusing to meet either his uncle's gaze or that of his cousin. His uncle seemed to tower over him and he realised he was afraid of him. Oh, he knew well what Society would think of him, but he couldn't help it. It was just the way he was, the way he'd been born. Terence had made him realise that. He'd said that it really wasn't anything to be ashamed of, even though it could never be admitted. It was against the law. He had always pushed the thought of his father and mother's reaction to the back of his mind, but now his uncle was forcing him to face facts that hurt, confused and humiliated him.

'You'll not disgrace this family. I'll not have your mother and father's memory sullied by the likes of you. Oh, no! Nor will you put Jess through any more heartache than you already have. You'll pull yourself together. Put all . . . that behaviour behind you and get married like any normal man!'

'Married!' Patrick almost screamed the word. He didn't

want to get married. The thought was so repulsive it made him feel ill.

'Yes, married. That way there will never be any scandal attached to your name . . . our name. Providing you behave yourself – and, by God, I'll see you do! – it will be the making of you, Patrick. I firmly believe that.'

'I . . . I can't . . . won't get married!' Patrick was struggling desperately against a tide of events that were threatening to overwhelm him. He couldn't let his fear of his uncle ruin his entire life. 'I *won't* get married, do you hear me? Do you understand that?'

Tom's face became an ugly shade of puce and his eyes were hard. 'So, you want me to ruin you? To sacrifice the family's name and reputation and see you in jail? I will, if I have to. You think about that! Not a single decent soul in this entire city would have anything to do with you. Your life would be one of destitution, degradation and loneliness and no one in this family would lift a finger to help you!'

Patrick felt as though he'd been physically struck across the face. He knew by his uncle's tone of voice and demeanour that he meant what he said. And he could tell by the look on Ronan's face that he supported his father in everything. 'You can't! You're not serious!'

'I've never been more serious in my life. How do you think you would survive jail? How would you survive at all with no money, no home, no family or friends? I'll do it, Patrick, by God I will!'

The colour had drained from Patrick's face. Oh, God! The picture his uncle's words painted so vividly was of a life not worth living. He couldn't live like that. He *wouldn't* survive prison. Nor could he involve Terence in any of this. His uncle and cousin would be delighted to see Terence go to jail. But married! Was the alternative they were forcing on him really so bad? It looked to be the lesser of the two evils. Miserably he nodded his agreement. It had been bad enough living without Terence but he had thought that when Jess had calmed down he'd be able to talk her round. He hadn't known about . . . this.

'Does Jess know . . . about . . . ?'

'No, she doesn't and neither does your Aunt Jo and that's the way it will remain or by God I'll break your neck!'

'I suppose you have someone lined up?' He prayed they hadn't but his hopes were dashed as his uncle nodded.

'I do. Catherine Grainger. A pretty, pleasant, quiet girl. Lives with a maiden aunt, someone your Aunt Jo knows.'

'But . . . but . . .' Patrick was struggling to take everything in. 'Will she?'

'I think she'll be agreeable, and *you* will make every effort to be charming and pleasant to her.'

Pleasant and charming! Dear God, he couldn't even bring himself to think about this unknown girl in that way and if he married her . . .

'Can I go now?' he croaked. He had to get out of this room, to get some fresh air in his lungs, to try to think . . . to come to terms with all this. He had to go and speak to Terence.

'Yes. I'll let you know what she has to say and then we can arrange for the two of you to meet. Remember, not a word of this to Jess or your aunt.'

He reeled from the room and out of the house, barely

closing the front door behind him. Oh, it was all too monstrous to contemplate.

Patrick was too distraught really to notice the depressing streets through which he stumbled, or the dilapidated house in which Terence Shay rented a room. He had been here just once before and had been upset that his friend was forced to live in such conditions. The sun had disappeared and heavy grey clouds now threatened rain. He picked his way across the debris that littered the broken and worn steps and wrinkled his nose at the unappealing smell that permeated the hallway.

Shay was surprised to see him. If he'd known about the visit he would have tidied both himself and the place up.

'Pat, what are you doing here? I thought we were supposed to meet in town tomorrow. You know this place upsets you.'

'I'm just far too upset to notice any of this!' Patrick was near to tears.

'My dear chap, come in and sit down. What's happened?' Shay took a half-empty bottle of cheap whiskey from the mantelpiece and poured two measures. He noticed that Patrick's hand shook as he took the glass. His friend looked terrible, as if he'd had some awful shock. Had that bitch thrown him out too? He had cursed himself for a fool a thousand times. To massage his wounded pride and slake his desire for revenge on that little slummy, he had thrown away a good, comfortable home where he could continue his liaison with Patrick in privacy, safe in the knowledge that Jess suspected nothing. He had even been contemplating the not-too-distant day when his fortunes would recover and he would once again want for nothing. And he'd thrown the whole lot away.

'I had to come! Oh, God, it's just too terrible!'

'Has she thrown you out?'

'No. It's far worse than that. I was sent for by my uncle. They . . . he and Ronan know, Terence. They *know*.'

Shay's eyes narrowed. This was something he'd not expected. 'How?'

'They said we were seen.'

'By whom?'

Patrick shook his head and held out the glass. Shay refilled it. This was worse than he had thought.

'I don't know, but not Jess.'

'That bloody brat. It had to be her!' Shay exploded. *She* was responsible for all this. For the fact that he now had to live in this stinking slum. That he could no longer afford good clothes, good food or drink. That he was no longer looked up to as he had been before by the staff and other members of his club. And what was she? A crafty, sneaking little slummy! And Jess? Oh, Jess was a fool if she couldn't see through her. If it weren't for that brat he was certain he could have eventually got round Jess, even to the point of getting her to give Patrick some sort of stake in her business which would mean access for himself, through Patrick, to her money. All that was gone now. Patrick's voice broke into his thoughts.

'It doesn't matter now, they're forcing me to get married!'

'Married? Who the bloody hell to? You don't know anyone,' Shay demanded. This was even worse.

'Some girl my Aunt Jo knows.'

'This is preposterous! They can't force you to do *anything*, Pat. You've more than reached your majority. Take no notice of them, it's all a bluff.'

'It's not. They said they'd ruin me, even see me in jail and they meant it. I *have* to do it but I can't even bear to think about it.'

Shay looked thoughtful.

'Terence, what am I to do? What will happen to us?' Patrick pleaded.

Shay began to pace up and down the tiny room, deep in thought.

'For God's sake, say something,' Patrick begged in desperation.

At last Shay sat down. 'Look, Pat. Go ahead with it, keep them quiet, pacify them into thinking that you're that kind of a man. We'll have to stop seeing each other for a while, but when things have sort of died down . . .' He shrugged expressively.

'I don't think I can go ahead with it.' Patrick had expected more sympathy.

'You'll have to be brave, Pat,' Shay soothed. All they had to do was bide their time. Eventually he'd find a way of working this mess out. A way for them to be together again, for ever. He cared a great deal about Patrick. Oh, at first he'd used him as a stepping stone to a firmer foothold in Society, but genuine affection had grown between them. He couldn't envisage being with someone else, yet he still wanted all the things in life that money could bring him and Jess had that money. He had to gain access to her money.

'Have another drink and we'll talk things over. Yes, this is another obstacle, but you know we've always managed to overcome them before.'

'Yes, you're right. We . . . we'll think of something,' Patrick replied, more calmly. A little of the original shock was wearing off. Perhaps it would all work out.

Jess was utterly amazed when she learned from Johanna that Tom and Ronan had actually persuaded Patrick to meet Catherine. Johanna was bringing her to supper on Saturday evening.

'You really don't mind meeting her?' she'd asked him quietly.

'Uncle Tom was most insistent. What could I say?'

'But you do realise that . . . that they want you to do more than just *meet* her? I told Aunt Jo that marriages aren't arranged in this day and age.'

'He spelt it out clearly, Jess. I . . . I agree with him. It's time I settled down and, as I don't know any girls, let alone suitable ones . . .' He shrugged. She'd never know how hard those words had been to say.

'Well, if you're sure, Patrick?'

He'd managed a tight smile. 'As sure as I'll ever be, Jess.'

Tilly was annoyed that she wasn't to be allowed to stay up. 'If Patrick marries her, she'll come to live here, won't she?'

'Yes.'

'So why can't I meet her too? I live here as well.'

'Tilly, I don't want her to have any distractions. If things go well, then you can meet her next time. Now be a good girl and don't sulk,' Jess had replied firmly.

The dining table looked well, she thought, surveying her

handiwork on Saturday evening. There could be nothing to fault there and she herself had dressed with care. Not too fancy but at the same time not too informal. Patrick seemed to have taken a bit more care than usual with his appearance, she thought. Maybe that was a hopeful sign.

'Are you nervous?' she asked him as he poured himself a drink.

'A bit, but I suppose it's only natural.' He tried to sound nonchalant but he was terrified of meeting this girl.

'You've never really said much about . . . it all.'

He shrugged. 'What is there to say? Uncle Tom had made his mind up.'

'But it's still up to you, Patrick. It's your life.'

Again he shrugged. 'She can't be all that bad if Aunt Jo likes her.'

'Well, we're about to find out,' Jess replied as the sound of the doorknocker reached their ears. Johanna was always punctual.

Jess was surprised at how young and pretty Catherine Grainger was and also how small and dainty. She had an oval face with large blue eyes framed by a cloud of corn-coloured hair. Her hands were tiny as were her feet encased in cream-coloured leather pumps. Her complexion was pure English rose, pale pink and white.

'Catherine, I'm so pleased to meet you,' she said with sincerity after Johanna had introduced her.

'It's very kind of you to invite me, Jess. I may call you that?'

'Oh, of course. We don't stand on ceremony, do we, Patrick?'

Despite his dread and misgivings Patrick had to admit

that the girl was very pretty and she appeared to be shy too. He hoped she would be easy to get along with. He pulled himself together. He had better make an effort to be polite at least.

'I'm so glad you agreed to come, Catherine,' he said pleasantly, taking the tiny hand that was extended to him.

Johanna and Jess exchanged relieved glances.

Catherine was very nervous. Ever since her aunt had informed her that Mr Patrick Brennan, the nephew of a trusted friend, had indicated that he was interested in her she had felt apprehensive. Oh, she knew only too well that her aunt would be glad to get her off her hands and in a way she would be glad to go. Life hadn't been very happy at all after her parents had been killed. She still missed them terribly. She didn't really mind that this would be an arranged marriage. She had never walked out with anyone before and so had no one to compare Patrick with, and he did seem, at first appearance, to be pleasant. And he appeared genuinely happy to meet her.

She knew she was coming here with nothing much to offer. No money, no family of any standing in Society, no accomplishments and no ambition. The latter two Jess apparently had in abundance. She had of course wondered about the more intimate side of marriage. Not that she knew very much about it. Her aunt had told her virtually nothing. She was nervous about sharing a bed with someone she hardly knew, but surely all young brides were? She had pushed it from her mind. It wasn't really proper for well-brought-up young ladies to think about such things, or so she'd been told. However, she was prepared to be a good wife, a good sister-in-law and in time a good mother. All she really longed for was a family of her own to fill her lonely life.

Gradually she relaxed. Patrick was most attentive although twice she caught him gazing into space, a look of sadness in his eyes, and she wondered if he had been disappointed in love before. She had liked Jess instantly even though she was a little in awe of her: Jess was far more self-confident and spirited than she herself was. That probably came of being a successful businesswoman. It was a lovely home, too. Far more comfortable and cheerful than her aunt's house. No, if things carried on like this, then she would have no objections to marrying Patrick Brennan and coming to live here with him and his sister.

When Johanna and Catherine had departed Jess poured herself a glass of sherry and sank down on the sofa.

'Well, I think that went very well. I liked her a lot. What did you think?'

Patrick contemplated his drink. 'She's far prettier than I thought she would be. She's a bit shy though.'

'I'd say that's a good thing. Do you think you could become . . . fond of her?' Jess asked tentatively. Patrick had seemed to get on well with the girl. She was very sweet.

'I . . . I think so.'

'Patrick, you don't *have* to do this if you really can't stand the idea. Arranged marriages are very old-fashioned.'

'Jess, I think I can trust Aunt Jo's judgement.'

Jess nodded. It looked as if he had given up on his friendship with Terence Shay and for that she thanked God. She was certain he would be far happier now he had accepted the fact that marriage would be the best thing for him: a wife, a secure home and future, and then maybe, in time, a family.

'I think Mam would have liked her too.'

'And don't forget Father,' Patrick added with a trace of bitterness in his voice. His father would never in a million years have understood him because he could never be the son Martin Brennan would have been proud of.

Chapter Twenty-One

———◆❈◆———

AFTER SOME INITIAL UNEASINESS, to everyone's relief Patrick and Catherine seemed to get on very well. But, as Johanna said, it was very easy to get on with Catherine, she was such a pleasant, thoughtful girl. A small, quiet wedding was planned for October, a month away, for, as Tom said, there was no use beating about the bush. Patrick must seize the bull by the horns for you never knew if the girl would indeed change her mind.

Patrick was hiding his despair well; only on the few visits he'd dared make to Terence Shay did he betray his real feelings.

'So, she's pretty and quiet and pleasant. Maybe it won't be so bad, Pat,' Shay had tried to pacify Patrick on his last visit.

'She really isn't bad, Terence, in fact I'd say she's a very nice girl if only I didn't have to marry her.'

'But you do and I've told you, Pat, I won't abandon you. I'll think of something.'

'I know you will, but . . . but if only I didn't have to go

through with it. I don't know if I can!' Patrick cried despairingly.

'You've *got* to, Pat, or suffer the consequences.'

Patrick shuddered at the thought. 'They're all getting into such a state over it. All the endless fuss and performance that seems obligatory with a wedding.'

'Who is paying for it?'

'Jess, of course. That skinflint aunt of Catherine's won't put her hand in her pocket for much.'

Shay nodded. Jess wasn't short of money. Her business was going from strength to strength. She could well afford to pay for this charade. A thought struck him. 'Is she going to give Catherine an allowance? Or by any chance is she going to give *you* something?'

'I think she's going to give it to Catherine. After all I do have a job though it pays a pittance. Certainly not enough to support a wife on.'

Terence Shay looked at him speculatively. 'And do you think Catherine would be amenable to handing it over to you?'

'I should think so, if I needed it.'

Shay nodded. If they could invest that money it would be a start. 'We could put it to good use, Pat. Invest it. Build a fortune. And then if you were no longer dependent on Jess for a roof over your head . . .' He shrugged.

Patrick grasped at the straw. 'By God, you're right! If I had money of my own, enough money, I could buy my own house and then I could have more freedom. I'll wait until we're . . . settled and then I'll get that money from Catherine. It shouldn't be hard.'

'You see, Pat, things will work out. Give it time.' Shay

poured them both a drink. 'Here's a toast to your wedding and Catherine's money.'

Patrick raised his glass. 'I'll certainly drink to Catherine's money.'

Drink was on the list that Jess was making for the small reception she was planning. Johanna was drawing up a guest list and she and Catherine were sitting around Jess's dining table for the discussions.

'It's going to be very small, Jess,' Johanna commented.

'I know, but we haven't got many friends or relations. Are all the Dempseys coming?'

'Yes. Would you mind if I invited Elinore, Jess?'

'Of course not. Isn't she a friend of your aunt too, Catherine?'

'Yes, she's very nice,' Catherine answered shyly. She could hardly believe that she was going to have so much money spent on her. Her dress was costing what she considered to be a small fortune. She thought herself very fortunate. She really did like Patrick, he was very kind and gentle and thoughtful. She was certain that in time she would grow to love him and while he didn't show her much affection she hoped that that would come. After all, there was nothing wrong in being reserved and polite. She also felt very fortunate to be coming to live in this lovely house. She liked Jess and little Tilly and Johanna. She felt a special affinity to Jess, after all she too had lost both her parents in tragic circumstances. She almost had a ready-made family. They had all shown her so much affection already, far more than her aunt had ever done. And she was delighted that Jess was even going to give her an allowance. Money to spend on whatever she fancied! That was something she'd never had in her life before.

Johanna looked apprehensively at Jess. The question had to be broached but she hoped it wasn't going to cause a row.

'What's the matter? You're looking very worried,' Jess asked her aunt.

'What about Tom, Jess?'

The question had also occurred to Jess. She sighed heavily. 'Well, I can't not invite him, especially as he's been so . . . good getting Patrick to think about his future. We'll be meeting on what I suppose you could call "neutral ground". But, Aunt Jo, please don't expect me to greet him with open arms.'

Johanna shook her head. 'Oh, Jess, I do wish you could put the past behind you. He's changed so much.'

Jess fiddled with the pen. She *had* to invite him to the wedding but she couldn't forgive him entirely. 'It's . . . it's . . . too difficult. I can never forget that but for him, Mam would still be alive. She would have been organising all this.'

Johanna nodded. She was in a difficult situation but at least Jess wasn't excluding him. Perhaps it was a start on the road to reconciliation.

Tilly was far happier these days, Jess thought as she watched the child exclaim over the beautifully made clothes Johanna had supplied for the new dolls. Jess had bought them for Tilly's birthday which was on the same day as Patrick's wedding. The air of watchfulness, caution, unease about her evident when Terence Shay had lived with them had gone.

'Aunt Jo is very good to have got those finished in time, especially with all the plans for the wedding.'

'I know, but she promised me them for my birthday and she never breaks a promise.' Tilly was very excited. It was going to be a very special birthday. She was going to be bridesmaid to Catherine and they were going to go to a hotel for the reception and she knew that Catherine had bought her something special. She'd told her. She liked Catherine.

'Well, you'll have all day tomorrow to dress them up, it's time for you to get ready. Have you had a good wash?'

'Yes,' Tilly replied indignantly.

Jess took the pale blue organza bridesmaid's dress from its hanger and slipped it over Tilly's head. There were little pearls sewn around the neck and the short puffed sleeves. It had a wide sash of white satin ribbon and she had a headdress of white and blue satin ribbon and the daintiest white satin shoes.

'You look like a little princess!' Jess exclaimed and Tilly was lost for words as she gazed at her reflection in the long cheval mirror in Jess's bedroom. She loved the way the skirt stuck out. If her mam could see her now she wouldn't recognise her at all, she thought.

'Now, don't move. I've to go and help Catherine dress,' Jess instructed. Catherine hadn't wanted to go to the church from her aunt's house so Jess had volunteered.

'Can I come too?' Tilly pleaded.

Jess sighed. 'As long as you promise to sit still and not chatter nineteen to the dozen. And will you stop fiddling with that sash? You'll have it all grubby.'

'I'll bring my dolls.'

Jess raised her eyes to the ceiling. Tilly never went anywhere without her 'family' these days, if she could help it.

Catherine had been given the spare bedroom just for the

night. On their return from honeymoon she would move into Patrick's room.

'Oh, Jess, I'm so nervous,' she cried when Jess and Tilly entered.

'I think you're supposed to be. It's all part of the ritual. I hope it's all right, but Tilly begged to come too.'

'Oh, Tilly, don't you look lovely!' Catherine cried with sincerity.

Jess smiled. 'Let's hope she stays that way. Now, let's start to make you lovely too.'

The white silk taffeta dress was slipped over Catherine's head and Jess did up the row of tiny buttons at the back. It was very plain but well cut which suited Catherine's petite figure. Too many frills and flounces would have made her look over-dressed. The sleeves were long and tight; the cuffs were decorated with bead embroidery as was the high neckline. The embroidery, becoming more elaborate, extended the full length of the long train. A small wreath of silk orange blossom was placed over Catherine's swept-up blonde curls and a veil consisting of yards of silk tulle was attached to it.

Jess stepped back to admire her handiwork and thought that any man, let alone Patrick, would be delighted to have such a truly beautiful bride.

'Oh, don't you all look absolutely gorgeous!' Johanna exclaimed, clasping her hands as she entered.

'Catherine looks like a vision from heaven, doesn't she?' Jess enthused.

Johanna kissed Catherine's cheek. 'Oh, my dear, Jess is right. Patrick will be delighted with you.'

'And you look very smart, Aunt Jo,' Jess complimented her

aunt who had chosen a biscuit-coloured fine wool two-piece edged with brown satin ribbon. Her hat, shoes and gloves were of the same shade of brown and as it was an autumn wedding she had opted for a sealskin muff.

'Now, we can't let Patrick catch even a glimpse of her, it's bad luck.'

'Haven't they gone to the church yet?' Jess asked. Ronan was to be best man and had arrived an hour before. Despite all the fuss, Jess had noticed a coolness between her cousin and her brother, and she hoped they hadn't had a disagreement about something.

'Just about to leave as I came up. Tom was going straight there with the Dempseys, apart from Edward.'

'I'll go and make sure, I think it's about time we left too,' Jess said, smiling. 'I'll ask Edward to come up now.' She had been relieved that Edward had agreed to give Catherine away, as the girl had no male relations.

Patrick and Ronan were in the hall and again Jess noticed the tension between them.

'You should both have gone by now!'

Patrick ran his finger between his collar and his neck. It was far from warm but he was hot and the collar was choking him. He felt ill at the thought of the events of the day ahead of him.

'Jess, you look lovely,' Ronan said quietly. It made him angry that she should have such a brother. She deserved far better. The familiar feelings began to stir in him as he looked at her. Why, oh why did they have to be so closely related? And why was she seeing so much of Edward Dempsey? He was certain that dour man was just stringing her along but he had no right to tell her that – or to tell her anything.

Jess smiled and reached up and kissed him lightly on the cheek. It was a gesture of affection, of thanks, nothing more, but he wanted to sweep her into his arms and hold her and kiss her. He steadied himself. One misplaced love affair in the family was enough.

Jess had turned to Patrick and kissed him too. 'Patrick, I hope this will be the happiest day of your life, now get off, the pair of you!' She laughed as she shooed them towards the front door.

She found Edward alone in the sitting room.

'Is it time?' he asked, getting to his feet.

'Yes. The carriage will be here any minute.' She laid a hand on his arm. He really looked very handsome in his grey morning suit. 'You're sure you don't mind doing this, Edward?'

'Of course not and, Jess, can I say you look beautiful?'

She smiled. 'Thank you, Edward, but Catherine will outshine us all today. Which is how it should be.'

He didn't think that was possible, not in his eyes at least. The deep rose pink Jess had chosen flattered her colouring, its plain lines showing off her slim figure. Her wide-brimmed hat, decorated with pink and black ribbon and gleaming black feathers, suited her face. She looked elegant, smart and very lovely. And he knew in that moment that he had never loved or wanted her more.

He took her hand. 'Jess, I know that this isn't the most suitable time, but... have you thought about what I mentioned?'

Jess's heart sank. It wasn't the right time but she couldn't ignore the question totally. 'Edward, we'll talk about this later. This evening, when everyone has gone. I promise.'

He didn't know what to think. Was it good news or was she waiting for more time and privacy in which to let him down gently? But there was nothing he could do except wait. He nodded. 'Then I'll see you in church, Jess.'

All through the ceremony and the reception that followed Jess was distracted. It was hard to keep her thoughts entirely on her brother and his new bride or the fact that, for the first time since her mam had been killed, she and her uncle were under the same roof and there had been a brief, if stilted, conversation between them. How exactly did she feel about Edward Dempsey? she asked herself as she watched Tilly talking animatedly to a pained-looking, overdressed Aideen. He had been wonderful today: calm, steady, authoritative and thoughtful. Those were his best qualities. If she was really truthful she just didn't know what she wanted but how was she to tell him that?

'A penny for them?'

Ronan's voice broke into her thoughts and she smiled. 'They're not worth it.'

'You look very serious. Are you worried about them?' He nodded in Patrick and Catherine's direction.

'No, not them. Me. I was thinking . . . deciding whether or not to end my days like Catherine's aunt. A spinster.'

He felt a wave of jealousy wash over him. 'Don't tell me that dry stick Edward Dempsey has proposed?'

Jess looked up at him, startled by his tone. 'And if he has?'

Ronan was struggling with his emotions. 'You don't *have* to marry . . . anyone, Jess.'

'But what if I feel as though I should?'

Oh, God! This was worse than he thought. 'Do you . . . love him?' He found it hard to get the word out and harder still to banish the image of Jess in Edward Dempsey's arms.

'Oh, Ronan, I don't know what I feel or what I want, but I have to give Edward some kind of an answer.'

'Jess, you're not . . . you're not going to agree!' Suddenly the room was stifling. No! No! She couldn't *marry* Edward Dempsey. She couldn't marry *anyone*!

Jess was concerned. She'd never seen Ronan like this. 'Ronan, what's the matter?'

He had to regain control of himself. Pick his words carefully. 'Jess, you know I'm very . . . fond of you.'

'I know that, Ronan. We've always been close, even as children.'

'I don't want to see you hurt. You've had too much pain and heartache in your life already and—'

'You think Edward is too old and staid for me? He's not *that* bad really, when you get to know him. He's kind, generous, steady, sometimes humorous – in his way – and quite handsome.'

'But do you *love* him, Jess?'

Jess sighed. 'I just don't *know*, Ronan. Really I don't!'

His spirits lifted. 'Then don't commit yourself, Jess, please?' he begged.

The relief he felt was almost tangible as she squeezed his arm and smiled and said, 'I won't, Ronan. I promise.'

Maybe there was *some* hope after all.

Thinking of her conversation with Ronan, Jess had reached her decision by the time Patrick and Catherine had left for the railway station, the guests had departed and Tilly was in bed, but she suspected not asleep. The child was thoroughly over-excited.

'Well, I think that all went very well, don't you?' she asked Edward as she poured herself a sherry and him a whiskey.

'It did. She's a quiet, pretty little thing. I hope they'll be happy.'

'Oh, so do I.'

'It must be a relief to you, Jess. I know he's caused you some sleepless nights.'

'He has, but, please God, that's all behind me now.'

'And what of the future?'

She sipped her sherry thoughtfully. 'I promised you an answer.'

'You did. I . . . I don't want to pressure you, but . . .'

She smiled. 'I know and it's not fair of me to keep you dangling.'

'So, have you reached a decision?'

She nodded. 'I'm very fond of you, Edward. You're kind and thoughtful and very reliable . . .'

'But rather dull and unimaginative.' He smiled wryly.

'No! I wouldn't say that,' she protested. 'I want to be fair to you so I . . . I think that perhaps we *should* see more of each other, it might help us to understand each other better. But I don't want to commit myself to anything more serious just yet. Can you understand that?'

He was disappointed but hid it well. He had hoped she *would* commit herself, but she had at least agreed that they should go on seeing each other, and more frequently. She hadn't turned him down flat, dismissed him with a carefully worded rejection.

'I can't ask for more than that, Jess, and you are being honest with me, for which I thank you.'

She smiled at him. 'It's only what you deserve, Edward, I just couldn't string you along.'

He finished his drink and rose. 'Then when may I see you again?'

'Whenever you like, Edward.'

'Dinner on, say, Tuesday evening?'

'That would be lovely. And thank you, Edward, for all you've done today. It went really well.'

He smiled his thanks. I hope our wedding day will go as well, if it ever arrives, he thought to himself before he took his leave.

Chapter Twenty-Two

'THEY'VE ARRIVED! JESS, THEY'RE home!' Tilly ran into the kitchen full of excitement.

'Oh, heavens, look at the state of me!' Jess cried, wiping her hands and quickly removing her apron. She'd been cleaning out the kitchen cupboards, one of the jobs she'd promised herself she would do for over a month now.

Tilly was already ahead of her when she reached the hall. She glanced quickly in the mirror and tidied her hair.

'Did you have a wonderful time?' she asked Catherine, giving her a quick hug.

Catherine nodded while Patrick busied himself with the luggage.

'You must be worn out. Come and have some tea.'

'I'd like to have a wash first, and get changed, Jess, if you don't mind. Travelling makes you so . . . grubby,' Patrick excused himself as Jess led his wife into the sitting room, followed by Tilly. He just wanted to be alone for a few minutes. It had been a nightmare: all that embarrassing fumbling; his fight to overcome the revulsion he felt; Catherine's tears and apologies. For the entire time they'd been away all he'd wanted to do was go home, but now that he was here he knew things were not going to get any better. In fact they would be worse. He would be under scrutiny. Jess would expect some signs of affection between them and he found it hard even to touch Catherine, take her hand, kiss her cheek. In time Jess would notice and then the awkward questions would begin. No, life wasn't going to be better now he was back. He had to see Terence. He just *had* to.

He sat on the bed and stared around the familiar room. A room he must now share with Catherine. He felt trapped. Panic began to rise in him and he had to fight hard to keep it at bay. He mustn't show any sign of how desperate he felt – already.

He got up and took off his jacket. Terence would understand. Terence would comfort him and bolster his spirits.

'So, tell me all about it? Was it a nice place? What about the hotel?' Jess asked as she placed the tea tray on the side table.

'Oh, Llandudno is very nice, Jess. It's very smart,' Catherine enthused. 'Lots of very big hotels and shops. We used to walk the whole length of the promenade each morning after breakfast and even though the weather was cold it was bright and sunny. One day we went out in a boat although I was a little scared, and another day we went right to the top of the Great Orme. The view was breathtaking. And I went shopping. Oh, Jess, I had a wonderful time. Money of my own to buy whatever I liked. It was such a treat.'

'And the hotel?' Jess was pleased that things appeared to

have gone very well. They seemed to have done quite a lot of things together. Just as a newly married couple should do.

'Very grand. The suite was so comfortable and the bathroom was huge and so modern.' Catherine pushed away the memories of those awful nights. It had been her fault, she was convinced of that. She was so naïve, so inexperienced that poor Patrick had become flustered and embarrassed and then she'd broken down in tears. It had been so different during the day. Patrick was more relaxed, he seemed to enjoy walking along the beach and the promenade and he had said he was perfectly happy to wander off on his own while she went shopping. But the nights! She had begun to dread dinner because she knew what was to follow.

'What's the Great Orme?' Tilly interjected.

'It's sort of like a big cliff.'

'A mountain?'

'No, more like a hill. There are two of them. One at either end of the bay. The other one is called the Little Orme. Perhaps Jess will take you one day.'

'I might just do that, when I get more time to myself.'

Catherine became concerned. 'You should take a holiday, Jess. You work so very hard.'

'I know, but I have so much to think about.'

'I bought you something, a little gift, and one for Tilly too.'

'Oh, you shouldn't have.'

'It's the least I could do, you've been so good to me.' Catherine delved into her bag and brought out a small box and a much larger one. She handed Jess the small box.

Jess exclaimed in delight as she opened it. It was a brooch in the shape of the Welsh dragon. It was enamelled in red and green with spots of gold leaf and semi-precious stones setting off its eyes and claws.

'It's lovely, Catherine, thank you!'

'Look! Look, Jess! I haven't got one like this!' Tilly cried, holding out a doll dressed in the national costume of Wales.

'It's very special, Tilly. You must take care of it and not go taking its clothes off and then putting them back on by the minute.'

The child nodded, fingering the tall-crowned black hat gingerly. Fancy Catherine going to all the trouble to find a special doll for her.

'Right, let's have some tea and then you can unpack, Catherine, and I'll put the kitchen back together again,' Jess laughed.

To his dismay it was three days before Patrick found the chance to go to see his friend, a circumstance that annoyed and frustrated him immensely.

'So, you're back, Pat. How did it go?'

Patrick flung himself down in a battered easy chair. 'Terrible! God, I need a drink!'

Terence Shay poured two tumblers of cheap whiskey. Patrick looked ghastly, as though he hadn't slept properly for over a week. It upset him. 'That bad?'

'Worse. I could hardly bring myself to touch her.'

'Put it out of your mind. Think about the future,' Shay instructed briskly.

'What future? I'm tied to her for ever!' Patrick moaned.

'Did you ask her about the money? It's the money that's important, Pat. Important for the future . . . our future.' He didn't want to know about the honeymoon and he didn't want Patrick to dwell on it either.

In the time Patrick had been away he'd comforted himself with thoughts and plans of how best to invest the money. He'd studied the papers and journals and calculated the dividends and returns. If everything went to plan he would be out of this rat-infested slum in six months. But he had to keep Patrick interested and focused; after all, it was for their future.

'No, I just never got round to it. Oh, the days weren't bad. She's not . . . demanding, she's a good listener. I managed to get off on my own too for a few hours while she went shopping, but the nights . . . Oh, God, it was terrible!'

'Well, now you're back at work you won't have to spend so much time with her and you can make excuses, say you're tired, you're worried—'

'But I can't even show the simplest signs of affection towards her and Jess is bound to notice and start to ask questions. What can I do?'

'You'll have to force yourself, Pat! We can't have Jess getting suspicious. Surely it's not too much to ask?'

'Oh, I suppose not, but life is going to be hell, Terence!' Patrick whined.

'Concentrate on the money, Pat.' Shay was irritated by Pat's attitude and the fact that he hadn't already broached the subject of the money with Catherine. It was the solution to his problem, their problem, and pussyfooting around, whining and complaining, wasn't going to help anyone. He often admitted to himself that Patrick was a fool, a selfish, weak-willed fool, but he was also his ticket out of this place and back to a substantially improved lifestyle.

'I'll mention it to her, Terence, as soon as I get home tonight. I promise,' Patrick agreed.

'Good. Drink that up and we'll have another and then . . . then we can discuss things in more detail.'

Patrick felt a little cheered. Terence was right. The money was the important thing.

He found Jess alone when he returned home.

'Catherine has only just gone up. We thought you'd be in earlier.'

'Sorry, Jess. I was detained, you know how it is when a few chaps get together for a drink.' He'd told her he was meeting some friends from work, just a bit of a social occasion. One of them was getting married at the weekend.

'Don't be apologising to me.'

He managed a smile. 'I'll go and apologise to Catherine then.'

She nodded and turned back to the column of figures she was poring over. He knew business was good, so she could afford Catherine's allowance; he wondered if he should ask her for a little something for himself? She knew his salary wasn't generous. But no, he didn't want to cause a fuss. He would have money of his own soon enough.

Catherine was brushing out her cloud of curls. They framed her face like a halo and made her look very young and child-like, Patrick thought irritably. He noticed with some consternation that she was wearing an obviously new and rather pretty nightgown.

'I hope you didn't mind me not waiting.'

He turned away from her. 'No, of course not.'

'Did you have a good time?'

'Oh, not bad. You know how these things are. I . . . I want to talk to you, Catherine.'

She turned to face him. 'What about? You look very serious, Patrick.'

'Money. Your allowance in fact.'

She looked confused. 'What about it?'

'Well, you know my salary is no more than a pittance. We can never hope to have a place of our own—'

'Do you want one? This is a lovely home,' she interrupted.

'I know it's very comfortable, but one day I would like a home of my own. No man wants to live with his family for ever, Catherine.'

She looked disappointed. 'What has my allowance got to do with it?'

'Well, if you would turn it over to me I could invest it wisely and it would earn us a good dividend which we could save for a home of our own.'

She looked puzzled. She didn't understand words like 'invest' and 'dividend'. 'You want me to give it to you?'

Inwardly he sighed with relief. He'd known she wouldn't offer any resistance. 'Yes. You have to admit that you don't want for anything. You have far more than you've ever had in your life before, you told me that yourself.'

Catherine was perturbed. She was quite happy here and Jess had specifically said it was 'her' money, not Patrick's. She had emphasised that.

'Yes, but . . . Jess said it was *mine*. That it was nothing to do with you.'

He was irritated. 'She's far too bossy! That's Jess all over.'

Catherine didn't want to give up her new-found wealth. It had been such an exhilarating experience to buy whatever took her eye, but neither did she want to upset Patrick. 'Perhaps if I asked her advice about investing?'

'No! I don't want you to mention it to Jess!' That was the last thing he wanted.

'But why? Surely she won't mind me investing or saving or . . . something?'

She wasn't going to give it to him! he realised with shock. She'd never shown this stubborn streak before.

'Because . . . because a man damn well has his pride and self-respect, Catherine! She'd go on and on about us having a comfortable home here and why would I want to buy another one?'

As Catherine didn't want to move to a house where she would be alone all day, without even Tilly around to talk to, she refused to see the sense of his argument. 'But she'd be right, Patrick, and I . . . well, I'd be on my own all day. You'd be at work.'

He lost his temper. 'So, you'd be happy for us to live here for ever? You'd be happy to see me beholden to Jess for the rest of my life? Happy to see me humiliated by having to ask Jess for money?'

She was confused and upset. She'd never seen him angry before. 'No! No, of course I wouldn't, Patrick! But I . . . I just don't understand! I've never had any money of my own and I . . . I . . . like it. I like it a lot. Please, please, Patrick, don't make me give it up. I'm sure if I went to Jess and explained how you feel—'

He rounded on her. 'Don't you say a word to Jess, do you

hear me?' He was furious. Damn the stupid little bitch! She was going to hang on to her allowance like grim death and if she went to Jess and even breathed a word of this there would be a terrible row.

Catherine was becoming a little afraid of him. He was very angry now. 'I'm sorry, Patrick. I won't say a word, but if . . . if you're short of money you can ask me, rather than go to Jess.'

Patrick pressed his lips firmly together. Ask her! Go begging to her for money! The stupid, selfish, empty-headed, stubborn little bitch! Couldn't she see that that was almost as bad as going to Jess? She was hell-bent on frustrating all his plans.

He was icy cold now. 'Just forget it, Catherine! If you're quite content to see me humiliated by having no real wealth to speak of for the rest of my life, then you can't think much of my feelings!' He turned away from her and walked out of the room, anger, frustration and disappointment washing over him. How was he going to tell Terence about this? And what could they do now?

Jess hadn't noticed the change in Catherine, but Tilly had. Catherine was much quieter. She hardly laughed any more and whereas before she'd always been interested in whatever Tilly had had to tell her, now she barely paid her any attention.

'Jess, I don't think Catherine likes living here any more,' she confided as Jess finished hemming one of her pinafores.

'Whyever not? What has she said?'

'Nothing, but she never laughs and she isn't really listening when I talk to her.'

'Oh, Tilly, you're imagining it. You talk nineteen to the

dozen all the time, no one can get a word in edgewise!'

'I don't! She used to read to me sometimes but now she says she's too tired. She doesn't go out to work like you do, so why is she tired?' It was inexplicable to the child.

Jess looked thoughtful. Was there really something wrong? Had she not been taking enough notice? Well, she'd find out for herself what was the matter with her sister-in-law – if anything.

Her opportunity came that evening. Tilly was in bed and Patrick had gone out after supper, saying he was going to see a friend from work who was having some problems with his landlord and needed moral support.

She had noticed that Catherine seemed very subdued over the meal and that when Patrick had said he was going out, she'd looked at him pleadingly but he'd ignored her.

'Catherine, I . . . I can't help noticing that you seem quiet. Is there something wrong? Is it something I've said or done?'

Catherine was startled. 'No! Heavens no, Jess! It's not you.'

'Then is it Patrick? I don't want to pry, it's really none of my business, but is everything all right between you? Is he treating you well?'

Catherine bit her lip. Ever since the row Patrick had been very cool towards her when they were alone and she was miserable about it. She had tried to apologise, to bring the conversation around to the argument but he gave her no opportunity. He cut her short each time she opened her mouth. He'd not made a single move to touch her either. He turned his back towards her every night.

'Catherine, you can tell me. I hate to see you unhappy,' Jess urged.

Catherine was so worried that she thought what a relief it would be to confide in Jess. 'Oh, Jess! It's all my fault! I know it is!' she blurted out.

'What is?' Jess prompted.

'We . . . we had an argument.'

'What over?'

She remembered how angry Patrick had been, forbidding her to mention any word of the disagreement over her allowance to Jess. 'Oh, something . . . stupid, but it's not *just* that.'

'Patrick doesn't usually sulk.'

'Oh, Jess, it's . . . well . . . he finds it hard to . . . to touch me. We . . . we've never . . .'

Jess felt an uneasiness creep over her. What was Catherine trying to tell her? That the marriage had not been consummated? If so, it must be terrible for poor Catherine.

'You mean he's never . . . ?'

Catherine shook her head miserably. 'No and, oh, Jess, I know it's my fault!'

Jess took her in her arms. 'It can't be *all* your fault. Has Patrick said anything?'

'No. No, we don't talk about it. And then we had that stupid row . . . !'

'Do you want me to talk to him?' It was something she really didn't want to do. It was a very private, personal thing, but she would if it would help.

'No! No, really, Jess! He would be so angry with me. I know he would.'

Jess was relieved – to an extent. 'I could just talk to him generally.'

Again Catherine shook her head. 'No, it's just me being

280

silly. I . . . I didn't know what to expect, you see. Perhaps in time . . .'

Jess nodded but a thought had come to her with such cold clarity that she was shaken. Catherine had said she hadn't known what to expect and she remembered Mam saying the very same thing about her tragic younger sister Carmel. In the end Carmel had found it so unbearable that she'd killed herself. But no, Catherine wasn't like that. She herself wouldn't allow the situation to degenerate to that extent. Catherine and Patrick would sort things out in time. But still, she was worried, and wondered if she should consult Johanna. After all, her aunt was older and experienced in these things, which she herself was not.

Chapter Twenty-Three

———❧———

'PAT, WHAT'S HAPPENED?' SHAY could tell by Patrick's face that all was not well.

'It's Catherine! My bloody stupid, selfish, bitch of a wife!'

Shay took him by the arm and propelled him to a chair. His eyes narrowed as he poured Patrick what he could see was a much-needed drink. What was the little cow up to?

'What has she done, Pat, to get you in this state?'

'She won't give up her allowance!' Patrick knocked back his drink in one gulp and held out his glass for another.

Anger stirred in Shay. 'I thought you said she would be no trouble? That she'd give it up easily?'

'I thought she would!' Patrick laughed bitterly. 'My wife has a stubborn streak. She likes having money of her own.'

'But she doesn't like *you* having any!' Shay snapped. 'I honestly thought you would persuade her.'

'I tried, but no, she was going to ask Jess's advice, would you believe? Jess! Who told her the money was for *her* alone.'

'I hope you stamped on that idea very firmly, Pat?' The girl was proving to be a menace.

'I did! Oh, indeed I did, and I've hardly spoken to her since the row. She couldn't give a fig for me or my feelings . . .'

As Shay half listened to Patrick's tirade, he realised it was time for drastic measures. He was furious not only with Jess and Catherine but with Patrick for being so weak as to not be able to force his wife to agree to his plans. Unless Shay did something at once they had no future at all.

Jess was the main obstacle and she'd been more than a thorn in his flesh for a long time now: she and that brat and now this Catherine, who wasn't so pliable as she'd first appeared.

'I can see I'm going to have to take a hand in this, Pat,' he said when Patrick had at last finished ranting, exhausted.

'What can you do, Terence? You know Jess hates you.'

Shay'd given this a great deal of thought. It had been tucked away at the back of his mind as an emergency plan. Well, the emergency had arisen.

'But if Jess were incapacitated in some way, she would be glad to hand over the business to you.'

Patrick laughed mirthlessly. 'She'd have to be on her death bed before she'd do that.'

Shay stared into his drink for a few seconds before he spoke, and when he did it was slowly and with deliberation. 'I don't think so, Pat. Just ill for long enough to be grateful to you if you stepped in to save the business from going to rack and ruin. The business she has worked so hard to build up.'

'How the hell is she going to get so ill? She's as fit as a fiddle.'

'There are ways,' Shay answered cautiously.

Patrick stared at him. 'Ways? What kind of ways?'

'It's well known that small amounts of certain . . . substances can cause debilitating illnesses.'

Patrick looked at him with dawning horror. 'You can't mean . . . ? You don't mean poison? For God's sake, she's my sister!'

Shay realised he hadn't put it well. 'No! Not poison, Pat! Drugs. Just enough to make her "incapacitated".' He grasped Patrick's arm. 'Just think of it, Pat. With Jess half drugged, she wouldn't know what was going on. Think of the money we could cream off. More than enough to get out of the predicament we're in. Think about it! It won't be harmful to her in the long run. The doses wouldn't be enough to make her really ill, let alone kill her. Do you think I would go so far as to poison her?'

Patrick was wavering. 'What . . . what kind of drugs?'

'Drugs that would make her tired, sleepy, unable to concentrate.' He had to be more persuasive. 'Drugs a doctor wouldn't suspect, even if he were called in. The family certainly wouldn't suspect and even they couldn't object to you stepping in to save her business from disaster. It's the perfect answer, the perfect plan, Pat! You know how you hate being beholden to her. You know how much you hate your life and your wife.'

'You're right, but it . . . it won't harm her?'

'I give you my word it won't. But I'll need you to help me. You'll have to slip them into her drinks.'

Patrick still prevaricated. 'I don't know about this, Terence, it's risky.'

Shay was losing patience. 'For God's sake, Pat, do you want to be dependent on her for the rest of your life? Do you want to have to go on living with that stupid little bitch they forced you to marry?'

'No! No, I'd do anything rather than face that!'

'Then listen to me. I know where I can get a powder made up. It's the only way, Pat. The only way out for both of us.'

Slowly Patrick nodded. Terence was right. He couldn't stand a lifetime living the way he did now. He'd sooner be dead than face it. He *did* trust Terence. His friend wouldn't seriously harm Jess.

'Good. Just keep thinking of the future – our future – and leave the rest to me.'

'You're sure this stuff isn't too strong?'

'Certain. What you need to do, Pat, is start some kind of routine. Make tea or cocoa or some kind of drink for all of you every evening. Start now, so it won't seem odd, then next week I'll come late one night with the powder and slip it to you. I know it would be easier and safer if you came here to collect it, but I want to go on seeing you, Pat. You do realise that?'

'Of course and I want . . . need to see you.'

'Well, after it's begun to take effect, I could even move back in. She wouldn't care.'

'Everyone else would.'

'To hell with them all, Pat! I'm sick of living in this pig-sty! You'll need help with the business. You know nothing about it. Two heads are better than one and I'm good with figures.'

Patrick was at last convinced. 'We'll do it! By God, we will! She's dictated to me for far too long and so have the others, and you've lived for far too long like this.'

Shay smiled slowly. He'd known he could persuade Patrick. Now it was just a matter of time before he could get his hands on as much of Jess's money as he wanted.

Jess was surprised when Patrick offered to make them all cocoa the following evening.

'It's very thoughtful of you, Patrick.'

'Well, these dark nights are miserable and you're often tired, Jess, as am I, and I know Catherine is fond of the drink,' he'd replied amiably.

Jess was glad to see he was including Catherine. Perhaps they were getting over their initial difficulties.

She had decided against informing Johanna, for the time being, thinking that it was still early days and that it had been an arranged marriage after all.

It quickly became a ritual; Patrick even joked about it, and Jess was glad to see his change of mood. They'd also fallen into the habit of discussing the day's events and Patrick always seemed interested in the business and her problems and ideas.

'So, you really think that feathers, as decorations, are falling out of favour?' he asked.

'I do. Oh, it won't happen overnight, but I'm starting to look at alternatives.'

'Such as?'

'Artificial flowers and fruit.'

'Won't that be very expensive?'

'Obviously I've considered that. If I can get the right girls and train them, buy the materials at cost, it might work. I'd just make up some trial lines. Find simple things to start with, something easy to make.'

'Where would you find the materials?'

'I don't know yet. I've got to make enquiries. I've also thought of making beaded motifs, ready to be sewn onto evening dresses and ball gowns. It would save hours of work. There are young girls who are quite skilled at beadwork, so I hear, and who at present are paid buttons for it – and they work from home, often in very bad light. My workrooms are spacious, light, airy and warm: I'm sure I could tempt them to come and work for me.'

'You'd have to look at the costs carefully, Jess,' Patrick advised. She certainly had a good business head on her shoulders, he thought. He wished he was as smart.

'I know. But I really do think we have to carry other lines if we're to continue making a good profit.'

'Don't be over-taxing yourself. You work too hard as it is,' Patrick said solicitously. Let her go on thinking like this, talking like this: it suited their plans very well.

He'd received word at work from Terence that he would come to the house at midnight that night and that Patrick should leave the back door unlocked. He felt nervous but tried not to let it show.

He'd made the cocoa and they'd had their discussions and at eleven Jess said she would go up. He said he had some work to do. He'd brought it home as they were so very busy.

'Don't *you* tire yourself out, Patrick,' Jess had warned but she was smiling.

'I won't. Catherine, I think I'll sleep in the spare room tonight. I don't want to disturb you when I come up, it might be late,' he offered. He didn't want her to wake and find him missing. She might decide to come down and look for him and he couldn't risk that.

'That's very considerate of you,' Jess said as Catherine, looking a little disappointed, also rose.

Catherine was indeed disappointed. He had been much more pleasant to her of late. He seemed to have forgotten the row and occasionally he kissed her cheek or gave her hand a squeeze, and she'd hoped they could try again. Clearly not tonight though.

When Patrick was sure they were both upstairs he got up and went into the kitchen. It was a foul night, he thought. The rain was lashing against the windowpanes and the wind was making the door rattle. Terence would be cold and wet. He'd need something to warm him up. It was a long journey and at this time of night transport was thin on the ground. He took two glasses from one of the cupboards and then went back into the sitting room for the whiskey. He spread the papers he'd deliberately brought home with him across the sofa and side tables and then began to pace slowly up and down, watching the clock. The time dragged interminably. The fire died back to ash and he placed the guard around it, then willed the fingers on the clock to move.

At five to midnight he opened the door and listened. There was no sound in the house. All that could be heard was the wind and the rain. Taking the whiskey bottle he went quietly into the kitchen and turned the lamp down until the room was in shadow. Then he sat at the table, waiting, beads of perspiration on his forehead.

He was certain that Terence's plan would work, it was just this thing of him actually having to administer the drug. What if he gave her too much? Or not enough? What if Johanna or the others got really suspicious? Or Catherine, or even that little pain in the neck, Tilly? Oh, it was no use letting his imagination run away with him. He'd be letting Terence down and Terence really cared for him and that and their life together was all that really mattered.

He didn't hear the back door open, but was relieved to see Terence slip quietly in. His coat was saturated and rain dripped from the brim of his hat.

'Good God, you're soaked! Come here to the fire,' he hissed.

'It's a bloody foul night out there.'

'You should have got a cab.'

'What with, Pat? I've barely enough to keep body and soul together.'

'Well, you're getting one back. You'll catch pneumonia. Here, drink this.'

Shay gratefully gulped down the spirit and felt a bit warmer. If he'd had any doubts about what they were going to do, the weather tonight had certainly banished them. As he'd trudged through the dark, wet streets, hanging on to his hat, with the icy rain stinging his face and hands, he'd sworn he'd not spend another winter like this: forced to live in a damp, draughty room with hardly any heat, with insufficient bedding to keep him warm and often no food in his belly. The wetness and dirt from the pavements seeped through the holes in the soles of his boots; his thin, shiny jacket and top coat barely kept out the worst of the winter chill. As he walked to work each grey, miserable morning he cursed the fact that he hadn't even the tram fare. This plan *would* work. Soon he *would* have money enough for all the necessities and, better, luxuries of life.

'Did you get it?' Patrick asked.

He delved into the inside pocket of his jacket and brought out a small box. 'Put half a teaspoon in her drink every night. It has an accumulative effect, so don't expect it to work at once. It's better that way. Less suspicious.'

'The cocoa has become a ritual: no one suspects. She's thinking of trying other lines to increase business. I've told her she's working too hard and Catherine's heard me.'

Shay smiled grimly. 'Good. I knew I could trust you, Pat.'

'How long will this last?' Patrick fingered the box.

'A week. I'll come again on the same day next week and for as many weeks as it takes.'

'Is that wise? Couldn't you have bought more?'

'It's not exactly cheap, Pat.'

'Don't worry about the money. I have enough.'

'Good. I'll need more. Now, give me another shot and then I'll have to be on my way. It'll take me hours to get back.'

Patrick refilled the glass and took some notes from his wallet.

'Don't worry, Pat, soon all our troubles will be over,' Shay said confidently, glancing around. Soon he'd be back here and Jess would have no say in the matter. Soon they would be rich and living together with that little fool Catherine as a sop to Society and respectability. He knew how to handle her, even if Patrick didn't. All that mattered was that no one outside these four walls knew what was going on and he'd make sure they didn't. Oh, Jess's days of lording it over them were numbered. And since it would be Patrick who would be administering the drug, not him, he couldn't be blamed if things went wrong.

Tilly wasn't sure what had woken her. There was a storm raging outside the bedroom window so she supposed it must have been the wind. The storm didn't alarm or frighten her – she was used to them – but she tossed and turned restlessly, arranging and rearranging the collection of dolls that shared her bed. Maybe if she had a drink and a biscuit she could get back to sleep? She didn't usually get up in the night but then she usually didn't wake up either.

She shivered as her bare feet came into contact with the polished lino and she felt around for her slippers. She didn't want to light a lamp or the gas in case she woke Jess or Catherine, so, clutching her dressing gown to her, she slowly felt her way to the door, then onto the landing and, one by one, down the stairs.

It was better when she reached the hall, there was a light on in the sitting room but that also meant that someone was up. Was it Jess or was it Patrick? She knew Jess would scold her but Patrick wouldn't. And if she was very, very quiet he wouldn't even know she was down here. She didn't try to peer around the door to see just who it was, she sidled along the wall towards the kitchen.

The door was open a crack and there was a very dim light burning and as she crept closer she was certain she heard voices. Was it Jess? Was it Catherine? She pressed her eye to the keyhole. It was Patrick and someone else. She screwed up her eye to see better and then stepped backwards, shocked. It was *him*! It was that Terence Shay! What was he doing back here? Jess wouldn't know about this, she was certain of that. Why had he come in the middle of the night and in such weather? Oh, God, what if they caught her spying on them? She began to sidle her way back towards the stairs and then she heard the back door close quietly and the key being turned in the lock. He'd gone but Patrick would be out soon. She couldn't let him find her here. She began to ascend the stairs quickly. She'd got as far as the half-landing when Patrick reached the bottom of the stairs and then the beam of an oil lamp caught her.

'What are you doing up?' Patrick hissed, shocked at the sight of her. How much had she seen and heard?

'I . . . I . . . was thirsty. The wind woke me up and I couldn't get back to sleep,' she said, eyeing him warily.

'Did you come to the kitchen door?' he demanded.

'No! No, I'd only just got down here. I . . . I didn't know you were still up. I didn't want to wake anyone, that's why I was creeping around in the dark.'

He didn't know if she were telling the truth but there was nothing he could say. 'Get yourself back to bed. Jess will be angry if she knows you've been creeping around the house at this hour.'

Tilly nodded and went up the remaining stairs.

Why had *he* been here? Should she tell Jess? But Patrick would probably deny it and say she had been dreaming and there would be a row and she didn't want that. She'd say nothing but she'd be watchful, just in case Terence Shay came again. If he did, then she'd tell Jess.

Patrick watched her go with mounting apprehension. Had she seen anything? He'd better concoct some story to tell Jess, just in case she had. Terence was right, he thought savagely. The brat was a menace and needed watching.

Chapter Twenty-Four

T HE WAITING FOR PATRICK was a nervous time. He slipped the powder into Jess's cocoa each night, taking great care that no one came into the kitchen and keeping the powder well hidden. He had carefully measured out each nightly dose into small envelopes which he kept locked in the top drawer of his dressing table. It was much easier to hide an envelope than the box.

On the second evening Jess said she felt unaccountably tired.

'I've told you, Jess, you're working too hard. You're worrying yourself to death over finding new lines. Try to take things easier,' he urged.

'Oh, Patrick, if only I could. I've talked Mrs Simpson at Heald's into trying some beaded appliqué pieces. Now I've got to get them made up and costed.'

'How will you do that, Jess?' Catherine asked. She thought Jess was terribly clever but agreed with Patrick that she worked too hard.

'Mary, my supervisor, knows a couple of young girls who do beadwork at home. She's going to ask them if they'll help out. I'll buy the materials of course and we'll go from there. Oh, I really can't keep my eyes open. You'll have to excuse me.'

'Finish up your cocoa, Jess. I'll wash up,' Catherine offered.

Patrick smiled at her. 'You're very helpful, Catherine.'

She smiled back. 'It's the least I can do.'

Patrick leaned back in his chair and began to relax. It was working. They were on their way. Thankfully Tilly hadn't mentioned anything to Jess, so she probably hadn't seen or heard anything.

By the end of the week Catherine was getting worried.

'Patrick, I don't think Jess is very well.'

'Why is that?' he asked from behind his newspaper.

'She's so tired all the time. She's half asleep when she comes in from work and she was telling me she has a terrible time getting up and getting through the day. She says she can't concentrate.'

'She's working too hard. All this rushing around finding homeworkers and buying materials and seeing buyers and dressmakers. *I've* told her. *You've* told her, Catherine.'

'I know.' She sighed. 'But you know she won't take any notice of me. Do you think I should mention it to Aunt Jo?'

Patrick took a deep breath and continued to hold the paper up before his face. 'No. Why worry her? She has enough to worry about with Uncle Tom's health. I'll have a serious talk with Jess first.'

She seemed to be satisfied, he thought, which was just as well as Terence was due the following evening.

'Oh, by the way, there's a bit of a panic on at the office at the moment so I'll be bringing work home with me tomorrow. I'll work in the dining room and then sleep in the spare bedroom.'

'You're working too hard too, Patrick. It was very late when you came up last week.'

'How do you know?' He was instantly suspicious.

'I woke up. Oh, I don't know what time it actually was, but there was a light under the door of the spare room. I didn't disturb you, but you'd obviously only just come up.'

'Well, if you wake up again, you can be reassured that I'm working away like a beaver down here.' He hoped that would pacify her and deter her from coming down to investigate. But he would warn Terence just the same.

Jess had been so tired that he'd had a hard time keeping her up long enough to have her cocoa, but he'd insisted it would help her get a good night's rest and then maybe she would feel better in the morning.

He'd spread out his work in the dining room and lit the lamp in the kitchen and waited patiently until he heard the back door open quietly.

'Come on in to the fire. I've a drink ready to toast our success.'

Shay looked pleased. He'd been worrying all week that at the last moment Patrick might change his mind. 'So it's working?'

'Yes. She says she can hardly stay awake all day. I've gone on and on about her working too hard and Catherine is so concerned that she wanted to inform Johanna.'

Shay was startled. 'Good God! What did you do?'

'I told her Aunt Jo has enough worries and that I'd have a serious talk to Jess. I haven't, of course.'

'Did that seem to quieten her down?'

'It did, but she woke last week.'

'She doesn't suspect anything?'

'No. As an added bonus I get to sleep in the spare room once a week. I tell her I don't want to disturb her when I'm working late here at home. Don't worry about her. She's no threat.'

Shay took another box from his pocket and Patrick handed him two banknotes.

'There is something though, Terence.'

'What?'

'Tilly.'

Shay's expression changed. 'What's that brat done now?'

'After you'd gone last week, I caught her on the half-landing.'

'Christ Almighty!'

'I'm certain she didn't see or hear you, otherwise she'd have told Jess. She said the storm woke her and she wanted a drink. I don't even know if she had got to the bottom of the stairs.'

'Watch her, Pat. Watch her closely. She's a real danger. Always sneaking around, poking her nose into things.' Shay was furious. It would be very risky now to move back into this house. Jess would soon be past caring and Catherine he could cope with, but that child visited Johanna and she would be certain to tell her and then Johanna would tell Ronan. He was almost certain that it had been Tilly who had discovered his and Patrick's secret, Tilly who had caused all this trouble. He wished there was a way to get rid of her permanently, but there wasn't. Even half drugged, Jess wouldn't stand for anything happening to her precious Tilly.

'She'll make it difficult for me to move back here, Pat.'

'Oh, surely not?' Patrick was disappointed.

'Better to be safe than sorry. Tilly would tell Johanna and she would pass it on to Tom and Ronan. But don't worry, I'll still visit you and if you are in the spare room . . .' He shrugged and smiled. 'It won't be too bad and it won't be for ever.'

When Patrick went upstairs he was relieved there was no sign of either Tilly or Catherine. Why should there be? he asked himself. Then he smiled. And of course Jess would be dead to the world.

At the end of the week, after Edward had called twice and found Jess so exhausted that she had to excuse herself and cry off from their proposed outings, he was worried.

'Patrick, there's something very wrong with Jess. She's never been like this: absolutely exhausted, no energy at all, hardly able to stay awake.'

'Well, Edward, I've told her and told her but she takes absolutely no notice. She insists on working herself into the ground.'

'I really do think you should call in the doctor. It might be something more serious.'

Patrick could see by the grim, determined look on Edward's face that it would not be prudent to disagree. He sighed. 'Very well, Edward, if you think it's necessary.'

'I most certainly do.'

'Right. I'll send Tilly around to Dr Chambers with a note.'

'I'd be very relieved.'

'I'm worried about her too, Edward,' he said with what he hoped was convincing sincerity.

'Is Jess really sick?' Tilly demanded, worried. Jess was never ill. She had been very tired lately but everyone said that was because she worked too hard.

'No, I think she's just overtired but we're getting a bit concerned, so it's to be on the safe side. Now don't dawdle on the way.'

Tilly and the doctor arrived back together and after a brief discussion of Jess's condition Patrick showed him up to his sister's room.

Jess struggled to get up. Her head was heavy and her limbs felt like lead.

'Lie back. Now, Miss Brennan, what seems to be the matter? Your brother is worried about you.'

'I just seem to be so tired all the time, doctor. I wake up tired and it's a struggle to get through the day. I find it very hard to concentrate.'

'Are you eating, Miss Brennan?'

'Yes. Oh, not as much as normal but I'm not starving myself.'

'And have you been taking anything? Laudanum or something similar?'

'Heavens no! I only took laudanum once and I felt so terribly ill afterwards that I've never touched it again.'

He frowned and took her pulse, looked down her throat, sounded her chest, checked her eyes and ears, and shook his head. 'I can't find anything wrong with you but I'm going to give you a tonic and you must take things easier. Your brother tells me you're working too hard. It could just be nervous exhaustion.'

'I'll try, doctor.'

'You *will*, Miss Brennan. There is no point working so hard that you make yourself ill.'

Jess lay back on the pillows. Perhaps she really should take Dr Chambers's advice. She certainly couldn't go on like this.

By the end of another week Edward was so worried about her that he went to see Johanna who was very concerned and immediately went to see her niece.

'Aunt Jo, I just don't know what's wrong with me. The tonic Dr Chambers gave me has done no good.'

'Jess, you're not anxious . . . inside . . . about something, are you?'

'No. I'm not really worried about anything. Oh, I had started to think about expanding my lines but, since all this started, I haven't done anything about it. I'm just tired all the time. So exhausted that I can hardly get out of bed in the morning and I'm so . . . light-headed that it's making me clumsy and forgetful.'

'Jess, this is dreadful. I think we should get a second opinion.' Johanna was afraid that Jess was going into a decline. She'd seen it happen before.

'Perhaps you're right. Things are getting so bad that without Catherine's help in running the house, the Lord alone knows where we would be. And Tilly is getting upset.'

'I know. She's afraid something might happen to you.'

Jess was alarmed. 'Oh, please tell her nothing will!'

'Then I'm going to see Dr Chambers and ask him if he can recommend something – a specialist of some kind. Everyone is disturbed about this, Jess. Even Patrick is looking troubled.'

'And he's been so good, Aunt Jo, he really has changed. He even insists on bringing me my cocoa at night and stays with me until I go to sleep – which doesn't usually take long.' She smiled apologetically.

'Well, I'm glad of that. Now, you go back to sleep. I'm going to call on Dr Chambers.'

Dr Chambers arranged an appointment for Jess to see Dr Marsden in Rodney Street and Johanna and Edward went with her. Patrick, too, insisted on going.

'I'm very uneasy about her too, Aunt Jo,' he'd insisted when Johanna said they could manage without him.

They all sat in the waiting room while Dr Marsden gave Jess a thorough examination. Then he called them all in.

'Thankfully, Mrs Kiernan, I can find nothing seriously wrong. Miss Brennan has told me a little of her ... er ... background and I think this may be a delayed mental process. The tragic death of her parents, the temporary drastic change in her lifestyle, her efforts to build her business: all these things take a mental and emotional toll and although outwardly she seemed to have coped with them, inwardly ... well, they tend to catch up with you in time.'

'Is it a mental illness?' Johanna almost whispered the words. Mental illnesses had such a terrible social stigma attached to them.

'I wouldn't define it as a definite form of mental illness, more emotional. It's just as draining as physical illness.'

Patrick endeavoured to look sympathetic. 'So really she's just . . . exhausted? Emotionally exhausted?'

'Yes, an apt description.'

'And what is the cure?' Edward asked. He didn't doubt the man's expertise but he thought it all sounded a bit inconclusive, to say the least.

'Rest and possibly a change of air.'

'Oh, I couldn't go away!' Jess cried in alarm.

'You should rest, Jess.' Edward was firm.

'But the business?' Jess pressed. 'I . . . I've worked so hard, I couldn't just let it go . . .'

Patrick thought the opportunity was God-given. How could his motives possibly be doubted now? 'Jess, would it help if I took over for you, just until you're well again? I have to admit I don't know much about it but I could at least "hold the fort", so to speak. You could hardly call the job I have important.'

Edward looked at him closely but found nothing but sincerity in his face.

'I think that would be an excellent solution, Miss Brennan, and if you won't consider a change of air, then you *must* rest.'

'I'll see that she does,' Johanna said firmly. She felt it was very unselfish of Patrick to help out like this. 'And Tilly for one will be delighted that you will be staying at home in future.'

'And so will Catherine. She says the days can be lonely,' Patrick added. Everyone was in complete agreement with the solution. Jess was even adamant about not going on a holiday which would have made things difficult for him. If she had gone away he wouldn't have been able to give her the drugged cocoa each night and she would soon have recovered. When Terence came next he would be able to report the complete success of their plan. Soon he would be free, free of them all.

Jess had felt certain that at the end of a week she would have felt much better, but here it was almost two weeks later and all she did was sleep. She tried not to worry about the business. Patrick assured her that nothing serious had gone wrong and that he was learning the ropes quite well, according to Mary, her supervisor. He assured her they were all coping, both at work and at home. Catherine was proving herself very adept at running the house and it gave her something to do all day. She also took a keen interest in Tilly's welfare, so Jess had nothing at all to worry about. She just had to get well.

'But I'm not, Edward,' she said fretfully when he called to see her.

He frowned. She was getting thinner and her complexion was becoming dull; her eyes were ringed with dark circles.

'Are you eating properly, Jess?'

'Yes. Catherine is very good. She brings my breakfast and lunch up and I try my best to go down for supper.'

'I think you should see Dr Marsden again.'

'Oh, Edward, what good will it do? You heard what he said. It's not a physical thing. It's emotional and there's no medicine for that.'

'Then maybe you really should think about taking a holiday. Just for a week, Jess? Patrick has surprised us all, you'll have to agree.'

She nodded slowly. 'You could be right, Edward.'

He sighed with relief. He was desperately worried that she

would never recover and he simply hated to see her like this. 'Good. Where would you like to go? I know the weather this time of year isn't at its best, but I hear the Isle of Man is very pleasant. I've never been there myself.'

'I've never been anywhere.'

'Then let's discover the Isle of Man together.'

Jess managed a wry smile. 'Without a chaperone? Oh, how people would talk!'

He smiled back. 'We could take Tilly.'

'Much as I'm sure she'd love to go I don't want to take her out of school. There are all sorts of activities for Christmas coming up: a carol concert, a nativity play, a party. She's been excited for weeks and I've been worried that I might not be able to attend them.'

'A week away and you'll be fit and well again, able to keep up with everything and enjoy all her little escapades. Do you think your aunt would come with us? While you are still so under the weather you'll need some help, feminine help.'

'I think she would be delighted. It's a long time since she had a holiday.'

'Shall I make the arrangements?' he pressed, not wishing to give her time to change her mind.

'Yes please, Edward.'

'Then I'll leave you to get some rest, but I'll call tomorrow.'

'Thank you. You are being so kind and thoughtful. Will you ask Aunt Jo?'

'Of course. Now rest.'

Patrick met him in the hall. 'Everything all right, Edward?'

'Fine. She's getting anxious that she's not improving but I've managed to persuade her to take a holiday. We're going to the Isle of Man for a week. It'll do her the world of good. Now I'm off to see Mrs Kiernan, to tell her the good news and ask her to come with us. Jess will need some help and we also need a chaperone. I know we can trust you to keep the business going, you're doing a good job, Patrick.' He smiled. 'We'll make a tycoon out of you yet!'

Patrick forced himself to smile back but he felt as though an icy hand had gripped his throat. Bloody Edward! Bloody interfering Edward Dempsey! How the hell could he stop her going away for a week? The answer was that he couldn't. Johanna would agree wholeheartedly and what could he say? He would be accused of not wanting his sister to get well.

He went into the sitting room and poured himself a drink. He'd just have to resign himself to the fact that it might take longer. She would certainly feel better when she returned, but it would only be a matter of time before her mystery 'illness' returned.

Johanna thought it an excellent idea and Edward booked them into the Excelsior Hotel on Douglas Promenade. They were sailing on the *Lady of Man* on the evening of December 4. They all prayed the weather wouldn't be bad.

Tilly had been upset that she wasn't included in the holiday.

'I don't want you to miss any of the excitement at school,' Jess had explained.

'I won't! We've got ages to Christmas yet.'

'But you have to practise – rehearse, or you'll forget your lines. And you know you've promised to help make the decorations. You can't let Miss Fielding down now. Besides, I'm sure you would be bored just going for walks with Edward and me and Aunt Jo. I promise I'll take you there next summer for a week. It will be lots of fun then. You can play on the beach – paddle or swim in the sea. You certainly can't do that at this time of year.'

Thus mollified, Tilly had turned her efforts to helping Jess and Johanna pack.

'You will make sure she doesn't catch cold, Edward?' Catherine fussed as they stood in the hall waiting for the cab that would take them to the docks. She too was relieved that Jess was taking a holiday and she didn't mind in the least looking after Tilly and running the house.

Jess was muffled to the eyes in a heavy wool coat with a huge fur collar and matching fur hat that covered her ears. As an added precaution Johanna had insisted she wrap a cashmere stole around her.

Jess had laughed at the reflection of herself in the hall mirror. 'I look like one of those funny Russian dolls.'

'The night air can be treacherous. I do hope that wind doesn't get any stronger.'

'I don't think it will and it's quite a clear night, so there probably won't be any rain,' Edward said reassuringly.

'Remember, you promised you'd visit everything so you can tell me all about it,' Tilly pressed.

'I will and I'll bring you something too. *You* remember that you promised to be good for Catherine!' Jess reminded her, giving her a quick final hug as the sound of wheels and hooves came to their ears.

'There's the cab now. Come back fit and well and don't worry about anything here. We will all cope,' Catherine urged, holding the front door open for them. Her new responsibilities had given her more confidence.

Despite the hour and the weather the docks were still busy. Edward found a porter for their luggage and escorted them onto the *Lady of Man*. He had booked cabins for them all and insisted on escorting Jess and Johanna to theirs first.

'It's been a long day, Jess, you need your rest now,' he said firmly.

'Oh, but I wanted to be on deck to see us sail out,' Jess protested, although she did feel tired.

'You can be on deck when we come back. You'll be much better then and besides, there really isn't much to see.'

'The moon is quite bright,' she protested rather weakly.

'Edward is right. You need your rest. Travelling is tiring,' Johanna agreed. She didn't want Jess to be on deck as they sailed down river and out into the estuary and the bay. It was a journey Martin Brennan had made so many times, and she wanted nothing to remind Jess of her loss. She was quite determined that this holiday was going to restore Jess to health and she was very glad that Edward was with them. If only she could encourage Jess to accept him she was certain Jess's life would be much easier. He had money, he was steady, he would accept Tilly. Patrick and Catherine were getting on well. Tom had been right. Marriage had been the making of Patrick. Look how well he was doing with Jess's business. No one would ever have believed it. Jess could leave the running of the business in Patrick's safe hands.

They had all slept well and Jess did feel a little better.

'It's a beautiful day and I've a cab and a porter waiting,'

Edward informed them as he shepherded them towards the gangway.

On deck Johanna breathed deeply and looked around. 'Oh, you're right, Edward. It's a lovely day and how pretty it is.'

Jess had to agree. Although cold, the day was bright and fine. The weak winter sunlight danced on the rippling wavelets of the wide, sandy bay, which curved in a perfect semicircle. The fine hotels along the promenade were pristine in the morning sunlight and horse-drawn trams could be seen moving backwards and forwards along the wide, tree-lined thoroughfare. Out in the bay the tiny island, no more than a collection of rocks with a lighthouse, looked less sinister than it did by moonlight.

'Oh, I feel so much better already. I think I'm going to enjoy this little break,' Jess exclaimed as Edward directed the cab driver to the hotel.

Chapter Twenty-Five

A FTER FOUR DAYS JESS felt like her old self. She was sleeping far less, eating more, was alert, interested and could concentrate.

The weather was holding. By day it was clear and bright with no wind to speak of. By night the sky was a deep indigo scattered with stars, the moon milky white with a halo of light surrounding it that foretold of heavy frost.

They fell into the habit, each morning, of walking the length of the promenade and catching a tram back. They had been to Peel with its pretty harbour where the fishing fleet tied up, and its ruined castle on St Patrick's Isle. They had been to see the Laxey Wheel that pumped water from the mine beneath where men sweated in the darkness to extract the tin and copper and small amounts of silver.

Edward had hired a small boat and planned to take a picnic to Niarbyl Head and see the seabirds and other wildlife on the steep cliffs there. Johanna had refused point blank to go.

'I couldn't! I just *couldn't* go out in a small boat! I'm not a good sailor and I'm terrified of being so close to the sea. And what if the weather changed? I believe it can.'

'Oh, Aunt Jo, you're priceless,' Jess laughed.

'We're not going alone, Johanna. The owner of the boat is coming along too. I couldn't sail it on my own. I wouldn't know where to start,' Edward urged.

'No, thank you, Edward. It's something I just can't do. I'll stay here and do some shopping. There are some lovely shops along the promenade, very quaint. You two go and enjoy yourselves.' She had tried on a number of occasions to cry off from their outings, wanting Jess and Edward to spend more time together, but her ventures hadn't been very successful – until now. This was the perfect opportunity. She was telling the truth. She was terrified and she was a terrible sailor. She'd even felt queasy on the ferry coming over and the sea had been calm then.

So they went without her. Edward carried the picnic basket and a heavy tartan rug while Jess was well wrapped up and carried two large umbrellas, in case the weather did change.

The burly Manxman who owned the small *Nickie* helped them down and got them settled before he cast off.

'It's a grand day for it. You shouldn't need those,' he said with a smile, indicating the umbrellas.

Jess laughed. 'Better safe than sorry.' She settled back while Edward tucked the rug over her knees.

It was very invigorating she thought as she watched the coastline slip past and the breeze generated by the boat ruffled the feathers on her hat. She was sure now that whatever had been wrong with her was over and done with. She was fully recovered. Edward had been right about this holiday.

They put ashore in a small secluded rocky cove and their captain lit his pipe and settled down for a rest. Edward carried the basket and the rug and helped Jess over the damp shingle to a grassy hillock overlooking the tiny beach.

Jess settled herself on the rug and gazed out to sea. Edward had been so good to her. He had known what was best for her and had taken control of things. Where else would she find a man like him? She knew she should talk more seriously to him about their future but still she held back. Oh, what was the matter with her? What more did she want? she asked herself irritably.

'You're miles away, Jess,' Edward said quietly.

She pulled herself together. 'I was just thinking how peaceful it is here and how good of you to bring me.'

'I had to do something, Jess. I could see you slipping away before my eyes. I was getting desperate.'

'I'm so glad you did, Edward. It's just what I needed.'

'Promise me you won't hurl yourself into that damned business the minute we get home?'

She laughed. 'Well, not the minute I get home at least.'

'Patrick's doing quite well on his own and I think it's good for him.'

'He never seemed to enjoy anything he did before.'

'Because he was never in charge. He was always an underling. Now he probably feels he's working for the "family business". It's much better for his pride, his self-esteem.'

Jess looked thoughtful. 'I never thought of it like that.'

'You have to admit he's changed, Jess.'

'Oh, he has. Do you think it would be better for him if I played a lesser part in the business?' Much as she didn't really like the idea, if it helped Patrick's confidence she would do it. She didn't want to see him slip back into his old ways.

'I do, Jess. I really do.'

She nodded. 'It's agreed then. Now, let's not waste any more time on the business or Patrick. I'm starving. What have they packed for us?'

Patrick fretted and fumed to himself and was short-tempered with both Catherine and Tilly. He should have done *something*. *Anything*, to have stopped Jess going away. And to add to it all Ronan had called twice, ostensibly to see that Tilly was behaving herself, as he said he'd promised Johanna he would. Patrick felt it was more likely to see if *he* was behaving himself. He was relieved that Terence was coming tonight.

He'd made sure that both Catherine and Tilly were asleep and that he'd spread out Jess's ledgers and order books on the dining-room table before he went into the kitchen to wait for Terence.

Midnight came and went and there was no sign of Terence. Patrick began to get seriously worried. What could possibly have delayed him? Hadn't he been able to get a further supply of the powder? Had he been injured? Was he ill? The questions circled round and round in his head as he paced the floor. Had he – oh, God! – abandoned him? That was a thought too terrible to contemplate.

At ten past one he was debating whether he should go to bed. He wouldn't sleep but it would be warmer at least. The fire in the range was nearly dead and he didn't want to risk fetching more coal to make it up because of the noise. He was still hesitating when the door slowly opened.

'Terence! Thank God! I'd nearly given you up!'

Shay was not in a good mood. 'There's a bloody riot going on along Scotland Road! It took me hours to get past them, sneaking around the back-cracks and the police cordons.'

'What and who . . . ?'

'The usual drunken rabble complaining about their lot! I've no patience with them!'

'Well, you made it safely.'

'Pour me a drink, Pat. I'm worn out.'

Patrick did as he was asked.

'And how is Jess this week?' Shay asked, standing close to the dying fire.

'She . . . she's not here.'

'Where the hell is she?' Shay demanded.

'I couldn't do anything about it, Terence. I couldn't stop her, it would have looked suspicious. Edward Dempsey insisted she go for a holiday and Johanna's gone with them!'

'That bloody interfering martinet!'

'They've gone to the Isle of Man. They'll be back on Friday.'

'Did they take that brat?'

'No. Something about not wanting her to miss school. But it's not too bad really, Terence. It just means that it will take longer. As soon as she's back I'll start giving her the powder again.'

'And what if someone realises that it's only at home that she gets ill?'

'Then so what? That fancy doctor said it was emotional. Sort of all in the mind. Connected with all the tragedies. Maybe we could persuade her to move away from Liverpool altogether for her health. Then we wouldn't need to give her the drug at all.'

'We might at that, Pat. Good idea. Well, I won't have to go for more of this stuff this week. It will save us a couple of pounds. Opiates don't come cheap. How much do you think we can syphon off from her accounts this week?'

'I've got the ledgers and order books in the dining room. You're the one with the head for figures, come and take a look. I have to be very careful. Ronan checks her accounts.'

They pored over the books, Shay making notes and totting up figures, Patrick with his arm around Shay's shoulder. Neither heard the door open or saw Catherine standing in the doorway, her hand to her mouth.

'Who? Patrick, who . . . is . . . this?' she stammered. It was very late. She'd found the door to the spare room open and Patrick had not been in bed, so she'd come to beg him to finish up for tonight.

They both spun around, Patrick's face flushing, Shay with narrowed eyes.

'Catherine! What the hell are you doing snooping around?' Patrick demanded, feigning anger.

'I'm not snooping, Patrick! It's very late, you weren't in bed . . . Who is this?'

'A friend. A friend from work, he . . . he's come to help me with the books.'

'Why has he come in the middle of the night? Why did you have your arm around him? I don't understand, Patrick!'

'She's got too much to bloody well say!' Shay growled. This was something else he could do without. His plans had been going so well – up till now. Why did Patrick have to leave everything to him? All the skilful planning had had to be done by himself. Couldn't Patrick understand it was for *their* future, and help him?

Catherine stepped backwards. She didn't like this man. He looked menacing and rough and he'd sworn. Fear began to well up inside her. She made to turn away.

Shay let out a cry and sprang forward. He grabbed her by the shoulder and dragged her into the room.

Catherine screamed in fear and pain.

'For Christ's sake, shut her up, Pat! Shut her up!' Shay snarled.

Patrick looked helplessly on. What would Catherine do? Would she go to Ronan as soon as she could and tell him? That would be the end of everything!

'She's been snooping! Haven't you? Haven't you?' Shay shook a terrified Catherine who tried to protest. 'You'll say nothing about any of this, do you hear, girl! Not a word to anyone! I was never here.'

Catherine was now so frightened she couldn't speak.

Shay hit her across the face twice, hard, her head snapping from side to side with the impact. 'Not a word or I'll kill you! I mean it!'

'For God's sake, Terence!' Patrick cried aloud. He'd never seen him like this before.

'Pat, I . . . *we're* not going to have her ruin everything, the sneaking little bitch!'

Catherine tried to pull away but he hit her again and she fell, banging her head on the brass fender. She didn't move.

'Oh, God! She . . . she's dead!' Patrick clung to the back of a chair for support.

Shay knelt down and gripped her wrist. 'She's not. Just unconscious. Pull yourself together, Pat!' he shouted. Everything was going wrong. All his carefully laid plans were falling apart before his eyes. Patrick was a fool! A useless fool! 'What's the matter with you? If she doesn't come to, say you found her like this. Say she must have . . . tripped or fainted. Don't lose your nerve now, Pat! We have to stick together in this. We can't throw away our future just because the stupid bitch saw us together. Control yourself! Pat, what the hell is wrong with you?'

Patrick's face was a mask of fear and his eyes were fixed on the open doorway.

Shay turned and fury flooded his face as he caught sight of Tilly. Another sneaking, snooping little bitch. How he hated her. *She* was responsible for *all* this! He let out a roar and jumped to his feet.

Tilly turned and ran. Panic tore through her as she raced for the stairs. She'd lock herself in her bedroom so they couldn't get to her. They'd hurt Catherine! *He'd* shouted he'd kill her and he'd hit her and she'd fallen and wasn't moving! *He* wasn't supposed to be here! Jess had thrown him out. But he was back. He must know that Jess wasn't here. Patrick had let him come back and now he'd killed Catherine!

She screamed in fright as Shay caught her and she began to kick and yell. What was he going to do to her? Was he going to kill her too? Terror gave her strength and she renewed her efforts to escape from him but he was too strong for her and he dragged her into the kitchen.

'You've hurt Catherine! I'm going to tell Ronan you hit her! You've killed her! Jess said you couldn't come here. I'll tell her! I'll tell everyone what you've done,' she screamed.

'She's seen too much, Pat! She *will* tell!' Shay was so furious that his rage was like a red mist descending over his reasoning.

Patrick was white and shaking. He'd not bargained for anything like this. 'Oh, God! Terence, what are we going to do?'

Tilly bit hard into the flesh of the hand Shay was using to cover her mouth and tried to kick out again.

'You little bitch!' Shay roared, catching her around the neck.

Tilly was terrified. She'd never been so afraid in all her life. And now everything was getting dark, she couldn't breathe and she had no strength left. Shay shook her like a rag doll and in a couple of seconds her short life was over.

Shay took his hands from her throat and let her limp little body fall to the ground.

'Jesus! Oh, Jesus! You've killed her!' Patrick was almost hysterical.

Shay was trying to compose himself. 'The little bitch knew too much, Pat! You heard her. She said she'd tell everyone. I *had* to do it! Did you want us both to go to jail! To lose everything! Because of a little slummy like that?'

'But . . . we . . . we'll . . . hang for this!' Patrick was crying and slobbering in fear and shock.

'We won't! I'll get rid of her before Catherine comes round. Pull yourself together, Pat, for God's sake, or we *will* hang!' Shay began to pace up and down, his mind working swiftly. 'We'll tell them you had a row with her and she . . . she ran away. Go and get a bag and some of her things. For God's sake, *move*, Pat!' he shouted, shoving Patrick towards the door.

Patrick stumbled up the stairs and into Tilly's room where the lamp was still burning. He dragged a small bag from a cupboard, then, opening the wardrobe, he snatched a few things and stuffed them into the bag. Suddenly he sat down on the bed. Oh, God, he was going to pass out! He felt sick! He dragged up the sash window and breathed deeply. He'd never meant any of this to happen. Now Tilly was dead and Catherine unconscious – and maybe she'd die too! Terence would have to find a way out of all this for them both or they'd both swing from the end of a rope! He swayed, his eyes closed, then forced himself to go downstairs with the bag.

The kitchen was empty. He poured himself a large whiskey, his hands shaking so much that he slopped a good deal of it. He gulped it down and was pouring himself another when Shay came in.

'What have you done?'

'I'll take care of it. I said I would. I won't leave her here.'

'Where? What?' Patrick stammered, refilling his glass for the third time.

'I'll take her back with me. They might find her washed up or in the dock in a couple of days or weeks, depending on the tides. Did you get her things?'

Patrick indicated the bag. 'What about Catherine?'

'Get her to her bedroom. Lay her on the floor and then if she's still out cold in the morning, say you found her like that. She must have tripped and fallen. Lay her near the fireplace, so it looks as though she hit her head.'

'But what if she . . . she tells?'

'She won't! She can't, Pat! Remind her of what I said I'd do. Tell her I meant it. Convince her, Pat. Surely you can do that? You *do* understand how much is depending on that?'

Patrick nodded miserably. 'What will I tell her about Tilly?'

'Say you had a row and you shouted at her and then in the morning you found she'd packed her bags and gone. Where, you don't know. Use your bloody imagination, Pat, for God's sake! Now, I'd better go. Put all these damned lights out or you'll have the neighbours wondering what's going on. I won't be able to come here for a while. Until things settle down. You've enough opiate to give Jess and, Pat,' he finished grimly, 'you'll *have* to make sure she takes it or all this will have been for nothing!'

Suddenly the room was empty. Empty and cold. Bitterly cold, Patrick thought, shivering. Oh, damn Catherine! He forced himself to go back into the dining room. Why? Why had she come down? He tried to pull himself together and bent down and shook her shoulder, praying she wasn't dead too.

She groaned and stirred and he almost burst into tears of relief.

'Patrick? Patrick, my head . . . It . . . hurts.'

He helped her to sit up and she looked at him in confusion. 'What happened?'

'You fell. You banged your head.'

The dazed look left her eyes. 'That man! That man hit me! Has he gone? Has he gone, Patrick?'

'Yes! You're not to tell anyone he was here. No one, Catherine!'

'He . . . he said he'd kill me!'

'And he will. He meant it, Catherine. You have to forget *everything* that happened tonight!'

She looked scared. 'Tilly! I thought I heard Tilly's voice.'

'You didn't!' he lied. 'Tilly's in bed!'

'Oh, Patrick, I don't understand . . .'

'Let me help you to bed, Catherine. Remember, not a single word. You promise?'

'I . . . I . . . promise, Patrick,' she whispered. For the first time she wished she had never set foot in this house. Never even set eyes on Patrick Brennan.

It was with some relief that Patrick carried her up the stairs. He laid her on the bed and covered her and she clutched his hand.

'Patrick, I'm frightened and my head hurts.'

'Just lie there, Catherine. I'll go and get you something to make you sleep,' he soothed.

She lay back and stared at the ceiling until he returned.

'Drink this, it's only laudanum, it'll help you sleep.'

She drank it slowly and then lay back. He stayed with her, without speaking, until her eyes closed. Oh, would this dreadful night ever end?

Chapter Twenty-Six

———◆◆◆◆———

THE WEATHER HAD BROKEN the day they left for home. Showers of hailstones driven by a howling gale sheeted down on the *Lady of Man* as she made her way across the Irish Sea through towering waves.

Johanna had never felt so ill or so afraid in her entire life. She was convinced they were all going to die. She clung to the edge of the bunk and begged Jess not to leave her. Jess, although a little queasy, was trying to bolster her own spirits.

'Aunt Jo, we're not going to die! It's just because you're so seasick that it all seems worse. Try and get some sleep. Edward won't let anything happen to us.' But she told herself she wouldn't be entirely happy until they were safely tied up at the Landing Stage and her feet were on firm ground again.

They were all pale, tired and very thankful when the ferry at last sailed up the Mersey, battered and with sections of her rail missing, torn away by the sea.

'If I never have another holiday in my life, I won't care!'

Johanna declared as Edward helped her into a cab. She was still shaking and queasy.

'Such a pity that that journey had to spoil an otherwise perfect week. But we're home safe and sound now,' Edward consoled her.

Jess smiled at him. 'It was perfect, wasn't it? Still, I'm glad to be back.'

'Jess, you remember what you promised?' Edward reminded her.

She laughed. 'I know. I'll leave Patrick to get on with things. Anyway, I'll have enough to do now with Christmas being so close.'

'The first thing I intend to do is have a bath and then I'm going for a rest. They will have managed quite well without me, so another day won't do them any harm,' Johanna said thankfully as the streets slipped by them.

'I can't see me getting much rest. Tilly will want to know *everything* and will no doubt have a catalogue of complaints about Patrick,' Jess mused.

Jess knew something was wrong the minute they arrived home for both Catherine and Patrick were waiting for her.

'Patrick, why aren't you at work? What's happened?' she demanded.

'Jess, Aunt Jo, Edward, I hope you had a good trip, but I think you'd better all come in.' Patrick had been dreading this moment and he'd rehearsed over and over what he was going to say.

'Catherine, what's wrong with your face, child?' Johanna cried. Catherine's face was a mass of bruises and she looked pale and apprehensive.

'I . . . I . . . had a fall. It's nothing. It looks worse than it is,' Catherine replied, near to tears. Patrick had impressed on her over and over again how important it was not to let them suspect anything untoward had happened to her. It was going to be hard enough for him to explain Tilly's absence. It hadn't been easy to explain it to Catherine.

'Have you seen Dr Chambers?' Johanna pressed.

'It's not necessary, Aunt Jo. Catherine feels perfectly all right. As she said, it just looks worse than it is.'

'So, if it's not Catherine . . . ?' Jess queried.

'It's Tilly,' Patrick said quietly.

Jess was instantly alarmed. 'Tilly? What's wrong?'

Patrick thrust his hands into his pockets. Oh, God, this was the dreaded moment. He just hoped he could be convincing. 'I . . . we . . . had a huge fight. About something totally stupid. She . . . she's gone, Jess.'

Jess stared at him in disbelief. 'Gone? Gone where?'

'I don't know, Jess. Truly I don't.'

Catherine could stand it no longer. She burst into tears. 'Oh, Jess! We didn't know what to do!'

Patrick glared at her. 'Catherine, pull yourself together! It's not your fault. It's mine.'

Johanna, although very concerned, put her arms around the weeping girl.

'Patrick,' Jess demanded, 'what happened? Where is she? When did she go?'

'I told you we had a terrible fight. Next morning when Catherine went to wake her, she'd gone. She took a bag of clothes with her. I've searched and searched. I've asked the neighbours but . . . nothing.' He spread his hands wide.

'How long has she been gone?' Edward demanded. Poor Jess. This was the last thing she needed. Couldn't Patrick be trusted even to keep control of things on the domestic front for a few days?

'Three days.'

'Three days!' Jess cried. 'What did you say to her, Patrick?'

'Oh, Jess, I don't really remember! Something along the lines that she was a pest, a burden, a worry to you. She yelled back that she hated me. She didn't want me living here and if I wouldn't go then she would. I didn't take any notice of her, Jess! She . . . she's just a child!'

'Oh, Aunt Jo, Edward! We've got to do something! We've *got* to find her. She's not used to living on the streets now.' Jess was utterly distracted.

'I don't suppose it's something you forget easily, Jess,' Patrick said.

Jess rounded on him. 'Patrick, how can you say such a thing?'

'Could she have gone back to Hunter's Yard?' Edward asked.

'No, I went there and asked,' Patrick said. It had been one of the first places he'd gone to establish his story's credibility.

'You've checked the offices and the workrooms and the stockrooms?' Edward asked.

Patrick nodded.

'Oh, I shouldn't have gone away! I shouldn't have left her. I should have taken her with us,' Jess cried.

'Jess, you can't blame yourself,' Edward said, glaring at Patrick. What kind of a fool was he to be arguing with a twelve-year-old child?

'I do!' Jess cried, near to tears.

Edward took charge. 'I'll go straight to the police and notify them. Ask them to search.' All the good the holiday had done Jess was being undermined.

'What good will it do? There're thousands of kids roaming the streets of Liverpool. She's only one of them,' Patrick said dismissively. He didn't want the police involved in any way.

'I'll go just the same,' Edward said firmly.

'Aunt Jo, come up with me to her room. Let's see what she's taken or if she's left me some sort of a note.'

'I've looked, Jess. She hasn't.'

Jess turned on her brother. 'Patrick, this is all your fault! If . . . if anything has happened to her I'll never forgive you!'

'It's *not*! Jess, you spoiled her! She was getting completely out of hand!' Patrick blustered. He'd steeled himself for this. He prayed he'd thought of all eventualities and appropriate answers. He just hoped he was convincing. But he was frightened.

Jess stormed from the room followed by Johanna.

'You go through the drawers, I'll look in the wardrobe,' Jess instructed, rifling through Tilly's dresses and coats.

'She doesn't appear to have taken anything. No underclothes or stockings,' Johanna reported. Everything was neatly in place. Tilly was quite a tidy child.

'She's taken some dresses and a coat. See if she's left a note anywhere, Aunt Jo, please?' Jess begged.

Johanna searched but found nothing. 'Oh, Jess, I'm so sorry. What a homecoming! What on earth possessed her to run away?' It was just too bad of Tilly to do something like this. But Patrick must have really upset her for her to leave when she had been so full of the forthcoming Christmas activities. She had pleaded to be allowed to make mince pies for the party. Like Edward, Johanna laid the blame at Patrick's door. Tilly wasn't a difficult child if you knew how to handle her, but Patrick obviously didn't.

Jess sat down on the padded window seat. Something wasn't right: why had Tilly taken no underclothes or stockings? Her gaze rested on the bed: there was something else she hadn't taken.

'Her dolls! Aunt Jo, she's left her dolls!'

Johanna looked a little confused. 'Well, there's so many of them, Jess.'

'But she never, never goes anywhere without them, not after what Terence Shay did to them. She'd have taken them or at least one or two. They're all here, every single one!' A deeper fear began to take hold of Jess. 'Oh, Aunt Jo, I'm afraid! I . . . I don't think Patrick is telling the truth.'

'But Jess, what else could have happened?'

'I don't know, but I'm going to find out.'

Johanna followed Jess as she ran downstairs and back into the sitting room.

'Jess, what's wrong now? You look terrible!' Patrick cried. He'd hoped all this wouldn't drag on, but the ordeal wasn't over yet.

'She's left her dolls!'

He stared at her blankly. Dolls? Had Jess lost her reason? 'Dolls?' he said, looking mystified.

'Tilly would never go anywhere without her dolls!

Catherine, you know that!' she appealed to her sister-in-law.

Catherine started to cry. She was frightened and she hated to see Jess so upset and worried.

Inwardly Patrick froze. Her bloody dolls! Why in God's name hadn't he thought of that? But it was so . . . petty!

'Jess, she couldn't possibly have taken that collection off with her. She would have needed a suitcase!' he said, trying to sound reasonable.

'I *know* Tilly! I *know* she wouldn't have left all of them! Patrick, I want to know what exactly happened. I demand to know.'

'Oh, for God's sake, Jess, I told you. She was ranting and raving, saying she wouldn't stay. She just ran away, that's all! Children often do!'

Jess glared at him. 'I don't believe you.'

Patrick appealed to his aunt. 'Can't you do anything with her, Aunt Jo?'

'Jess, this isn't helping. I think Patrick is right. She just ran away, not thinking. If she was so angry and upset, do you think she would have been bothered about her dolls?'

'Yes I *do*!' Jess persisted.

'Well, I don't. Now, let's have a cup of tea and calm down. Edward has gone to the police station, that's all we can do. Let them look for her. Getting into such a state isn't going to do you any good, Jess. You have to think of your health.'

'Oh, damn my health!' Jess cried, flinging herself into a chair, already feeling exhausted. She would never rest properly until she got to the bottom of this and found Tilly. That was all that mattered.

* * *

By the following afternoon there was still no word of the missing child and Jess was distraught. The police, with Patrick, Ronan, Tom and Edward, had searched every single place any of them could think of where she might have gone.

Johanna was very worried not only about Tilly, but also about Jess's health and that of Catherine. There was something very wrong with the girl: she seemed to be in another world and kept dissolving into tears. Johanna had made Jess go to bed and try to rest and was determined to have a talk to Patrick's young wife. She made a pot of tea and took it into the sitting room. They were alone. All the men were out.

'Catherine dear, sit down here beside me and we'll have some tea.'

Warily Catherine sat.

'Is there something wrong, dear? Apart from Tilly's disappearance?' Johanna asked gently.

'No. No, really!' Catherine cried. Oh, how she wished she could confide all her fears to Johanna. She was certain that that terrible man was responsible for Tilly's disappearance. Like Jess, she *knew* Tilly would never go away and leave her 'family'.

'How did you manage to fall? You do look as though you should have had Dr Chambers to see you.'

'I . . . I tripped over the rug.'

'Where was Patrick? Didn't he hear you fall?'

'He was downstairs . . . working. I . . . When I came to, he was bending over me. He was very concerned.' Catherine held tightly on to her cup, afraid she would spill the tea. Her hands were shaking.

'And so he should be. I really can't understand why he didn't call the doctor.'

'Really, it's nothing.'

Johanna placed a hand on the girl's arm. 'Catherine, if there was anything wrong between you and Patrick, you would confide in me, wouldn't you? It must be very hard not having your mother to discuss . . . things . . . with. I do know that marriage can be difficult at times. Tom's sister Carmel found it particularly so.'

Catherine knew about Carmel Kiernan and couldn't keep back the tears. 'Oh, Aunt Jo, I . . . I wish Patrick . . .' She couldn't go on. If she said anything more it might open the flood gates and she'd say something she'd regret and then that man would kill her, just as she was sure now that he'd killed Tilly.

'What about Patrick, dear?'

Catherine shook her head. She'd said too much.

Johanna patted her hand. Upset as she was the girl wasn't going to open up to her – yet.

She relayed her conversation and her worries to both Tom and Ronan that night.

Ronan had serious misgivings about Patrick and the row that had apparently caused Tilly's disappearance. Privately he agreed with Jess about the dolls and he was certain Patrick wasn't telling the truth. He hated to see Jess so upset and worried, especially as his mother had said she had made a remarkable recovery. He'd hated, too, the thought of her being away with Edward Dempsey, but the presence of his mother as chaperone had comforted him a little. He had no right to have such feelings, he told himself, but it didn't help ease the burning jealousy.

'I'm going to have a talk with Patrick. See if I can get anything more out of him,' he informed his parents.

'I wish you would, although he does seem genuinely worried,' Johanna replied. 'As for poor Catherine, I can't get her to tell me what's wrong, but she's very, very upset.'

Tom and Ronan exchanged glances. Both felt that Catherine's story of her fall wasn't exactly true. Patrick knew far more than he was telling them.

Ronan found Patrick tired and irritable and he'd had quite a few drinks.

'Drowning your sorrows?' he asked curtly.

'What the hell do you want? Can't a man get a bit of peace in his own home?' Patrick shot back.

Ronan glared at him. He was pathetic. 'What really happened to Catherine? Father and I don't believe a single word of that tripping up and falling business. You hit her, didn't you? What did she do to annoy you? Demand what any young wife would? That her husband show her some love and affection?'

Patrick flushed. 'You mind your own bloody business! That's between Catherine and me! And for your information, no, I didn't hit her and that's the truth!'

'Someone did. Was it Shay? Has he been here? Have you had him here while Jess has been away?' Ronan demanded. He wouldn't put it past Patrick.

Patrick's eyes narrowed. 'You go to hell, Ronan! What I do is my own affair.'

'Not if it's under Jess's roof, it isn't! *Was* he here? Did Tilly see him? Was that what caused the row and made her run away? What did you and that . . . creature say to her?'

Patrick got to his feet. 'Get out of here, Ronan! I know how you feel about Jess. It's jealousy that's eating you up inside. Jealousy towards Edward Dempsey! Well, you can never have her!'

Ronan caught him by the lapels of his jacket as fury surged through him. 'If you hurt her in any way, and that includes harming Tilly, I'll . . . I'll kill you with my bare hands! I swear to God I will! You're right, I can never have her any more than you can have that . . . that evil genius Shay. And if you lay a finger on Catherine again you'll be sorry! You're a weak, despicable excuse for a man! Only someone like you would beat a woman!'

Although afraid, Patrick found the strength to push him away. 'Get out of here! I've never touched Catherine!'

'And that's part of the trouble, isn't it? How long do you think you can go on like this? She's bound sooner or later to confide in Mother or Jess. What will you do then? How will you explain that away?'

'Get out! What I do is my own business! And this is my home, whether you like it or not! Get out!'

Ronan stormed from the room. He'd meant what he'd said. If Patrick ever hurt Jess, he'd kill him and damn the consequences.

'Well, what did he say?' Tom demanded.

'He's sticking to his story but I'm sure Shay has been round there, and I'm equally sure it was he who hit Catherine.

Patrick didn't deny it but I can't prove anything.'

'Those two are up to no good, Ronan. By God they're not! It's Jess's money they're after and Shay will stop at nothing to get it, you mark my words. He's manipulating or blackmailing Patrick.'

'Do you think poor Catherine is in any real danger? Is it our fault?'

'We did it for the best, Ronan.'

'It doesn't seem to be turning out like that. If anything has happened to Tilly, it may be Catherine next! God, sometimes I think we should have left well alone.'

'Nonsense! Let Patrick disgrace us? Think what it would have done to your mother and Jess if he'd been caught and sent to jail.'

'What about Catherine?'

'Shay won't be fool enough to try to harm Catherine, not now. Patrick is bound to tell him we're suspicious. It might even cause them to pause and think about whatever it is they're up to.' Tom was firm.

'I just hope you're right, Dad. For Catherine's sake, I hope you're right.'

Chapter Twenty-Seven

IT WAS A WEEK SINCE Tilly had disappeared, Jess thought dejectedly as she gazed out of the bedroom window at the gun-metal-coloured skies from which the cold rain descended unrelentingly. She had suffered agonies of fear and despair, wondering what had happened to the child. Was she lying somewhere, hurt, hungry, frightened? Tilly was now used to a comfortable, safe home. It was so cold at night. Oh, God! Was she lying freezing, in some doorway or alley with not even a blanket to cover her? Soaked by the cold rain, alone, crying. It just didn't bear thinking about. She was torturing herself. Oh, where was she? It still disturbed her terribly that no one, except Ronan and Catherine, thought it very odd that the child had left the dolls she loved so much. If she *had* forgotten them what did that mean? Had she in fact run away or had someone driven her away? Patrick was adamant about the row, but could she trust him? And there had been some argument between him and Ronan. Nor was Catherine herself at all. What in God's name had gone on in this house while she had been away? Oh, what kind of a Christmas was this going to be now?

Catherine's voice broke into her thoughts. 'Edward is here to see you, Jess.'

'Has he any news?' she asked, her eyes searching Catherine's face.

Catherine shook her head. 'No. He just wants to see you, Jess.'

The flicker of hope died as Jess followed her sister-in-law downstairs.

'Edward, I thought . . .' She spread her hands helplessly.

'I'm so sorry, Jess. I came to see if you would like to go out this evening?'

Jess shook her head. 'Thank you, Edward, but . . .'

He hated to see her so distressed. 'Jess, you can't stay in for ever.'

'I know, but everywhere is so festive. Oh, Edward, I can't bear it! She was so looking forward to Christmas! All the activities at school, making decorations, helping me to decorate here and bake and . . . and I've got her presents. They're just waiting to be wrapped!' She couldn't stand it any longer and burst into tears.

Edward took her in his arms. 'Oh, Jess, we've searched everywhere! If there was some way I could find her, bring her home . . . I'd move heaven and earth to do it! I hate to see you so upset. I know how much you loved her, but you can't spend your life mourning.'

'But I can't just forget her!'

'Of course you can't, but your life has to go on. You're going to make yourself ill again.'

'I feel so ill now, Edward!'

He looked concerned as he stroked her hair. 'Are the symptoms back?'

'Yes. I feel so exhausted, as if I'm walking in a dream – a nightmare!'

'And are you sleeping as much?'

'Yes. I go to bed thinking I won't sleep a wink, worrying about her, but I do!'

Edward felt cold fingers of fear clutch at his heart. If the tragedies of her past life had caused her illness last time, what kind of effect would Tilly's disappearance have on her now?

'Jess, maybe we should go away again? Perhaps for Christmas, if you're dreading it so much?'

'No! No, I couldn't go away, Edward. What if there was news? What if she's found and is ill and needs me?'

He sighed. It had only been an idea. A straw to clutch at.

Johanna came round later that evening as she did almost every evening now, prompted by Ronan.

'How is she, Catherine?' she whispered as the girl took her coat and hat.

'The same, Aunt Jo. Edward came this afternoon.'

Johanna nodded and went into the sitting room.

'How are you, Jess? I believe Edward called?'

'He did. He's worried about me.'

'We all are.' Johanna thought how pale her niece was, and she was losing weight again.

'He wanted me to go away, for Christmas, but—'

'Jess, won't you consider it? It's going to be very hard for you,' Johanna coaxed.

'How can I?'

'Aunt Jo, I don't think that's such a good idea. She's had so much upset and upheaval,' Patrick said.

'We would still be here. If there was any news we could contact you,' Johanna pressed.

'No. No, really, Aunt Jo, I couldn't.'

'Aunt Jo, leave it, please? I'll make the cocoa. Will you have a cup?'

'I'd prefer tea, Patrick, if you don't mind,' Johanna said, annoyed with him for not giving her his support.

'Would you mind if I had tea too tonight, Patrick? Sometimes cocoa is so cloying.'

Patrick sucked in his breath. Damn! 'But you like cocoa, Jess. It helps you sleep, you know it does.'

'Patrick, I slept very well without it when I was away. I'll have tea.'

'But, Jess, when you were away things were . . . different. Now, with all the worry, I'm sure cocoa would be best for a good night's sleep.'

'Patrick, for heaven's sake, let her have tea if she wants it!' Johanna cried. Why on earth was there all this fuss over a bedtime drink?

Patrick couldn't protest further. Cocoa was strong and sweet and disguised the taste, but he dare not risk it in the tea in case it was too obvious. Damn Aunt Jo! He just hoped Jess wouldn't demand tea every night. Maybe he could talk to Catherine, persuade her to try to influence Jess. He didn't hold out much hope. Catherine was terrified of him and seldom spoke to him and that was something he was certain Johanna would notice sooner or later. Oh, God! The whole terrible business was affecting his nerves and he slept badly these nights. Remorse and fear were now his constant companions.

Jess felt a little better the following morning and managed to help Catherine around the house, but she was still heartbroken over Tilly. The child's plight was constantly on her mind. Johanna came in the afternoon and Edward in the evening, but by then she felt so weary and bowed down with heartache that she couldn't concentrate.

'I really think Jess should go up soon, Edward,' Patrick managed to whisper.

Edward nodded his agreement. Jess looked far from well.

'Right, I think it's time for cocoa,' Patrick announced, trying to muster up some semblance of good humour.

'Good idea, Patrick,' Edward concurred.

'I'll have tea, Patrick, please. I didn't feel as heavy-eyed this morning. Perhaps the cocoa isn't agreeing with me.'

Patrick's heart dropped like a stone and he had to check himself before he could speak. Did she suspect? 'It's never had that effect on you in the past, Jess, and it's become a sort of . . . nightly ritual. A family ritual, hasn't it, Catherine?' He tried to sound amiable but a little hurt.

Catherine nodded wordlessly.

'Oh, well, if you're going to make such a fuss . . .' Jess said irritably.

'Jess, I'm sure Patrick means well,' Edward said gently,

trying to keep the peace. Things were already strained between brother and sister and he wasn't at all sure that Patrick was telling the entire truth about Tilly. Oh, the child was impetuous but he couldn't help feeling that if she had indeed run away, by now she would have come to her senses and returned home, penitent and no doubt chastened by her experiences.

Jess drank her cocoa without further protest and, half an hour later, said goodnight to Edward and retired to bed.

She fell asleep immediately but her dreams were troubled with images of Tilly. Tilly calling out to her. Tilly hurt and lost in a dark place where Jess couldn't reach her. She was crying for Jess and for her dolls.

Jess woke with her hair sticking to her forehead with perspiration and her nightdress clinging clammily to her body. She was shaking uncontrollably. Oh, God! What was happening to her? She felt ill. Very ill. Her head was pounding and her throat was sore. She'd have to get a drink. Her mouth felt dry, her tongue furry and the cloying stickiness of the cocoa was still strong in her mouth. The cocoa! She had told Patrick she didn't want it, that it didn't seem to agree with her. It had been the truth – she now felt terribly sick. She would have to go downstairs and get a drink.

After Jess and Catherine had gone to bed Patrick had washed up carefully as he always did. How long would Jess go on searching for Tilly? She was getting very difficult to handle, especially over the matter of the cocoa. Oh, there were times now when he wished he'd never let Terence talk him into any of this. He often had nightmares where he could see the hangman's noose and feel someone propelling him forcefully towards it and he always woke in a lather of sweat. Things seemed so much worse during the hours of darkness. During the day he could cope well enough. He could find things to occupy him, but the evenings were long and tense. Catherine watched him fearfully and never spoke. He tried to behave normally but he could never entirely put aside the dread of the ritual of the cocoa, followed by the long, hellish hours when sleep wouldn't come.

He was about to turn out the gas when he heard the gentle tapping on the back door.

'Terence! God, am I glad to see you!' he said thankfully.

'How are things, Pat? I'm sorry I couldn't come before. It wasn't safe.'

'She's still searching for the child and I had a bit of a scare with Ronan.'

'What kind of a scare?'

'He doesn't believe my story. We forgot about her damned dolls! We should have got rid of them. That's why Jess won't really believe me either.'

'Christ! I forgot about them! But surely it doesn't matter now?'

'No, but I'm having trouble getting her to take the powder in the cocoa.'

Shay was worried. 'Pat, you've *got* to give it to her.'

'I know but it's easier said than done! Oh, God, Terence, what a bloody mess!'

'You're not losing your nerve, are you? Remember the consequences!'

'No, I'm not, but it's not easy.'

'Are you still running the business?'

Patrick nodded.

'Good. I'd wondered about that. And Catherine?'

'Catherine is terrified of me. She hardly speaks.'

'Is that a bad thing?'

'No. I don't suppose so, but . . .'

'But?'

'But I'm afraid that she'll lose her senses one day and tell Aunt Jo everything!'

'You'll have to make sure she doesn't, Pat,' Shay warned. 'Or else . . .'

Patrick was horrified. 'Jesus! Terence, we . . . you can't . . . Catherine can't disappear!' he stammered. 'She can't run away! I'd have Ronan and Uncle Tom down on me like a ton of bricks, you know I would!

Shay was concerned. It was a good thing he'd decided to pay Patrick a visit to bolster his courage. 'Let's hope it doesn't come to that. Now, shall we discuss all this further . . . upstairs?'

Patrick glanced around uneasily. 'Isn't it safer down here?'

'You *are* losing your nerve, Pat. Jess is asleep, Catherine is asleep and there's no sneaking little brat to spy on us. Let's go up.'

Patrick nodded slowly.

Jess had dragged herself to the door of her room, after pulling on her dressing gown and feeling for her slippers. It was cold, bitterly cold. She felt more awake but still very sick and shivery. The landing was in darkness but there was a sliver of light under the door of the spare bedroom. Why was Patrick sleeping in there? What was wrong between him and Catherine? She had been too preoccupied with Tilly of late, but she had begun to notice that Catherine hardly ever spoke to her husband and she never smiled or laughed these days. Jess leaned against the wall as a wave of nausea swept over her. Oh, she was too ill to think about them now; and she was too ill to manage the stairs: she'd fall, she was certain of it. She'd ask Patrick to go down and bring her up a drink.

She knocked on the door and then listened. She was sure she'd heard him moving around. She knocked again, feeling dizzy.

'Patrick! Patrick, I . . . need help!' She opened the door and her eyes widened. 'You! You!' she screamed.

'Jess! Get out of here!' Patrick shouted.

The sickness was fading, rage was sweeping through her. 'How dare you come here! How *dare* you!'

'You bloody fool, Pat! I thought you said you'd given her the cocoa?' Shay yelled.

'I did! I swear to God I did!' Patrick was in a lather of sweat with panic.

Suddenly it all became clear to Jess. Her illness. Her recovery when she'd been away. Patrick's insistence on making her cocoa. 'You've been poisoning me!'

'No! No, it wasn't poison!' Patrick cried.

'Liar!' she shrieked at him.

Shay caught her arm and pulled her into the room. 'If that little brat hadn't poked her nose into things that didn't concern her we wouldn't have needed to go to such lengths!'

Jess stared at him, horrified. His words were so clear. He

had said 'hadn't' and 'didn't'. He had spoken of Tilly in the past tense. 'What have you done to her? What did you do to my poor Tilly?'

'Jess, we didn't mean to . . . we had no choice . . .' Patrick whined.

Suddenly all the hours and days of worry and anguish and fear for Tilly manifested themselves in a surge of blind fury and Jess launched herself at Terence Shay, raking his face with her fingernails.

He yelled in pain and tried to grab her hands. 'You bitch! You bitch!'

'You killed her! You murdered her!' Jess howled, still lashing out at him.

'For Christ's sake, Pat, do something!' Shay bawled.

'No! No, Terence! Not Jess! She's my sister!'

Patrick's cries steadied Jess a little. This *monster* had murdered Tilly. He had probably beaten Catherine, and Patrick . . . Patrick had done nothing to help them! Her own brother had stood by while this fiend had beaten his wife and killed Tilly. He had even lied about it all. How could he? Oh, how could he?

Shay felt the roughness of the rope around his neck. He couldn't let it happen. He couldn't! Jess had to be silenced. Like Tilly. He lunged forward.

Patrick let out a yell and grabbed him and Jess turned and fled, realising in that instant that Shay would kill her too.

'Let go of me, Pat! Let go, you bloody fool. Do you want to hang?' Shay bellowed, shoving Patrick away. Patrick staggered, careered into the chest of drawers and slid to the floor sobbing in guilty fear.

Terror filled Jess as she reached the hall. Shay was not far behind her and he was going to kill her! She wrenched open the front door and ran out into the darkness. She had to get to Johanna's house! She *had* to! Ronan would save her! Ronan and Uncle Tom!

Shay's legs worked like pistons as he ran after her. He had to catch her before she could get to the main road where someone was bound to stop and help her – if anyone was around at this time of night. If she got away, it was all over! Determinedly and steadily, inch by inch, he was gaining on her.

Jess's heart was hammering against her ribs and her breath was coming in short painful gasps. She could hear his running footsteps behind her. Oh, how much further could she go before he caught her? If he did she was determined to scream so loud and put up such a fight that she would wake the neighbourhood.

He'd nearly caught her. A few more inches, he thought grimly. Just a few more inches and I'll have a secure hold on her dressing gown or her hair. He reached out but Jess shrieked, feeling him close behind her. Forcing herself onward, she reached the corner and collided with someone and fell sprawling to her knees.

''Ere, girl, watch where yer're goin'! A poor auld feller can't walk the streets of this city no more without bein' knocked off 'is feet!' The old tramp steadied himself, one hand on the wall.

Shay grabbed a streetlight to stop himself and leaned against it, wheezing. The old fool! The bloody old fool! But was it worth knocking him senseless? Jess would be away in the time it would take him to silence the old man. Was it just better to cut his losses and make a run for it? Where? Anywhere away from this cursed city. There were plenty of ships in the docks. He had some money saved. He could go back and get it and be away on the next tide. But what about Patrick? Oh, Patrick would be no bloody use to him now. The old man was helping Jess to her feet. It was time to go. Time to think about keeping his head out of a noose and to hell with Patrick! Let him fend for himself.

Jess too was panting hard but she managed to gasp her thanks to the old tramp before turning and breaking into a trot. As she reached the main road she turned. Shay wasn't following her. Oh, thank God! Thank you, God! she gasped. Now she had to get to Aunt Jo – somehow.

It seemed to take for ever even though she had begged a lift from a carter who was making his way early to the market with a load of sprouts and potatoes. She'd told him it was an emergency, that was why she was running in her nightclothes through the city suburbs. He'd accepted her explanation and hadn't tried to engage her in conversation. He'd let her down at the bottom of Walton Road and she'd run the rest of the way to Claudia Street.

With what strength she had left she hammered on the door. 'Jess! My God, what's happened?' Tom cried as he opened the door and she fell into his arms.

'Oh, Uncle Tom! Uncle Tom! It's Terence Shay! He tried to kill me!' Jess sobbed, the past forgotten entirely.

'Ronan, lad, give me a hand. It's Jess!' Tom called to his son who was halfway down the stairs, followed by a frightened Johanna.

'What happened?' Ronan picked her up and carried her into the kitchen. She was shaking like a leaf in the wind and she was half frozen.

'Johanna, make some tea, she's freezing and half hysterical,' Tom commanded, taking off his dressing gown and putting it around Jess.

'Jess, who did this to you? What's happened?' Ronan was beside himself with anger.

'Patrick . . . Patrick and Terence Shay have been poisoning me! They . . . Shay murdered Tilly and beat Catherine and . . . he tried to . . . kill me! I ran! Oh, how I ran!'

Johanna screamed and dropped the teapot.

'Where is that bastard now?' Ronan yelled.

'I don't know.'

'So where's Patrick!' Tom demanded.

'At home. I . . . left him . . . He didn't help me! Uncle Tom, he . . . he killed my poor Tilly! And Catherine is still there! She's on her own and Patrick or Shay might have beaten her or . . . killed her, I don't know!'

'By God, he'll swing for this! They'll both swing for this!' Ronan was shaking with the force of his emotions.

'Ronan, lad, go to the police! Tell them everything!' Tom instructed.

'Oh, Tom! Oh, Tom, how could Patrick . . . ?' Johanna cried, unable to believe what she'd just heard.

'Because he's been in the clutches of that twisted . . . that devil, Shay! Don't press me on it now, Johanna. You'll know the details soon enough. Shay influenced him, but he won't escape. By God! Neither of them will escape!'

Johanna gathered Jess in her arms. 'You poor, poor girl!'

Ronan left the room. He wasn't going to the police. He was going after Shay, but first he was going to see Patrick. Only after he'd finished with his cousin could the police have him!

Chapter Twenty-Eight

J ESS WAS STILL IN a state of shock. The events of the night were too horrific to take in. She was still shaking, her head was thumping and she couldn't seem to get warm at all, even though she was wrapped in blankets and Johanna had built up the fire. Johanna, stunned and confused herself, had bathed Jess's face and hands and attended to the grazes on her knees, sustained when she had collided with the tramp.

Tom paced in the background. 'I should have gone with Ronan! I should have paid more attention to what was going on in that house!' he fulminated.

'Tom, what could you have done? Will you calm down, please. Think of your health!' Johanna begged.

'Oh, Uncle Tom, I'm so sorry! *I* kept you away. I carried on not wanting to have anything to do with you, when I really could have done with your help,' Jess cried, filled with remorse.

'Don't upset yourself over that now, Jess. The past is just that. I'm only sorry that it took something like . . . this to make you see it.' Tom patted her shoulder. What the hell would he say to Maddy and Martin when he saw them in the next world? How could he explain how he had let their children down?

'Jess, drink this, then I'm going to call the doctor.' Johanna placed a mug of tea in Jess's hands.

'No, please, Aunt Jo, I'll be fine . . . if I can just sleep,' Jess protested. She was exhausted. She couldn't think straight.

'Will you sleep?'

'Yes, I think so. I'm so tired and so . . . muddled.'

'Well, I think tomorrow we should have the doctor.'

'I agree, Johanna.' Tom dropped his voice. 'This business is far from over, she's got more to face.'

'We'll help her get through it, Tom. The only good thing to come out of all this is that she is finally reconciled with you,' Johanna said quietly, her eyes full of tears.

Fury drove Ronan on. Throughout his journey to Jess's house he let his feelings and imagination run riot until he was utterly beside himself.

The house was in darkness but he barged inside without bothering to knock.

'Patrick! Patrick, where the hell are you?' he shouted from the hall. He heard a movement upstairs and took the stairs two at a time.

Catherine was standing on the landing, her hand on the banister. She was deathly pale and shaking.

'Where is he? Where's that snivelling little bastard?'

Catherine couldn't speak. She had been woken by Jess's screams and Shay's shouting. She had seen and heard everything and had been reduced to abject terror, cowering back against the wall when first Jess and then Terence Shay had run past her. She hadn't even been able to go and see how Patrick was; she had crawled back to bed. Now she could only point to the spare bedroom in reply to Ronan's demands.

Patrick was still crouched on the floor. The whole world had come crashing around his ears. He didn't know if Terence Shay had caught Jess and if he had . . . what had happened to her. And Terence? He would never have believed he could be so violent and cruel. He had killed once and would do so again and it would be Jess – his sister! Oh, God, why had he let it all happen? He should have made some effort! He had huddled here for what seemed like an eternity, cold, shivering, dazed and petrified.

Ronan dragged him to his feet. 'Where is he? Where's that murdering bastard?'

'Ronan! Ronan, please? I . . . I never meant anything like this to happen! Oh, God, help me!'

'Don't bank on Him to help you! You'll hang for this, Patrick, and there's only one place you'll be going then!'

'Jess? Where's Jess?' Patrick pleaded.

'She's safe, he didn't get her! No thanks to you!'

'I . . . I . . . didn't mean to hurt her! It was only stuff to make her sleep!'

Ronan hit him hard across the face and Patrick squealed in pain and fright.

'Where is he? Answer me, Patrick, or I'll break your bloody neck!'

'Gone! I don't know, Ronan, I swear to God I don't know!

He went after Jess, that's the last time I saw him!'

'Where does he live?'

'Hopwood Street. I never meant to hurt Jess or Tilly. He killed Tilly and took her away! Oh, God, I never meant any of this and now—'

'Who gave her the poison? You or Shay?'

'It . . . it was me but he bought it. He suggested it. It wasn't poison, Ronan, you've got to believe me!'

'Why were you giving it to her, if not to kill her?'

'For . . . for her money. The business. I . . . we wanted money for a house and—'

'You pathetic, despicable, spineless creature!' Ronan's temper snapped and he began to rain blows on Patrick who fell to the floor screaming. 'I'll make you pay for everything you've done to Jess!' Ronan roared, kicking Patrick who lay whimpering and groaning, trying to shield himself with his arms from the vicious attack.

Ronan was almost exhausted when Catherine finally managed to drag him away from Patrick.

'Ronan! Ronan, stop it! Stop it, you'll kill him!' she wailed, hanging on to his arm.

The mists of fury began to clear from Ronan's mind and he looked down at the prostrate, bloody body of his cousin.

'Ronan, he's not worth hanging for!' she said quietly.

Slowly he nodded. 'You're right, Catherine, he's not, but he'll remember that beating for the rest of his life and I hope he has scars so that every time he looks in the mirror he'll recall what he did!'

'You've got to find *him*! Terence Shay. He threatened to kill me and he killed Tilly . . .'

'I know,' Ronan said grimly.

'Shall I call the police?'

'No! No, not yet, Catherine. Leave it all to me.'

Catherine was afraid. She wanted the safety a policeman would bring to the house. 'What about Patrick?'

'Do whatever you think is best until I get back.'

He turned and left the room, ran down the stairs, through the hall and out into the street. Hopwood Street was his next destination.

He'd taken a cab and when he got there he'd roused the whole house where Shay rented a room. Two men, both of whom stank of stale beer and tobacco, and two women, old coats over their shoulders and hair hanging in greasy strands around their faces, all glared at him.

'Where is Terence Shay? Where's that murdering bastard?' he yelled.

'Gone, an' bloody good riddance! Cumin' 'ere an' makin' such a racket ter wake the 'ole bloody street!' the elder of the men replied.

'Gone where?' Ronan demanded.

''Ow the bleedin' 'ell should we know! Like Bert said, bloody good riddance!' the other man answered.

''E owed me two weeks' rent! Now 'e's done a runner!' one woman commented sourly.

'Did he have money?' Ronan asked.

'Iffen 'e did 'e wasn't 'andin' it over!'

'How long ago did he leave?'

'About an hour. Now, clear off an' let honest workin' men get some bleedin' sleep!'

Ronan went back out into the street. An hour ago. Did

Shay have money? What had Patrick said? That they were poisoning Jess for her money. He would never believe they meant her no harm, and he was certain that Patrick would have handed money over to Shay. Where could Shay go? He would realise that Jess had got help by now. Might even have called in the authorities. Half the police force of the city could be looking for him, for all he knew. Where would he go? He had to try to think like Shay. The man had to get away from Liverpool and quickly. By train? There were very few trains that left at this hour. The platforms would be empty, any searching policeman wouldn't have a hard job finding him. No trams were running. By ship! It had to be by ship, they left at all times depending on the tides, and sailed to the far corners of the world. He made up his mind. The docks. He'd search the docks.

It started to rain as he reached the Victoria Dock. He was going to do it methodically, starting with the Victoria and working his way to the Brocklebank Dock. The police at the dock gates knew of all the departures and expected arrivals, that at least would help him.

There were no ships leaving within the next couple of hours at the Nelson or the Bramley Moor Docks. At the Sandon Dock he was informed that the *Castletown Rose*, a 'bit of an old tramp', was due to sail in half an hour for Lisbon; 'and I hope the weather holds for them or they'll never make it in that rusty old tub' was the policeman's parting comment as Ronan thanked him and made his way across the slippery, damp cobbles and the rubbish that had accumulated on them.

The gangway was still down but there was no one in sight

so he went up. He walked along the deck towards the wheel-house where lights were burning.

'Here, you! What do you think you're doing?'

Ronan turned at the shouted question. A large man was approaching wrapped in oilskins but with a peaked cap that proclaimed his status as master.

'I'm looking for someone! Have you taken on any passengers in the last hour?'

'What if I have?'

'A darkish man? Not very tall, slim build?'

His question was met with speculative silence.

'He's a murderer! He murdered a girl, a child, and he's been poisoning another woman! Is he on board?'

'A child, you say? He's murdered a child?'

'Yes!'

'I'm having nothing to do with no murderer. He came aboard half an hour ago. Paid with a wad of money. Smarmy-looking feller. Are you the police?'

'Yes,' Ronan lied.

'Come with me, he's below.'

Ronan followed the captain down a steep companionway and along a dark, narrow passage that smelled of oil and brackish water until he stopped outside a door.

'In there. Then I'd be obliged if you'd get off my ship, we're sailing soon. I knew nothing about him being a murderer or poisoner, I swear!'

Ronan didn't knock. He flung open the door.

Inside the tiny, dimly lit, dirty cabin Shay had been sitting, trying to make plans. He'd got this far safely, he had money . . . He uttered a strangled cry as the door burst open and Ronan Kiernan filled the opening.

'You murdering bastard! You thought you'd got away with it!' Ronan said coldly.

Shay put up his arms to defend himself but Ronan grabbed him by the shoulder and yanked him to his feet.

'Get going! You're going nowhere, except jail!' He pushed the cowering figure along ahead of him. There wasn't room for Shay to try to fight, but once on the open deck he turned and struck Ronan hard.

Ronan hadn't been expecting it. He bellowed in pain and rage and then lashed out. Shay staggered and half fell but Ronan dragged him to his feet and hit him hard in the gut. Shay doubled up in agony.

'So, you thought you could rob Jess blind? You poisoned her, you murdered Tilly, you beat Catherine and then you tried to kill Jess! It's a bloody pity you can only hang once!'

'Get him off my ship!' the captain roared. 'We're almost ready to cast off and I'm not missing the tide!'

Shay had struggled to his feet. He had to get away from Ronan. He had to hide. He knew they were about to sail. If he could hide for just a few minutes he'd be away free. He turned and began to run across the deck.

Ronan sprinted after him. Did the fool think he could get away? There was no escape for him.

As Shay reached the rail on the starboard side Ronan caught him. Shay struggled with all his strength and managed to get a foot on the second rung of the ship's rail. Ronan seized him but Shay twisted out of his grasp and swung his leg over the rail.

'Oh, no, you don't, Shay! You'll get what's coming to you!' Ronan shouted, grabbing for him again.

Shay slipped, snatched at the air, cried out and then fell.

Ronan stood staring at the empty space where seconds before Shay had been wrestling and cursing.

'I'd say that's the end of him!' The captain looked over the side of his ship to the oily, murky water below that was being churned into a dirty cream-coloured froth. 'Can't no one survive in that. We're getting up steam. The screws are turning. He'll be sliced to bits by the blades.'

Ronan gripped the rail. Shay might have cheated the hangman, but he hadn't cheated death.

'Now, will you get off my ship! You can make your reports out when you like but I'm not missing the tide! And if you ask me, he's no loss to Society!'

Ronan turned and walked towards the gangway. There would be no report to the police about Shay but what about Patrick? Could he be allowed to get away with everything he had done?

As soon as Ronan reached the dockside the gangway was hauled up. He walked to a small, grubby-looking café on the dock road that was open all night. He needed time to think.

Catherine knew Patrick was badly beaten, but was afraid to call either the police or a doctor.

'Catherine! Catherine, help me?' Patrick moaned through swollen lips. 'Please? For the love of God, don't leave me to die. Catherine?'

She bit into the back of her hand, still frightened and yet feeling pity for him.

'Please, Catherine? I . . . I never meant to . . . hurt you!'

She couldn't leave him here. He might die and then how would she feel? There had been enough violence and terror this night. 'Lie still, Patrick. I'll help.'

She bathed the blood from his face and managed to get him onto the bed.

'Patrick, is it really bad?' she half whispered.

'Got to . . . get . . . to . . . Jess . . .' he mumbled. Numbed with shock and agony though his mind was, he knew he had to tell Jess the truth. That he hadn't meant to harm her, that he hadn't killed Tilly. It had all been Terence's fault.

'Can you walk?' Catherine asked. There was nothing she wanted to do more than go to Johanna. To someone who would sort out all this mess.

Patrick tried to sit up but fierce stabs of pain shot through him. 'Get . . . get . . . a cab, Catherine, please?' he begged.

Catherine was afraid to leave the house and go out in the dark silent streets to look for a hackney carriage; only the thought of getting to Johanna's and safety drove her on. It took her nearly half an hour but at last she saw one approaching and hailed it.

'What the hell happened to him, luv?' the driver asked when she led him upstairs to help her.

'He . . . got in a fight.' It was all she could think of, and of course it was true.

'You sure you don't want to go to the hospital?'

'No! No, I'm sure. If you could just help me to get him downstairs. We . . . I'm taking him to my aunt's.'

Somehow between them they got Patrick downstairs and into the cab, but he was barely conscious and Catherine felt near to collapse. She gave the address and leaned her head against the back of the cab interior. Would this terrible night ever end? she wailed to herself, unconsciously echoing her husband.

Johanna was horrified. 'Oh, my God! Catherine! Thank God you're safe! Patrick! What happened?'

'Ronan. Ronan came and . . .' Catherine's nerves finally snapped altogether and she broke down.

Johanna took her in her arms. 'Ronan? Did Ronan do this?'

Catherine could only sob.

'Tom! Help him!' Johanna appealed to her husband. She had already been shocked by the night's earlier events, now she was visibly distraught. She couldn't believe her son was capable of such violence.

'I'll get him into the kitchen. Jo, you take her upstairs to Jess.'

Johanna led Catherine away and Tom half carried his nephew into the kitchen. He despised Patrick, he was furious with him and God knew he thought he deserved to be punished, but he too was shocked by his son's behaviour.

'Uncle Tom! Jess . . . I didn't mean to hurt her! I . . . I didn't kill . . . Tilly. You *have* to believe me!'

'I believe you, lad,' Tom answered. This was all that snake Terence Shay's fault.

'I . . . I . . . can't help . . . how I . . . am.'

Tom didn't reply. His nephew's behaviour sickened him.

'You will tell . . . Jess?'

'I'll try and explain. Lord God, this family has suffered so many tragedies!' Tom shook his head sadly. And the worries weren't over yet. Ronan obviously hadn't gone to the police as he'd told him to do. Where the hell was he?

Chapter Twenty-Nine

———◆———

RONAN HAD SORTED EVERYTHING out in his mind. The *Castletown Rose* had sailed and God knew when she would be back in Liverpool, and he was certain that the captain would make no formal report when he did return. The man wanted no trouble and, besides, he thought Ronan was a policeman.

When Shay was fished out of the dock it would be looked on as an accidental death. People often fell into the dock and drowned or, if they were unfortunate enough, fell in the path of the ships' propellers as Shay had done. (If you were lucky and you were fished out alive it meant at least a night in hospital as the waters of the docks were so polluted they were full of all manner of deadly diseases.) But Ronan felt he couldn't stay in Liverpool now. For a long time an idea had been forming in his mind. There were plenty of opportunities for a young man in South Africa. The country was being opened up and was said to have huge reserves of gold, silver, copper and other metals. Somehow he'd persuade Jess to go with him. They could start a new life there, away from all the memories this city held for them. They would be happy.

That left Patrick. Patrick had to be punished for his part in all this. He had been defrauding Jess of money from her business, trying to poison her and, even if he didn't physically take part in the murder of that poor child, he had aided and abetted Shay, his evil mentor. Patrick wouldn't, *couldn't* escape retribution. He'd go to jail. It was one more reason to get Jess away from here. He was sure his parents would take poor Catherine in.

The house was in darkness but the first rays of the grey December dawn were streaking the sky when he finally got home. He let himself in quietly and stood listening. Everywhere was quiet. He needed a drink and tiptoed down the hall.

He was surprised to see his father sitting in the dark kitchen. The only illumination came from the banked-up fire.

'I thought you'd have gone back to bed.'

'Where the hell have you been? You didn't go to the police as I told you to do.'

'No. I went after those two. I had to!'

'Did you have to beat your cousin half to death?'

'I . . . I lost control, that's all! You would have done too if you'd seen him. That pathetic excuse for a man, lying cowering and crying like a baby! How do you know, anyway?'

'He's here. Catherine brought him. The poor girl is half out of her mind!'

'He's *here*? You let him in? You're . . . harbouring him?'

'What else could I do?' Tom demanded.

'We'll have to go to the police. He can't get away with this! He'll have to be punished.'

'Your mother got the whole story out of Jess, out of them both, and I've been sitting here thinking about it all and terrible though it is, we can't afford to have Patrick go to jail. Think of the trial! Everything would come out – everything! God knows how it would affect them all: your mother, Jess and Catherine. We *can't* bring all that suffering and humiliation on them. Not after all they've been through. Scandal has torn this family apart once already. We *can't* stand it again, Ronan, and this time it would be ten times worse. It would destroy us all.'

'But Patrick should pay! He's caused all this! It's *his* fault!'

'Patrick would die in jail. It would be a living death for someone like . . . him. He'd never survive and I won't have that on my conscience. He's suffered enough and so has poor, innocent Catherine. I've regretted many things in my life, lad, but nothing so much as ruining that young girl's life. I made a huge mistake, God forgive me, in thinking she would be good for Patrick. At least I've the rest of my life to try to make amends to her. No, Ronan, we can't involve the police no matter how many heinous crimes have been committed. Tilly's dead. It's over. Let's bury it and try to help the living.'

Ronan could see the sense in his father's words. He sank down in a chair and dropped his head in his hands.

'What did happen to Shay?'

Ronan looked up. 'I followed him to where he was living but he'd gone. I guessed he'd gone to the docks. I went after him, caught him on board a tramp steamer just about to sail.'

'And?' Tom leaned forward.

'There was a fight; he . . . he fell overboard. The ship was getting up steam, he was caught by the screws.'

'He's dead?'

Ronan nodded.

'And so?'

'The ship sailed. The captain thought I was the police. He wanted no trouble. There's no need to worry. If and when they find him it will look like an accident.'

Tom nodded slowly. 'Your mother, Jess and Catherine will have to be told about Patrick, but not yet. Let them recover a bit first.'

'Jess should get away from here. Away from all this.'

'I agree but whether she will is another matter. Well, it's nearly dawn. We'd both better try and get some rest.'

'I'll find it hard, knowing Patrick's under this roof!'

'We'll sort all that out later,' Tom said heavily. He was getting too old to deal with such traumatic events.

Jess woke with a leaden feeling in her head. She turned over and opened her eyes. Where was she? What had happened? Then she remembered. Between them Patrick and Shay had killed Tilly. Tilly was dead. Oh, her poor, poor Tilly! How could she ever forgive Patrick? It didn't matter that he'd been drugging her for some purpose, nothing mattered except that she would never see Tilly again and would always be haunted by the events surrounding her death. The tears slipped slowly down her cheeks and she buried her face in the pillow.

Johanna found her still weeping when she came in an hour later.

'Oh, Jess, I'm so so sorry about poor Tilly! She saw Shay beat Catherine and then walked in on him and Patrick going through the books from your business. She threatened to tell us and Shay . . .' Johanna couldn't go on. She'd been very fond of the child.

'Patrick could have had all the money he wanted. He only had to ask. He knew that!'

'He wanted it for a house of his own.'

'He could have had that too!'

'He was in the clutches of that wicked man – that devil! But he – Shay – is dead.'

'How do you know?'

'Ronan went after him. There was a fight, on a ship, and he fell overboard. He drowned.'

'I'm glad! I'm *glad* he's dead!'

'So am I. And Patrick has suffered too. Ronan . . . Ronan beat him terribly! I am so shocked, Jess.'

'Ronan beat Patrick?'

Johanna nodded. 'He's so bad that I'm going to send him to the hospital. I'm sure he has broken bones and maybe even internal injuries.

Jess stared at her. 'No! Surely Ronan wouldn't have done that?'

'I couldn't believe it myself. But I really think I should have the doctor to see you as well as poor Catherine. She's in a terrible state, she was there.'

'Oh, God, Aunt Jo! Why has all this happened to us?'

'I don't know, I really don't. All we can try to do now is get over it as best we can. We'll have to talk again, Jess, later, when everyone is a little calmer, myself included.'

Jess shook her head. There was so much to think about. 'Yes, later.'

Johanna got up. 'Would you like me to send for Edward?

He'll hear soon enough and it might be better if he heard it from us?'

'Yes. Yes, I owe him that much.'

Jess lay back on the pillows. She could hardly take everything in, so much had happened in so short a time, but Ronan beating Patrick! Ronan beating anyone! It was so unlike him – or was it? He did have a temper. She'd never witnessed it but she'd heard Aunt Jo tell her mother about it. And what was she going to do about Patrick? At least Shay was dead and she no longer had anything to fear from him. As Aunt Jo had said, he was an evil man: the hold he had had over her brother must have been very powerful.

She was dozing, half in and half out of sleep, when Ronan disturbed her.

'Jess, Mother wouldn't let me come up sooner. I'm so, so sorry. How are you?'

She sat up. 'Dazed, confused, full of grief and regrets.'

He reached out and took her hand. 'Shay's dead. I followed him, there was a fight and he fell into the dock. You've nothing more to fear from him, Jess. He got what he deserved. It wouldn't have been a . . . quick or painless end.'

A shudder ran through her, but she had no wish to know all the details of how Terence Shay died.

He held her hand tightly. 'Jess, you've been so brave, so strong! I . . . I love you!' It was out. He hadn't meant it to be like this but now it had been said.

Her eyes widened. 'Ronan! What do you mean?'

'What I said! Oh, I know we're cousins but that can't be helped! I love you. I want to be with you always! I've made up my mind that, when this is all over, I'm going out to

South Africa to start a new life and I want you to come with me! You'll be away from here, away from all the terrible memories!'

Jess was stunned. She couldn't believe what he was saying. 'But . . . Patrick!' was all she could say.

'Oh, damn Patrick to hell! It's where he deserves to be – with Shay! It's you who matters, Jess. You and me – us!'

Jess uttered a frightened cry. This wasn't true! Ronan couldn't be serious. He was saying he loved her and wanted to marry her but she didn't, couldn't love him – especially not now he'd shown a side she had never dreamed he possessed.

'You've beaten Patrick half to death!'

'He deserved it! Come away with me, I beg you. Can't we put all this behind us?'

Jess was out of the bed. He was mad! He must be! How could she go away with him? She wrenched open the door and fled down the stairs.

'Jess! Don't run away from me!' Ronan called after her.

She turned and faced him, gathering herself. 'Ronan, don't you think I've been through enough? I don't love you! I can't love you! Maybe it's best if you *do* go away but I can't, *won't* come with you! Leave me alone! For God's sake, leave me alone!' Her tone, the disgust in her face, left no possible doubt that she meant what she said.

She turned towards the kitchen door, her hand on the knob. 'I don't know if I want to see you again.'

Ronan gripped the banister rail. He'd lost her. He'd lost her for ever. He'd have to leave. He couldn't stay here any longer.

* * *

Jess looked out at the patch of blue sky beyond the window. Daylight was fading; fingers of dusk were already creeping across from the east. She leaned her arms on the sill. Oh, what a day it had been. She had had to face still more revelations and try to make some impossibly difficult decisions.

Aunt Jo and Uncle Tom had both been alarmed when she'd burst into the kitchen and blurted out everything Ronan had said.

'I can't believe it! Tom, has he lost his reason?' Johanna had cried.

'It's not unheard of, Jo, but Jess is not for him. Maybe . . . well, maybe it is better if he goes away,' had been her uncle's reply.

There had then followed the disclosure that Patrick was not as other men, something which, after the initial shock had worn off and on reflection, she realised explained a lot of things about Patrick's behaviour. She wondered if she would ever be able to forgive him for the part he had played in her beloved Tilly's death but even that, she acknowledged, was all due to the corrupt influence of Terence Shay. She wasn't sorry he was dead and she prayed it would be a lesson Patrick had learned well. But his injuries at the hands of Ronan were something he wouldn't forget and neither would she.

She raised her head and looked across the tiny patch of darkening garden. And then there was poor Catherine. It had amazed and then angered her to learn of her uncle and Ronan's part in that disastrous marriage.

'How *could* you? Oh, how could you do such a thing?' she'd cried.

'Jess, I've never been more sorry in my life but you have to believe that we honestly thought it was for the best. That it would make Patrick behave . . . normally,' Tom had said emphatically and sincerely.

Johanna had said nothing, she had just shaken her head sadly.

Poor Catherine indeed, Jess thought. She too had suffered and she was still so young. She would have to try to think of something that would give the girl some purpose in life, some comfort and compensation for the terrible things she'd endured. Her head had begun to throb and she passed her hand wearily across her eyes. And what of herself? What kind of future lay ahead for her? She knew what her mother and father would have expected of her. Everything that had happened could be overcome, in time. She had borne so much heartache in the past and she had fought on against fate – but did she want to go on struggling alone? Were her young shoulders broad enough, her spirit indomitable enough? She was weary, the events of the last few days had drained her emotionally. Oh, it would be so good to have someone else to turn to, to bring her worries and troubles to. The image of Edward's concerned and considerate face came into her mind. It was such a dear face. A feeling of great peace spread through her, banishing the chill, comforting her. Dear, dear Edward. Was this love? This feeling of warmth and security? He was always there when she needed him. Staunch, unwavering, caring. So unlike Ronan and yet he loved her just as much. She'd made him wait for so long. Too long. Now, the time for waiting was over. Of course she loved him. How could she have doubted it? She wanted to spend the rest of her life with him – if he'd have her after all the revelations of the day. It was a small doubt and one she dismissed. It was unworthy of Edward, he was the one man in the whole world she could rely on. He wouldn't let her down.

She got up slowly and drew the curtains. Darkness had overtaken the house and the garden and the city she loved so much. Edward would be arriving soon and he would have his answer and they would put the past behind them.

'When daylight comes I'll start again, Mam. A new day, a new life, a new beginning for me and for Patrick,' she said softly.

Epilogue

———◆———

'QUICK, CATHERINE, CATCH HIM before he falls in!' Jess cried.

Catherine ran lightly over the grass and snatched up the toddler who had been making his way determinedly and with some speed to the edge of the lake where two children were throwing bread to the ducks.

'Martin Dempsey, you little scamp, you have your poor mama heart-scalded!' Catherine struggled with the squirming tot.

'Come here to me. You'll get all wet and then Papa will be cross!' Jess laughed. They came to the park on Sundays whenever they could, and on other fine days too.

'What has that child been doing now?' Edward asked, a bemused smile on his face as he watched his wife and small son.

'Don't ask!' Jess laughed again. 'Do you think we could persuade Aunt Catherine to take you for a nice walk, Martin?'

'Ducks! Want to feed the ducks!' Martin stated firmly.

Jess grinned. 'He looks just like you when you're reading the newspaper!'

'Oh, surely not, Jess?' Edward protested.

'I'll take him to the pavilion, they might have some bread and then we can feed the ducks. Shall we do that, Martin?' Catherine coaxed.

Edward sat down beside Jess as they watched the pair walk towards the pavilion.

'He is like you, Edward, thank God!'

'Why thank God? His mother is beautiful, kind, generous, vivacious and a survivor!' He took Jess's hand and squeezed it.

Jess squeezed back. She didn't regret her decision to marry Edward. A decision made the same day that Ronan had made that outburst, nearly three years ago now. She became serious. It had been yet another terrible day with shouted accusations from Uncle Tom, tears and pleas for explanations from Johanna and Catherine. In the middle of it all Edward had arrived and had been a tower of strength and she'd known then that the decision taken as daylight faded that day was the right one. For the rest of her life she wanted him to take charge of things, cherish and protect her.

'No regrets, Jess?'

She turned and smiled at her husband. 'You must have been reading my thoughts, Edward. No, no regrets at all. I couldn't have got through it all without you.'

He patted her hand. He, too, would never forget that day and all the terrible secrets that had been revealed. He sighed. Ronan had been packed off to South Africa in an alarmingly short space of time. Patrick had recovered and he and Tom had had a long talk to the troubled young man and a short while later they had all gone to see him off to start a new life in Canada. Catherine had opted to stay with Johanna and he wasn't sure whether, even after this length of time, the girl really understood about her husband's 'problem' as he always referred to it.

'Have you heard from Patrick recently?' he asked.

'Not me, but Aunt Jo had a letter last week. He's doing well, so he says. Building quite a business out there. He has his own place now and quite a lot of . . . friends.'

Edward raised an eyebrow. He wasn't going to ask Jess whether the friends were male or female. Maybe both. He was sure that after the terrible experiences Patrick had gone through here, he would be very careful in future how he chose his 'friends'.

'Would you like to go out there, Jess, for a holiday? Say when Martin is older?'

'Yes, I think I'd like that, Edward.'

'Do you miss him?'

'I do. He's my brother when all is said and done and I . . . I . . . can't be responsible for my brother's sins. I've even forgiven him for Tilly. I'll never forget her, but it wasn't his fault entirely.'

'Terence Shay was an evil man, Jess.'

She nodded. She didn't want to dwell on those dark days. They were all behind her now. She was a Dempsey, not a Brennan, and she had her own family to look out for. But she had never forgotten her mother's promise to the families who lost men on her father's ships, and, with Edward's help, she had founded the Trust Fund for the Widows and Orphans of the Brennan Line. Now that was done, she could look to the future.

'Edward, have you thought any more about my business?'

He laughed. 'Oh, Jess! I thought you said that now no fashionable woman would be seen dead with feathers in her hats or on her dresses?'

She laughed. 'They won't! But there are plenty of other things.'

'You are incorrigible, Mrs Dempsey! Don't we have enough money?'

'I was thinking of Catherine. In fact, I've been thinking about her for quite a while now. She needs something in her life. Something to devote her time and energies to.'

Edward nodded. She was right. Catherine's life had no purpose and probably never would have. Unless something happened to Patrick she was not free to remarry, should the poor girl ever wish to do so. Her experience of marriage was not happy. 'Yes, I think you're right.'

'She'd need me to help of course, to start with, but it could only be for a couple of months anyway. After that I'll have enough on my plate with Martin and another . . .'

Edward took her hand. 'Jess! You're telling me we're going to—'

'Be parents again,' she finished and kissed him lightly on the cheek. 'Would you like a daughter this time?'

'Jess, as long as it's healthy I won't mind.'

She settled in the crook of his arm, secure and happy. 'If it is a girl can we call her Tilly?'

'You can call her anything you like, but I think Magdalene – Maddy – would be nicer.'

Jess bit her lip. Perhaps Edward was right. The name Tilly would evoke too many unhappy memories. Her son had been named for his grandfather, why not call a daughter after her mother? 'Yes. Maddy would be nice.'

'And if she has all the qualities of her mother and grandmother she'll go far in the world, just as the first Maddy did.'

'I think Mam would have approved of you, Edward. I really do.' Jess laughed and planted a kiss on his forehead.

From Liverpool With Love

by

Lyn Andrews

In 1920s Liverpool, Jane, her little brother Alfie and their mother Ellen have faced the horrors of the workhouse together.

But when Ellen dies, two very different paths open up for the siblings.

Jane is sent to work in the Empire Laundry and builds a new life for herself with the neighbours who take her in. She finds solace there and the promise of a happy future when she falls for Joe, their eldest son.

But Alfie absconds from the workhouse and embarks on a life of crime. When their paths cross once more, Alfie turns on his sister. His plans will jeopardise every happiness she hoped for . . .

Available now from

HEADLINE

Heart and Home

by

Lyn Andrews

Cathie Kinrade is all too used to hardship. Growing up on the Isle of Man in the 1930s, she sees her da set sail daily on dangerous seas while her mam struggles to put food on the table. Cathie has little hope for her own future, until a chance encounter changes her fortunes for ever.

Fiercely determined, Cathie leaves for Liverpool, a bustling modern city full of possibility. With a lively job as a shop girl in a grand department store, and a firm friend in kind-hearted Julia, Cathie has found her niche.

But the discovery of an explosive secret could put everything at risk. And when love comes calling, Cathie's new friends fear that she may be set to trust the wrong man with her heart . . .

Available now from

HEADLINE

Liverpool Sisters

by

Lyn Andrews

It is 1907 in bustling Liverpool. Thanks to their father's success, sisters Livvie and Amy Goodwin are moving to leafy Everton. But tragedy strikes when their adored mother Edith dies in childbirth. The girls are still missing Edith every day when Thomas introduces their new stepmother-to-be – a woman just a few years older than Livvie.

Thomas is an old-fashioned man, who expects to make the important decisions in his daughters' lives. He plans for Livvie to marry a wealthy neighbour's son – not Frank Hadley, the kind and handsome factory manager Livvie is attracted to. Livvie's relationship with Frank is a dangerous enough secret, but her interest in the Suffragettes could drive Thomas to the edge.

For the Goodwin girls, the happy future they once took for granted is far from certain . . .

Available now from

HEADLINE

Lyn Andrews

'An outstanding storyteller' *Woman's Weekly*

The House On Lonely Street
Love And A Promise
A Wing And A Prayer
When Daylight Comes
Across A Summer Sea
A Mother's Love
Friends Forever
Every Mother's Son
Far From Home
Days Of Hope
A Daughter's Journey
A Secret In The Family
To Love And To Cherish
Beyond A Misty Shore
Sunlight On The Mersey
Liverpool Angels
From Liverpool With Love
Heart And Home
Liverpool Sisters

Now you can buy any of these bestselling books from your bookshop or direct from Lyn's publisher.

To order simply call this number: **01235 827 702**
Or visit our website: **www.headline.co.uk**